little black dress

· IT'S A GIRL THING ·

Dear Little Black Dress Reader,

Thanks for picking up this Little Black Dress book, one of the great new titles from our series of fun, page-turning romance novels. Lucky you — you're about to have a fantastic romantic read that we know you won't be able to put down!

Why don't you make your Little Black Dress experience even better by logging on to

www.littleblackdressbooks.com

where you can:

- ❤ Enter our **monthly competitions** to win **gorgeous** prizes
- ❤ Get **hot-off-the-press** news about our latest titles
- ❤ Read **exclusive** preview chapters both from your **favourite** authors and from brilliant new writing talent
- ❤ Buy **up-and-coming** books online
- ❤ Sign up for an essential slice of romance via our **fortnightly email** newsletter

We love nothing more than to curl up and indulge in an addictive romance, and so we're delighted to welcome you into the Little Black Dress club!

With love from,

The *little black dress* team

Mary Carter is a freelance writer and a graduate of the American Academy of Dramatic Arts in New York City. After five years of acting, temping and waiting tables, she won a scholarship for her second degree in Sign Language Interpreting at the Rochester Institute of Technology. She currently lives in Manhattan.

Also by Mary Carter

She'll Take It

Accidentally Engaged

Mary Carter

little
black
dress

First published in 2007 by
KENSINGTON BOOKS

First published in this paperback edition in Great Britain in 2007
by LITTLE BLACK DRESS
An imprint of HEADLINE PUBLISHING GROUP

A LITTLE BLACK DRESS paperback

5

978 0 7553 3533 6

Typeset in Transit511BT by Avon DataSet Ltd,
Bidford-on-Avon, Warwickshire

Printed and bound in Great Britain by Clays Ltd, St Ives plc

Headline's policy is to use papers that are natural, renewable and
recyclable products and made from wood grown in sustainable forests.
The logging and manufacturing processes are expected to conform to
the environmental regulations of the country of origin.

HEADLINE PUBLISHING GROUP
A division of Hachette Livre UK Ltd
338 Euston Road
London NW1 3BH

www.littleblackdressbooks.co.uk
www.hodderheadline.com

Accidentally Engaged

Mary Carter

Prologue

It all started that fateful evening when I allowed myself to turn over the first card. It was from the Major Arcana, Trumps Zero, The Fool.

He's the grinning idiot, the class clown, the one who eats oysters despite the Red Tide warning, the guy who lowers his car for increased speed and agility, despite the fact that it's a Saturn.

Most Tarot card decks show The Fool standing at the edge of a cliff, not watching what he's doing. He's daydreaming, he's staring off into the sky, he's mentally composing his grocery list. In other words, he's terminally out of milk.

He's also one step away from plunging thousands of feet to his death.

And it's not like anyone didn't warn him. (Hence, his name.)

If a nonfoolish man were carefully and strategically walking down a path and suddenly plunged to his death due to large foliage, overgrown trees, or poor city planning, we'd all feel sorry for the guy, maybe even drop a bundle of flowers or light an outdoor-only nonflammable candle at the accident site. Maybe even shed a few tears. We're reasonable people. And even if we didn't go that far, we certainly wouldn't blame the guy for dying.

But if there were clues pointing to the impending disaster scattered along the way, such as small forest animals running at top speed in the opposite direction, a strange, stale feeling of doom hovering about the suddenly stilled air, or a large, neon sign blinking *Danger! This path ends in a perilous cliff!*, we probably wouldn't be so sympathetic when The Fool blindly forged ahead and plummeted off the face of the earth. Most likely we'd say, 'I told you so.'

In my defense (because a fool always has one), at the time I thought I was doing the reading for someone else. It's only now as I stand at the edge of the cliff, one step away from taking the fatal plunge myself, that I can see everything so clearly.

Daily Horoscope — Pisces

*Your kindness will be tested. Stand up for yourself
fish-woman!*
*A placemat collects silver, while a doormat just
collects dust . . .*

'Clair, please. Just do this one for me. It's just one little
reading. Please, please, please, please, *please*.'

I pulled my beaded, green purse protectively to my
side where my Tarot cards were resting peacefully in their
box, happy to be done for the day.

'Why won't you do it?' I said, trying to sound mature
and reasonable when what I really wanted to do was jump
up and down and whine, 'I want to go home, I want to go
home!'

'Because I know the girl. I sort of – used to date her. I
just . . . she's kind of . . . I can't get into this right now
Clair,' my friend and colleague, Brian Shepard, said. He
glanced over his shoulder as if someone were stalking him
and then lowered his voice to a harsh whisper. 'She's
standing right *over there*. Please. Please, please, please,
please.'

I contemplated Brian like a lizard stares at a fly right
before its slimy, red tongue shoots out and wraps it in
deadly saliva. Not that I didn't sympathize with his plight.
It's truly difficult to do a reading for someone you know.

Family and friends hit me up all the time for free readings, but I was always worried I'd let the things I already knew about the person subconsciously influence the outcome. Like the year I was nine and my brother Tommy broke his leg in a motorcycle accident. The cards said he was entering a long period of rest and introspection, and I happily relayed this to him.

But instead of praising my astounding psychic abilities, my brother glared at me like I was a Happy Meal sans the fries and the prize. 'Duh, Clair. Incredible talent you got there. Hmm ... broken leg – period of rest. What a wanker. If you're so psychic, why didn't you predict the accident, huh?' I stared at him, dumfounded. 'Why'da let me break my Mother-Fudging leg in the first place, lunatic?'

But as bad as it was to give someone a 'duh' reading, it paled in comparison to giving them the *exact* answers they wanted to hear, and then spending the next twenty-three Christmases listening to – say your sister Abby – getting smashed and shouting, 'Clair you said I'd be married with two identical, blond, extremely brilliant twin boys and living in Quebec, Canada, by now. Where are they, Clair? Where are my two twins? Where is my tall, entre-preneurial, Canadian husband and my two twins? Eh? Eh? Is Santa bringing them this year, Clair? Is he? Is *he*?'

It took superhuman strength on my part not to shout back at her at the top of my lungs, 'Twins *means* two, Abby. You don't say "two twins"; it's redundant! Obviously they must get their brilliance from their tall, entrepreneurial, Canadian father!'

Besides, I gave her that reading when I was *twelve*. It took me years before I could take off my psychic training wheels. Abby, on the other hand, still hadn't let it go. The above tantrum was *last* Christmas. I'm thirty-two and she's thirty-eight, and she still blames me for her naked ring finger and barren womb. I also told her she would lose her left eye in a freak mining accident, and you don't see her holding me responsible for that one not panning out.

'Come on, Clair. Are you going to do this one for me or not?' Brian whined.

We both knew I was going to do it. I was a complete pushover by nature, and as my three ex-husbands could attest, I have never been able to resist a man on his knees. But that didn't mean I wasn't going to milk it a little before giving in. Especially since I had already put my Tarot cards away, taken down my sign, and packed up the yellow silk scarf I used for my ten-card Celtic spread.

'If I do this – and I'm not saying I will – what are you going to do for me?' I said. Brian sighed, folded his arms across his chest, and tried to match my intimidating gaze while I studied my reflection in the spoon hanging around his neck. It was starting to turn his Adam's Apple slightly green, but Brian refused to take it off. He was determined to bend it with his mind, twist it into tiny knots using only the Power of Thought. He'd been wearing it a little over a year and a half.

'You could charge them double,' Brian said, jerking his head toward his tent. 'The two of them are walking advertisements for Gucci, Prada, and Coach.'

'I don't care if they're carrying gold bricks,' I said. 'I'm not charging anybody double.' Brian sighed and ran his hands through his hair. He wasn't exactly a handsome man, slightly elflike in appearance, despite his six-foot frame. His blond hair was curly and static, ears splayed out like television antennas, his nose terminally pink. On the plus side, he had sparkling emerald eyes, a full head of hair, and a charismatic aura he never failed to inflict on women. How else could you explain a tall, lanky elf-man getting so much tail?

Although, according to my best friend Karen, he had a very large package, so that could have accounted for a hefty percent of it. She unwrapped the said package in the upstairs hallway at my birthday party last year after drinking four shots of tequila off his stomach. Incidentally, all I got was a cheap crystal ball and a pair of orange-striped gym socks.

'God, you're such a Girl Scout. Fine. Do this for me and I'll fix you up with my friend Scott.'

'Brian,' I warned. He knew full well I wasn't going to go out with his friend Scott, or John, or Jeff, or T-Bone, or any of the other men he'd tried to push on me the past year. I was on a long, long, hiatus from men. As a bona fide recovering in-love-aholic, I was officially cut off.

'Okay, okay, calm down. Do this for me and I'll switch places with you tomorrow.'

Our booths were stationed at the Chicago Psychic Fair, in the gymnasium at the Healing Arts Community Center. We were sandwiched in between booths on acupuncture, massage, herbal remedies, yoga, and vegetarian cookies. I had the unfortunate luck of being next to a vegan fanatic whose booth was covered with pictures of bloody cows. Although I was all for the humane treatment of animals, I couldn't ignore my inner carnivore; I'd been craving a cheeseburger all day.

Brian's booth, however, was across from homemade fudge. Whereas the sugary scent drew customers to his vicinity, the bloody cows scared them away from mine. His offer was generous, but I couldn't take him up on it.

'I'm not here tomorrow,' I told him.

'What do you mean you're not here tomorrow?'

'I'm going on my pilgrimage,' I bragged. Every year, for the past three years, I'd taken a road trip. It was the only thing that had kept me sane – and single – since my last divorce. This year I needed it more than ever.

'Who's here instead?' Brian asked, his voice rising in pitch and cracking like he was going through puberty. He started fingering his spoon. 'Don't tell me it's Dame Diaphannie. You know I can't work with "Double D." ' Not wanting to get him started on her, I reached into my purse and touched the gold-embossed envelope I'd been carrying around the past week like a time bomb strapped to my chest, hoping Brian would pick up on it and ask me about it. Ed, my third husband, 'the one that was supposed to stick,' was getting married.

Alexis, his twenty-four-year-old ballerina-bride-to-be, took it upon herself to invite me to the blessed event. If I didn't get out of town, I might just show up. And at the toast, I might very well raise my glass and announce to everyone how Ed said he'd always love *me*. How he'd stood on our back porch one humid Friday evening, still dressed in his work clothes, and tearfully confessed that he didn't want to be married. How he hoped I'd find it in my heart to forgive him. How he had really, really, really tried because of how much he loved me – but, he just wasn't the marrying type.

Oh, yes, I needed my pilgrimage. My sanity was at stake. Brian was still ranting about Dame Diaphannie.

'That cow listens in on my readings and corrects me when I'm doing my best work.'

'I know. . . .'

'Last time she actually yelled over the curtain, "It's never gonna happen, honey: he's having an affair with your sister." '

'She's out of control,' I agreed halfheartedly, as images of her colorful turbans, stick-on rubies, and sandalwood incense floated through my mind. She spoke in tongues, smoked two packs of cigarellos a day, and occasionally rolled her eyes back in her head as if she were having a full-blown epileptic fit during readings. I pulled the invitation out of my purse and waved it hypnotically in front of Brian.

'Did I mention Ed is getting married?'

'About seventeen times,' Brian said, throwing a worried glance at his booth. Crushed by his lack of enthusiasm, I mentally blew black smoke over his aura, like a manic-depressive maid sprinkling the dust back on the furniture instead of polishing it off.

'Do the reading, Clair. I know you could use the money.' He had me there. I had a stack of bills at home, all accruing late fees.

'Fine,' I said, dropping my purse on the card table with a thud. 'Let's just get it over with.' I was unpacking my cards when suddenly Brian put his hands on my shoulders and turned me to face him.

'Um . . . Clair?'

'Yes?' I said, startled at his intensity.

'Rachel is . . . uh . . . the sensitive type – you know? A little . . . uh . . . *wound up*, I guess you would say.'

'I'm sure I'll survive,' I said.

'It's not you I'm worried about. It's her. She's extremely . . . uh . . . wound up.'

'Wound up, wound up. I got it. Don't worry, Brian. I won't add any of my own vibes, I'll just read the cards.'

'Perfect. But – still – be careful.'

'Don't give it a second thought,' said I, the fool.

Daily Horoscope — Pisces

Cheer up, things will get worse.

My first impression of Rachel Morgan was that she was a woman in a lot of pain. She reminded me of a poodle just out of the bath, staring at you with big, pleading eyes. But despite her obvious distress, she was a stunningly beautiful woman.

She had fresh-from-the-salon blond hair cut in a bob, eyes the color of the Aegean Sea, and a body straight from the gym/tanning bed/Pilates/Bikram Yoga. Whereas I looked the part of a gypsy, with my voluptuous, slightly thinner-than-hour-glass figure, curly brownish-gold hair, green eyes, and my favorite trait – olive skin – Rachel Morgan was pure Super Barbie. She also had the unique quality of being both beautiful and nonthreatening; I had just met her and I wanted to hold her hand, become her new best friend, and tell her everything was going to be all right.

Her friend, Susan, on the other hand, trim with dark hair and hazel eyes, would have been considered beautiful too, except for the dark aura hovering about her, and the fact that she was staring at me like a makeshift slingshot, pulled tight and poised to plunge a rusty pocketknife into my side at the slightest provocation.

'Won't you sit down,' I said, gesturing to the two empty chairs across from me. My cards were out of the box and lying face down on my grandmother's yellow silk scarf. Susan and Rachel sat down and looked at the cards as if they were a wild animal. I stifled a giggle; unnecessary laughter was a detriment to my mysterious aura.

There are seventy-eight cards in a Tarot deck, divided into the Major and Minor Arcana. 'Arcana,' deriving from the Latin word *arcanus*, means 'closed' or 'secret.' The trump suit, or Major Arcana, is composed of twenty-two cards. Each card has a picture that shows a behavior, action, or possible future event. The cards are also named and numbered – in the Major Arcana they go from One to Twenty-One. The exception to this is The Fool, he is number Zero.

That leaves the Minor Arcana, consisting of fifty-six cards divided into four suits: Swords, Cups, Coins, and Wands. There are fourteen cards in each suit, numbering from Ace to Ten, and four face cards: Page, Knight, Queen, and King. Like playing cards, (which originate from Tarot cards) there are hundreds of decks and styles, and professional readers often have quite a diverse collection at their disposal. I was no exception.

But since I had taken an immediate liking to Rachel, I had decided to use my personal favorite, a Medieval-style rendering of the Major and Minor Arcana, with intricate, hand-painted figures whose vibrant colors hadn't faded a bit with the passage of time.

They belonged to the first psychic in my family, my maternal grandmother, Isabella Ivars, who passed her gift on to me, along with her cards. They are hers and they are mine. This was the deck I used whenever I wanted answers to my own questions; they're my way of speaking to my grandmother, asking for her guidance. Rachel and Susan sat silently and watched me spread the cards out. 'I take it this reading is for you,' I said to Rachel.

She nodded but did not speak, which is how I preferred it. There was nothing worse than a chatty Querent. I finished shuffling the deck and asked Rachel to cut them from left to right into three distinct piles. Her hands trembled as she followed my directions. Once again working left to right, I had her gather the piles and place them on top of each other. As I reached for the top card, Susan's hand shot out and stopped me.

'Just a minute. I need to pay you. Rachel, this is on me, remember?'

I opened my mouth to tell her she could pay me later, but we were already in motion. Susan pulled me to the farthest corner of the tent. 'There's something you should know,' she said in a low whisper. I glanced at Rachel who was intently studying a large diamond ring on her right finger.

'She's getting married and she has cold feet,' I said.

Susan's mouth fell open like the lid of a rusty mailbox. She glanced at Rachel who now had her hands folded in her lap, obscuring the ring. I didn't normally resort to such parlor tricks, but I had low blood sugar, was late for my pilgrimage, and didn't like this woman at all.

'Good guess,' she said, composing herself. 'She's marrying my brother Jack—'

'You know,' I said, pulling away from her, 'the less I know the better.'

'You don't understand. This reading has to go well.'

'I don't control what the cards say. But don't worry, even if the reading is – say, less than favorable – she has the power to change any possible outcome.'

'Listen to me,' Susan hissed. 'Rachel is totally freaking out, okay? She had some kind of weird dream last week and suddenly she's confused. Confused,' she said throwing her arms up. 'We've been planning this wedding for two years. We've invited two hundred prominent guests, Chicago's best ice sculptor, and a famous Fusion caterer from the East.'

'I see,' I said. 'But—'

'Not to mention the thirteen bridesmaids who have been dieting their asses off – literally – just to fit into their custom-made gowns. And then there's the ten-foot fountain of Dom Perignon, a cake so exquisite it should be a federal crime to slice, and a collection of flowers so exotic they're going to make the Garden of Eden look like home-grown herbs on a window sill.' Susan took another microstep toward me. Her breath smelled like cold, hard mints, and her voice poured out like wet cement. 'Rachel Morgan is going to marry my brother in two weeks, and if you say one negative word to her about it, I'm going to make your life a living hell. Do you understand?'

'I understand perfectly,' I said.

'Good,' Susan said, holding out two crisp one hundred dollar bills for the twenty-five-dollar reading. I turned away from the cash and headed to my table where Rachel sat cross-legged on the chair, her skinny leg bouncing up and down like a jack hammer.

'I'm sorry,' I said to Rachel with the most comforting smile I could muster. 'But I can't do this reading.' I gathered my grandmother's cards and started putting them back in the box. Rachel shot out of her chair like a rogue astronaut ejected from the space shuttle.

'Why can't you do it? It's something bad, isn't it? Oh God, you've got a bad vibe.'

'No, no, no. Nothing like that,' I tried to assure her. 'It's late, that's all. I thought I had time for this but I—'

'What did you say to her?' Rachel turned on Susan. 'What did she say to you?'

'Look – a Tarot card reading isn't for everyone,' I explained. 'I can tell just from looking at you, your expectations are too high.' I looked her in the eye.

She didn't budge.

'You've come to the wrong place for the answers you seek,' I said waving my hands mysteriously and slightly rolling my eyes back in my head. Rachel started to cry. I sat down, pulled her down to her chair, and took her hand. 'Maybe we could just talk,' I said. 'Susan tells me you're getting married. That can be a scary thing. I should know, I've done it three times myself.'

'Oh, now there's someone you should be taking marriage advice from,' Susan said. 'Let's go, Rachel.'

'Three times?' Rachel asked, horrified.

'Yes,' I admitted. 'But the first one doesn't really count because I was only eighteen and the second one was in Vegas, so – really, technically – I guess you could say I've only been married one, one and a half times at the most.'

'Rachel, let's get out of here,' Susan insisted.

'If you had it to do over again?' Rachel started to say. 'I mean . . . did you have doubts?'

'Did I have doubts,' I said. 'Good God yes. Of course I did. I had that little voice, you know?' Rachel nodded, which is the only excuse I can come up with for not repairing the broken dam that was my mouth. 'Marriage is a huge – I mean huge – commitment,' I continued. 'I was way too impulsive. You can't even imagine the things I never even thought of—'

'Miss,' Susan said.

'I mean the things you learn about a person,' I railed. Susan was now physically trying to pull Rachel out of the chair. I was oblivious.

'You think you know him – and *wham* – you find out the man you married paints his toenails black when there's a full moon. Or that he doesn't like the way you sip tea. Like there's a right and wrong way to *sip tea*. Or he suddenly stops having sex with you because the blouse you wore the week before reminded him of his mother.'

'His mother,' Rachel repeated in a deathly whisper.

'Miss,' Susan said again, louder.

'Believe me, there are going to be days when you can't stand the way he looks, smells, talks, and even *breathes*.' Rachel's beautiful face had turned to stone. I didn't notice. 'But the worst part is when you know – when you just know deep down in your bones – that the man who said he'd love you forever doesn't want to see, taste, smell, or touch you anymore either.'

'Miss. You are *very* unprofessional,' Susan roared. That stopped me. She was right. What was I doing? This whole thing with Ed had me all out of whack. Not to mention staring at bloody cows all day. It was really messing with my mind. All I could think of was Ed – Ed and the ballerina covered in blood. And I wasn't a violent person at all. I was a Pisces. We're humble and kind. Peace loving. We're not like – what was her name?

'What's the name of the girl who hacked up her parents with a hatchet?' I asked Susan and Rachel. This time both of them started to back away. Oh, God. I needed to get away from other human beings as quickly as possible. But seriously, what was her name? Lucy?

'I'm so sorry,' I said to Rachel. 'I am being very unprofessional. Let's get back on track here, shall we? Let's just see what the cards have to say.' But Rachel had gone white.

'Susan, would you mind waiting outside the tent,' she said. 'I want to be alone with Clair.'

Susan shook her head and locked eyes with me. 'Susan. I want some privacy,' Rachel persisted.

Susan hesitated but relented under Rachel's steady gaze. 'I'll be right outside,' she said.

'Look,' I confessed when we were alone. 'Susan told me you've been having bad dreams. Maybe I can help you interpret them?' Rachel Morgan sat straight in her chair, put her palms flat down on the table, and stared at me without a single tear left in her eyes.

'Just deal the cards,' she said, like we were playing Black Jack in Vegas.

'I thought you wanted to talk—'

'No. I've heard enough. I just want you to deal the cards, and in a very loud voice – so Susan can hear – I want you to tell me that marrying Jack Heron would be the worst mistake I could ever make in my entire life.'

'Whoa,' I said. 'I didn't mean to freak you out—'

'A deadly mistake.'

'I mean just because my marriages were complete and utter failures—'

'Please,' Rachel begged. 'Get me out of this.'

'I'm sorry,' I said. 'I can't continue this reading. I'm normally very professional. It's just that my third husband, Ed – the one I thought would stick – he's getting married again. To a fucking ballerina. And it's just really messed me up you know? I mean even though we've been over for a long time. Three years.' I felt tears come to my eyes. 'He said he'd love me forever.' I took a deep breath and tried to compose myself. 'A fucking ballerina,' I repeated bitterly.

Rachel's hand flew out and landed on top of my deck. 'Deal the cards,' she said again. 'Tell me not to marry Jack.'

'Please don't touch my cards,' I said, trying to regain some semblance of composure. 'You know I can't just tell you that. The cards will say whatever they have to say.' Rachel removed her hand from the cards but kept it planted on my side of the table.

'Lizzie Borden!' I shouted. 'Lizzie Borden took an axe, gave her parents forty whacks.' Rachel stared at me. 'Sorry,' I said. 'I just remembered that.' Rachel leaned in.

'Here's one for you,' she hissed. 'Do you remember the Runaway Bride?' Her formerly diminutive voice had flatlined into a frightening monotone. I had just decided I should become the Runaway Psychic, shove everything in my bag and get the hell out of here, but something stopped me. Okay, if you must know, I kind of wanted to know where she was going with this. I took her hand, lifted it, and put it back on her side of the table. We eyeballed each other for another few seconds. Then I nodded for her to continue.

'If you don't help me out of this mess, you're going to know me as the Suicide Bride. I'm going to shoot myself in my Vera Wang wedding gown in front of two hundred well-dressed guests and my unsuspecting groom. I'm going to wait until right before I say, "I Do," put the barrel in my mouth, and say your name.'

'What?' I said, completely thrown out of the riveting melodrama by the mention of my name.

'I'm going to say, "Clair,"' she said, spotting my business card at the edge of the table, ' "Clair Ivars has my blood on her hands."'

She was so convincing I found myself staring at her milky, white face as if droplets of blood would drip from her pouty lips at any second. She smiled with her perfectly straight, white teeth, and leaned in for the kill. 'And then,' she said, whispering as if we were on a first date, 'I'm going to squeeze the trigger, and put a bullet through the back of my head.'

I must admit, part of me was a tiny bit tempted to ask her how she was going to enunciate all that with a gun in her mouth, but I reined myself in. There we sat, the psychic and the psycho, staring each other down, as red, pulsing, energy danced above our heads.

'You need professional help,' I said as quietly and gently as I could.

'What I need is for you to do this reading,' she shot back. 'What I need is for this reading to tell me *not* to marry Jack Heron. What I need,' she said her voice rising to near-panic level, 'is for you to yell it out, so that the Ice Pick out there hears you! *Capice*?'

I held my breath and quickly ran through my options. What did Brian say? She was a little ... *wound up?* I was going to kill Brian the minute I saw him. Maybe I'd skip my spiritual journey. Killing Brian would be my spiritual journey. First I'd torture him, then I'd kill him. I didn't know a thing about torture except that it usually involved duct tape. *Get duct tape*, I mentally jotted down.

I was in an impossible situation. I wanted to argue with Rachel, tell her that no one in his or her right mind was going to blame me for her actions – that even if I did give her a bad reading, people would still blame *her* for canceling her wedding by shooting herself in the back of the head, not *me*.

Wouldn't they?

Maybe I should have just kicked her out and told 'the Ice Pick' about her threat. Surely, the Ice Pick would have believed me and not her.

Wouldn't she?

At the least, she wouldn't want to see blood on a perfectly good Vera Wang wedding gown.

Besides, what woman in love lets a Tarot card reading

stop her wedding? Obviously, this woman wasn't in love. And she was too gutless to end it herself.

In the end, I didn't do it for her. In the end I did it for Jack Heron, whom I had never met, but surely he didn't deserve this kind of fate. Either she would go ahead and marry him and he'd be stuck with someone who really didn't love him for the rest of his life, or she *would* put a gun in her mouth during the wedding vows and blow her brains out, and he would be forever known as the guy who was literally left at the altar by the Suicide Bride.

And, whether it was logical or not, if anyone could manage to understand her mumblings with the gun in her mouth, I would be forever known as the psychic who couldn't predict a suicidal bride to save her life.

This too shall pass, I said to myself as I glanced toward the curtain, picked up the first card, and laid it face up on the table. You don't have to be psychic to know what it was. I've already told you.

It was, indeed, The Fool.

Daily Horoscope – Pisces

One girl's best friend can be another's worst enemy.

'What does that mean?' Rachel asked as we stared at The Fool. I was using the ancient Celtic method, a ten-card spread in which the cards were laid out face down in the shape of the Celtic cross.

'This card represents you, the Querent,' I answered carefully. Rachel made an upward motion with both hands, indicating I should pump up the volume. 'The Fool indicates one who is plowing ahead foolishly in his or her current situation,' I resumed in a louder voice. Rachel gave me a thumbs-up and I responded with a dirty look; I didn't like interruptions during my readings.

'Now we'll have to see how the rest of the cards play out, but this tells me you are in a state of confusion and you need to watch where you're going. This covers you,' I said as I turned over the next card. It was The Magician.

'Why is he upside down?' Rachel asked.

'He's reversed,' I said. 'It changes the meaning.' I studied her for a moment before speaking. 'You're trying to control your environment,' I said. 'One might even say you're trying to manipulate things to go your way.'

'Get on with it,' Rachel hissed.

'The next card will show us the obstacles you face in your current situation,' I managed to say without strangling her. Rachel leaned forward. She was so engrossed in the cards, she didn't notice Susan creeping back into the tent, lingering in the corner. I turned over The Devil.

'My future Mother-in-Law,' Rachel gasped.

'The Devil actually represents a struggle between good and evil,' I said. 'Or less dramatically, you will encounter a struggle between right and wrong.'

'I'm telling you, it's Madeline Heron. She's the devil.'

'Rachel!' Susan said. Rachel's face turned white as she registered that Susan was in the tent.

'I'm sorry, Susan. But your mother is . . . difficult,' she hissed, like a balloon letting out all its air.

'Nonsense. She's just a successful woman. Like Martha Stewart,' Susan asserted, once again taking the seat next to Rachel.

'What does she do?' I asked. Normally I would stick to the reading without engaging in idle chitchat, but I was hoping to stall the reading, trying to figure out a way out of the lies Rachel wanted me to tell.

'My family owns and operates one of the finest rare wine cellars in the world,' Susan bragged. 'Perhaps you've heard of us? Heron Cellars? My brother has also just started to market and promote our own distinct label of vodka. Heron Estates Vodka?' I had never heard of it, so I shook my head.

'That's not the official name,' Susan said. 'Jack's holding a contest to name it. You know. Like they do at the zoo. When a baby panda is born.'

'They do it with elephants too,' Rachel added quietly.

'Ah,' I joked. 'I'm sure children everywhere are hitting the bottle and putting on their thinking caps,' I said, miming downing back a shot and then tapping my head. I drew two blank stares from the pair across from me.

'We're not encouraging *children* to drink vodka,' Susan said icily.

'You misunderstood us,' Rachel said, horrified at my

comment. 'Children are a precious commodity. Children are our future.'

'Well I love vodka,' I blurted out before she broke into song. I was quite the connoisseur of vodka if I did say so myself.

'Anyway,' Susan continued, 'you should see it in stores soon if Jack gets his way. Which he always does,' she added with a glance at Rachel. Rachel locked eyes with me, silently pleading for help.

'Our estate is nestled in the Shawnee National Forest,' Susan said. 'In fact, Rachel and I will be heading there after this for the big engagement party.'

'Engagement party,' Rachel laughed. 'Your mother has invited every business associate she's ever known and is probably charging them four hundred dollars a plate.'

'Rachel doesn't have an eye for business,' Susan explained to me. 'There's no harm in combining your engagement party with a little wining and dining. Besides, a portion of the profits are going to help . . . some charity. Manatees, was it? Or poor African children. I can't remember which.'

'I can see how you would get them confused,' I said.

'Jack insisted on it. He's the CEO. And a softy. He doesn't have a head for business. Or for wine for that matter. Hence the whole vodka thing. I think it's a big mistake, but once Jack makes up his mind, that's it.' I glanced at Rachel. She kicked me underneath the table and subtly mimed putting a gun into her mouth. She wanted me to get to the 'Don't you dare go through with this wedding' part of the reading. I was starting to feel her pain. The sooner I finished this reading, the better. I turned over The Page of Swords.

'You have to watch out,' I said. 'You have an enemy. He or she may try to thwart your efforts in achieving your goal.'

'An enemy?' Rachel whispered dramatically. She glanced at Susan who shook her head. Rachel twitched her nose at me. I turned over The Four of Cups.

This is where I veered off the ethical psychic path a little.

I wanted them gone.

I wanted to go home.

Normally, The Four of Cups represents a 'friendly' warning. It means that you are standing in the way of your own happiness. It's your own negativity causing the problem, nothing else. If you would just drop the chip on your shoulder, everything would be fine. I decided to stretch the truth a little. I let out a little gasp. Susan and Rachel leaned in.

'The Four of Cups brings you a very, serious warning,' I said. 'Things are not right, they are not balanced.'

'Oh, God,' Rachel said, manufacturing a tear.

'It's just a game,' Susan said. 'Don't be so dramatic.'

'This is behind you,' I said, turning over The Two of Cups. Susan glanced behind her. 'I mean this is in Rachel's past,' I said as Susan blushed. 'This represents love, marriage.' I could have interpreted this as the preparations for the wedding, coming to a close as the day approached. But that evening was anything but normal. I glanced at Rachel one more time. She nodded her approval.

'I'm sorry, Rachel,' I said, giving her what she wanted, 'this card is telling me that for you, for this particular relationship, love and marriage are a thing of your past.'

Rachel clutched her hands up to her mouth. 'I knew it,' she cried.

'That's ridiculous,' Susan said, leaping out of her chair. 'Take that back.'

'This is your immediate future,' I said, ignoring Susan and turning over The World. This is a very positive card. It means all of your goals are possible to achieve; in other words, you hold the world in your hands. 'Oh no,' I exclaimed. 'This is *awful*. Rachel, I'm sorry. I've never had such a strong, negative reading. The cards are warning you – if you go ahead with this marriage,' I said, 'it's going to be a total disaster.'

'No,' Rachel said, churning out tears so real that I was

momentarily stunned. It reminded me of a pasta Play-Doh maker I had as a child. You turned its red crank and it oozed out little wormy strings. Tears poured down Rachel's face so fast, I found myself looking for her crank.

'Can't you see what she's doing?' Susan said, standing up. 'She's messing with you. Let's go, Rachel.'

It was time for me to end this. I turned over another card. It was either luck, or fate, but either way the card I turned over was Death.

Now the Death card simply means that life as you know it is about to take an abrupt turn. It rarely means a physical death – it simply means a sudden change. But that's not where I went with it that evening.

'This couldn't get any worse, Rachel,' I said, standing up. 'Do not,' I said in my most menacing voice, 'marry Jack Heron. If you do, you will regret it the rest of your life. What little will be left of it,' I said, holding up the Death card and turning it to face her.

I know, I know, I know. Straight into the deep end, round the bend, over the rainbow, down under so far I would have to learn to love vegemite sandwiches. But Rachel had made it clear she didn't want to marry the poor guy – so actually I was doing them both a huge favor.

And as far as 'the Ice Pick' was concerned, surely she would recover. She could throw herself into her charity work and go swim with the manatees – or poor African children.

'It's like my dream,' Rachel whispered. 'It's exactly like the warning in my dream. I can't do it, Susan. I can't marry Jack.'

'These are parlor tricks, Rachel,' Susan screamed. 'Do you hear me? This woman is not psychic. She's a vulture.'

'Hey,' I said. 'I am *not* a vulture. A vulture would have taken the two hundred dollars you offered me to give her a positive reading.'

'What?' Rachel screeched, turning on Susan. 'How could you? You knew I needed to hear the truth.'

'The truth? You call this the truth? It's lies, Rachel, all lies. She's scamming you.'

'I'm not scamming anyone,' I said. 'In fact, forget the twenty-five dollars. Good day ladies.' But Susan wasn't finished.

'If you're so psychic, why don't you prove it?' she said, black-marble eyes glowing like those of a wild animal, in the middle of the night. 'Tell me one thing about me that you couldn't possibly know.'

'Look,' I began.

'One thing.'

'I'm not going to—'

'Because you can't.'

Sticks and stones—

'You're a con artist—'

May break my—

'Preying on innocent victims—'

Bones—

'You're a phony – a freak.'

'Your husband *is* sleeping with the nanny,' I blurted out. 'You've known it for months, but you refuse to confront him because you're afraid he'll leave you.'

Susan staggered back, as if my words were a physical force, pushing against her chest. Guilt came crashing down on me. 'I'm so sorry,' I said, reaching for her. But I was too late. Susan burst out the flaps of the tent, leaving me in their wake. They swayed rapidly in and out, like a giant finger shaming me. Rachel stared at me.

'I knew Harold was a slime,' she whispered. 'He hit on me, too. Although ... the nanny? I didn't see that one coming.' She let the thought drop and stared at me. 'How did you know?' she asked, taking a step toward me, her voice deathly quiet.

I didn't answer her; I ran out to catch Susan, but was greeted only by a silent, shiny gym floor and a row of condemning, empty tents. Suddenly Rachel tapped me on the shoulder, nearly killing me with fright.

'What did the cards really say?' she asked. 'About me

marrying Jack?' I couldn't believe my ears. For a moment, I didn't know how to answer.

'They said – I didn't – you wanted—' I stumbled over my answer like a firewalker with a wooden leg.

'Tell me,' Rachel begged. 'Am I doing the right thing?' The cards rose in my mind as I stared at her. Truthfully, they had predicted an amicable marriage; okay, maybe even a *great* marriage, but did it matter if she was willing to go to such lengths to end it? This woman was seriously off balance. Someone had to think of her poor fiancé here.

'Yes,' I said, crossing my fingers behind my back. 'I think you're doing the right thing.' She stared at me for a moment and then nodded solemnly. Then, she turned away before I could decipher whether those were real tears in her eyes this time, or if it was just the way the gymnasium lights were reflecting on them. In a guilty fog, I went back inside my tent and started to clean up. I wondered again how I had ever let myself get into this mess, grateful it was over. Tomorrow was a new day. Tomorrow I would forget all about this and start my journey. My mood picked up a notch. I would learn a lesson from this and move on.

It wasn't until my cards were put away for the third and final time that day that a shiny object sitting smack dab in the middle of my table caught my eye. Dumbfounded, I crept up on it as if it were an exotic insect. I put my face as close to it as I could without going blind, and simply stared.

There, sitting in the middle of my table, shooting off specks of light like a bouquet of Fourth of July sparklers, was a three-carat, diamond engagement ring.

Daily Horoscope — Pisces

The light at the end of the tunnel just went out.

I stared at the ring, took a deep breath, and fought the urge to skip it across the floor of the gymnasium like a pebble across a pond. Although I had been married three times, only Ed, husband numero tres, had given me a diamond. I was eighteen with numero uno, and we wore mood rings. I was twenty-five with numero dos, and we tattooed the symbol for infinity on our middle fingers. By the time I hit the big *30*, I was older and wiser, and I told the-one-I-thought-would-stick straight up I wanted a diamond ring.

I should have been a little bit more specific.

I should have asked for a diamond large enough to see with the naked eye. It was small 't' tiny. But we were broke and he meant well. Besides, if you squinted at it just right (and held a magnifying glass up to it), it seemed a tad larger. I spent the entire summer leading up to our wedding squinting and swiveling my head around at different angles for maximum, precious-gem, enlargement. 'Why are you squinting?' Ed finally asked me after several weeks of it escaping his attention.

'It makes it sparkle,' I said holding out my hand. 'You try it.'

'Get the knife, we're going to be late,' he said instead of

turning his head and squinting like I had reasonably requested. That was the weekend he talked me into four days of 'survival' training in the backwoods of West Virginia as a 'fair trade' for the premarital counseling I had insisted we attend.

The trip was hell. My new hiking boots gave me blisters, I hadn't even thought to bring a sports bra, and *one of us* forgot the food backpack, or the *feed bag* as Ed had been calling it all day.

I'll give you a hint – it wasn't me.

I was in charge of the *vodka*, two bottles that were weighing down my backpack, swishing and clinking together as I tried gingerly to step over protruding roots of large, angry elm trees. Ed, instead of comforting me and assuring me that he would find a way to feed his low-blood-sugar fiancée, (i.e., use his new hunting knife to spear a tasty fish or skin a small, aging rabbit whose long, happy life in the forest was coming to an end anyhow and therefore he didn't mind dying a swift and painless death so that I wouldn't pass out) – my future husband – instead – completely ignored me.

He was too busy plowing full speed ahead, hacking down vines in our path with such gusto that, after four hours of hiking and taking furtive, bitter swigs off of one of the bottles of Grey Goose, I had myself entirely convinced that Ed had lured me out here to kill me.

I was about to start dropping bread crumbs when I realized all over again that we didn't have any bread crumbs because the idiot I was going to marry had forgotten the bread. And then I wondered if, despite months of telling me I didn't look fat, Ed secretly thought I was fat, and that's why he didn't bring the feed bag; he was trying to starve me out.

By the time we pitched our tent and discovered that Ed had wrapped the feed bag inside the tent in an effort to streamline the number of bags he had to carry, I had convinced myself that it had been part of his master plan all along. He wanted me to think I was going to starve (or be hacked to pieces), so that when he pulled out the silver dried packets of ready-to-eat Beef Burgundy and Penne, I would be whipped into a grateful, ravenous, sexual frenzy.

And it worked! I was completely fired up.

And drunk, too, but what's hiking without a couple a hundred little swigs along the way?

But instead of ravishing me, Ed fell asleep five minutes after drinking his meal and hitting the sleeping bag. So I mixed my beef dinner with the rest of the vodka, wandered out into the pitch-black to pee, and ended up wiping myself with poison ivy. Then, what with all the screaming, blaming, and itching that ensued, it wasn't surprising that it wasn't until we were on the silent, fuming drive home that I even noticed my diamond ring was missing. We never went back for it, and that was the one and only diamond I had ever owned.

I picked up Rachel's ring and experienced such an intense rush of emotion that I almost dropped it. I couldn't believe I was one of those women illogically drawn to a shiny object. After all, I had finally realized that marriage wasn't a destination, it was a pit stop. One I was never going to visit again. After all, three times the charm, three strikes and you're out, three's a crowd.

Marriage and gypsies don't mix.

But the ring was so pretty. I didn't have to squint to see this one sparkle. In fact, I probably should have been wearing sunglasses to protect me from its brilliant glare. *Precious*, Smeagol from *Lord of the Rings* whined, and, like a slap across the face, I came out of my daydream. Horrified, I looked down at my hands. They were poised to place the ring on my left finger. I was dying to put it on. The next thought hit me like an unexpected gush of wind. *No woman in her right mind would leave this ring in the hands of a total stranger*.

Turn it into a beautiful necklace, bracelet, or earrings, sure. Sell it on eBay or craigslist to the highest bidder, okay. Trade it in for new breasts, absolutely.

Or – if the woman had been betrayed or dumped or

humiliated – toss it out to sea, smash it with a hammer, shove it down the throat of her beloved. I understood the depths scorned women were capable of, and could rationalize just about any behavior, no matter how odd. But leave this ring on my table, in the hands of a total stranger just because of the premarital jitters, a few frosty toes?

Never.

And yet, here it was.

Fearing to make skin contact with the ring again, I picked it up with my sleeve, dropped it in a little pouch I used to keep crystals in, and carefully placed the pouch in my purse. How much was this rock worth? More money than I made in a year – or ten. Before I could do anything rash, like putting it on, I needed to get this thing home. Without dropping it. Or swallowing it. Or projecting, 'Mug me!' like a drive-in movie. I hopped on my bus, avoiding eye contact with everyone. Too obvious. Could anyone else feel the heat rising from my purse?

I lived in a studio apartment on the fourteenth floor of the Almeda Brownstone on Maxwell Street in downtown, Sweet Home, Chicago. My place was small, but I loved its wood floors, brick fireplace, and large arched doorway into the kitchen. I also had a great peek-a-boo view of the Sears Tower from the kitchen window. All I had to do was stick most of my body out the window, crane my head to the left, and voilà! I had a view. But the best part was rent that didn't drain my lifeblood.

Whereas most Tarot card readers have to keep a day job in addition to plying their psychic craft, my tiny place allowed me to make my living solely reading cards. I had also given up cable, high-speed Internet, text-messaging, voice mail, match.com, and all extracurricular shopping. I bought generic groceries and thrift store clothes and hardly ever ate out. It was a bit of a drag leading such a predictable life, but I was 'living my dream.'

I used to do readings in my living room, but then I got a stalker and that put an end to that. Since the stalker, I've kept home and work separate. Besides, it helps avoid burnout. I was getting weary of people thinking that either I was a total kook or I knew everything under the sun, with absolutely no latitude in between. And believe me, there's no empathy for a psychic having an off-day. No one is impressed if your readings are 'close.' Clients love to scrutinize every detail, dig out your mistakes, and use them against you. I've learned not to take it personally; I know I'm not perfect, I'm just waiting for the rest of the world to catch on.

Despite my flair for reading the cards, as I've already told you, I didn't get lotto numbers, I had no idea where Jimmy Hoffa was buried, and I had a complete blind spot when it came to predicting my own future – especially when it came to love.

Hence, my three failed marriages.

But I didn't have time to obsess on my inadequacies; the minute I got home I was going to pack for my road trip. As far as the ring was concerned, surely Rachel would change her mind, track me down, and take it back. And even though she had written down Jack Heron's address on the back of one of my business cards and placed it underneath the ring with the words 'Please Return To:' didn't mean I was obligated to do it.

Was I?

Surely she would call any minute. She took my business card, didn't she? She must have. Yes, she would definitely call. If I didn't hear from her within the hour I'd call Brian and get her phone number. No way was I going to babysit the Hope Diamond for a suicidal bride.

Finally, the bus pulled up to my stop. I couldn't wait to grab my black leather duffel bag, throw in enough clothes for four days, and get out Clair's Spiritual Road Map and Spinner. I had this down to an art. I never made reservations, I didn't pre-plan, and I never knew exactly where I was going until I spun the wheel. The wheel was from SORRY!, a child's board game I picked up at a sidewalk sale.

The spinner was a cardboard circle with a plastic red

arrow pointing in the direction of four colors: yellow, red, blue, and green. I used the colors to represent North, South, East and West. I'd take out a map, always starting with Chicago, spin the wheel, and whichever direction it pointed, I'd go! My driving range was between three and eight hours. Once I got going in the right direction, I would stop wherever I wanted to, turning off where it 'felt right.' It was one of my few chances to drive too – I always took the bus in the city – and I relished the chance to hop in a rental car and hit the open road.

Not all of life was predestined and I, more than anyone, needed frequent reminders of that fact. A week of exploring and solitude and I would be right as rain! I'm sure by the time I was done I'd be ready to send Ed and the ballerina a Cuisinart. I couldn't wait to find out where I was going this time.

Spontaneously, as I thought this, the image of the little board game spinner rose to mind. I tried to flick it toward my new destination, but it was stuck. Stubbornly, I mentally tried to spin it again. It didn't budge. As I walked the five blocks to my apartment, I tried not to let the vision get me down. *It's not a premonition. Besides, if the wheel is literally stuck, I'll use something else.*

I arrived at my building to find Mrs Romero, my downstairs, token-crazy neighbor, sitting on the stoop of our brownstone, chain-smoking, twirling a baton, and singing in Spanish. 'Hola, Mrs Romero,' I said.

'Buenas noche,' Mrs Romero sang. 'You out late again.'

'Trabajo,' I replied, trying not to breathe as she blew out a plume of carcinogens. 'Working.'

'Devil's work,' she said, dropping her singing voice, lapsing into a guttural growl and shaking the child's baton in the vicinity of my breasts. 'You stop messing with Lucifer!' From now on, I'm telling everyone I meet I'm in insurance. Or I'm a car dealer. That way, when they accuse me of doing the Devil's work, at least there will be some validity to their claims. I looked at Mrs Romero and forced a smile.

'Do you like ballerinas?' I asked impulsively. Her baton suddenly swung around and smacked my ankle.

Hard.

'That *hurts*,' I yelled, clutching my purse and hobbling up the rest of the steps before she could strike again. 'Mrs Romero,' I said when I reached the top of the stairs, 'you cannot hit me, do you understand? Nada. No hitting. If you do it again I'm calling Andrea.' Mrs Romero rolled her eyes. 'I'm sure she wouldn't appreciate her tenants smacking each other around with childhood props,' I added.

Mrs Romero flashed a knowing smile, the one that always convinced me she wasn't as insane as she was pretending to be. Out on the steps she chain-smoked, shrieked in Spanish, wore layers of gaudy clothing, and wielded a silver baton, while inside she probably sat down with chamomile tea and did the *New York Times* crossword puzzle.

Genius actually, and when I hit the age where I could no longer use my sex appeal to get my way, I was going to act completely bonkers too. I planned on living in an old folks' home in Florida, where I would cheat at Bingo and gossip with the other old biddies about the impossibility of finding a good man in this sea of Viagra. Then, if dared by other giggling blue-hairs, I would pee in the hot tub, run naked across the manicured lawns, knock down plastic, pink flamingos, and make beaded water bongs out of our empty cans of Ensure.

I may not have had a clue about my immediate future, but at least I had a long-term plan.

But empathizing with Mrs Romero and her faux insanity didn't make her any easier to deal with. She was here when Andrea bought the building ten years ago, and I had only been here a year and a half, making me the low man on the tenant totem pole.

Furthermore, Mrs Romero had been a complete sweetie to me until she found out what I did for a living. And it's not like I came out and told her I was a Tarot card reader. My deck of cards fell out one day when I was digging through my purse for my keys. I scrambled to pick them up, but I was too late.

Mrs Romero promptly flipped out, reaching for my cards while furiously screaming Bible quotes at me. She had gotten a hold of The High Priestess and was about to crush her between her righteous fingers, when I went all mother-bear-cub crazy. Nobody touches my cards unless I give them permission.

I reached for my card, but when my hands touched hers, I was immediately engulfed in sadness. I felt a yearning so great, I couldn't let go of her. I concentrated all my energy on sending her waves and waves of white light. I summoned earthly sources of heat: sun, fire, and lava poured out of me and wrapped protectively around her, offering their warmth. I called on my idea of God: soaring, snow-peaked mountains, roaring, monstrous oceans, and acres and acres of rolling green hills. I sent them all to her, eye-to-eye, hand-to-hand. Some might find religion inside a stained-glass church, but my salvation was the everlasting outdoors.

Mrs Romero dropped my card like it had been chopped out of her hand. We never spoke of it again.

Since then, we've lapsed into a predictable pattern of interaction. She swears, snarls, smokes, and preaches under her breath, while I speak a few words of polite Spanish to her (namely because I haven't learned any *impolite* words in Spanish yet), and then I extricate myself from her presence as quickly as possible.

Striking me was an unwelcome development. Not that I intended to fight back – it just wasn't in my nature to harm a four-foot, eighty-pound, seventy-five-year-old woman, even if she was wielding a glittery weapon.

As I limped up four flights of stairs, I tried to think happy, calming thoughts.

Road trip! A cute little motel somewhere, a deserted beach, a country road where I could walk for miles and miles. A week without my cell phone or the national news;

a week without clients desperate for news of love and fame and money. A week without soaking up everyone else's emotions like a sponge. A week without Dame Diaphannie blowing cigarello smoke in my face, or Brian fingering his spoon. A week just for me.

Again, the image of the board game spinner appeared before me, with the plastic red arrow refusing to budge. To make matters worse, my ankle was already starting to swell. But it turned out I wasn't going to get a chance to ice it any time soon. There, looming in front of me, blocking my front door, was my stalker.

I should have seen this coming.

Daily Horoscope — Pisces

When going to hell in a handbasket, don't forget to pack a snack.

S he was sitting cross-legged at my front door, camped out, barring me from immediately entering, flinging off my underwire bra, and looking for my spinner. Her name was Terri Lang, and she was the reason I stopped doing readings in my home.

'Clair, finally!' Terri said, uncurling her muscular legs and jumping up as I approached. I didn't even try to stop the groan from escaping my lips.

'Terri,' I said. 'This isn't a good time.'

Terri first came to me nine months earlier. She had seen my ad for private readings on craigslist and was at my front door forty minutes after I e-mailed her back. She's twenty-two, with spiky, mahogany hair, more tattoos than skin, and piercings in so many places it's a wonder I can read her with all that metallic energy in the way.

Unfortunately, her silver accoutrements may actually enhance my abilities, for she's one of those clients I can read without much effort at all. During her first visit she had been in turmoil over losing her driver's license, and because she was starting a new delivery job that required her license, she was in a complete panic. I was her last resort.

As I was doing her reading, the image of a glove compartment, in a vehicle with a driver other than her at the wheel, kept coming to mind. I was about to tell her the license was in someone's glove compartment when I realized I was looking at a picture taped to the glove compartment. Then I saw the color yellow.

'Did you take a cab ride recently?' I asked her.

'Yes, I took one here,' she said breathlessly.

'No. Before here.'

She scrunched up her nose and thought. 'Um – yep – I take 'em all the time.'

'Well, your license was left in a cab.'

'The cards are telling you that?'

I hesitated. No, the cards weren't telling me that. The practice of doing Tarot was one in which you attempted to get your conscious mind out of the way by allowing it to focus on something concrete, such as the cards and their meanings, so your unconscious mind could come through and speak without interruption. It was like your conscious mind was a screaming toddler, and you had to shut it up with a sucker so you could think. In this case, the Tarot was the sucker, I was the thinker.

If no thoughts of your own came through, you could simply read the literal meaning of the cards, a skill that only involved memorization, nothing psychic by any means. There are plenty of 'straight' readers, those without the gift – those whose thoughts remain hidden regardless of their practice – but others, like me, had moments of genuine intuition as we tapped into the energy of the other person. I didn't go into all of that with her.

'That's what I'm getting,' I said.

'Well *which* cab? What's the license number?'

'I don't do numbers. Let's continue with the reading and we'll see if I get anything else, okay?'

I turned over the next card and was attacked by busty twins chewing gum. Wrigleys.

'It was the cab you took when you went to Wrigley's Field for the baseball game,' I said. Her mouth dropped open. 'Just figure out what night that was—'

'Last Wednesday—'

'Call the cab company. Hopefully they'll have your license.'

She called from my apartment – not exactly what I had in mind, but when it turned out they had her license, she gave me a hundred-dollar tip. At the time I was thrilled.

I've been cursed with her ever since. She shows up at all times of day, without calling, at least three times a month, with a new crisis. Who should she date? What's her next career move? How can she get her mother off her back? Does dreaming about men with long hair and shaved legs make her a lesbian transvestite? Is she pregnant? Is her brother a serial killer? Should she buy an iguana?

Finally, three weeks ago, I told her if she couldn't call ahead for an appointment, I was going to have to sever our relationship. *Apparently*, I thought as she stood blocking the way into my home, *her definition of sever is slightly different than mine*. Suddenly, fog filled my cramped apartment hallway like a bathroom filling with shower steam. Words started to take shape in the air, slowly coming into view as I stared at Terri. The first letter was 'V.'

'Vodka,' I said, and Terri screamed so loudly my neighbor across the hall opened his door and peered out.

'Sorry, Mr Holland,' I said, glaring at Terri. He shook his head at me and retreated back into his apartment like a pissed-off turtle.

'Sorry!' she echoed as I opened the door to my apartment. Uninvited, Terri followed me in.

'Terri, you have to leave now,' I said, marching directly to my kitchen and making a beeline for the small drawer where I kept the map and the spinner.

'But you knew I was coming,' Terri said, following me inside like a little lost puppy.

'I did *not* know you were coming. I never know when you're coming.'

'If you're—'

I whirled around and put my finger up to Terri's pierced

lip. 'I swear to God if you say "If you're so psychic, you'd know when I was coming," I swear to all the forces in the Universe, I will kill you right here and now with my bare, psychic hands. It's been that kind of a day and I have no doubt I could summon the will to do it. Do you *hear* me?'

Terri's eyes widened and she nodded. 'You are so totally rock on,' she said in awe. 'That's *exactly* what I was going to say. Like you should have your own TV show dude. Like John Edwards.'

'John Edward,' I said. 'There's no "s." And I told you. You can't just show up on my doorstep like this, Terri. This is my home. I *live* here. Do you get it?'

'But you said "vodka," ' she said, thrusting a magazine page in my face. 'See? vodka!'

I turned away from her and yanked opened my kitchen drawer. Spatula, packets of Splenda, bottle caps, matchbooks, penguin magnet, movie stubs to *Memento* – apparently I hadn't cleaned out this drawer in a while. Where were my map and spinner? I tore through the drawer twice. Nada. I always kept the map and spinner in this drawer. I never put it anywhere else.

'Clair! I have to win.'

'I'm not listening to you, Terri. I'm not even going to ask you "win what?" I'm going to find my map and my spinner and go on a *cleansing spiritual journey*.'

'All right, all right. Turn your freak light down.'

'Go away.'

I stomped over to my bedside table, yanked it open, and started rifling through it like a sleep-deprived baggage inspector with an axe to grind.

The spinner had to be here somewhere. I dug deeper. Margaret Atwood's, *The Handmaid's Tale* (paperback), *The Tibetan Book of the Dead* (hardback), stale cinnamon gum, scissors, love notes from Charles (ex number two); obviously I hadn't cleaned this drawer out in a while either. No map. No spinner.

'You see this, Terri?' I said, shaking my arms up and down like I was trying to relinquish a basketball that was superglued to my palms. 'I'm looking for something.' Terri was standing near my bed, twirling her hair. I advanced on her like a tiger. 'I've lost something,' I yelled, as her fingers froze mid-twirl. 'I don't have all the answers,' I screamed. 'I don't have all the answers!'

I knew this wasn't all Terri's fault. But in fairness to me it had been a terrible day and Terri had been given a strict warning never to just pop up on my doorstep again. I'm afraid losing the spinner was making me blow my top.

'But—'

'You know what else?' I paused for breath while she held hers. 'I don't care whether or not you get another tattoo, color your hair purple, date your second cousin—'

'Third cousin, once removed—'

'Travel to Thailand, get liposuction on your calves, or buy another iguana. Now go home!' I ended my tantrum by dropping to the floor like a puppet whose human arm had been severed and stared underneath my cavernous bed.

'What are you looking for?' Terri chirped from above me. 'I'll help you find it, and you can help me win the contest.'

'I'm not listening to you. I'm not listening to you. I'm not listening to you,' I said while I waited for my eyes to adjust to the darkness.

'All I have to do is come up with a name and develop a logo for their label,' Terri yammered behind me.

'Like they do with baby pandas at the zoo,' I couldn't help saying.

'Exactly,' Terri cried, clapping her hands. 'The winner gets ten thousand killer smackaroos, darling. Killer.'

Terri was one of those people who called everyone, regardless of status or age, 'darling.'

'I'm a killer artist, Clair,' Terri yammered on. 'You said so yourself.'

'I did?' I said, feeling like Helen Keller at the water pump, as my eyes finally adjusted and the lumpy shapes underneath my bed suddenly took on names. Dust bunnies, Stephen King's *Bag of Bones* (hardback), a hammer (protection or picture hanging device), a single black sock, *Bridget Jones' Diary* (paperback), *Eight Minutes in the Morning* – because who couldn't lift weights for a mere eight minutes every morning? (apparently me) – and a half empty (or half full) box of Trojans. Obviously it had been *a really long while* since I'd cleaned underneath this bed. Who *was* the last man I had slept with?

Charles, I thought glumly. Last year. Christmas. I had started reading his love letters one night, which led to thinking about him, which led to remembering our fabulous sex life, which led to dragging out the wedding pictures, which led to an hour of rationalizing how it wouldn't hurt to call and say hi, which led to calling him and begging him to come over.

I think he knew this would happen. I think the only reason men write love letters is because they've discovered they're a sexual insurance policy against a future breakup. A man knows there'll come a day, a week, a month, or even a decade later when she'll come across one of those letters and call in a weeping, lustful, pathetic attempt to revive the love they once had. Which is exactly what I did.

Love letters are the gateway drug to sex with your ex.

And ex number two was a beautiful man. He was strong and sexy and all consuming. God what a beautiful man. What a kisser. What a lover. What a laugher, what a storyteller, what a body, what a cuddler, what a comedian.

What a pothead.

Our marriage ended when I realized his 'Once in a while I like a little smoke' was more accurately a 'Can't live without it' thrice-daily ritual. Even when we went to my parents' house and slept in my childhood bed he had to light up 'a fatty' in the house because it was too windy to light up outside. He lay in bed in his FUCK MILK, GOT POT? T-shirt, humming 'Strawberry Fields' and rolling a joint. I begged him not to, I warned him that although my mother may not have my powers of perception, she had a nose that could put any hound dog to shame. And who could smoke marijuana in a room that still boasted Holly Hobby wallpaper and a pink pony lamp?

Apparently, Mr-Until-He-Blows-Pot-Smoke-in-My-Mother's-Face-Do-We-Part.

'Relax, Clair,' Charles said as he let out a cloud of heavy gray smoke. 'Her room is all the way downstairs.'

'You don't know my mother,' I said, fanning the smoke with my hands and opening the window a crack.

'For Christ's sake,' he yelled, shutting the window. 'It's freezing in here.'

'My mother,' I hissed, pointing up at the ceiling.

'Clair, she's been asleep for hours. Besides, if she smells anything she's going to think she's having a nice little sixties flashback.'

'You can't go one night without it, can you?' I whisper-yelled. 'You're an addict.'

'Stop being so dramatic. It's just a little puff. It helps me sleep.'

'Fine. Tell that to my mother.'

'Like even if she smells it your mother's gonna come busting in here. Give me a break.'

I rolled over, tense and on the verge of tears.

'All right, baby. This is the last puff and I'll put it out, okay? Then I'll go get that can of air freshener your mother buys in bulk—'

I giggled despite myself.

'—what is that stuff, blueberry pancake or lavender shit? Personally I think it smells like wet wabbit.'

I laughed into my pillow so my mother wouldn't hear me.

'What's up doc?' Charles said, infused by my laughter. He made his Bugs Bunny face, twitching his nose, chattering his teeth, and – disgusting but undeniably funny nonetheless, grabbing his carrot-dick. I howled. He took advantage of the moment to take a big drag, just as my mother burst into the room as if it were on fire, asking if we knew what that 'funny smell' was.

What Charles didn't realize, as he removed his hand from his groin and hid the joint behind his back, was that my mother knew *exactly* what that funny smell was. She had been through it all with my brother Tommy. Charles, thinking she was as naïve as she was pretending to be, held the smoke in his lungs and shook his head 'no' as his cheeks turned fire-engine red. She stood and stared him in the eye until he collapsed into a coughing fit, expelling marijuana smoke like a train belching exhaust. Then his coughing fit turned into a laughing fit, which turned back into a coughing fit as my mother glared at him.

So you see, despite his charm, our marriage went to pot.

But last Christmas, I thought maybe, just maybe, the trauma of Losing Me had knocked him straight, he had just been too ashamed to call me. So I broke the number one rule governing holidays, breakups, and PMS:

NEVER EVER PICK UP THE PHONE AND CALL YOUR EX.

He came right over and within seconds of his arrival we were making love. I had been right this time! Before I knew it, a whole hour had gone by, and there had been no mention of Mary Jane. We were cuddling in bed, staring into my electric fireplace, content with each other and the Christmas spirit. 'I got you a present,' Charles said, reaching for his leather jacket sprawled at the foot of the bed. He handed me a beautiful little box, wrapped in shiny gold foil, topped with a big red bow. I opened it happily, carefully lifting the fragile, glass object out of the box.

It was a battery-operated Santa Claus bong. When you inhaled through the chimney, Santa's bulging glass eyes glowed red.

'Clair!' Terri said, her head appearing underneath the bed on the other side. 'Just look over the contest rules. That's all I'm asking. Look over the rules and see, you know, if anything comes to you.'

I threw myself on my bed and buried my face in my

pillow. Terri sat on the edge of the bed. 'Just look it over,' she said. 'Then I'll go.'

I held out my hand and she slipped the torn-out magazine page into it.

'Cute, isn't he?' she said, referring to the picture of Jack Heron staring out at us from the magazine article. 'For an old guy.'

'Yes,' I answered, scanning his bio underneath the article. 'A whole thirty-six. Ancient.'

'But cute. Probably married though.'

I shrugged, stopping short of saying, *he was about to be, but thanks to me his fiancée has flown the coop.* Instead I kept my mouth shut as I studied the picture of tall, smiling, dark-haired, ancient Jack Heron.

The Universe was drawing me to Jack Heron like he was a refrigerator and I was magnetic poetry. You might think it strange, but it was par for the course for me. Call it 'zeitgeist,' 'a funny feeling,' or 'a series of unbelievable coincidences,' we all received signs now and again about our lives. And when the Universe called, I always answered. You should too.

If you don't, they send a registered letter. If you rip up the letter and throw it in the trash, they send a messenger to the door. If you shut the door in the messenger's face, they'll burn down your house and a cute fireman will knock you over the head with what's left of your grandmother's dining-room table where the message has been clearly branded into the charred wood. It was becoming impossible to ignore the beacon that was Jack Heron, blinking in my face.

This was the guy she didn't want to marry? He was a male siren if I ever saw one. I would crash myself against his rocks any day. I studied the picture again. Dressed in a dark gray Brooks Brothers suit, Jack Heron leaned up against a tree. He wore a mischievous grin and gave the illusion that he was looking directly into your eyes, reading your mind. Tall, a full head of black hair, navy blue eyes. He was sexy through and through and he was going to make a million Chardonnay lovers start hitting the vodka.

'Clair,' Terri whined. 'What do you think?'

I skimmed over the details of the article. As Susan and Rachel had mentioned, Jack Heron was holding a contest for a nonprofessional to name and design the new line of vodka. Not a bad marketing ploy, I thought.

'I was thinking of a French worm,' Terri said excitedly.

'Come again?' I said.

'Ooolala,' Terri suddenly yelled. I took a step back. 'That's what the worm would say, darling. "Ooolala."' I nodded in response, trying not to laugh.

'What's funny about that?'

'The worm is in tequila, Terri. This is vodka,' I said.

'I know that. I just thought a worm drunk on vodka would be a nice twist. You know? They wouldn't see it coming. And he'd be wearing a killer beret, darling.'

'One normally thinks Russia when they think vodka,' I said.

'Think, Clair. If the worm is Russian, how can he have a killer beret?' Terri demanded. 'Although I guess he could wear a killer fur parka.'

'Da,' I said, handing her back the article as Terri frowned. 'Do that,' I said, ultimately losing the battle and busting out laughing.

'Clair!'

'I'm sorry, Terri. Really. Go with that. Nothing is coming to me.'

'Well, hold it again, darling,' she said, once again thrusting Jack Heron in my face. 'Get a vibe.'

'No.'

'I have to win.'

'Then come up with something on your own, Terri,' I said, marching over to my bookcase. 'I'm sure you can do it if you try,' I said, handing her *Fortune-Telling for Dummies*.

Terri glanced at the book and then shook her head. When I refused to say anything more, she threw the book on my bed, stomped over to the door, and yanked it open. 'Some psychic you are,' she said.

'That's what I've been trying to tell you,' I answered as the door slammed shut in my face. At least she was gone. But the article, complete with Jack Heron's smiling face, was still lying on my bed. A mere two hours ago, I had never even heard of Jack Heron. Now, I had his face on my bed and his ring in my purse. Was it a sign? No. It was a test. The Universe was testing me to see if I would drop my spiritual journey and allow myself to get sucked into other people's problems, or would I, for once in my life, stand up for myself, be uncharacteristically selfish, and focus just on me?

Well, I'd show them. Rachel was Brian's ex-girlfriend. I had three ex-husbands and not once had I pawned one of them off on him. I had already booted out my stalker; it was time for the diamond to disappear, too. I grabbed my cell phone and clicked it open.

Daily Horoscope – Pisces

Little white lies might lead to an even bigger surprise . . . or not.

'Jesus,' Brian said for the third time. 'Jesus.'

'Mary and Joseph, too,' I added, adjusting the mirror in my rented Saturn. I was still sitting in the rental lot, I had just argued with the salesman about getting the extra accident insurance, and I had a few phone calls to make before dropping off the ring with Brian and heading north. I never did find the spinner and decided I would just get in the car and head out. That was the meaning of a true spiritual adventure. But I had to get my phone calls in now, because once I started the car, I had to turn my cell phone off for the week.

Besides, I have never been able to drive and talk at the same time. My best friend, and maid of honor at all three of my weddings, Karen, moved to Seattle six months ago and she *only* calls me while driving. Our conversations are always interspersed with the random, 'Get out of the way fucker,' 'You bastard!' And 'Put the espresso down and *drive* mugger.'

'I told you Rachel was wound up,' Brian bragged. 'Didn't I? I mean I just had this feeling.'

Whereas I had moments of genuine premonitions and psychically obtained information during readings, Brian did not. He was a straight reader, and my abilities made him crazy with jealousy.

That, and his unrelenting quest to bend a spoon with his mind.

'So, Brian,' I said, finally getting to the point, 'I'm just going to drive to your place and drop off—'

'I mean I barely even talked to her, yet I knew she was wound up!' Brian continued excitedly. The air in the Saturn became heavy.

'That doesn't count,' I said. 'She's your ex-girlfriend. So of course you're going to know something like that.' Silence. Now the air was slightly wet. Sticky.

'Brian?' I said.

'About. That.' Brian said. The back of my neck tingled. 'She's not exactly my ex-girlfriend.'

'What do you mean?' Brian laughed nervously. 'Brian? You mean *girlfriend* is too heavy of a word? You mean, like, you just went on a few dates?'

'I wish,' Brian said. 'But you believed me, didn't you? You believed someone that hot would date me!' I gripped the phone.

'Brian,' I said, forcing myself not to yell. 'Why did you lie?'

'I'm sorry, Clair. Believe me, I would have loved to do her cards. She was hot.'

'Brian, I'm counting to three—'

'All right, all right. She asked for you. Satisfied?'

'She asked for me?' I repeated.

'I thought you knew her,' Brian dared to say.

'Brian,' I said, chucking maturity out the window of my rented Saturn and yelling at him. 'You know I didn't know her.'

'Well I do now Clair-bear, but when she asked for you—'

'Why not just tell me she asked for me? Why all the games?' I heard Brian sigh like he was the one who was being put out, and I waited while he wrestled with his explanation.

'Look. She goes, "I'm here to see Clair Ivars," and I go, "I'd be happy to read your cards, Baby" (I know for a fact he didn't say 'Baby'; Brian couldn't flirt his way out of a paper bag, but in the interest of hearing his confession I didn't interrupt.)

'And she goes, "Sorry, I need to see Clair Ivars," and I go, "Oh you know Clair," and she goes, "No." '

'Why not just tell me that?' I barked when I couldn't stand anymore 'I go–she goes.'

'Because, it was like she thought you were Edgar Cayce or something,' Brian said, speaking the name of the famous psychic with awe. 'And I was chopped liver. So I just—'

'Lied to make yourself look like a complete stud and keep from flattering me,' I finished for him.

'I don't like how I sound when you put it that way, Clair.'

I stared out the window while I pondered this new information. Where did Rachel get my name? If someone had referred her, it seems only natural that it would have come up in the conversation. 'Hi, I'm Rachel. So-and-so said you were great.'

I did have a few regular clients, but most of them were locals, and I was hardly a cause célèbre. I didn't do readings on the phone, or the Internet, and I was hardly a card-carrying member of the psychic network.

'I apologize,' Brian interjected in the middle of my thoughts. 'Although I don't see how that would have changed anything. And hey – you've got your adventure, right?'

'What do you mean, "I got my adventure"?' I demanded.

'Your spiritual . . . whatever it is.'

'Pilgrimage,' I hissed.

'Technically, Clair, a pilgrimage is a journey to a specific locale.'

'It's a metaphor, Brian. It's a journey to my spiritual center. And I do end up at a "locale," just not one that's pre-planned.'

'So this time it is planned,' Brian said. 'Nothing wrong with that.' If it weren't for the fact that I still needed to talk to him, I would have banged the cell phone on the dashboard until the tiny little electronic pieces smashed all over the uninsured leather seats.

'My spiritual journey is one of solitude,' I stressed. 'Not dropping off diamonds for runaway brides.'

'Well I don't see what choice you have. We don't have her phone number, but you do have time off, a rental car, and a very expensive item that doesn't belong to you. Could the signs be any clearer?'

'I don't even know how to get there,' I said.

'The Heron Estates is nestled in the Shawnee National Forest,' Brian answered. 'Home to wineries, rolling hills, and wildlife.'

'And how would you know that?' I growled.

'I just pulled it up on Yahoo!. It's easy: south on 57 until you hit Route 13 to Harrisburg.'

'But I'm going north.'

'I suggest you drive three hours tonight, find a motel, and drive the rest in the morning.'

'He is really good-looking,' I said out loud, looking at Jack Heron's picture for the umpteenth time. For kicks I had taped his face to my glove compartment. 'Why would she walk out on a guy like this?'

'Loosen the buns, Princess Leia,' Brian said. 'You're just dropping off the ring, remember?' I glanced at the picture again.

'Oh. My. God. You're thinking of having sex with him, aren't you!' Brian yelled.

(One of the hazards of being friends with another intuitive.)

'No, I'm thinking of how heartbroken he's going to be when he finds out the love of his life has dumped him,' I lied.

'Maybe he'll fall madly in love with you,' Brian said. 'Maybe you two were destined to meet.'

I ignored the white and yellow rays emanating from the

direction of the glove compartment and turned my sarcasm on full blast. 'Great idea, Brian. I'll just say, "Hi, Jack. I'm Clair. I just pushed your emotionally fragile fiancée over the edge of her marital precipice with my Tarot card reading and she's called off the wedding. Here's the rock back. Hey, is this seat taken?" '

Brian didn't reply. He didn't have to. We both knew the psychic spinner had been spun. Despite the fact that I wanted to go north, something, or someone, was pulling me south to the good-looking, vodka-making groom. I just hoped he wasn't the type to shoot the messenger.

Daily Horoscope – Pisces

Attention all shoppers. Scratch that. Attention to the shopper who has purchased and returned three already. We're completely out of men. And we won't be getting any more in until you're dead. Have a pleasant day.

After hanging up with Brian, I left a message on Karen's machine, briefly filling her in on my adventure, started the car, and only then did I call my parents. This was in case they actually answered, so I would have the perfect excuse not to talk to them.

'I'm driving,' I'd say. 'I'd love to talk but there's a minivan passing me.' My mother had been deathly afraid of minivans ever since a *Dateline* hidden camera special captured several rolling over as they tried to maneuver their boxy girth around orange cones. Mom even steers clear of them in parking lots; she won't even walk down the row if there's one in sight. It takes her four hours to go to Costco, half of which she spends circling the parking lot searching for unstable minivans on the verge of keeling over on unsuspecting bulk foods.

Luckily, no one answered the phone at home either and I left them a vague message about work and travel, threw in that I was eating well and taking calcium supplements, asked about the health of the Ivars clan in general, and then hung up, feeling slightly guilty and edgy in addition to resentful to all of them for making me feel that way. Although I knew they loved me to death, and never said as much to my face, my family was slightly ashamed of me. My only saving grace was that they were ashamed of Abby and Tommy too.

I'm sure my parents told friends at cocktail parties that all three of us had been adopted from alcoholic, drug-addicted, mentally ill, teenaged parents, which would explain our general lack of ambition and absence of offspring.

Even so, I stood out. In addition to my three failed marriages, I was a *psychic* – a word, a job, a thing they had never quite wrapped their brains around.

Of course my mother had always accepted my grandmother's 'gift,' talked about it as a matter of fact, marveled over it, and regaled us with all her favorite stories of my grandmother's psychic abilities, such as the time when my mom was nine years old and had decided to take a bubble bath while my grandma had gone to the grocery store.

'It took her forty minutes in those days to get to the A&P,' my mother would say. 'It was only twenty miles from our house but she was terrified of driving and wouldn't go more than fifteen miles per hour. We were having the Clearys over for dinner that evening and she was out of milk and butter. Mr Cleary liked his butter so—'

'Get on with it, Trudy,' my father would always say at this point.

'Yes, dear. Anyhow, she parked the car. The store was crowded because it was Labor Day weekend; it was absolutely packed with people cramming the last of summer into their carts. Watermelon—'

'Trudy, we don't need the grocery list,' my father interjected again.

'It's irreverent,' Abby would add.

'Irrelevant,' I'd say.

'I just said that,' she'd say.

'She waited in a long line,' my mother would cut back in, speeding up slightly so that the end of the story always came out with a heightened sense of urgency, 'got right up to the counter, started putting her groceries on the counter—'

'And a little voice told her to go home,' my brother would cruelly interject from the corner.

'And out of nowhere,' my mother would continue as if he hadn't spoken, 'she heard a little voice telling her to *go home*. That's what it said. *Go home now*.'

My mother would look at us then, one by one, forcing us to return eye contact.

'My mother, a woman who would rather cut off her left hand than leave a store with groceries sliding up the counter, *ran* out, jumped into the Chevy Nova, and *sped* home. She must have gone seventy-five miles an hour,' my mother said, shaking her head and bracing herself against the dining-room table as if she were in the car.

'She rushed upstairs and found me passed out in the bathtub. She smelled the problem right away – gas leaking out of the pipes. I was moments – make that mere seconds – away from losing consciousness and drowning in my bubble bath. If she hadn't come home at the *exact moment she did*, none of us would be here. None of us.'

The story was always followed by silence and a slight feeling of shame, as if we were somehow to blame for the incident in the first place. Now *that* was a gift. I always wondered why my father didn't mention that *he'd* still be here if my grandmother hadn't made it home in time, but to his credit, he never did.

'Did she go back for the butter?' my brother always asked after the guillotine of silence had lifted. It always cost him dessert, but he had to say it anyway.

But somehow when it came to *me*, it wasn't a *gift*, it was a 'silly notion.' Apparently, in my family you're not a real psychic until you've saved an innocent child from drowning in bubbles.

'When are you going to get this silly notion out of your

head, Clair?' my mother often said. 'You're a grown woman with a brilliant mind and a college degree. Why don't you do something with it?' I had a liberal arts degree in Philosophy. Did I really need to philosophize on the uselessness of 'doing something with it'? In the end, I decided not to waste my breath. Everybody knows that families are the number one cause of sucking all the psychic energy out of your life force. Just thinking of them ignited my need for meditation and solitude.

That and the three-hundred-pound diamond I was carrying with me like a noose around my neck.

I tried to shut everything out as I drove; this was still my pilgrimage after all, even if at the moment I was driving down a quickly darkening highway with spotty radio reception, leaving me no choice but to listen to Harry Chapin sing 'Taxi Driver.'

I rolled down the windows and allowed the cold, streaming wind to whip my hair into a frenzy while I unleashed a few primal screams. I was woman, I roared. And when the picture of Jack Heron started flapping at the edges, threatening to blow away forever, I didn't lift a finger to stop it. But he didn't blow away; instead, his handsome, brooding face stayed squarely on the glove compartment, staring at me from time to time.

Daily Horoscope – Pisces

Mother Nature might be a beauty, but her daughter is a bitch.

After five hours of driving south on 57 in the dark, singing cheesy songs, I started looking for a motel. I loved nighttime in strange, seedy, little motels. I especially relished ones that were slightly falling apart, that had fluorescent pink lights on the blink, lopsided vending machines filled with evil, sugary things, and slightly musty, flowery bedspreads.

Unlike my search for true love, finding a truly seedy motel was easy. The King's Ransom beckoned with his rusty crown, boasting $29.99 rates. I had that weary feeling of peace you get when you're too tired to worry about your life. I was happy despite the television only getting channel two, the vending machine only spitting out stale peanut butter crackers, and drinking water the color of sunrise. I didn't care, because I wasn't alone. I had my Tarot cards. And Jack's face taped to the bedpost, but there's a perfectly good explanation for that – I had consumed a half a bottle of red wine from The King's Liquor, which was conveniently located right next door to The King's Diner. Finally, it was time to do my cards.

I just wanted to get a little insight into my pilgrimage. A little direction, some gentle guidance. Besides, I needed a distraction. I had taken the diamond ring out and placed it on the rickety nightstand. There it sat, cushioned on its purple, velvet pouch, sandwiched in between the Gideon Bible and the Shawnee National Forest Yellow Pages. I should have put the ring away, I should have ripped Jack's picture off the bedpost, but I didn't. The diamond was my night-light; Jack, my strong, silent one-night stand. Besides, my romantic insanity had a shelf life; by this time tomorrow Jack would have his ring back, and I'd be off on my adventure. And given the fact that I was once again dying to put the ring on, leaving it on the nightstand seemed a very sane compromise.

Surely the cards would straighten me out. First I did the Celtic Spread. Chock full of advice about getting in touch with my inner self, facing my fears, shutting out negative voices but – funny – no mention of a man. I mean, not that I was asking about love, but normally there is at least one card that somehow relates to love. And even if they weren't talking about me and Jack, you think the cards would at least talk about my strange situation here. After all, it wasn't my choice to give up part of my vacation to chase after Jack Heron – you think the cards would at least mention it – you know, speak of the slight detour I was planning on taking before getting down to spiritual business.

Maybe I was doing the wrong spread. That's it. There were hundreds of Tarot card spreads, and if you weren't getting the answers you sought, sometimes it simply meant you had the wrong spread. Easy fix. I gathered the cards up, reshuffled them, closed my eyes, and concentrated. I got it. I would do the Three Card Spread. Simple, yet effective. Past, present, and future.

Ace of Swords. Reversed. *Self-destruction*.

What? Okay, perhaps I had been a tad self-destructive in the past. Just giving into Rachel's demands was self-destructive. Besides, that's my past. Card two will illuminate my present situation.

Page of Coins. Reversed. *Bearer of bad news*.

But that's so obvious. Of course I'm the bearer of bad

news. The card can also mean selfish and self-involved, but obviously in my case it was bearer of bad news. Why were the cards wasting my time telling me something I already knew? Okay, no worries. It's the third card that's the important one. The third card will clarify the future. How this is all going to end. I closed my eyes and turned it over.

Eight of Swords. *Uncertainty. Take precautions to avoid possible losses.*

Huh? They're telling me my future is uncertain? Everybody knows the future is uncertain, that's why we read the Tarot in the first place! Avoid possible losses? Could they be any more vague? Take precautions could mean anything from putting on your seat belt to using condoms. What . . . was I suppose to take precautions against everything?

I swept the three cards up and shuffled the deck again. Obviously, in this situation, three cards weren't enough to illuminate my path. I should do the five-card spread.

The Two of Wands. It could mean complete failure, a loss – or simply that something unexpected will happen. Which was it? Oh God. It's got to be unexpected, right? Because I don't know what to expect. So that makes sense. Or maybe it's telling me not to lose the ring. Take precautions. *Protect the ring at all costs.* Okay, okay, I could do that. But what about me? Was this all about Jack and his stupid ring? What about my spiritual journey? The next card will answer that one. The next card will be about me.

The Ten of Wands.

I can do anything! I can achieve anything! That was much better.

Except.

The Ten of Wands is a tricky card. It comes with a caveat. Basically, it's a 'be careful what you wish for' card. The very thing you *think* you want more than anything in this world could make you absolutely miserable. Kind of like finding out the man of your dreams is actually your worst nightmare.

What did that mean? Were they talking about love here, or were they talking about my spiritual growth? How could spiritual growth make me miserable? How many cards were left? Wait a minute – that couldn't be the end of the spread.

I had it. I should have done the Gypsy Spread. With twenty-one cards. That should do the trick.

How could all twenty-one cards be vague, misleading, and insulting? Well, I wasn't going to take this lying down. I sat up on the bed and furiously reshuffled the cards. I did the Horoscope Spread. The Relationship Spread. The Full Moon Spread. The Quarter Moon Spread. The Single Woman Spread. The Nymphomaniac Spread (that one took up the entire bed), The Witches Spread, The Tree of Life Spread, The Women Who Love Too Much and the Men Who Sleep with Them and Never Call Them Again Spread.

Finally, when I couldn't get any sweatier, shakier, or more confused, I did The Last Chance Spread. By this time I didn't even know what the cards were saying. They were blurring into one vague, cryptic message. In the end Queens were holding Swords and Knights were spinning Cups and High Priests were flipping Coins. They all mocked me. *Be careful, your future is uncertain.* I fell asleep with The Knight of Cups, the messenger of true love, clutched to my unfulfilled, beating heart.

Even though I had estimated it was only another hour and a half to the Heron Estates, I was awake by six the next morning, eager to see the Shawnee National Forest, eager to spot an eagle or deer along the way, and especially eager for a freshly brewed cup of joe. As I shifted through the contents of my purse I found myself touching the small velvet pouch where I had returned Rachel's engagement ring, wanting to reassure myself to its existence.

I stared glumly at the pot of brown sludge the clerk had referred to as coffee, debating my options while my caffeine addiction battled my sense of self-preservation. I knew there wouldn't be a Starbucks between here and the estate, a fact I had already confirmed with the aforementioned clerk, Sammy. The twenty-something, un-shaven, snarly boy had yet to do anything but grunt at me; he was engrossed in sheets of postage stamps, holding them up to the light like they were hundred-dollar bills at a bar. I stared at the red, plastic name badge hanging askew on his blue jacket and thought about the stack of bills in my car I had yet to mail. I should bring them in right now and get them off before I got nailed with the various late fees, but I didn't want to spend another second in this motel. I just wanted coffee.

'Hey,' I said as brightly as I could manage, when he still hadn't acknowledged me. 'Can we make a fresh pot of coffee?' Whereas some people hate the use of the royal 'we,' I figured he'd be less defensive this way, and I was ready to jump over the counter and grind beans with my teeth if it were the only way I'd get some real coffee. His answer came in the form of fire. He flicked a match, held it up, and watched it burn down to the tip of his thumb. Only when the flame licked over his dirty nail did he look at me.

'It's fresh enough,' he said, dropping the spent match on the counter and lighting another.

'How long has it been?' I said, pouring myself a cup of the lukewarm sludge, working my way toward a plan. 'Since you quit smoking,' I added, pounding on the container of dried creamer, trying to loosen enough to lighten my science experiment.

'Do I know you?' Sammy suddenly shouted.

'It's been what? Five days?'

'NO,' Sammy said. 'Like six. Six and a HALF.'

'Don't worry. You'll get through it this time,' I said.

Fuck you, Sammy said back to me, although it wasn't out loud. 'Try nicotine gum,' I offered. He rolled his eyes but I knew he had heard me. 'Listen. I'll give you twenty dollars and tell you exactly how you're going to get through nicotine withdrawal, if you make a new pot of coffee and scare up some real cream.'

Twenty minutes later I was back in my Saturn, marveling at the concept of supply and demand, licking stamps and sipping my twenty-five-dollar cup of coffee. Sammy, not thrilled with my advice to meditate, chew gum, and practice Tai Chi, raised the price five bucks, so I made him throw in the stamps. I hadn't expected him to actually agree to it; it just goes to show that when you really need something, the Universe will provide. He even smiled at me when he turned them over! That, my friends, is charisma. When my tongue had gone numb from licking, I tossed the bills aside and pulled onto the highway. If I didn't see a mailbox along the way, I'd mail them from the estates.

Before long I had left 57 South and was driving along Route 13 toward Harrisburg. This would take me through Shawnee National Forest toward Hidden Lake near where the estates were located. I knew (whether through psychic abilities or common sense) that the Heron Estates would be partially hidden and a challenge to find, but I had a good head start and felt up to the challenge.

More importantly, I was enjoying myself. This part of the drive had been well worth the wait. Tall pines, spruces, and elms hugged the winding road, standing guard with their arms outstretched as birds jockeyed for the best branches; the ones high up in the air with sky and lake views squabbled over them like they were rent-controlled apartments in Manhattan, while chubby squirrels tumbled in and around the thick bases. I felt a surge of inane jealousy at their joy; how long since I had felt such wild abandonment, and when would I feel it again?

Just as the thought hit my brain, so did the feeling. Complete euphoria. I was suddenly, deliriously happy. I laughed out loud. I took a deep breath. I felt fully alive and instead of driving, I felt like I was floating down the highway. I relished the fact that I wouldn't trade this exact moment for anything else in the world. I was the luckiest girl on the planet, and if I was feeling slightly sorry for myself, it was just because I didn't have anyone to share it with.

I couldn't believe how bright the colors were outside

my window. Look how many shades of green! The sun was heaven on my cheeks. The world was a beautiful place. I wanted to pack it inside, put it on ice, feel like this forever. I rolled down the window, turned off the radio, and welcomed in the great outdoors.

I was a city girl at heart, but it didn't mean I couldn't appreciate a little wildlife. The air smelled like lavender and rain, a product of the numerous lakes, streams, and rivers that lay in wait just beyond the trees, along with hiking trails, campgrounds, and scenic views. (I read the brochure in the motel.) I had been driving about an hour, yet it was still early enough that not another soul was in sight.

Strangely enough, my thoughts turned to marriage. *Something old, something new –*

Seriously, Clair, stop this right now. I glanced at the glove compartment, wishing I had left Jack's picture up after all.

Something borrowed –

Stop this right now!

I'm happy right now without a man, I thought. *Right this very moment.*

Something blue –

And then, everything went black.

Daily Horoscope – Pisces

Saturn is passing through your Venus today. You're so fucked.

I had just rounded a curve, enjoying the slight downhill glide that followed, when a large, bluish black blob flew directly into my window, obscuring the world from view. It was like driving through a car wash and being assaulted by monstrous, black, soapy brushes. Enveloped in the black and blue shadow that was smothering my entire windshield were two black eyes boring into me like a dentist's drill. The sound of my own screams filled the air and my chest was so tight I thought my lungs had been punctured by shards of glass. I hadn't been speeding. Between hugging the winding roads and taking in the scenery, I was being extra cautious, but now suddenly I had the sensation of being airborne; the car was soaring off the ground.

'Don't panic,' I said out loud as a hodgepodge of irrelevant safety advice poured into my brain. *Tap the brakes. Steer into the turn. Stick your whole fist down its throat* (attack dog). *Pee on it* (snake bite? sting ray?). *Don't break the seal* (drinking/peeing advice). *Get low to the ground and breathe into a wet cloth, wash your hands, change your sheets once a week, wear clean underwear, let sleeping dogs lie, don't hold a golf club in a lightning storm, always wear a condom!*

My life didn't flash before my eyes. Instead, I saw a blinding, white light, felt the car shake as if I were going down the first steep hill on a rickety, wooden roller coaster, and then, before I could formulate a coherent thought, I was slammed into a wall of brown and green. It took seconds (which felt like hours) to realize the jarring feeling was due to the Saturn hitting the ground and bouncing, and the green-brown walls flying past me were actually trees, for the car had veered into the woods.

Who's driving this thing? With a growing sense of panic, I realized it was supposed to be me, and it was then that I instinctually slammed on the brakes, bringing my right foot down as hard as I could while gripping the wheel as if it were a life raft, ignoring all 'softly tap the brakes' advice, wanting nothing in the world but to stop. Finally, I felt the car jerk to an abrupt stop, but my relief was temporary; it turns out the experts are right, slamming on the brakes at high speed is a risky little thing to do. The car (and I) flipped onto its side, dangled at the acrobatic angle for a few heart-pounding seconds, and then flipped over. Fifteen minutes of communing with the God of Nature and I was completely upside down.

When the initial fear passed, anger surged through me. How could this have happened? Why didn't I get any kind of warning, any premonition, any strange feeling that something wasn't right? Quite the contrary, seconds before the impact I had been oblivious and happy. *Something blue*, my inner voice said. They gave you, *something blue*. That's not fair. That wasn't a real warning.

But was I functioning? Was anything broken? Could I move? Was I dead and the afterlife was really an upside-down Saturn?

So far I had been afraid to move anything but my head, which apart from pounding into my skull, seemed to be in working order. I wiggled my fingers. Yes, they moved too. Realizing it was still running, I lifted my shaking, right hand and turned off the engine. Strange how everything still works upside down. Slowly I lifted my left foot, then my right. I took off the seat belt, working up the courage to try the door. I knew if it didn't open I would panic. I don't like small spaces, and if the door was stuck I was going to have a major meltdown.

I reached to my left and pawed the door. Where was the handle? Everything might be working, but things change position when they're upside down. I finally located the latch, lifted it, and gave a push. To my relief it opened about a foot until it stuck in dirt. *That's okay, I just have to figure how to crawl out.* I looked at the opening and then considered the position of my body. Since the top portion of the car wasn't as wide as the bottom, it was going to be a tight squeeze. I was going to have to turn myself around and go out head first, slithering like a snake. I had just managed to turn stomach first onto the seat and head out when I realized I didn't have my purse.

For a moment I considered leaving it; for all I knew this car was leaking gas and would blow up. *Never run back into a burning building for material possessions!* Mind you, I didn't see or smell smoke, but I wasn't going to take any chances. I didn't need to grope around for my purse, I needed to get the hell out of there.

On the other hand, my cell phone and the diamond ring were in the purse, so it was worth taking a few extra minutes to look for it. I'm sure if the car had actually been on fire, I wouldn't have taken the time to retrieve it. But without my phone and wallet and the ring, I didn't have much chance of getting myself out of this mess. I found it on the ceiling in the back. I was briefly grateful I had used my zippered purse; all the contents were still safely inside. I grabbed it, turned over on my stomach, wiggled out the door, and screamed.

There, standing his ground just a few feet away, with his massive wings outstretched like a cobra spreading its hood, was the largest blue heron I had ever seen. Under normal circumstances I would have been thrilled to see this beautiful, prehistoric-looking bird up close, but he was the last thing I had expected to see when I crawled out of the car. And he looked terrified. Of me. My screaming was working us both into a state of severe agitation, but I couldn't stop myself. He lifted his massive wings and flapped away, but not before turning his head to glare at me again, as if saying, *How dare you run into me with your Saturn.* He didn't appear hurt in the least, just incensed. Could that really have been what flew into my windshield? If so, it certainly wasn't a good omen.

As I crawled along the pine-needled ground, I tried to remember the details of the rental car insurance policy. I vaguely remembered arguing with the guy about 'extra' insurance. Nothing irks me more than being pressured into 'extra' insurance, especially at the post office. You *pay* them to mail your package and they turn around and ask if you'd like to *guarantee* its delivery. If I'm not paying for delivery, then what am I paying for? If I didn't want to guarantee delivery, wouldn't I just shove my mail in a bottle and toss it out to sea? I was becoming more and more concerned that I *hadn't* ordered the extra insurance.

I glanced around; I was just off the main road, but hidden from sight by a canopy of trees. I'd have to stand in the road in order to be seen. I wanted to call a taxi, but there was a shocking lack of Yellow Pages in the wilderness.

Hitchhiking was always an option, although one I'd never been stupid enough to take ever since I saw the movie *The Hitcher* with C. Thomas Howell, where he stops at a diner and finds a finger in his French fries. I forget what that had to do with hitchhiking. Now that I think of it, it should have been a thumb instead of a finger. Of course! Who writes these things? Why didn't they make it a thumb? The very thumb that moments earlier had been stuck out onto the highway, beckoning strangers to stop. Then, 'The Hitcher' could have driven by with an axe and hacked it right off! Maybe it *was* a thumb and I just couldn't remember. Whatever happened to C. Thomas Howell? He was cute.

I could call Jack Heron and ask for a lift and a tow truck

in exchange for his diamond ring. I didn't like the idea of being alone out here with such a valuable rock. Not that anyone would know I had it, but what if they decided to check? I started to walk to the main road, grateful I wasn't wearing heels. In fact, my attire was very woodsy – green Gap cargo pants, black tennis shoes, and a black, long-sleeve tee. My unruly curls were pulled back in a black silk scarf and I was wearing only a touch of makeup, and that was because I didn't want to scare any poor woodland creatures.

I was tempted to go for a hike; according to sign posts, I was only four miles from Garden of the Gods and six from Devil's Backbone, both of which sounded intriguing.

Maybe on the way back.

I pulled out my business card with Jack Heron's address and remembered there was no phone number. Stupid, stupid, Rachel. 'Information, how may I help you?'

'I'd like the number for the Heron Estates.'

I breathed a sigh of relief when seconds later I was automatically connected to the number. Why didn't I think of calling information before? I know this option probably cost me another seventy-five cents, but when you've just tipped your rented, extra-insurance-less Saturn upside down, rule of nonhacked-off thumb says it's okay to splurge a little.

'Heron Estates, how may I direct your call?'

'Jack Heron, please.'

'He's not available. How may I direct your call?' the bored female voice said.

'Listen. It's urgent I speak with Jack,' I said, hoping the I-know-him-on-a-first-name-basis trick would be the thread that sewed this conversation up.

'*Jack* isn't available,' she swatted back. 'How may I direct your call?'

'Susan, please,' I said, knowing that Susan would never take my call if she knew who I was.

'Susan who?'

Shit. She was married and I certainly didn't know her last name.

'Jack's sister,' I said. 'And it's *still* an emergency.'

'No one is available to speak with you. How may I direct your call?'

'Gee. How *can* you direct my call if no one is available to speak with me!'

'I can send you to voice mail.'

'Fine.'

She put me on hold. Then the line went dead.

It took only ten minutes to reach the road; I was happy to realize my car hadn't plunged too far off the main stretch. I wondered if I had also violated some 'mustn't drive through national forest' rule in addition to the whole 'extra insurance' thing. I was probably in a lot of trouble, so I might as well pick a wild flower; at least then I'd have something pretty to put in my jail cell. I tried to memorize the area so I'd know where to send the tow truck. Would anyone believe this wasn't my fault?

A giant blue heron smashed unharmed into my windshield, flipped my car, gave me the evil eye, and flew off.

It was so ridiculous that even *I* didn't believe it. And it was an occupational hazard that I had an extremely high tolerance for the bizarre.

This had not been a stellar couple days. My planets must be seriously out of whack. First there was Brian goading me into doing Rachel's reading. Rachel goading me into breaking her engagement, Susan goading me into proving my psychic abilities, and finally a grungy motel clerk with a serious attitude goading me into buying a twenty-five-dollar cup of complimentary coffee.

Last but not least, blue herons flying into uninsured rental cars.

Left, left, left, right, left.

I hobbled along the road all the while on a sharp lookout for flying monkeys.

Minutes later, my scarf had slipped out of my hair,

allowing sweaty curls to cling to my cheeks, my stomach was growling, and large, red blisters were forming on my angry feet. Why didn't I spend the twenty-five dollars on bottled water and healthy snacks instead of a lousy jolt of caffeine and a few stamps? Which reminded me I had left the stack of bills back in the car. Forget it, I wasn't going back for them. Where was this place? And where were all the cars? I had already made peace with my thumb-less future and was ready to hitch a ride. I had also decided to call information for a cab, or call Brian, or even dial 911, but my cell phone was dead.

If only that switchboard girl had patched my call through! Should I have told her about the diamond ring? She probably wasn't even at the estate, I realized. She was probably sitting at a switchboard in a cubicle somewhere doing her nails and taking personal calls on line four. It didn't matter now. I almost screamed with joy when a white pickup truck rumbled by. It didn't stop at first, and I started to run after it, screaming, waving my hands, sending all my psychic energy its way. I saw the red brake lights come on in the distance and a kick of dirt as the truck squealed to a stop. Then slowly, it started moving backward.

It was a beat-up little truck, packed with men and lawn equipment. *Boys with Rakes* was written across the side in faded blue paint. Three men were squeezed in the front cab and another five were in back, sandwiched between lawnmowers, rakes, and shovels. As it neared, I could also make out a long lump of burlap taking up the entire middle of the cab. It was probably a tree they were off to plant and if they let me in, it was going to be a tight squeeze. The men ranged in age, size, and color. The youngest looked to be about twelve, the oldest pushing sixty. The driver, a muscular, young Latino, leaned over his two cab mates and shouted out the window.

'I'm Jorge. You need a lift?'

'I'm Clair,' I shouted back. 'I'd love one.'

Jorge flashed me a grin. 'Where you goin'?'

'The Heron Estates,' I said, hooking my thumbs safely in my pockets. 'You know it?'

'I sure do. It ain't far. You want to sit up here with me and the girls,' he said ribbing his two muscular front seat mates, or you wanna go back there with the snakes?' I glanced back at the men in the cab.

'You mean the rakes?' I said. All of the men laughed. Again, I had a good feeling about them; they were all smiles, except for the oldest one who simply contemplated me with the patience of a river on a lazy Sunday afternoon. He reached down to help me into the back of the truck, the muscles in his arms easily hauling me in. One by one the men scooted over politely, making room for me at the head of the large burlap bag.

I ran my eyes over it as the truck pulled back onto the highway and picked up speed. Up close it didn't look like a tree at all. My eyes traveled down the length of it, and when I got to the end I stared in horror. My intuition (and common sense) had failed me again. I was about to lose more than my thumb. For sticking out underneath the burlap lump was a pair of pointy cowboy boots. I was sitting next to a tall, dead man.

Daily Horoscope – Pisces

Seize the day! Slip Sleeping Beauty the tongue.

People have been predicting their own deaths for centuries. Sullivan Ballou, a famous Civil War soldier, wrote, '[D]eath is creeping around me with its fatal dart,' just before he was killed in the Battle of Bull Run; Abraham Lincoln saw himself lying in a coffin in a dream a few months before he was shot; and it's even rumored that President Kennedy foresaw his own assassination. But here I was, about to be pushed over to the other side, absolutely livid that I hadn't seen this coming. Quite the opposite – I had liked these grungy gardeners. What is the point of being psychic if you can't save your own hide?

The youngest of the gardener/murderers saw me looking at the body. His thin lips spread into a wide grin. He moved forward and reached for the tip of the burlap bag, near the dead man's head. He wanted me to see him.

'That's okay,' I said, scooting back as far as I could. I looked over the edge of the truck at the highway whizzing by. Would I rather die by jumping? Before I could make my move, the elderly gardener/murderer who'd helped me up said, 'That's Sleeping Beauty.'

Oh God. It wasn't a dead man at all. They'd killed a freakishly tall woman. Before I could stop him, the young gardener/murderer yanked the burlap sheet down as my hands flew over my eyes.

'Maybe you could play Prince Charming and give him a wake-up kiss,' another voice joked. I parted my fingers slightly, knowing I'd have to face up to the dead man.

Who, remarkably, was breathing.

I took my hands down and looked full on. It wasn't a freakishly tall dead woman at all, it was indeed a live man. I let out my breath and giggled. The nonmurdering gardeners laughed with me. I was grateful they didn't know the real reason I was laughing. I studied the sleeping man before me.

It was hard to get much of a read on him; he was scruffy and wore large sunglasses with a turned-around baseball cap. His hands were folded against his T-shirt. I leaned in to read it. GARDENERS LIKE IT DIRTY was written in bold white letters. I blushed as the men around me laughed. I tried not to linger on his chest or muscular arms; I suddenly appreciated how a little gardening could do wonders for the biceps.

'He's had a rough night,' the gardener next to me said. The youngest one held up a cell phone.

'You kiss, I take a picture,' he said. The rest of the men leaned in eagerly, awaiting my answer.

'It would get him good. Right?' the youngest said, watching me hopefully.

'She's gonna do it,' one said.

'She ain't gonna do it,' another countered.

'It would get him good.'

They flattened themselves against the truck, giving me full access to the man they called Sleeping Beauty. I don't exactly know why I decided to do it. Maybe it was simply the relief I felt that I wasn't going to be murdered with a rake. Or maybe it was his full lips. Even hidden behind a baseball cap and sunglasses, I could tell this was one sexy, sleeping gardener. There was always a chance that he would wake up and clock me midkiss, but it was too late to worry about that, I was already straddling him as the men laughed and cheered me on. What the hell, it was just a kiss.

I leaned close to his face, staring at the stubble on his strong jaw line, so close I could feel his breath on mine and see the tiny lines in his lips.

'She's gonna get him good.'

I lowered my body onto his, hyperaware of my crotch lightly touching his and my breasts mashing into his chest. Softly at first, I touched my lips to his lips. I giggled out of embarrassment as the men clapped. I wasn't going to give them a real show, and it was nothing but a light, feathery kiss. But just as I was about to dismount the gardener, his arms shot out, wrapped around my waist, and pulled me back down. This time our lips met with full force, and I was swept up in a tidal wave, knock-down, drag-out, take-me-under-and-let-me-drown kiss.

Good God, I was going to have to take up gardening.

Like an out-of-body experience I could hear the men whooping and hollering, but I couldn't pull away from the suction of his lips. Even if I wanted to. Which I didn't. Kissing him felt like I was being transported into another realm. It was as if he and I were completely alone, our lips and bodies two proverbial lost puzzle pieces finally joined together. His mouth was soft and strong and I was impressed that despite 'tying one on' last night, he had fresh breath. He must have popped a mint before passing out in the truck.

Our tongues met and my floodgates opened. That's when I tried for real to pull away. I wasn't the type of girl who liked an audience, even with a kiss like that. This time he let me go. I scrambled back to my spot, wiping my lips and not daring to look at the man who was now sitting up, staring at me through his sunglasses.

'Whew, she got you good!' one of the men yelled. The sleeping stranger laughed along with the men.

'She sure did,' he said, sunglasses aimed right at me. 'If this is a wet dream fellows don't you dare wake me up,' he said with a slow smile.

'Hey now,' the older one barked. 'None of that talk.'

'Sorry, Bob,' he said, tipping the back of his baseball cap. 'It was a bad joke. Ma'am,' he said to me. 'My apologies.' He shook his head and wolf-whistled as the men laughed again. But I felt like a total idiot. Embarrassment covered me like a hot, wet cloth. He could obviously see the redness in my cheeks and yet he wouldn't stop staring at me. I wished he would take his sunglasses off; I can always read people better when I can see their eyes.

'Who are you?' he said.

'Just a girl catching a ride,' I answered.

'To where?'

'The Heron Estates.'

'What for?'

Gee. You give the guy one, long, passionate where-have-you-been-all-my-life kiss, and he's all 'what's your life story?'

'It's personal,' I said. He didn't answer, but I saw his shoulders shrug.

'Suit yourself,' he said. 'Just makin' conversation. Thought we should be polite since we just had our tongues in each other's mouths and all.' The rest of the guys laughed as I blushed.

'I'm sorry. No more questions.'

'Thank you.'

'What's your name?'

I glared at him. So he was cute and the kiss was downright electrifying. But I had just been following a dare, not cultivating another stalker. I didn't owe him any small talk. I just wanted to get to the estates, find Jack Heron, and give him back the ring.

'Sorry. That was another question, wasn't it?'

'If you don't mind – I would really like to just keep to myself and enjoy the rest of the ride.'

'No problem.'

'Thank you.'

'You're welcome.'

I closed my eyes, wanting nothing more than to get to a place where I could get out of my sweaty clothes—

I left my overnight bag in the Saturn.

Great. Jack was going to think I was a beggar who had stolen his three-carat diamond ring. Why didn't I think of how this was going to look? I was going to have to find a bathroom and clean up before meeting Jack. Susan wasn't going to welcome me with open arms, and even if she did, she was way too thin for me to borrow any of her clothes.

'What do you do? Besides hitchhike and kiss?'

'I'm in futures,' I said, shutting my eyes, hoping he'd take the hint and leave me alone.

'Really. Any predictions?' *I opened my eyes and stared at him.*

'Excuse me?'

'You know – any hot stock predictions?'

'If you don't mind,' I said. 'I'd rather not talk about work. I'm on vacation.' I closed my eyes again.

'I'm glad you're not the talkative type,' the guy said. 'Wouldn't want you telling my girlfriend about that jaw-dropping kiss.' I ignored him. He must be really good-looking under the hat, glasses, and stubble. Average men are never that cocky. Just like a guy to have to slip it in there that he had a girlfriend, too.

'It was just a dare,' I said. 'They made me do it.'

'She got you good,' the young one piped in again.

'She did indeed,' the stranger said. Then thankfully, he finally shut up. For a few seconds. 'Feel free to do it again,' he said. 'I dare you.' I fully intended to snap back at him with a witty, biting comment, but instead I found myself laughing with the rest of the guys. 'You have a nice laugh,' Sleeping Beauty said from his prone position. I crossed my legs tighter and tried to get the phrase GARDENERS LIKE IT DIRTY out of my head. I was glad he couldn't see me blushing.

Twenty minutes later the truck slowed down, pulled off the main road, and just as I thought Jorge had gone crazy and decided to plunge me into the trees for a second time that day, we were suddenly moving along a dirt path barely wide enough to accommodate the truck. The only markers were two large boulders on either side of the path with HERON painted on the left boulder and ESTATES on the right, in cursive, cobalt blue. I never would have found it on my own.

Crashing the Saturn was meant to be. I shook off the voice, and closed my eyes. My stomach tightened as we wound up the path, ascending up a little hill and then straightening out for another hundred yards. Shortly afterward the trees cleared, the dirt road became a paved blacktop, and an expansive green lawn spread out in front of us like an Astroturf ocean.

'Thank you,' I called to the men as I hopped out of the idling truck and took in the stretch of lawn before me. I was particularly struck by a massive castle looming in the distance. 'It's gorgeous,' I said out loud.

'I guess,' Jorge said, turning off the truck as the gardeners piled out. 'If you don't have to mow it,' he said with a wink. They had been headed here all along, and I didn't even know it. Humiliation 2-Psychic Powers 0.

'Who are you anyway?' Jorge asked, ignoring the twenty-dollar bill I held out. 'Cleaning girl? Kitchen? Caterer?'

'Umm . . . ring bearer,' I said, clutching my purse. Jorge studied me like a nonartist taking in Michaelangelo's Statue of David for the first time, and then nodded. To my relief, the man I had kissed was no longer paying attention to me, he was conferring with the other gardeners. It wouldn't have mattered anyway; we were soon distracted by a flurry of motion heading straight for us from the direction of the castle. The gardeners instantly spread out and busied themselves. I hadn't lost all my psychic abilities – I knew in my bones the tornado winding its way toward us was none other than Jack Heron's mother Madeline.

She was lean and tall, six feet one or so. But as she drew close, I realized it was her eyes that commandeered your full attention, carrying her well past six feet, transforming her into a long, lean giant. They were alert, amber orbs with specks of black, the eyes of a screech owl. Once she locked them on you, Game Over, you were pinned. One wouldn't call her a beauty, but her strong, thin face conjured up the word 'handsome'. The lines on her face looked like they had been sketched on, and could be erased at a moment's notice. Her thin, pursed lips were pulled tight and a long worry line lay across her forehead like a log across a creek. She had wispy dyed-black bangs, chopped and hanging like a theatre curtain, her cheekbones stood out like mountain peaks, and her nose sloped up and suddenly dropped off like a ski-lift.

I took a step back as she pointed her manicured fingertips at Jorge, her diamond tennis bracelet bouncing up and down as she repeatedly jabbed her finger in the air toward him. When she stopped fingering him, she jabbed at her watch. 'Late, late, late!' she cried. 'We have tables and tents to set up, they're supposed to be there right now. Do you see any tables and tents set up?'

Jorge actually looked around as the others in his group silently unloaded mowers and rakes from the truck. 'Mother, calm down,' Susan said, stepping forward from behind Madeline. I quickly ducked behind Jorge and his rakes.

'I'm sorry, Mrs Heron,' Jorge said. 'We'll work quickly, make up for lost time.'

'This is coming out of your pay you know,' she replied. I wanted to stand up for them and defend their late arrival, for I was partly to blame for it, but I couldn't risk Susan recognizing me – I would be thrown off the premises immediately, and I didn't come this far to turn back now.

I had decided on the bumpy ride over here that not only was I going to personally give Jack Heron back the ring, but I was going to confess the whole sordid tale from the moment Susan and Rachel stepped into my tent. It was the only way I was going to relieve myself of the backpack of guilt I had been heaving around ever since I delivered the unethical reading. The blue heron had been an omen, one I couldn't ignore, and I didn't need the cards to tell me that coming clean was the only way I could set things straight.

The gardeners started to move, spreading across the lawn like lightning bugs set free of their glass jar, while Madeline Heron lauded over them, chirping orders. This gave me a chance to slip away, keeping to the right where I could hide behind a string of large white delivery trucks parked along the circular drive like a strand of boxy pearls, and wind my way up to the castle.

For there was no other word to describe the house. Its stone walls towered above the grounds, boasting two turrets, protruding from the roof like bookends. It was only as I got closer that I noticed details too small to be seen from afar: stained-glass windows, statues of maidens, and arched, gleaming doorways whose towering heights made me feel small. The main entrance was marked by a heavy brass knocker, and if you trailed your eyes upward, you'd see a family crest painted into the alcove above. A home fit for a family of wealthy giants. Perfectly trimmed pine trees flagged the perimeter and colorful summer flowers were hung, planted, and strewn about the massive wraparound porch.

I found myself scanning the area for knights in full armor charging me with outstretched swords, or at the least an alligator-filled moat, but finding none, I made the surprisingly simple ascent up the front stone steps until I reached the door. *So this is where my vodka money goes*, I thought to myself as I reached out to touch the large brass knocker. *I get a hangover, and they get a freaking fortress.* And it was as this word came to mind that I realized, despite its outward magnificence, the place was cold and quiet, as if a low cloud of sorrow dominated every nook and artist-chiseled cranny.

I suddenly yearned for my parents' modest three-bedroom house in the suburbs of Illinois. I wanted to sit on the front porch with Abby, peeling corn and bickering, as we often did on summer evenings when the strain of our dysfunctional family had settled down, graduating into a sense of humor, acceptance, and (despite all our collective faults) belonging. *Money doesn't buy happiness, it just leases it*, I thought as I prepared to enter.

Just as my fist was clenched in preknocking position and pulling back for the first hit, the door swung open and a pile of people laden with tablecloths, candles, and baskets of flowers crashed out like a wave, almost knocking me over. I took the opportunity to peek inside. A marble floor greeted me in the entrance, reflecting the light of the massive crystal chandelier hanging above it. Just beyond the entrance I caught sight of a gleaming spiral staircase, winding up toward the sky.

A short, bald man dressed in a dark blue suit fastened his eyes on me with such intensity that I was forced to acknowledge his gaze. I had hoped to sneak into the house unseen and look for Jack. Given the size of the place, it could take hours, if he was indeed in here. The man herded the small group out the door while raising his index finger to me; I was to wait for him.

I considered making a run for it; surely my comparatively long, lean legs could run faster than his short, stubby ones, but he had a commanding presence and I had no doubt he could summon longer, faster running legs if the necessity arose. The sooner I found Jack, gave him the ring, and confessed, the sooner I could get out of here and get on with my road trip. I briefly thought about finding the gardener I had kissed and having a quickie before taking off. It would certainly be a promising start to my adventure. But I soon dismissed the idea, as I remembered his smug showboating as he shamelessly kissed me; he was definitely the type to kiss and tell.

'May I help you?' the man asked politely as he returned to his post as gatekeeper, blocking my previous view of the entrance.

'I'm here to see Jack,' I said as all other creative excuses flew out of my head. The man tilted his nose toward me like a bloodhound sniffing around a crime scene.

'Are you now?' he said as if I had just proclaimed my intentions to pee on the lawn.

'Yes, I am,' I said. 'I have something for him. I also need the ladies room, and some water would be heaven,' I added. His expression changed like a slideshow, sarcastic to incredulous in seconds flat.

'You must be out of your mind. I told Master Heron that contest was a bad idea—'

Master Heron? You've got to be kidding me. So this is how the other half lives! In stuffy suits with Victorian vocabulary. Once again, I longed for home.

'—You'll have groupies on the lawn! I told him. And here you are. How you got this close I don't think I even want to know—'

'I'm not here about the contest—'

'You are trespassing on personal property and I have no qualms calling the authorities—'

'Rachel sent me,' I interrupted. The man stopped jabbering and stood stone still.

'Rachel? Rachel who?'

'Rachel Morgan. Jack's fiancée.'

The change in his demeanor was immediate. His eyes brightened as if shades had suddenly been drawn open, filtering sunlight into his irises. Whereas moments ago I would have described his eyes as dull and brown, now they were alive and glowing, like copper pennies basking in the sun.

'Dear, dear, dear. What is our girl up to this time? Everyone is in quite a flutter wondering where she is, you know.'

Just then a familiar, jarring voice cut through our conversation. 'Anderson, the gardeners arrived late,' Madeline yelled from the steps. 'I'm docking their pay two hundred dollars.' It was too late to hide. Madeline Heron had descended on us like a storm cloud. I couldn't help but think of the Tarot card reading as the Devil's card danced in front of her.

'Who is this?' she said, noticing me but addressing the question to Anderson.

'I'm a friend of Rachel's,' I said when Anderson failed to voice a response. 'I'm also the reason the gardeners were late.'

'Where is Rachel, why is this woman dressed like a lumberjack, and what on earth does she have to do with my gardeners?' Madeline asked Anderson, as if I didn't speak English and he was my personal interpreter.

'I was in a car accident,' I said.

'On second thought,' Madeline said, moving past me into the house. 'I don't care. I don't have time for this. Tell Rachel to meet me on the veranda. Her fitting is in one hour. Anderson, find Rachel's friend something more appropriate to wear and don't forget two hundred less for the lawn boys.'

With that, Madeline Heron was gone as quickly as she had come. I was in the process of looking down at my 'inappropriate attire' and working myself into an emotional tantrum when Anderson lightly touched my elbow.

'I'll show you to the ladies room,' he said. 'Then I'll make you a nice cup of tea.'

If it hadn't been for the attendee in the restroom, waiting patiently for me to finish with a monogrammed towel thrown over her arm, I would have stayed in there for hours. The same marble floors that greeted me in the entry were spread across the bathroom floor. Matching painted bowls masquerading as sinks beckoned from the counter, reaching out to me with gleaming silver swan-neck faucets. Everything was perfect except for my bedraggled reflection in the gilded mirror. No wonder Madeline had rejected me. I was a mess. If I had been wandering the streets of Chicago with a cup of coffee, do-gooders would have been chucking change into it.

My hair was knotted and frizzy from the truck ride, and dirt adorned me from head to toe. I had almost forgotten I was in a car accident and had spent the morning crawling in dirt and frightening prehistoric birds. Upon seeing what I looked like, I couldn't believe the gardener had actually enjoyed kissing me; I guess his T-shirt was right, he really did like his girls dirty. I giggled and then splashed my face with cold water, hoping to quiet my tingling nether regions.

I washed my face, spritzed some water on my hair to bring back the natural curl, and tried to brush the dirt from my clothes. Maybe I would let Anderson find me 'something pretty to wear' after all.

The more I thought about it, the more it made sense. If I was going to meet Jack Heron face-to-face and break his heart, it was only right that I look as sexy as possible while doing it.

Daily Horoscope – Pisces

Today's horoscope is not fit to print. (Really. It would have seriously bummed you out.)

Anderson handed me a dress the minute I stepped out the door. 'You'll find plenty of towels in there,' he said. 'If you need anything, Miss Solar can attend to you.' I trotted back to the bathroom, wishing Miss Solar would leave.

'I'll be right outside if you need me,' she said, as if reading my mind.

I stripped off my clothes and stepped into the glorious shower. It was cathartic wiping away the remaining traces of dirt on my body with a warm, soapy washcloth. The shampoo and conditioner smelled like ripe peaches. I wanted to stay underneath the waterfall forever, but since I had already shampooed, conditioned, shaved, and exfoliated, I didn't have too many excuses left to use up all of their hot water. In my little studio in Chicago, I could go exactly twelve minutes before the water turned ice cold.

I stepped out of the shower and wrapped myself in luxurious towels, fighting the urge to lie down on the tiles, wrapped in warmth like my sister and I would do when we were little after a long bath. Our mother would come in and rub our backs as we lay face-to-face giggling. 'Snug as two bugs in a rug,' she would say, and we'd stay wrapped in her attention for as long as we possibly could.

I really have no one to blame for turning out so weird; unlucky for me I'd had a pretty happy childhood.

I dried myself off, picked up the dress, and was astonished and slightly embarrassed to find undergarments tucked into the dress. They were silky, blue, and exactly my size. I put them on, and strutted a little in the bathroom, marveling at how sexy I looked. I even turned around and glanced at my ass, which was when my head popped back up and scanned for a hidden camera. I didn't see any, but you never knew in a place like this.

Next I picked up the dress, pulled it over my head, and immediately wiped a clear spot in the middle of the foggy mirror, so I could shamelessly peer in and admire myself. I looked stunning. It was as if the dress had been tailormade for me. It was sky-blue, with a plunging neckline, slimming waist, and full skirt that ended midcalf. The shade of blue made my green eyes glow against my olive skin. My breasts were accentuated while the rest of me disappeared underneath the A-line cut. When my little voice chided me for being so narcissistic, I immediately bound and gagged it. I deserved to feel beautiful.

Fleetingly, I thought of the gardener I had accosted in the truck, wishing I had a making-out-with-a-complete-stranger do-over so that I could be wearing this dress. Not that he hadn't seemed to enjoy me just the way I was—

Enough. That was a shameless thing I had done. Quite unlike me. And now that I was dressed like a lady, I wasn't going to rehash my slutty morning. I had other things to think about, like where had this dress come from?

Madeline, Susan, and Rachel were all tall and thin – this dress was built for someone with a little more curves. Someone like me. Anderson had even given me shoes to match, blue sandals with gorgeous leather straps that tied above the ankle. I twirled around in front of the mirror and then opened the other small bag I had been handed. Lotion. Deodorant. Toothbrush and paste. Makeup. Perfect for my complexion. Something odd was happening here, and once again I had the sensation of being in a dream.

But instead of running screaming from the place, I expertly made up my face, brushed my teeth, and lubricated every inch of my body. A girl never knew when her next brush with dirt was going to be. When I was done, I threw away the clothes I came in, so that when it came time for me to leave they couldn't ask for the dress back unless they wanted me streaking across their lawn. I left the ladies room a much prettier woman than when I had gone in.

If Anderson was astonished by the change, he didn't let on. He simply led me into a drawing room and sat me on a plush rose couch in front of a tray of tea. 'Whose dress is this?' I asked casually, as if I wouldn't physically fight for it with every lotioned inch of my body if he thought I was ever giving it back. 'It fits me perfectly.'

'I thought it might,' Anderson said. 'I used to be in the theatre.'

His answer made absolutely no sense, so I concentrated really hard on squeezing lemon into my black tea. 'You were an actor?' I asked after I had completely strangled my lemon and Anderson still hadn't clarified his thespian confession. It was hard to imagine this furtive little man having any kind of a stage presence.

'Goodness no,' Anderson confirmed, shaking his head as if I had said something distasteful. 'I was in costumes. This place has seen a million parties over the years. Some guests take things with them, others leave things behind. I'm glad it fits.'

He's lying. I am the first and only person ever to wear this dress. And the under-wear? You're telling me I'm wearing panties a past guest had carelessly flung into the hedges after downing too many glasses of bubbly at the garden party? Maybe you're an actor after all. You're definitely a liar. But then again – how could this dress have been bought for me?

I smiled politely and drank my tea while he stared unapologetically. I looked around the room half expecting to see it cordoned off with a thick, red rope, as if we had snuck underneath it while the museum curator snoozed.

Family photographs on the fireplace mantle were the only personal touch in the room; the rest was a festival of antique furniture, oil paintings, thick, gorgeous Persian rugs, and interesting art spilling out of every corner like stuffing bursting out of a pillow. I suddenly felt like I was going to hyperventilate, so I focused on a gorgeous crystal vase to my right. It was tall and gangly, a deep yellow glass whose uneven pieces were sporadically arranged, overlapping like tiny bricks, a prism rock-climbing wall.

I wanted to know its origin, its make, and its value, just in case I accidentally bumped into it and sent it shattering across the floor. With the run of bad luck I was having this morning, it wasn't out of the realm of possibility. I cleared my throat. Anderson raised one eyebrow. *What famous glassmakers do I know? Stuebing?* I smiled and cleared my throat again. Anderson raised the other eyebrow, equally exercising his frowning muscles.

'Um,' I said, shifting uncomfortably and jerking my head to the vase. 'Is that a Stubbing?'

'A stubbing?' Anderson said, looking somewhat alarmed.

'I mean a Stuebing.' I wished I had a long cigarette to inhale. Right now I could be blowing smoke out, covering up my Freudian slip with white fluffy plumes. 'Or is it a Waterford or a Bedford?' I said with an air of authority, as I brought my teacup up to my mouth. As an afterthought, I quickly stuck out my little pinky, but it was immediately seized by a cramp. And not just any little cramp. It was a middle-of-the-night-Charlie-Horse-twisting-your-calves-like-a-dominatrix-squeezing-a-dish-rag-catapulting-you-awake-making-you-swear-off-wearing-heels-for-the-rest-of-your-life cramp.

'Fuck,' I squealed as my pinky convulsed and the china cup threatened to splash tea over its side. I wasn't even the cussing type, but I was in too much pain to formulate any upper-class epitaphs. 'Jesus, God. Fuck. Ow, ow, ow.' Anderson popped out of his seat and even reached his hand out to me, but instantly froze to his spot. Whether it was the result of hearing the F-word uttered twice in the midst of such luxury, or he was running over the impropriety of touching a lady's naked pinky in public, the end result was that he had been zapped into stone, seemingly incapable of helping out city guests writhing in country pain.

Luckily my good hand eventually saw to it to take the cup away and place it back down on the saucer so that I could hold my poor little pinky and massage it back to normal. Anderson simply watched all of this in silence, as if it were an everyday occurrence that a stranger would dress up, play tea, and scream in pain in the sitting room. As the storm blew over, I smiled and wiggled my pinky at him so he could see that no real damage had been done. It was slight, but I saw a smile leak out of his lips and from its proper place at his side, his little pinky waved weakly back. Then, once again, we lapsed into silence.

I bravely picked up my tea again, this time keeping all digits curled in. 'And thank you for the makeup,' I said when I could no longer bear listening to myself swallow.

'You're quite welcome.'

'I have an unusual skin tone. It's kind of olive. Most foundations are made for the ivory gals. Sometimes I have to search for hours' – I realized I was babbling and cut straight to the point – 'but the foundation you gave me was a perfect match. Someone left that behind as well?'

'Madeline's daughter, Susan, has her own line of cosmetics. Again, my theatre background had a hand in choosing the right tones for your complexion. And the shoes? They're the right fit?'

'Like Cinderella,' I laughed. 'Although you left out the handsome prince.' He didn't laugh or move his eyebrows. I coughed. 'Thank you,' I finished lamely.

'Well,' Anderson said, 'I knew with a house full of bridesmaids this weekend I'd better be prepared.'

Duh, Clair. The engagement party. I had almost forgotten.

'I'm not exactly a—'

CRASH. Something above us was erupting like a volcano. The sound was so loud, I was immediately thrown back into the couch, my teacup trembling as I stared at the ceiling. Anderson sprang from his place on the sofa, no stone statue this time, quite the opposite, his entire body in motion. 'Excuse me,' he said, bolting to the winding staircase.

'Would you like me to go with—'

'NO.' It was the first time his voice had risen to anything other than a calm refrain; he had practically shouted at me.

'It's quite all right,' he said, regaining his composure and bowing slightly as if to make up for his outburst. 'Please. Make yourself at home. I'll return momentarily.'

I was too jumpy to sit down and finish my tea, so the second he left I walked over to the fireplace. Unlike my tiny one at home, this one was massive with a large mirror hanging above a mantle where a dozen, perfectly framed family photos were lined up like loyal toy soldiers. As I scanned the row, dying to see a picture of Jack, another one grabbed my attention.

Smiling out at me was the face of an older woman; she was in her seventies at least, but beneath her wrinkles lay the face of a beautiful woman. Her hands were clasped under her chin, and she radiated the look of someone who had just been given good news. There was something familiar about her. A feeling of homesickness spread through me – like the time I was eight and went to camp for the first time. I didn't realize I was actually holding the picture in my hands until I heard Anderson clearing his throat behind me.

'Please don't touch the photographs,' he said.

'I'm sorry.' I quickly placed the picture back on the mantle. 'Is everything all right up there?'

'I'm afraid I have an urgent matter to take care of,' he said, ignoring my question. 'You'll find Jack out back.'

'Out back?'

'Yes. The wine cellar.' Anderson pointed out the large picture window, indicating the woods behind the house. 'Take the path directly behind us. It will lead you to the cottage. You can go out through the kitchen. If you're lucky you'll find Jack before Madeline does. I wouldn't be the one to break the news to her if I were you.'

'Break the news?'

'She's going to hit the roof as they say. As for Jack . . . well. He's not expecting this you know. And he's certainly not expecting you.'

I stared at Anderson, at a loss for words. The ceiling vibrated from another loud crash. Anderson stood perfectly still but his eyes looked up at the ceiling and when they focused on me again, it almost seemed as if he were pleading for help. I stepped toward the staircase in concern. He held up his hand.

'Everything is perfectly fine,' he said as we heard the sound of glass being shattered and the chandelier began to sway. I took another step.

'You'd better catch Jack while you can,' Anderson said. Swish, swish, swish. 'It's very sensitive to vibrations,' he said of the dancing light fixture, as if trying to convince himself.

'It would seem so,' I said. Anderson simply pointed again in the direction of the exit. 'Good luck to you then, Clair,' he said to my retreating back.

Daily Horoscope – Little Red Riding Hood

Go back bitch. He's going to eat you alive.

It wasn't until Anderson disappeared up the winding stairs and I was making my way through the massive stone-tiled kitchen and out the back door that it hit me. I had never told him my name. But he said it as clear as day. *Good luck to you then, Clair.*

Had I told him my name and I just couldn't remember? Maybe I had said it instinctively, like you do when someone tells you theirs. That was it. He must have held out his hand and said, 'Hello, I'm Anderson,' and I must have held mine out and replied 'Hello, I'm Clair.' And then I must have added – 'I'm here to break awful news to Jack,' for he hinted at that as well. Okay, now that was stretching it. No way would I say, 'Hello, Anderson, I'm Clair. I'm here to break awful news to Jack.' So how did he know? Was Anderson a fellow intuitive? I didn't get that feeling about him, but all signs were pointing to the fact that I was having a very off psychic day. There was only one other explanation. Susan must have said something to him.

Or Rachel herself, even. Perhaps Rachel had tearfully confessed to Anderson that she planned on leaving Jack. It eased my mind a little to realize there were several explanations that fit, so I didn't turn around and go after him. There would be time to grill him later. Besides, the truth was, I was jumping out of my skin like a little girl on Christmas Eve. Because just beyond the kitchen was a carved wooden door leading outside. And just beyond the door to the outside was the woods. And in the woods was a path. You see where this is going I'm sure, but I'm on a roll. Into the woods and through the path was a cottage. Where I would find Jack Heron. *The* Jack Heron. The man whose handsome face had stayed glued to my glove compartment. Despite my common sense telling me I was acting like a total idiot, I was so giddy I had completely forgotten I had come here to break his heart.

The path through the woods couldn't have been more than twenty yards. The cottage was made of stone and wood, so quaint and stoic I felt as if I were in a Shakespearean village. There was no need to knock, the front door was wide open. It wasn't until I stepped into the cool, dark interior that I remembered this was a wine cellar. When my eyes adjusted to the dark, I saw the back walls lined floor to ceiling with bottles, complete with a long wooden bar and several wooden tables. The floor beneath me was concrete and directly across from the entrance was a set of French doors, leading out to a patio.

'Hello?' Water dripped an off-beat, nonsensical answer in the distance. I stepped up to the bar, eyeing the bottles of vodka lined up along the back wall below the wine racks. A plain, tan label was attached to the bottles, with Heron Vodka typed across the top and blank labels below, no doubt awaiting the new name and graphics of the contest winner. I wondered what the entries looked like so far.

'Hello? Jack?' I said, even though it was obvious he wasn't here. I headed out to the patio where I was assaulted by sunlight. My eyes had just adjusted to the dimness of the cellar, and I wasn't prepared for the sudden burst of brightness. I closed them for a moment, allowing the sun to lick my lids. After a while I opened my eyes and took in the little oasis.

Somebody had done an amazing job creating a perfect Zen garden. A slice of bright blue sky hovered above the canopy of trees where birds were flitting from branch to branch, chirping, trilling, and flitting about like kids on a playground. The bricks were warm from the sun so I slipped off my sandals, relishing the heat on my weary feet. Peonies, begonias, and lilies sprouted from thick clay pots; fat, red roses sang along the edge, and a hammock was strategically positioned in the corner, which caught the bulk of the shade. Despite the lack of a breeze, the hammock was swaying slightly as if some unseen slumberer had just sprung up and run away.

But the pièce de résistance was the large fish pond sunk into the middle of a patio, as if it were a huge mirror and the bricks its elegant frame. I took a step closer to marvel at gold and yellow koi gliding effortlessly beneath water lilies bursting with life. It was no surprise I felt right at home; water is a powerful conduit for tapping into your psychic abilities. Scrying, the act of gazing into clear, reflective surfaces such as this pond, is the oldest fortune-telling technique around. Crystal balls were formulated to imitate the mirrorlike effects of a rippling pond. As I gazed into it, one by one, my strained muscles gave up their grip on my body. I felt like I was floating. It wasn't long before the warm bricks cajoled me into lying down. I continued to stare into the pond as I lay beside it, feeling my breath deep within my body, imagining the birds singing just for me, wrapping myself in the scent of jasmine. I closed my eyes, and was gone.

'Clair, over here.'

It's my grandmother's voice, she's calling to me. I can't see her; I'm walking in a wall of fog. *'Over here,'* she calls again. *'I'm right here.'* I turn the other direction and start walking. *'You're going the wrong way. I'm over here.'* Again, I turn. Her voice seems to be coming from everywhere at once. Suddenly her hands appear through the fog. They're reaching out to me and I try to grasp them with my own. But she slips away, instead of soft, wrinkled hands, I touch air. '*Clair,*' she cries. '*Your gift. What have you done with your gift?*'

I woke with a start. A man was kneeling on the other side of the pond, staring at me. He was dressed in a suit, as if he were going out to dinner and a show instead of bending on one knee by a fish pond. For a foolish moment, I thought he was going to propose. Underneath the black jacket protruded a bright blue dress shirt that made his dark blue eyes stand out like flashing lights on a pinball machine. He didn't look anything like his magazine picture. He looked a zillion times better.

'It's you,' I said. 'Jack.'

'Who are you?' Jack asked, clearly puzzled. Even the little frown line across his forehead was beautiful.

'My name is Clair,' I said, slowly sitting up and putting my hand up to my head; I was feeling a little dizzy.

'Are you okay?' There was concern in his deep, melodic voice. He stood and slowly approached me, his tall frame blocking out the sun so that I could look up into his eyes. Where was my cell-phone camera when I needed it?

'Jack.' Madeline materialized in the doorway, startling us both. 'There you are.' Jack reluctantly took his eyes off me and turned to his mother. Somehow, I managed to stand. Jack took my arm, steadying me as I wobbled.

'You again,' Madeline said to me. 'Where is Rachel?' she demanded. 'Did you tell her about the fitting?' Jack turned to me.

'You're a friend of Rachel's?' he asked.

'Jack this is no time to flirt with the bridesmaids—'

'You're a bridesmaid?'

'Apparently she rode in with the gardeners, although I still don't understand why.'

'I was in a car—'

'I told Anderson to dock their pay. They were late getting here and it's going to throw the schedule off completely.'

'Don't dock their pay,' I said. 'It's my fault they're late.

They gave me a ride.' Jack tilted his head to one side and stared at me.

'You're a bridesmaid?' he asked again.

'Is that so hard to believe?' I replied, suddenly insulted. Why couldn't I be a bridesmaid? Despite my new dress, could he take one look at me and see I didn't fit in with his high-society friends?

'I just . . . thought I met all of the bridesmaids,' Jack explained as his eyes swept intently over my face. Oh. Well, that made sense. I felt heat come to my cheeks as his eyes dropped to my lips and back to meet my eyes again.

'Well I'm not exactly a—'

'Jack,' Madeline interrupted. 'We have a situation.'

'A situation?' Jack said. Madeline looked at me. I turned to the pond and pretended not to be listening.

'She's at it again,' I heard Madeline say in a low voice. 'And I will not tolerate it this weekend. Do you hear me, Jack? I've had enough.'

'Calm down, Mother.'

'Don't you tell me to calm down. She's gone too far this time.'

'Let's take this somewhere private,' Jack said.

'Jack. All the people coming here tomorrow—'

'I know, Mother—'

'The investors. Do you want them to see and hear—'

'Let's talk up at the house,' Jack said, throwing a look to me. I buried myself in the pond again, making eye contact with a large goldfish.

Is she ever going to leave? The water gets twenty degrees colder when she's around.

I giggled. Jack and Madeline looked at me. 'Sorry,' I said. Jack came over and shook my hand as if we had just concluded a business meeting. His hand was smooth and manicured, his grip firm but warm. *Not a wet fish at all fellas.*

'What is your name again?' he asked, nervously dropping my hand and putting his in his pockets, as if he couldn't trust them not to wander all over my body.

'I'm Clair.'

'It's nice to meet you, Clair,' Jack said with a genuine smile. Madeline glared at me.

'Let's go, Jack,' she ordered.

'You head up first, Mother,' Jack said, still smiling at me. 'I'm going to just finish up with Clair.'

Yes, please finish me off. Up. 'Jack,' Madeline said, gripping his shoulder. He turned to her and lowered his voice.

'I heard you, Mother,' he said. 'And I said I'll be right there.' Madeline stalked off, but not before turning to give me a thorough eye-lashing. I was starting to understand why Rachel had called her the devil. 'So how exactly do you know Rachel?' Jack asked the minute we were alone.

'I uh—' I said, completely at a loss for what to say. Endorphins snowboarding through your body have a way of obliterating all rational thought. I took a deep breath and geared up for the confession. 'Jack. I'm here because—'

I was interrupted by a saxophone belting out 'Moon Glow.' Jack glanced at me apologetically and flipped open his phone.

'Susan,' he said. 'Yes. I know. I know. Mother was just here' – he winked at me as he listened to her, smiling until something she said made his face go slack. 'What? What do you mean missing?'

Uh oh. 'I'll be right there,' Jack said, snapping his phone shut. 'I have to go.' He headed for the door.

'I'm sorry,' I called after him. He stopped.

'About what?'

'Um . . . about Rachel,' I admitted.

Jack nodded, headed for the door again, and then stopped. 'What about Rachel?' he asked, turning back.

'Um . . . she's missing?' I said.

'What?'

'The phone call,' I said, pointing at his cell phone. 'Missing.'

'Oh,' Jack said. 'No, no. That wasn't about Rachel. It's my—' His cell rang again.

'We'll talk later,' he said. 'Okay?'

'Sure, but—'

'Good. It's a date.' He flashed me another killer smile and disappeared.

It's a date. Did you hear that? It's a date. Clair. It is NOT a date. You should be running after him instead of standing here smiling like a smitten schoolgirl. What kind of unfeeling empath are you? His fiancée has gone AWOL. You are here to confess your part in this mess, give back the ring, and get on with your trip.

I wandered back into the wine cellar, took a seat at the bar and put my purse on the counter, half expecting a bartender to materialize. I looked around. I was alone. It was quiet. To my left stood at least ten bottles of vodka. An orange was propped on a cutting board with a knife next to a shot glass. I looked around again. I picked up the shot glass. I put it next to me. I slid the cutting board over. I looked around. I sliced the orange. I put a piece of the orange in the shot glass. I looked around. I slid the cutting board away from me. I looked at the bottles of vodka. I reached out with my left hand and touched a bottle. I looked around. I slid the bottle next to the shot glass. I looked at the shot glass. I looked at the bottle, picked it up, and poured.

Oh wow. It was really, really, good vodka. Way to go Jack. Smooth and sweet, with the lightest touch of vanilla. And the fresh orange was a genius touch. The second pour I didn't even bother looking around. It had been a hell of a day. I deserved it. There were a ton of bottles here, I'm sure Jack wouldn't mind my discreet sampling.

The second shot went down as smooth as the first and while I was savoring the taste, I was struck with a brilliant idea. Okay, maybe it wasn't a brilliant idea, but it was my last chance. I looked around. 'Anyone here?' I joked. There was no answer. I looked at my purse. I looked around. I touched my purse. I looked around. I slid the purse next to me. I opened the clasp on my purse and quickly removed my hand. I distinctly looked away from the purse. Casually, still looking away, I dipped my hand in the purse and touched the velvet pouch inside. It couldn't hurt just to look at the thing now, could it?

Before I could talk myself out of it, I had reached into the pouch, pulled out the diamond ring, and slipped it on my left finger. It was a perfect fit. If I would have crossed my legs and done a few Kegel exercises, I would have had an orgasm. I held it out at arm's length, giggling at the thought of practical-old-me wearing such a rock. 'Of course you can see it,' I said, holding it out to an invisible Irish bartender. 'Jack sprang it on me last night. Under a full moon.' The bartender whistled.

'Congrats, Lassie,' he said, refilling my shot glass. 'This one is on me.'

'It's ginormous,' Brian's voice said. 'You always did like them big.'

'You're so lucky,' Karen wailed, grabbing my hand as drool dribbled down her chin. 'Can I be your Maid of Honor again?'

'We might just elope,' I said. 'Madeline is having a fit over the wedding preparations and Jack and I don't need all the fuss. We just want to be together.'

I laughed and mentally patted myself on the back for letting loose and fantasizing. Everyone is entitled to trot out their inner child and play. Especially after a horrific day and three shots of vodka on an empty stomach. I hopped off the bar stool, arm extended, ring flashing. I twirled around the cement floor, blinding nearby dancers with my happiness.

'Mrs Jack Heron,' I said dreamily. 'I'm Mrs Jack Heron.' If Gene Kelly could sing and dance in the rain at his age, I could sing and dance in the ring at mine. I twirled around some more. Suddenly, I saw Jack across the room. Our eyes met and we melted into each other over the crowd. He gracefully made his way over, beautiful blue eyes seeking me out, muscular arms reaching for me. 'How about a dance with your husband?'

'I'd love to dance, Jack,' I said as he took me in his

arms. When he kissed me, I couldn't help noticing it was the exact kiss I had shared with the gardener. No need to reveal this to my new husband. 'I love you, Jack,' I whispered as we twirled around the dance floor. 'I love you, love you, love you.'

'Oh. My. God.'

The music screeched to a halt as my imaginary stereo was ripped out of the wall. I recognized her voice immediately and a shiver played over my spine. 'I can explain,' I started to say as I turned to face Susan. But my voice was strangled shut before I could gasp out another word. Susan wasn't alone. Standing beside her was Madeline Heron. And standing beside Madeline, was Jack.

13

Daily Horoscope – Pisces

The stars say it's time to bare your soul. But not your thighs. Definitely keep those jiggly babies covered.

I tried convincing myself they hadn't heard any of my adolescent proclamations, but the looks on their faces abruptly shattered that fantasy. They were gaping at me, mouths opening and closing like goldfish flipped out of their bowls. I ran over to the bottle of vodka and pointed at it.

'This,' I said, 'is *very* good vodka. I mean good. Really, really, good.' They still hadn't moved, or uttered a single word. Jack looked as if he were going into shock. 'I didn't eat a single thing today,' I cried.

Three blind mice. Three blind mice. See how they stare. 'I was in a car accident,' I yelled, putting my hand up to my head and feeling around for a lump. 'I think I have a concussion.' Madeline Heron gasped, and for a moment I was touched by her concern.

'I'll be okay,' I said. 'I just—'

'The ring,' she yelled, pointing her long index finger at me. 'She's wearing the ring.'

'I can explain,' I said, mortified. This was like waking up from one of those humilating naked-in-public dreams only to find that you really are naked in public.

'I don't believe it,' Susan said, stepping toward me. 'You stole Rachel's ring?'

'Where is Rachel?' Jack demanded. He took two steps toward me and I took two steps back as if we were playing a demented game of Mother-May-I.

'Rachel gave me the ring,' I said, reaching to take it off. 'I came to give it back.' I tugged on it. It didn't budge. All three of them advanced on me, looking at the ring. Susan and I made eye contact. Madeline put her hand up to her heart. I wiggled the ring around my finger trying to ease it off. 'My fingers must be swollen from the heat,' I said, yanking on it as hard as I could.

'What do you mean she gave you the ring?' Jack asked. 'You mean – like to hold it for her?'

'Why would she ask a bridesmaid to hold her engagement ring?' Madeline countered. 'That's ridiculous.'

'Bridesmaid?' Susan sputtered. 'Bridesmaid?' Apparently, she didn't get the memo. I wished I couldn't see auras. Hers was putrid green, a clear sign of rage. It was getting really, really hot in here and despite intense efforts, I still couldn't get the ring off.

'Baby oil?' I shouted. 'Does anyone have any baby oil?' Silence. Blank stares from the studio audience. *They all ran after the stand-in wife – and cut off the ring with a carving knife . . .*

Madeline was indeed looking at the cutting board knife. 'Look,' I said, backing away from the counter so that I could make a run for it in case she snapped it up, 'Two days ago—' I stopped and looked at Susan. Little beads of sweat were breaking out on her forehead and her rage was turning yellow. Guilt mixed with a little bit of fear. Was it just two days ago she and Rachel came into my tent? Or was it yesterday? Maybe I really did have a concussion. Waves of dizziness came over me as I tried to remember.

'I remember you now,' Susan said. 'Rachel introduced me to you the other day. I'm sorry I didn't recognize you.'

'Oh,' I said. 'I, um – it's nice to see you again—'

'No worries, Mother,' Susan interrupted me. 'This is a dear, dear, friend of Rachel's.'

'You are?' Jack said. I didn't answer. I had to see what was going to come out of Susan's mouth next.

'If she says Rachel gave her the ring, then Rachel gave her the ring.'

'Rachel's never mentioned you,' Jack continued.

'That's because – she's been out of the country,' Susan said. 'Where were you again?' she asked me. 'Italy?'

'It's just not coming off,' I said, ignoring the both of them. Madeline marched over, and pulled on the ring.

Did you ever see such a horrible sight—

'Ow,' I said. 'You're really hurting me.'

'You should have thought of that before you stuck it on your fat little finger,' she roared.

'I don't have fat fingers. It's the heat. And the vodka.' Jack stepped forward and put his hand on his mother's elbow.

'Mother. Let her go.' He replaced her hand with his own. 'Why don't you two go back up to the house,' he said. 'Hopefully Rachel is there by now. I'll be along with the ring in a minute.' They chose glaring over moving. 'I said I'll be right there,' Jack insisted. I was happy to see he wasn't a complete pushover, otherwise these women would have eaten him alive by now. When they finally left, Jack was still holding my hand.

'Come here,' he said, guiding me to a small sink by the bar. He placed my hand under warm running water and gently worked soap over my swollen finger. Ever so slowly, the ring slid up my finger. I looked up at Jack and our eyes held. There was no denying it, we had major chemistry. If we had a beaker, we could have blown something up.

'Were you really in a car accident?' Jack asked. His concern, combined with the stress of the day, turned on my water works.

'Yes,' I said, biting back the tears. 'And your vodka is good. But still – I don't know what came over me. I just wanted to look at the ring one last time. Then the next thing I knew I was putting it on and dancing and – obviously – I didn't mean for you to walk in when you did – I was completely mortified—'

'It's okay—'

'No, it's not. I was way over the top. I'm so embarrassed.'

'Clair, it's okay. But I still don't understand why Rachel—'

'I mean . . . I don't want you to think that I think I'm in love with you, you know?' His soapy hand, entwined in mine, stopped moving. 'I mean I don't think I'm in love with you.'

'Let's just—'

'I don't mean I don't *think* I'm in love with you – you know like I'm on the fence – what I mean is – I *know* I'm not in love with you.'

'Got it.'

'I mean nobody really believes in love at first kiss—'

'First kiss?'

'Sight. I meant sight.' Shit. Why did I have to keep thinking about that gardener? *Because kissing him was sexy. Daring. Because you can't stop thinking about him. What is he doing now? Mowing, trimming, whacking?* 'Weeding, I meant weeding,' I said out loud.

'What?' *Oh God. My crazy thoughts had gotten loose and were leaking out of my mouth.*

'Harder,' I said, changing the subject. 'I can take it.' Jack stared at me. 'The ring,' I cried. 'I meant the ring.' It was his turn to be mortified. Then he laughed and I laughed, and our eyes met again, and sparks flew around our heads. Jack yanked on the ring and although it inched up to just below my knuckle, it refused to budge any farther. I tried again too, to no avail. 'I am so sorry.'

Jack put my hand back under the water and rinsed the soap off. 'It's okay. We're just making it worse.' He took a nearby towel and patted my hand dry. Then, to my total surprise, he brought my hand up to his lips and kissed it. Our eyes met again and it took everything I had not to press my lips against his again, although I wouldn't have stopped there – I would have been up on the bar with my dress over my waist . . .

'We'll try again in an hour or so.' He smiled. I searched his face for an imperfection. Strong jawline, perfect nose, great lips, straight teeth, beautiful blue eyes with thick lashes. It was no use. His only imperfection was the ring on my finger. He was taken. In love. And still in the dark about his suddenly single status because instead of 'fessin' up like I was supposed to do, I was hitting the bottle and Dancing Without The Stars.

'How about one more drink?' Jack asked, dropping my hand like it was five hundred degrees. 'I think I could use one myself. And you can tell me how you know Rachel. And . . . your stint out of the country. Italy, was it?'

'I have to arrange a tow truck for my car,' I said, stalling for time. I didn't want to turn down another drink with Jack Heron, certain parts of my body didn't want to turn down a drink with Jack Heron, in fact I should have been pouring ice cold water straight down my dress just to get my mind off the five-alarm fire going on down there. But telling him the truth about Rachel was a sobering discussion that I was suddenly afraid to face.

'I know a guy,' Jack said, taking out his cell phone. 'Where exactly is your car?'

'Um . . . a little off into the woods on Route 13,' I said, feeling sweat break out on my forehead. 'Um . . . near Devil's Backbone? Well at least near a sign marker for Devil's Backbone.' Jack was nodding politely but staring at me with definite pity.

'Um . . . I'm going to need a little more to go on than that. Can you think of any other markers? Do you think there are skid marks on the road?'

'No. There couldn't be because I was flying.'

'Flying?'

'The car was airborne. Until I crashed and it flipped upside down.'

'Good Lord. You must have been terrified.'

'I thought I was going to die.' Jack hugged me. I buried my face in his neck, and was immediately intoxicated by his scent. He smelled like pine trees and cinnamon, with a trace of a wood-burning fire.

'How long had you been driving on Route 13 before the accident?' he asked, suddenly pushing me away.

'It's not far from where your gardeners picked me up,' I said. Now that man had an imperfection. A little scar hiding underneath the stubble along his jawline—

'My gardeners?'

'Boys with Rakes,' I said. 'They gave me a ride.' *And I gave one of them a ride*.

'Uh, okay,' Jack said. 'I'll speak with them. Do you know about how long you had been walking when they picked you up?'

'Good question,' I said. How long *had* I been walking? I honestly didn't know. The whole day was one big blur. 'Fifteen minutes to an hour,' I said confidently. Jack burst out laughing.

'I'll see what my buddy can do with that,' Jack said. 'And I'll make a few calls; the police could have towed it by now.'

'I tried to call 911,' I explained. 'But my cell phone had died. It's a rental car, too. I'm probably in a bit of hot water.'

'It was an accident. Don't worry, I'll help you out.'

'I don't know how to thank you.'

'Don't mention it. You're a friend of Rachel's,' he said, pouring a bucket of cement into my stomach.

'Jack. I'm not really—'

'Clair, I have to run up to the house. I'll call the tow truck on the way. Why don't you walk around the grounds? I'd invite you back with me but we've got a bit of a family emergency.'

'No problem. In the meantime I'll work on this,' I said, holding up the ring. As Jack looked at it, a flicker of anger momentarily darkened his handsome face. 'How did you get that again?'

'Rachel came to see me on' – Jack's phone cut in. He

looked at the screen and shook his head. 'Hold that thought,' he said. 'She's going to blow.' With that, he ran out of the cellar, leaving me with my hardening guilt. I shouldn't have stalled. And here he was being so nice to me. Family emergency aside, I had to tell him. I ran after him, calling his name. I couldn't see him; the thick cluster of trees made it impossible to see more than a few feet ahead. He could be just around the bend. I ran through the trail as best I could in wraparound sandals. Finally, I reached the clearing, panting like I'd run a marathon. 'Hello there,' a voice called out from a Weeping Willow looming to my right.

I let out a little scream and instinctively threw my hand up against my heart, as if trying to keep it from leaping out of my chest. 'It's okay, my dear,' an old woman standing under the tree said as she held her wrinkled hands out to me. 'I'm nothing to be afraid of.' I stepped into her hands and studied her face. It was the woman from the photograph on the fireplace mantle. The one I had been so drawn to. Her grip was soft from her sagging skin, but strong from the squeeze she was administering.

'I'm so glad you're here, my dear.' She was smiling and searching my face like she had lost something.

'I'm so sorry I screamed,' I said, feeling foolish. 'I just wasn't expecting to see you there.'

'That's quite all right, my dear. I'm Jack's grandmother, Elizabeth. And I've been expecting *you*. I've been expecting you for a long, long time.'

Daily Horoscope — Pisces

*Reinvent yourself. Change absolutely everything.
Please, I beg you, become someone, anyone other
than you. We're running out of ink.*

As soon as the words were out of her mouth, I burst
into tears. 'There, there,' she said, wrapping me into
a hug. It must have been a combination of the car accident,
the vodka, and my constant, niggling guilt. Or it could
have been her kind embrace. Six hours of driving with one
lousy cup of coffee. Attacking a gardener. Pretending to be
Jack's wife. Or maybe just a comforting, 'There, there,' just
like my grandmother used to say, was enough to break me.
I was suddenly sobbing helplessly in her arms.

And I thought proclaiming my love for a man I had just
met in front of him, his mother, and his sister was
embarrassing. Elizabeth Heron stroked my head while I
sobbed. After a few minutes, I felt better. In fact, I felt
great. I pulled away and accepted the handkerchief she
handed me. I hesitated as I brought it up to my eyes, afraid
to get mascara all over it. It was a dainty pink handkerchief
with the initials AB engraved in it. I wiped my face, blew
my nose, and almost handed it back to her when I stopped
myself just in time. Something about this woman was
bringing the five-year-old out in me. She took my hand, the
one with the engagement ring.

'It's a perfect fit,' she exclaimed. 'It was my ring you know.'

'I had no idea,' I said. 'It's beautiful. I tried using soap to get it off, but my fingers are swollen and it's stuck.'

'Get it off? Why would you want to take it off? Don't tell me you and Jack have had a fight.'

Uh-oh. I looked into her blue-green eyes as she searched me with concern. Then she broke out into another wonderful smile and took my face in her hands. 'I had cold feet too you know. Right before I married my Robert. Don't you fret, my dear; Jack can be molded into a wonderful husband.'

'I'm not who you think I am. I'm Clair. I'm not Rachel.'

'Don't ever give up on love. I'm eighty-five years old and I still miss my Robert. Even though he's been gone for a long time now.'

'I'm sorry.'

'He and Robert Junior, Jack's father, were killed in a car accident. Thirty years ago.'

'I'm so sorry,' I said helplessly. Life could be so difficult, this many years later and from the look on her face it was as if she had just received the news. Fresh tears threatened to spill over her wrinkled face. I wanted to touch her, but I held back. 'Jack was only five and little Susie was only eight.'

'It must have been horrible for all of you,' I said.

'They were driving through the forest, near Devil's Backbone. Nobody really knows what happened. There had been a storm, the roads were slick. The car was found—'

'Upside down in the woods,' I finished for her. She stared at me.

'Yes,' she said slowly. 'I take it you've heard the story.'

Oh God, what was happening to me?

'And there we were, Madeline and I, alone with a winery and two children to raise all by ourselves. Of course, Anderson pitched in—'

'Anderson?' I couldn't help but interrupt. I wondered if she was mixing people up again.

'Yes, dear Anderson. He's worked here for ages. Before Jack was born even. When my husband and son died, he stepped right in and became like a father to those children. Mind you some people said it didn't look proper – having the help suddenly act like they were part of the family, but between you, me, and the wine cellar, without him, Madeline would probably have gone completely insane. And who was I to interfere? Those children had already lost their father and their grandfather. And they loved Anderson. Just like he's always loved—'

She stopped midsentence to watch a butterfly flit past. Her mouth curled into a smile, and then she stuck her tongue out as the butterfly disappeared. She looked around, leaned into me, and whispered, 'Between you, me, and the Daylight Savings, I've never liked my daughter-in-law. And now she'll be your mother-in-law. Is that what has you so upset?'

'Mrs Heron—'

'Call me Grandma Elizabeth,' she said, gripping both my hands this time.

'Grandma Elizabeth,' I said carefully. 'I'm not Jack's fiancée. Rachel Morgan is Jack's fiancée.'

'I've been waiting so long for Jack to get married,' Elizabeth plowed on as if I hadn't spoken. 'Seeing him married, happy – away from that woman. That's what I want.'

'Madeline is a bit difficult,' I agreed. 'But I'm sure she loves her son.'

'And now you're here and the two of you will be married and as soon as you're happily off on your honeymoon I can go. Don't look at me like that. I know what I'm saying. Despite what they all say about me around here, I know what I'm saying. Between you, me, and the Democratic Party, I'm ready to die darling. I've just been waiting for you.'

I opened my mouth to refute her again, but stopped. Obviously she was senile. And she looked so happy. I was suddenly furious with Rachel Morgan. How could she put me in this position? Did she really want to give all this up? Was it all because of Madeline Heron? Or was the poor girl just having serious jitters?

Like Jack's grandmother said – that was perfectly normal. And I certainly hadn't helped matters. Quite the contrary; I had pounded the last nail into Rachel's cold-feet-coffin. I never should have allowed her to rope me into giving her a fake reading. Why, it was like convincing your doctor to give you a fake-terminal diagnosis!

What had I done? I needed to at least try and reach Rachel, make sure this was really what she wanted before breaking the news to Jack. This time I would tell her the truth about the reading. I would tell her the cards hadn't predicted disaster at all. I'd come clean about everything. Except maybe I'd leave out the bit about throwing myself about the wine cellar and pretending to marry her fiancé all the while flitting about with her diamond ring and a bottle of vodka like it was Mardi Gras.

I had to fix this. I would enlist Susan's help and together we would find Rachel and straighten out the whole sordid mess. 'Elizabeth, can I get you anything? Water? A sandwich?' I said, wanting an excuse to go to the house.

'Aren't you a dear,' she said, squeezing my hand tighter. 'See what a lovely wife you're going to make?'

'Wife?' Jack said from behind. I couldn't believe how adept he was at sneaking up on people.

'Jack, darling,' Elizabeth exclaimed, more schoolgirl than eighty-five-year-old grandmother, 'come join us. I'm just getting to know your beautiful fiancée.' I shook my head at Jack and tried to smile. But his face was set in a hard, grim line and he was staring at me like I was an 'assembly-required' toy with a million pieces.

'I can explain,' I squeaked.

'Grandma, I can't believe you're out here,' Jack said, ignoring me. Obviously he wasn't even going to attempt to put this toy together. He leaned down and kissed her on the cheek. 'Why didn't you tell us you wanted to go out? You scared us to death. I was just about to call the police.'

I was impressed at his genuine show of love for her, but also a little taken aback. Why did this beautiful, elderly woman have to tell anyone when she wanted to take a walk? 'I've missed this willow tree,' Elizabeth said, lurching forward and clutching it. 'I've really, really missed it.' She gazed at the tree, like an infant taking in the world for the first time. 'I used to read Jack stories under this tree,' she said to me. 'Didn't I, Jack? Didn't I read you stories underneath this tree?' Jack turned his head and wiped his eyes. Was he crying?

'You've made my day, Grandmother. You've made my day.' I was completely lost. Elizabeth smiled at Jack.

'Why I just had to come here, Jack,' she said. 'I had to come here and wait for your lovely bride.' Jack glanced at me, frowning slightly.

'Grandmother, my lovely bride has gone missing as well. Now will you come up to the house? It's time for your medicine and as I said everyone is all worked up over your disappearing act.'

'Do you hear that, darling?' Elizabeth said, bouncing my hand up and down. 'We're both missing. It's nice to be missed, isn't it?'

'They must love you very much,' I agreed.

'I told you he was a good man,' Elizabeth said, reaching out to snake her arm around my waist. 'And I can see from the way you're looking at him how much you love him. It's the exact same way I used to look at my Robert!' Jack gave me another indecipherable look as my face turned twelve shades of red.

'I've tried telling her I'm not Rachel,' I explained. 'It's as if she can't hear me.'

'The ring fits her perfectly. Don't you think, Jack?' Elizabeth said, holding up my hand to the light. The diamond caught a ray of sun and sparkled as if on cue.

'Personally, I think it's a little tight,' Jack said, folding his arms across his chest.

'Nonsense. It's a perfect fit,' Elizabeth argued. 'She's beautiful, Jack. Absolutely stunning. And she's sitting right next to me at dinner tomorrow evening.'

I waited for Jack to tell her I wasn't invited to dinner, waited for him to immediately escort me off the property. Hopefully Jack wouldn't cancel the tow truck. Not that the car would be in any shape to drive. I'd have to find another way back. No more rental cars. But there had to be a bus back to Chicago. *You could find that gardener and ask him to give you another ride.* My face flushed and I snuck a look at Jack to see if he noticed. But Jack wasn't looking at me, he was staring at his grandmother as if he had just seen a ghost.

'You want to – join us for dinner?' he said. 'You mean – sit at the table – with everyone?'

'As long as you sit on one side of me and she sits on the other,' Elizabeth said.

'That's amazing,' Jack said, throwing his arms around his grandmother. I looked at Jack for an explanation, but he was ignoring me. 'It's a deal then,' Jack said to my complete surprise. 'But only if you come with me now, take your medicine, and rest.'

'But I'm not going to be at dinner,' I cried. 'Mrs Heron—'

'Elizabeth dear. I told you to call me Elizabeth.'

'I'm not Jack's—'

'Darling,' Jack said, grabbing me around the waist and pulling me into him. Our faces were only inches apart. I could feel every button on his shirt press my body. I could smell his cologne and the faintest scent of sweat. I had only to reach up a few inches to feel his wavy hair in my hands. His belt buckle was cutting into my stomach and his heart was beating rapidly into my right breast. His hands, which were resting on my hips, flexed a clear warning. 'Let me get Grandmother up to bed, darling,' he said. 'Didn't you hear her? She wants to sit next to you at dinner tomorrow evening.'

'Yes but—'

'She hasn't had dinner with us for a very long time.'

'Okay, but—'

'She's taken dinner in her room every night—'

'I don't see what that has to—'

'She hasn't been out of her room at *all*,' Jack growled.

'I heard you, but—'

'For the past two years.'

That shut me up. Clueless psychic strikes again. *Two years locked in her room?* I looked at Elizabeth. She was still gazing at the willow tree. No wonder she was drinking in her surroundings like a parched child. I felt a tug in my heart. When Jack saw understanding creep into my eyes, he loosened his grip on my hips.

'I can make my own way up to my room if you love-birds want to stay here and smooch,' Elizabeth said happily. Jack let go of me and held his arms out to his grandmother.

'We'll have plenty of time for that,' Jack lied. 'Right now I want to take a walk with you.'

'I think this has been enough for one day,' Elizabeth said, smiling at me. 'And now that she's here, everything is going to be all right.'

'It is, it is indeed,' Jack said as his voice cracked.

'All the nonsense is going to stop now, right dear?' Elizabeth asked suddenly, grabbing my hand. Confused, I looked at Jack.

'What nonsense, Grandmother?'

'Just make it stop,' she begged, ignoring Jack and staring into my eyes. 'All right?'

'I'm sorry,' Jack whispered in my ear. 'She has trouble sometimes.'

'What are you whispering about?' Elizabeth barked. I was shocked by the sudden change in her tone. Jack put his arms around his grandmother. 'I'm sorry,' he said. 'I was just telling – Rachel – I was going to take you to your room now and tuck you into bed myself.' Elizabeth dropped her anger like a child ditching one beloved toy for another, the smile back on her face full force. 'Don't let him go, darling,' she said over her shoulder as Jack started walking her back to the house. 'Don't you dare let him go.'

I watched them leave, grandson and grandmother, arm in arm, on this breakthrough day, and I wanted to be happy for them, but I just couldn't summon my earlier joy. I couldn't shake the feeling I was missing several key pieces of this puzzle. One minute Elizabeth had been so happy, but the next – the way she gripped my hand and pleaded with me as if we shared some deep, dark secret. *Just make it stop.* Make what stop? Jack said she was confused sometimes, but I knew better than to ignore my little voice.

Elizabeth Heron was frightened of someone or something and she expected me – 'Rachel' – to save her. *Listen to yourself. You're being way too melodramatic. You're just in the middle of a wealthy, dysfunctional family with a grandmother who has been shut in her room for so long she has a few cobwebs in the attic.*

But my uneasy dread remained. I had to find Rachel and get to the bottom of this, if only to ease my own mind. But, until I could track her down, it looked like I'd be standing in for her at dinner. Only this understudy had yet to learn her lines.

Daily Horoscope — Pisces

Mysterious celestial influences converge, hitting you with a monkey wrench.

I headed up to the house, circumventing the rolling lawns and flower beds, trying to clear my mind. I was starting to lose all sense of time; I wondered how long I'd been here and if anyone was trying to contact me. I made a mental note to look for a cell-phone charger. Then again, if no one was trying to contact me, I'd feel like a loser. It was one of the things I hated most about not having someone in my life; there was nothing like the loneliness of knowing – no one knew you were away, no one was waiting for you to come back.

Charles called me six months ago from rehab, and I got all excited thinking he was going to finally make amends and apologize for the hell he had put me through. Instead, he asked if I could sneak him in some pot brownies. I was so angry I actually did make pot brownies and ate the entire batch with Brian. Brian wanted us to do practice readings to see if our insights were better when we were looped up on sugar and THC, but I was too engrossed with my refrigerator word magnets, writing a very creative fuck-you letter to Charles.

Brian got into it and wrote a fuck-you letter to his ex, and then, when we realized what incredible writers we were, we started the Fuck-You fridge novel. It began at the top of the freezer, ended at the floor, which is about how long our average relationship lasted anyway. We were convinced it was going to make us a million – the literary equivalent to the sticky note. We couldn't exactly figure out how to pitch it, however, since the fridge was such an integral part of the presentation. We waited so long that words started falling off, and then one day, when my forty-year-old brother, Tommy, was spending the weekend with me (I had accurately predicted the not going to college thing), I came in to find our Fuck-You fridge novel replaced with one sentence. 'Give Me Blow Jobs or Give Me Death.' That was pretty much the end of our literary careers.

In the distance I could see several white tents propped on the lawn like giant slices of Wonder Bread and people running around in various states of distress. But despite their anxiety, I could see that quite a bit of work had been accomplished already. The lawn, fresh from its buzz cut, smelled crisp and glowed such a brilliant shade of green I had to reach down and feel its soft tendrils, just to assure myself it wasn't Astro-turf. Tables were set up underneath the tents, adorned with fresh linen cloths and candles, and the adjacent patio and gazebo had been strung with little white lights. Excitement pulsed through me; this was the party of the century and I was going to be a central part of it all.

Because Jack's grandmother thought I was Rachel.

I needed to find Susan so we could hunt down the real bride-to-be and I could get my ass back to Chicago before the evil queen could cut off my head with a croquet stick. *I'm not going anywhere. Head or no head, I'm not going to miss this party.* I turned and ran straight into a man's chest, hitting my head on the exact spot I had banged up in the car accident. 'Ow,' I said, rubbing the lump. I had to squint to look up at the man who I was cursing under my breath.

'Mike Wrench,' he said, holding out his hand for a

shake as if a woman bouncing her head off his chest was a regular occurrence. I stared at him. He was dressed in a suit similar to Jack's, and he had obviously come from the shower for his thick hair was tousled and wet, and a dab of shaving cream was visible on his chin. 'This is the part where you tell me your name,' he said, still holding my hand and smiling.

'Mike Wrench you say?' I removed my hand from his grasp. 'I would have gone with the Mad Hatter.'

'Sorry?'

'It's just – people keep sneaking up on me,' I said, rubbing my head. 'And they all seem to know me or think they know me. I'm beginning to feel a little like—'

'Alice In Wonderland.'

'Exactly.'

Mike Wrench threw his head back and laughed. I pegged him to be in his early thirties, and he definitely had tall and handsome down. In fact, he and Jack could have been brothers. But there was something else about him. Something extremely familiar. I studied him again, trying to put my finger on it. Thick, darkish hair, hazel eyes. Impeccably dressed. Nice smile. He'd obviously lifted a few weights in his life.

'I need to get back to the house,' I said, still trying to sort it all out. Who did he remind me of? Suddenly his arms were on my waist and he pulled me around to him. Despite my little voice lecturing me that one of us should make a move to put some distance between our bodies, I remained pressed against him long after it occurred to me that I shouldn't be. He even felt familiar. Was this one of those past-life connections?

'Am I that easy to forget,' he said, cutting through my thoughts, brazenly running his hands up and down my back, 'or is it just cuz I clean up so nice?'

'Gardeners like it dirty,' I blurted out as his crisp blue dress shirt was replaced by the green T-shirt with white lettering. He laughed and since my stomach was flattened against his, I was forced to laugh with him.

'I certainly do,' he said. 'And I have a feeling you do, too. His flirting snapped me back to reality.

'You know,' I said, pulling away from him. 'I'm not normally like that.'

'Like what?' he said, letting me go but smiling like he knew I didn't want to.

'I just mean – it's not – I have to. I need to lie down,' I stammered. 'Alone,' I added when he gave me that look again.

'Just tell me your name.'

'It's Clair.'

'Clair De Lune,' he said. I stared at him. 'You're going to catch flies like that,' he said, gently touching my open lips with his finger.

'Clair De Lune,' I said. 'That's what my grandmother used to call me.'

'Ten years of classical piano,' Mike admitted. 'Debussy is one of my favorites.'

'I need to find Susan,' I said, suddenly terrified of the strange impulses running around my body. I wanted to kiss him again, too, just to see if it would be anything like that first kiss. 'I have to find Susan,' I said again louder, clutching my head.

'Okay, okay. I'll walk you up to the house,' he said, putting his arm around my waist. 'You can tell me things about yourself.'

'Like what?' I said as a feeling of dread came over me.

'You said you were in futures. Are you here checking out Heron Vodka as a possible investment?'

'Yes,' I said with confidence. 'Yes I am.'

Mike suddenly stopped walking and since his arm was latched around my waist, I stopped too. He turned me to him again, our bodies once more plastered together. 'I was hoping I'd run into you again,' he said. 'Was it just me, or was that one hell of a kiss?'

'It was just you,' I said breaking away. I stumbled forward and he followed.

'Oh really?' he said with a whistle. 'Could have fooled me.' If he was trying to push my buttons, it worked. I stopped and faced him.

'What's that supposed to mean?' I demanded. He shrugged, but the confident grin never wavered.

'You seemed awfully into it,' he bragged.

'It was a dare.'

'I see.'

'A dare.'

'I heard you.'

'Why are you smiling?'

'Because you're here.'

'You don't even know me.'

'So tell me about yourself.' I felt like he was playing games with me, talking me in circles. 'I have to get to the house.'

'We're walking to the house.' I looked down at my feet. Sure enough, we were walking to the house. The ground shifted, moving right and left as if we were skating across it rather than walking. Mike was whistling 'Clair De Lune.' I picked up the pace.

'Have I said something to upset you?'

'No. I just need to—'

'Get to the house.'

'Right.'

'Clair, I'm just going to say it. Waking up to find you on top of me, kissing me? It was hands down the sexiest thing any woman has ever done to me.' We stopped and stared at each other. In lieu of throwing myself into his arms and kissing him again in the hopes that it would be the second sexiest thing anyone had ever done to him, I took a step back and almost fell. The ground was spinning like a carousel. Immediately, his arms were around me, holding me up. 'Are you all right?'

'I need to lie down,' I said.

'I'll get you to the house.'

'I don't think I'll make it that far.'

'It's okay, I've got you.' It struck me, as he helped me

along the lawn, that I had no idea who this guy was, but the strangest part was how familiar he felt, how perfectly normal it felt to be tucked in his arms. It was official; I may not have been completely off it, but my rocker was definitely starting to tilt.

'So if you're an investor – then why does Madeline think you're one of the bridesmaids?' Mike Wrench asked nonchalantly.

'Oh,' I said, wiping little beads of sweat from my forehead. 'That was a simple misunderstanding.'

'So you're not a bridesmaid?'

'I am not a bridesmaid.' It felt good to tell the truth.

'But you are an investor?'

'I told you,' I repeated. 'I'm in futures.'

'Exciting business futures,' Mike said.

'You don't know the half of it,' I agreed.

'I'll be honest. Sexy and financially savvy. You're my dream girl.'

'What would your girlfriend think of all this?' I added, suddenly remembering his smug declaration in the truck.

'I don't have a girlfriend—'

'You said—'

'I lied. Once you dismounted you looked downright terrified I was going to attack you.' The wolfish grin was back on his face. 'And I'll be honest – I was tempted. But in the end I decided to be a gentleman. Thought the girlfriend thing might calm you down a bit.'

'Well, it didn't,' I said, using every ounce of energy I had to move forward. I felt like I was slugging through quicksand. I briefly wondered if the vodka had been poisoned. 'So why were you pretending to be one of the gardeners?' I asked Mike, hoping to steer the conversation away from me.

'I wasn't pretending to be one of them, you just assumed. Besides you didn't want to talk to me back then either. Remember?'

I didn't? The truth was, it was all kind of a blur. Except the kiss. I definitely remembered the kiss. That's right, I kind of freaked out about turning into a slut. The house loomed closer, perhaps another thirty feet away, but I really felt like I couldn't make it. I used talking to Mike as a pretense for stopping.

'You didn't really answer my question,' I said.

'Ask it again. I was distracted,' he said to my lips.

'Who are you?'

'I guess you could say I'm a friend of the family.'

'I see,' I said, although I didn't at all.

'And, I'm Jack's best man,' he added.

I felt a sudden, desperate urge to sleep. I started to get down onto the ground.

'Clair?' Mike said. 'Over there.' He pointed to a hammock several feet away. 'Think you can make it?' I managed to nod and headed for the hammock, Mike's arms firmly around my waist, guiding me. The minute I felt the heavy mesh underneath my body, I gratefully turned over and closed my eyes. Mike knelt down next to me. I could feel the heat of his gaze licking through my eyelids.

'Clair? Are you all right?' I tried to answer but my lips were sealed in cement. I felt his hands caress my cheek. 'It's okay Clair De Lune,' he whispered. 'I'm going to be right here when you wake up.' I didn't answer. I didn't even know if his lips really brushed my cheek, or if I had imagined it. I was already dreaming.

I was in a wedding dress I never would have been caught dead in. It was reminiscent of the Victorian Ages, with a high, choking collar, lacy sleeves, and a straight bodice flowing into a neverending train. I was carrying a bouquet of cash, and running through a cemetery. Even while dreaming it, I tried to decipher its strange meaning. Marry for money? Marriage is like death?

Despite hating the dress and its suffocating feel around my neck, I was irritated it was trailing the ground, wet with dew, and brushing over mounds of dead people. And then I tripped over a grave, my cash went flying, and I landed facedown in front of a headstone. I lifted my eyes, fully expecting to see my own name staring back at me. I leaned closer to the stone, making sure I was seeing things right. The name hadn't changed. It was carved in large, capital letters, etched forever in imitation marble: RACHEL MORGAN.

I woke to find Mike's face inches from mine. I screamed, forcing him to back away. 'You scared me,' I yelled. My heart was still tripping from the dream, my breath shallow. Rachel Morgan. What did it all mean?

'I didn't scare you,' Mike said. 'You were having a nightmare.'

'Are you sure it's over?' I asked, glaring at him.

'Are you always this cranky when you wake up?'

Why did I see Rachel's name on a headstone? Was she in any danger? Or was the dream simply telling me her marriage was dead? But I already knew that, after all I was instrumental in its demise. 'I have to find Susan,' I said, trying to get to my feet. But I had stood up too fast and now waves of blue and black fuzz washed over my eyes and the lawn was still spinning beneath my feet. Mike came to my rescue again, but I feebly tried to push him away.

'Please, let go of me,' I said.

'Fine. Fall then,' he said, releasing me. I stumbled, and then fell on my face. Mike ran over and crouched down. 'Jesus. I'm sorry,' he said. 'I didn't really think you were going to fall. Are you okay?' He knelt down on the ground next to me.

'Rachel's not coming.' The confession, aimed at the wrong person, shot out of me.

'What do you mean?' Mike asked. 'Why isn't she coming?'

'I need to talk to Susan,' I said, putting my hand up to my head, trying to will the waves of dizziness to pass.

'Are you wearing Rachel's engagement ring?' Mike asked, roughly picking up my hand.

'Uh – yes,' I said, pulling my hand free.

'I'm sure there's a good explanation?' Mike urged.

'I don't owe you any explanations,' I said. 'Rachel asked

me to return the ring to Jack,' I admitted. 'I was just trying it on, that's all. But it's stuck.'

'Rachel asked you to return the ring.'

'Yes.'

'The Rachel you said you didn't know.' Gee, this guy really pays attention. Go figure.

'That would be the one.'

'And . . . she's leaving him?' Incredulity was stamped on his face, ready to mail.

'You're his best man,' I said excitedly. 'Do you think *you* could break it to him?' Mike let go of me again, and this time he didn't even blink when I hit the ground.

'She left him?' he yelled down at me.

'Yes,' I admitted.

'And she sent you to do her dirty work?'

'Er.' He ran his fingers through his hair.

'Jesus, Clair,' he said. 'And here I was starting to like you.' I slowly picked myself up off the ground.

'Hey,' I said throwing my arms up. 'I'm just the messenger.'

'Just the messenger? Why are you wearing that ring again?'

'Women try things on. Shoes, clothes, jewelry, men. It's what we do,' I said. I was trying to make a joke; after all, he had certainly sprayed out his share of innuendos and sexist remarks. He didn't seem to find the explanation humorous.

'This is going to kill him,' he said. 'Do you realize this is going to kill him?'

Guilt sealed my mouth shut and we walked back to the house in silence. Mike was right, Jack was going to be devastated and here I was playing with the ring like a complete adolescent idiot. We reached the front door and stood staring at each other. I tried to get a read on him, but it was as if a giant padlock had been placed over his thoughts. Or maybe I was just too tired to practice my craft.

When he left me on the porch I was sure of only two things. One – I didn't realize how much I was enjoying his attention until he took it away, and two – I wasn't the only one with a secret. Mike Wrench was hiding something. I didn't know what – but he was definitely hiding something. Just before we had parted, a single word had appeared above his head, clear as day.

Liar.

Daily Horoscope – Pisces

Accusations fly. You should've taken the train.

Anderson greeted me at the door. 'Are you all right?' he asked. I shook my head. 'I need to talk to Susan.'

'She's in a family meeting.'

'Then I'm going to take a nap.'

'I'll show you to your room.' We walked up the set of winding stairs. At the top of the first flight we turned right down a long hallway and stopped at the third door on the left. 'You should find everything you might need in the closet.' Anderson opened the door revealing a tidy little guest room bathed in a light blue hue. 'Dinner is served at six sharp. If you miss it, you can always go into the kitchen and help yourself.'

'Is it true that Elizabeth Heron hasn't been out of her room in two years?' I asked him as he was leaving. 'I mean – before today?' Anderson stopped and looked at me.

'Yes. She secluded herself in her room,' he confirmed. I had a million questions. I wondered why she didn't leave her room, why with all their money they didn't get her help a long time ago – but mostly I wondered what had caused her to come out of her room – why now? Why today? Why did I have this feeling it had something to do with me? It was ludicrous I knew, yet I couldn't shake the feeling that my arrival and her venturing out were connected.

And what did she mean when she asked me if all the nonsense was going to stop? Was she was suffering from Alzheimer's or another form of dementia? 'I wouldn't go around asking anyone else about this if I were you,' Anderson said, walking to the door. I followed him.

'You sound just like Mike,' I said. Anderson stopped in his tracks and I had to screech on my heels not to run into him. Seriously, the man should come with brake lights.

'What about Mike?' he demanded. I had obviously pushed a button. Did Anderson know something about Mike that I didn't? I tried to concentrate on Anderson's thoughts, but all I could think of was Colgate toothpaste. This might sound odd to you, but I was used to it; you'd be surprised how intense people get with their mental shopping lists. I realized he was still waiting for me to answer his question about Mike.

'Nothing,' I deflected. 'I just meant – it seems like the two of you are . . . warning me, I guess you could say.'

'The Herons are a very private family,' Anderson acknowledged.

'I understand,' I said. Anderson looked as if he were about to run off. 'Wait,' I said. 'How did you know my name?'

'Pardon?'

'When I first arrived. As I was heading out to find Jack – you said, "Good luck to you then, Clair."'

'Yes?' he said, clearly confused.

'I never told you my name was Clair.' It was slight, but Anderson stiffened.

'You must have.'

'I didn't.'

'Then you must have misunderstood me.' We met each other's steady gaze. Anderson bowed slightly. 'It's never my place to argue with a guest.' He was gone before I could ask him anything else.

Sometime later, I awoke, drenched in sweat, heart pounding. I didn't know how long I'd been asleep, it could have been ten minutes or ten hours. I put my hands up and covered my ears to drown out the shouting. The raised voices were actually coming from downstairs, but physically, it felt like they were shouting directly into my eardrums. The energy in the house had a distinct, angry pulse. I knew it wasn't any of my business, but it wasn't my fault; if they were going to scream that loudly, they had to know someone was going to hear them. I slid out of bed, and entered the hall. I made my way down the winding staircase, using the sounds of shouting as my guide.

It was when I reached the doorway from where the sounds had originated that I realized I couldn't have possibly have heard them from upstairs; despite their voices ringing with urgency, they were barely speaking above a whisper. It hit me like a ton of bricks. I had heard them telepathically. I had experienced clairaudience, the act of hearing things not within the normal range, as opposed to clairvoyance, the act of seeing things. This wasn't the norm for me – this kind of ESP was 'way above my pay grade' as they say. Somehow, after several hours of being out of touch with my psychic abilities, they were back full force.

I didn't knock on the door, I simply opened it and stepped in, despite Anderson's former warnings not to disturb the very private Herons. I stood in the doorway and surveyed the room. It was a formal study bathed in books, leather, and wood. The room also housed a fireplace, wet bar, and mirrors. That's how I saw the three of them first, through their reflections in the wall-sized mirror behind the bar. They certainly didn't look happy. Maybe they knew about Rachel already.

Madeline was the first to spot me.

'Speak of the devil,' she said. *Funny, that's what they've been saying about* you. 'Why are you still wearing the ring young lady?'

'Because it's still stuck,' I said, giving it a tug to prove it to her. It slid right off. And onto the ground. Somewhere. 'Oh,' I said, dropping to the floor.

'Now look what you've done,' Madeline said crossly. 'Find that ring at once.'

'Mother, stop it,' Jack said, but he didn't sound too

happy with me either. Susan dropped to the ground with me to look for the ring. She was trying to catch my attention, sending not-so-subtle signals with her eyes. We came face-to-face underneath an antique pool table.

'Have you heard from Rachel?' I whispered. Susan's lips stretched into a thin, hard line. She nodded curtly.

'She's with her parents,' she whispered back. 'I tried to speak with her but she hung up on me.' While I was taking in this new information, I spotted the ring next to Jack's shoe. I crawled out from underneath the pool table and reached for it.

'Don't move,' I told Jack, reaching between his feet. Just as I laid my hand over the ring, Jack shifted his weight and stepped on my hand. I cried out, and he immediately hopped back. I lifted my mangled hand, convinced he had broken a few fingers.

'Are you okay?' Jack asked, kneeling beside me.

'I'll never play the piano again,' I said, looking him in the eyes. We stared at each other for what felt like forever while cartoon sounds of bells ringing and sparks flying between us swarmed through my head. Jack finally got the joke and busted out laughing. I laughed too, all the stress of the day building up and spilling over. Jack sat down, held his stomach, and laughed. I howled in response. Madeline and Susan stood over us with sour pusses. When Jack stopped laughing, I took his hand, turned it over, and put the ring in his palm.

'I'm so sorry,' I said.

'Hey – I've got it back now, it's no big—'

'I'm not talking about the ring,' I interrupted. 'I'm talking about Rachel.'

'What do you mean?' Jack asked. I took a deep breath and imagined Jack bathed in healing, white light.

'Rachel doesn't want to marry you,' I confessed. 'She sent me here to call off the wedding.'

'I don't believe it,' Susan said in a loud, dramatic voice. 'It's – *unbelievable*.' I gave her a look. She narrowed her eyes at me. Jack remained on the floor; he wasn't saying a word, but he was searching my face, as if waiting for the interpreter to show up and explain everything in English.

'Just who do you think you are?' Madeline Heron said, towering over me. 'Coming here with a story like that.'

'I'm sorry, Jack, it's the truth,' I said, ignoring Susan and Madeline. 'Rachel came to me on Friday night. She was – conflicted about the marriage. She had nothing but kind things to say about you – but – she just . . . didn't want to marry you. I'm sorry she didn't have the guts to come here and tell you herself, but there it is.'

'Friday you say?' Madeline interjected. 'That's not possible. Susan, didn't you spend all day Friday with Rachel?'

'Of course I did,' Susan said. 'All day. And I've never seen this woman in my life,' she yelled, pointing at me.

'You said you two had met,' Jack said. Susan retracted her hand.

'Yes, I did say that,' Susan sputtered. 'What I meant was – I swear – on my life – I didn't see this woman on Friday. With me. Or Rachel. Because I was with Rachel all day.'

'Are you sure Rachel wasn't out of your sight at all?' I said, pulling her out of the pool swimming when I really wanted to push her back under and drown her. Susan bit her lip and shifted her gaze between Jack and Madeline. 'Say, around six P.M.?' I prodded. Forget drowning her. Drowning was too gentle. If this woman didn't grab onto the rope I was throwing her, I was going to wrap it around her neck and hang her with it.

'Now that you mention it. She did say she had an appointment—'

'What kind of an appointment?' Madeline demanded. Jack got to his feet and staggered to a leather chair. Even though rich people couldn't get away from the harsh realities of life, I felt a stab of jealousy they got to do their sulking in soft leather chairs.

'Something about the florist, I think,' Susan muttered. 'She said she'd meet up with me later.'

'I made all the flower arrangements,' Madeline

exploded. 'Why would she dare meet with a florist?' Madeline stepped into Susan's space. 'Were you two secretly seeing florists behind my back?' Jack closed in on her, too.

'Did you meet up with her later?' he grilled. Susan closed her eyes. I almost felt sorry for her.

'No. She called and said – she had some things to take care of – she wanted me to come here without her.'

'How did she sound?' Jack asked. 'Did she sound . . . like she wanted to leave me?' His voice cracked. I wanted to throw my arms around him and kiss him. *Gardeners Like It Dirty. Stop it, Clair.*

'No. Of course not. She sounded completely normal. It's all her fault,' Susan said, pointing at me. 'I just know. I just have this – *feeling*. She *must* have said something to upset her.'

'Or worse,' Mike Wrench said from the doorway.

'Or worse?' I repeated. Jack stood up and Madeline Heron took a protective step toward him.

'What are you talking about, Mike?' Jack asked.

'Foul play,' Mike said. 'I'm talking about foul play.'

You Don't Have to Be Psychic to Know:

Your stock portfolio should be diversified.

It rains a lot in Seattle.

If he accuses you of 'foul play' instead of engaging in 'fore play,' he's just not that into you.

Daily Horror-scope

Speak up and clear the air. But don't cloud it with your dirty laundry.

I wasn't perfect, that was for sure. I was in love with love, I had a wacky job without health benefits or a retirement plan, and despite the fact he had just accused me of 'foul play,' I wanted to wrap my body around Mike like he was a tube of toothpaste and squeeze – but this was going a little too far. Did he think I was a kidnapper? A murderer? Or a plain old jewel thief? The very thought made me laugh. Unfortunately, I was the only person in the room laughing. The rest of them were staring at me like they had just revealed the ending to a Clue game. *It was Clair in the study with the candlestick!*

'Susan,' I yelled, trying to swallow my laughter. 'It's over, okay? I tried to keep you out of this—'

'We should call the police,' Susan yelled over me. 'She's crazy. She's totally insane! Nothing she says makes any sense.'

'Susan. If you don't tell them, I will,' I threatened. 'She just spoke with Rachel on the phone,' I said, pointing to Susan. 'Ask her.' All heads swiveled to Susan. Susan gasped and put her hands on her chest.

'She's holding Rachel for ransom!' Susan yelled.

'What?' I cried.

'Oh my God,' Jack said.

'I am not holding anyone for ransom,' I said firmly. Jack looked at Susan. She shrugged.

'It was just a guess,' she admitted.

'Did you talk to Rachel on the phone or not?' Madeline interjected. She may have been a walking stem of thorns, but at least she was confronting the issue head on. Susan looked at me.

'No,' Susan lied. 'I haven't heard from her since Friday.'

'Where did you last see her on Friday?' I asked. Susan glared at me again.

'I told you. Rachel said she had an appointment and that she would meet me at the estate later,' Susan said.

'Did she meet with you?' Mike asked me. 'Were you the appointment?'

'If you are holding Rachel for ransom,' Madeline interjected before I could answer him, 'you're not getting a dime from us.' I looked around the room for a hidden camera. I looked each of them in the eye. They were totally serious.

'Oh. My. God. It's like I'm on an episode of the *Twilight Zone*,' I said, throwing up my arms. They continued staring at me. Nobody yelled, 'Smile, you're on Candid Camera' and not one of them made a move to apologize. I lost it.

'I'm from *Illinois*. I grew up chucking corn on the back porch and reading *Nancy Drew*. I was a good girl. My older brother, Tommy, hold somebody for ransom – completely plausible. Or take my sister, Abby. Now she's insane. I used to give my allowance to boys she liked, just so they wouldn't tease her about her eye tooth. Otherwise she'd have nightmares and pee the bed and I was on the *bottom* bunk. I worried about everything. At twelve I wrote President Carter a letter a week. Had he heard about the ozone layer? Did he know they were clubbing seals in Alaska? I even told him my brother was growing marijuana plants in the middle of my mother's vegetable garden in case he wanted to make an example of him. The winter of my thirteenth birthday I thought I was going to burn in hell for masturbating with a turkey baster.'

I had been on such a roll that I didn't know what was building up underneath my tongue until I spit that little confession out. To make matters worse, I actually gasped out loud after I said it. And now somebody in the room was starting to snicker. I wanted to know who it was, but I was too mortified to look any of them in the eye. Why, why, why would I tell them about the turkey baster?

At least I didn't tell them that when I slipped back into the kitchen to put it in the dishwasher, my mother whisked it out of my hand with a, 'I was just looking for that,' and before I could make up some excuse about dropping it on the ground she dipped it right back into the broth and started basting the turkey. It was that Thanksgiving my Uncle Leo declared it the best turkey he had ever tasted, and I declared myself a vegetarian. He went on and on about how juicy and tender it was, so much so that by the end of the dinner I had branded him as a child molester. From then on I gave him dirty looks whenever he smiled at me and held myself as stiff as a board whenever he went to hug me.

I had never told anyone about that incident. How could I have betrayed myself like that? It was their fault. They were getting me all flustered with their ridiculous accusations. I still didn't dare look at Jack or Mike, but out of the corner of my eye I could feel them staring at my nether regions just in case another turkey baster was going to spontaneously pop out from underneath my dress.

'Oh just forget it,' I said. 'I can't believe this is my life. Up until Friday evening, I had never even laid eyes on Rachel Morgan.'

'I see,' Mike said, although what he was really thinking was *turkey baster, turkey baster, turkey baster*.

'Well, I don't see,' Jack said. 'I thought you were a bridesmaid?' he added, although what he was really thinking was *turkey baster, bridesmaid, turkey baster, bridesmaid*.

'See,' Susan said, pointing at me, 'Liar.' *Turkey baster, liar, turkey baster, liar.*

'Friday night Rachel came to my work,' I began.

'Liar!' Susan cried again.

'Perhaps you'd like to wait until after I finish a sentence to call me a liar,' I said through clenched teeth. I folded my arms and waited for a response. The motion of my arms across my chest tugged the dress down a tad and I couldn't help but notice Mike's eyes glued to my chest. Then he noticed that I noticed, and he looked away.

'Please let the woman finish,' he said to Susan.

'Rachel came to my work on Friday evening. She cried on my desk about her upcoming marriage – how she was having second thoughts. At first I thought maybe it was just cold feet. I listened to her. That's all. I asked a few questions. But her mind was made up. She ran out of my office. I ran after her – but she was gone. When I came back to my desk, the ring was sitting there along with Jack's address. I'm sorry, Jack. That's all I can tell you.'

Do not marry Jack Heron. It would be the worst mistake of your life—

'You're now saying Friday evening was the first time you laid eyes on Rachel,' Mike said.

'It's the truth.'

'Why would a total stranger wander into your office and spill their guts?' Mike asked. 'It doesn't make any sense.'

'I agree,' Jack said. 'Where do you work? What exactly do you do?'

'She's in—' Mike started to say. Susan cut him off.

'She must be a counselor,' Susan announced. 'A psychotherapist.'

'God help us,' Madeline muttered.

'Are you a psychotherapist?' Jack asked.

'If she is, Jack, that would be confidential,' Susan admonished. 'Wouldn't it, Clair?'

'The content of the therapy would be confidential, Susan, not her profession,' Jack argued.

'I'm not a therapist of any kind,' I said before the

conversation got any more out of control. 'I'm—' I hesitated. I could feel heat pouring off Susan. She was really starting to sweat. In a way, she was right. I *was* a type of therapist, bound by a code of ethics. Whatever was said in a private reading was a matter of the utmost confidentiality. I didn't have the right to 'out' Susan for coming to my booth.

'I'm in futures,' I said once again.

'And I'm in spirits,' Jack answered from the wet bar. We all watched him open a bottle of vodka, toast no one in particular, and pour it directly into his mouth.

Mike pretended as if he had never heard this revelation from me. 'You know, you don't really look like a finance gal,' he said, staring at my cleavage.

'Oh,' I said. 'But I do look like a criminal?' Mike gave a little shrug and tossed me a slow, sexy smile. I looked away.

'I can see you as a finance gal,' Jack said as he sucked on the bottle.

'You can?' Susan said, looking me over. 'Really?' I glared at her. *Either get on board with me sister, or you're going down.*

'Which firm are you with?' Mike asked.

'Downtown Chicago,' I said, answering Mike's question as vaguely as possible and hoping he wouldn't press me again. I didn't even know the names of any investment firms. At least they had started to calm down. Several minutes had gone by without anyone accusing me of breaking any laws. Now I just had to find my car and get the hell out of here. At this point, facing charges for plowing into a national forest didn't seem so daunting.

'What is the name of your firm?' Mike asked, still on the hunt.

'It's a private firm,' I said. 'I work for several public – *private* clients.'

'Public–private clients?' Mike asked. 'What does that mean?'

'I need another nap,' I said, heading for the door.

'And I still don't understand why Rachel came to you,' Mike said, preventing me from leaving. 'Was she in some kind of financial trouble?' Every head in the room turned to me as they awaited my answer. When nothing came out of my mouth, Madeline was the first to step up.

'Financial trouble? That's not possible.'

'Mother,' Jack said.

'I had her financial solvency thoroughly checked out,' Madeline revealed.

'What do you mean you had her checked out?' Jack asked.

'You're a very eligible bachelor, Jack,' Madeline said, avoiding Jack's gaze. 'You can't just marry anyone off the street.' *Like me*, popped into my head. Funny. Everyone had stopped talking and was staring at me.

'What?' I said.

'Yes, like you,' Madeline said. 'Exactly like you.' I felt the heat rise to my face. *I said that out loud?*

'Jack, did you get any word on my rental car?' I whined, trying to divert attention away from my accident-scene mouth.

'They haven't found it yet,' Jack said.

'I was afraid of that. It's such a long stretch of road and the car veered completely into the woods—'

'My friend assured me he's checked all sections of the woods along Route 13. You did say Route 13?'

'Yes. Maybe somebody already called the police. The car was completely upside down.'

'You walked out of an upside down car?' Mike asked.

'You didn't know about the accident beforehand?' Susan said. Everybody but me looked at her. Jack was the first to speak.

'How in the world would she have known about the accident beforehand?'

'It was just a joke,' Susan muttered.

'I don't get it,' Jack said. Mike stepped forward and made a point of looking me up and down, circling me as the theme tune from *Jaws* played in my head.

'Let's see. There's no car and you don't have a scratch on you,' he said.

'Just what are you insinuating?' I demanded.

'It just doesn't add up, Clair. Why would Rachel give a three-carat diamond ring to a practical stranger?'

'How should she know,' Susan cut in. 'She's not a mind reader,' she added emphatically. Thumbs-up, wink-wink. Good God. Why didn't she just paint a third eye on my forehead?

'We'd better get on the horn, Mother,' Jack said, slugging back the bottle. 'Cancel the engagement party.'

'We're not canceling the dinner,' Madeline said. 'We have investors coming, remember, Jack?'

'And where will we say my lovely bride is? Upstairs with a headache?'

'Well,' Madeline said, pacing the room. 'Now that Rachel's family and friends aren't coming – that just leaves our friends and families and the investors.'

'Fine. You have the dinner, Mother. I won't be there.'

'The investors have never met Rachel,' Madeline continued. 'For all they know,' she said, pointing at me, 'she could be Rachel.'

'I agree with Jack,' Susan said. 'He just lost his fiancée. How can you even think of continuing this charade?'

'This charade, as you call it, was Jack's idea in the first place,' Madeline retorted. Her anger was making her stand as stiff as a board; she looked seven feet tall. 'Don't forget this whole business about getting into vodka was your idea. I let you leverage a lot of money—'

'You let me?' Jack sputtered as Mike tried to fade into the woodwork.

'I'm still in control of the finances,' Madeline shouted.

'No, you're not. Grandmother is.' Silence cut through the argument and they both looked at me. I pretended to be immersed in the grandfather clock I was standing next to.

'Maybe on paper, Jack. We both know that woman isn't capable of making any real decisions.'

'All right, Mother, let's not get into this. I don't care anymore. I'm not going through with the dinner.'

'I agree with your mother, Jack,' Mike said, stepping forward. 'We have a lot of money tied up in this. If the investors back out now, we stand to lose everything. Not to mention you were supposed to announce the contest winner at the dinner. Remember? I'm afraid you're going to have to suck it up and get through it.'

'Who the hell are you to tell me what to do?' Jack yelled. Mike looked hurt, but didn't respond.

'Mike is just doing his job,' Madeline said. 'Even Elizabeth has authorized him to make the financial decisions.'

'Well I certainly didn't authorize him,' Jack slurred. 'I don't give a fuck what he thinks.'

'Robert Junior—'

'Don't call me that, Mother.'

'I won't have that language in my house. Do you hear me?'

'I'm not going to the party and that's that.'

'There you are, my dear,' a new voice interjected. Elizabeth Heron punctuated the doorway like an exclamation mark. We all stared. She was positively glowing. Could have been the outfit. It was causing all of our mouths to hang open like the victims of a mass-surprise party. Elizabeth Heron was wearing a wedding dress. And not just any old wedding dress. Elizabeth Heron was wearing the Victorian wedding dress from my nightmare.

Daily Horoscope – Pisces

*Just because you blow your stack. Doesn't mean
your stack has to blow away.*

Seeing Elizabeth Heron in her wedding dress
cemented the unwanted suspicion that had been
swirling around my head. She wasn't right in hers. Old
age will do that to you I suppose, and so will living with
the likes of Madeline and Susan Heron.

'Darling,' she called to Jack. He reluctantly put down
the vodka and approached his grandmother.

'You look beautiful, Grandmother,' he said, embracing
her.

'I'm so excited about your wedding – I just had to put
this old thing on again.' She held the material out,
modeling for us. 'What do you think, Rachel?' she asked
me. 'Do you like it?'

'It's beautiful,' I stammered. *Not so pretty when you're
running through a graveyard—*

'Would you like to wear it?' she asked me. I looked
around for help. They were all too cowardly to say
anything.

'Um . . . maybe later?' I said. Elizabeth laughed.

'I meant for your wedding, darling. Oh I know you
probably want something new and exciting. I just thought
– I don't know – you might want to wear this instead?'

'It's lovely, Elizabeth,' I said, 'but I've already ordered a Vera Wang—'

'How did you know that?' Jack interrupted. My face flushed. Elizabeth laughed.

'Darling, why wouldn't she know that? It's her wedding after all.' Jack gave me a concentrated look while Elizabeth slipped one arm through mine and the other through his. 'Let's take a walk,' she said. 'Just the three of us.'

'You want to go outside again?' Jack asked.

'Of course, my darling. Old people need fresh air you know. We're not fish.'

'Absolutely. But – maybe you'd like to change? You don't want to get your gown all dirty.'

'I haven't worn it in sixty-two years. It could use a little dirt.' Elizabeth grabbed my arm and started propelling me out the door. She was surprisingly strong.

'Elizabeth,' I said. 'I'm going to sit this one out.' I needed to make some calls of my own about the car. It was time I stopped depending on others to solve my problems for me. Besides being accused of being a kidnapper and a blackmailer, I was facing some real trouble in regards to the car accident. I couldn't ignore it any longer. Not to mention I had completely abandoned my spiritual adventure and I was not only starting to obsess on both Mike and Jack, but also I was dying, simply dying, to try on the Vera Wang wedding dress. For my own sanity, I had to get out of here. Where was my sponsor when I needed him? When was he getting back from Tibet?

'Darling,' Elizabeth said. 'I insist you come with us.' I looked at Jack for help. Elizabeth followed my gaze. 'Jack,' she said. 'Tell your beautiful fiancée she is coming with us.'

'You heard her, Clair,' Jack said. His face immediately paled. 'I mean, Rachel,' he added. 'I don't know why I called you Clair.'

'Clair De Lune,' Mike said.

'I really need to find my car,' I said, ignoring Mike. 'I'm sorry. I can't—'

'Pass up a chance like this,' Jack interrupted. I looked at

Jack and he met my eyes with a stern plea. 'Mike will look into your car. Won't you, Mike?'

'Of course, Rachel,' Mike said with a bow. 'I'll certainly do what I can.' He and I held eye contact. I wanted to slap him. And kiss him. And then slap him again. Or bite him. Yes, I definitely wanted to bite him. His lips curled into a smile, as if he knew what I had been thinking. I went back to wanting to slap him.

'Jack,' Madeline called as we were leaving. 'So is everything still set for tomorrow evening?' Jack looked at his mother for a long time. Then he looked into the smiling face of his grandmother.

'Of course, Mother,' he said. 'Everything is all set.'

The walk around the grounds should have been pleasant. Jack and his grandmother certainly seemed chipper, chatting about flower beds, the names of the birds littering the lawn, and the weather, while I stewed about Mike. How dare he goad me in there, call me out on every single little inconsistency and accuse me of 'foul play'? He knew he was just toying with me, but the others, I think the others really believed him for a minute. And now he says he'll look into my car? Maybe somebody should be looking into him. There were more secrets buzzing around him than Area 59. How would he like being pursued like a bloodhound? I was just the girl to do it, too. If I was staying. Which I was not.

I had done what I came here to do. Give the ring back, and come clean. Of course I left out the bit about being a Tarot card reader who terrified his fiancée and falsely predicted doom and gloom for the rest of their lives, but Jack didn't need all the niggling details, did he? I was so deep in thought, I almost ran into Elizabeth when she stopped near a cluster of rose bushes.

'This is much superior to looking out my window,' she said, yanking a rose petal off, holding it up to her nose, and closing her eyes. I felt Jack's eyes on me and when I looked up at him he mouthed *thank you*. I wanted to tell him that I didn't do anything and immediately confess everything I had done, but in the end I just mouthed back, *you're welcome*; the other bit would have been way too much for him to lip read.

I wondered again why on earth Elizabeth had spent the last couple of years locked in her room, but she was living proof that it's never too late to change. 'The children are out,' Jack said pointing straight ahead at two blond heads bobbing in a sandbox. Next to them, a middle-aged man stood swinging an imaginary golf club. As I looked at him, green slime began to ooze from his ears. 'Harold,' I said. Jack gave me a funny look. I pretended not to notice it.

'Is it Harold?' Elizabeth said. 'Is he – spending time with the children?'

'Susan fired the nanny,' Jack said. I was happy I wasn't eating or drinking anything; I would have choked on it.

'Why on earth would she do that?' Elizabeth said. 'I thought she was a lovely girl.' *So did Harold.*

'Pardon me?' Jack said. It took me a minute to realize he was talking to me. I had done it again, said something out loud that I thought was only in my head. What was wrong with me? How do I explain this one away? Sorry Jack, lately I can't tell the difference between saying something out loud and just thinking about it. But just look at the man. Isn't it obvious he was screwing the nanny?

'Clair?'

'Are they twins?' I asked of the boys, desperate to change the subject. I knew they weren't twins, one was a good head taller than the other. Jack made the introductions and I concentrated very hard on anything but the nanny as I shook Harold's slime-filled hand. I needn't have worried. Harold was as far as you could get from being any kind of empath; he wouldn't have known what I was thinking if I wrote it on his chest in blood. I'm sure he didn't even realize why his wife fired the nanny.

'Grandma Heron,' he boomed. 'I didn't know you were getting married.' He shook his finger at her. 'I would have bought you a china set.' Elizabeth giggled and smoothed out her dress with her wrinkled hand.

'It's been in my closet for sixty-two years. I just wanted to wear it one more time. Rachel and Jack have me thinking about my own wedding.'

Harold glanced at me. His eyes dropped down to my chest and lingered until I turned away. 'Any word on Rachel?' he boomed. I knelt down by the sandbox and introduced myself to the two boys while Jack and Harold talked. The taller of the two boys spoke first, proudly telling me his name was Mathew and he was seven. The smaller piped up he was Conrad and he was five, but his brother quickly made him confess to being four and a half. As the youngest myself, I sympathized with the plight of being bossed around by an older sibling and tried to console Conrad.

'Four and a half,' I said. 'That's a great age.'

'But it's not *five*,' Mathew interrupted.

'It's *almost* five,' I answered as Conrad's sand-coated lip started to quiver.

'I'm bored,' Mathew said, throwing down a chewed, plastic blue shovel.

'Let's go look at the pond,' Conrad cried.

'That's boring,' Mathew wailed. Harold stepped up behind me.

'Have any of your own?' he asked.

'No,' I said. 'But yours are adorable.' Harold nodded his head seriously as if we were discussing a new car instead of his children. I saw him looking at Jack again.

He knows something slammed into my brain like being hit from behind in a bumper car.

'Rachel,' Elizabeth said, holding her hand out to me.

'Rachel?' Harold asked, arching his right eyebrow.

'She's a little confused,' Jack said.

'Who's a little confused?' Elizabeth barked.

'Jack, you've gone and found another so quick?' Harold joked. When he saw the looks on our faces, he turned his smirk into a little cough. 'Well it's nice to see you again, Rachel,' Harold yelled as if we were all deaf. 'You're looking great. You've put on a few love pounds, eh?' He threw his head back and laughed uproariously. With a growing sense of panic, I tried to calm down the swarm of electrical anger in my brain, but I was too late.

'Dad,' Conrad said. 'My shovel just moved.'

Beautiful flowers, swaying trees, feel the sun kiss your face—

'Dad look, look it's moving. It's magic.' Luckily Mathew grabbed the plastic shovel hovering in the air several inches above the ground. Conrad looked at me with wide eyes. 'Did you see that?' he asked, pointing to the shovel. 'Did you see it flying?'

'Yes,' I said. 'I saw it.'

'Shovels don't fly,' Mathew yelled.

'They do, too,' Conrad yelled, pointing at me. 'She saw it.'

'Do shovels fly?' Mathew demanded, swatting the shovel at me. *Sometimes when I'm really, really stressed or really, really angry, all right, kid? It hasn't happened in a while. I thought I had it under control, but—*

'Dad, we're bored,' Mathew said, dropping the shovel.

'From flying shovels to boredom in seconds,' Jack laughed. 'You're a lucky man, Harold. I can't wait until Rachel and I have kids.' Hope and sadness danced the Tango around his face. I wanted to reach behind my back and hand Rachel to him like a bouquet of flowers. I also wanted to shake her and rip her little flower-heads off, but this was about Jack, not me.

'You're going to make a wonderful mother,' Elizabeth said, sneaking her hand into mine and swinging it like we were schoolgirls.

'Let's go look at the pond,' Conrad said. 'Fish,' he said to me, pointing in the direction of the woods.

'Sleeping beauty has already seen the pond,' Jack said. From the look on his face when I met his eyes, I wasn't the only one caught blurting out their private thoughts. Our eyes held for a minute and then Jack turned back to his grandmother. Again I felt the rush of being in love, followed by dizziness, followed by an urge to call Brian and confess that once again I was going over to the dark side.

Obviously, I'm not in love with Jack. *Gardeners like it dirty.*

Or Mike. I'm definitely not in love with Mike. I'm just having the sensations of being in love. My constantly tingling stomach. Obsessive thoughts about the person. Deviant sexual fantasies running through my brain every time either one of them looks at me like that. And Elizabeth wearing her wedding dress wasn't helping matters. It was ridiculous, but I loved wedding dresses. God help me, I did.

For my first marriage I wore my prom dress, for the second I wore a sequined flapper's dress that I bought at a carnival I was working, but for the-one-I-thought-would-stick, I wore a real, bona fide wedding dress. That I bought off eBay for three hundred bucks. Not that anyone would have ever known, if I hadn't gotten totally smashed at the wedding and revealed this in a loud voice to anyone who asked.

Regardless, I loved weddings. I loved falling in love. I loved the dress and the party, and the flowers, and the music, and looking longingly into each other's eyes. I loved having rice thrown in my face, and ripping open free toasters wrapped with silver bows, and finally having a penis to have-and-to-hold for the rest of my life. The best laid plans. Because here I was, thirty-two, and penis-less. Soy milk lasted longer than my relationships.

'I need to lie down again,' I yelled. 'I need to lie down.'

This caused Jack to look at me again, which caused us to maintain eye contact again. Our eyes held again until he looked away. Damn. I had wanted to be the first to look away. I had to catch his eye again just so I could look away first this time. But he wasn't looking at me, not directly anyhow, but he could probably see me out of the periphery of his eye and now not only had I not looked away first, now I was officially staring at him. Not cool. So not cool. Very unpsychic like.

'I need to lie down, too,' Elizabeth said. 'Jack, why don't you take Rachel and me to bed.'

I smothered a laugh as any sexual thoughts I had about Jack evaporated. Maybe I didn't need a nap after all. 'Rachel, you're going to sleep in the guest room next to mine,' Elizabeth said.

'Thank you,' I said, keeping my eyes glued to the grass so I wouldn't look at Jack. It was only then that I realized I had instinctively answered to the name Rachel. I had to get out of here.

'Where's your ring?' Elizabeth asked, grabbing my hand and inspecting it.

'I gave it to Jack for safekeeping,' I said.

'Nonsense. It belongs on your finger. Jack, I insist you put the ring back on Rachel's finger this instant.'

'Grandmother, let's get you up to bed.'

'I'm not going anywhere until you put that ring back on her finger.' She grabbed my hands and squeezed them between hers. 'You should never take it off, my dear. You need to feel it.' *I do feel it. All over. For two men at the same time. Which is exactly why I'm not putting on that ring.* 'Jack?' Elizabeth said. 'The ring?' Jack looked at me as he pulled the diamond out of his breast pocket and placed it on my finger. 'That's better,' Elizabeth said

Elizabeth stopped on the front lawn near the porch. 'I love this time of day,' she said, taking a deep breath and spreading her arms. Jack's face lit with a huge grin as he watched Elizabeth relish the pleasure of a walk. 'Why don't you kiss your lovely bride?' Elizabeth said, pushing me harshly to Jack. I cried out as my nipples collided with his chest.

'Grandmother,' Jack chastised. 'You're making her blush.' It was true, I could feel the heat feeding off my cheekbones.

'Go on, kiss her,' Elizabeth demanded. Jack gave me a peck on the cheek. 'You can do better than that,' Elizabeth growled. 'Can't he, dear?'

'I'm sure he can,' I blurted out. Jack tilted his head and looked at me as the fire returned to my face. He pulled me in again and kissed me on the lips. Elizabeth clapped. I did not. No fireworks. No sparks. Nothing happening in my nether regions. Mike was right. You don't experience the kind of kiss we had shared every day. What had happened to us in the truck – it was something special. Now, in the span of another kiss, I was no longer obsessing over two men. Now, I just needed to exorcise one.

'It's so nice to see young people in love with their whole lives ahead of them,' Elizabeth said.

'I couldn't agree more,' a voice from the doorway interjected. I looked up to find Mike staring at me. I pulled away from Jack and fought the urge to run up to him and explain. Jack and Mike exchanged a strange look.

'I'll walk you to your room, Grandmother,' Jack said, helping her up the stairs. I followed along silently, vowing I would find a way to somehow make this right. When I passed by Mike, he grabbed my hand and whistled at the ring.

'Didn't take long to get that back on your finger,' he whispered, not letting go of my hand.

'Rachel,' Elizabeth interrupted from a few feet ahead.

'Yes?' I answered without a second thought.

'Tomorrow I'd like to go over the plans for the wedding with you.' Mike dropped my hand. I looked to Jack for help.

'What do you mean, Grandmother?' Jack asked.

'Why, I want to know everything. The flowers, the dress, the bridesmaids. I want to be involved.'

'Mother and Rachel have already made those decisions, I'm afraid,' Jack said.

'Well they can share them with me, can't they?' she said sweetly, clasping her hands in front of her mouth. 'Or don't you want an old woman's opinion?' she bellowed suddenly, shaking her fist at me accusingly. I backed away.

'Of course we do,' Jack said. 'Clair – clarity is welcome!' he finished lamely. 'Rachel would be happy to – fill you in tomorrow.' He looked at me and I nodded and smiled like a weight-loss contestant caught scarfing a tray of double-fudge brownies before the big weigh-in.

'Happy to fill you in,' I repeated.

'Marvelous,' Elizabeth said, drawing me into an embrace. 'It's a date.'

Jack and Elizabeth disappeared up the stairs. Mike and I stood face-to-face. Silence hung between us like a sheet hanging from a clothesline in a torrential downpour. Mike closed the distance between us. His breath was on my neck, in my ear. He smelled amazing. Clean and spicy. I was thrilled he was going to kiss me again. All qualms of not wanting to have sex in a public place flew out of my head as I imagined him wrapping me around the spiral staircase, taking me on the stairway to heaven. To hell with the servants, they could dust around us. But instead of his lips, I felt his words.

'Getting yourself in pretty deep, *Rachel*,' he whispered. 'Don't you think?' I looked at him. *You're in deep, too. Way, way deeper than I am*. 'Pardon me?' Mike said.

It didn't take a psychic to see that my comment had set him on high-alert. I flushed at once again having accidentally spewed my thoughts like a water main without a shut-off valve.

'What did you mean by that?' Mike insisted.

'I don't know,' I said honestly. 'But I'm right, aren't I?' I added. Mike studied my face like he was trying to memorize it for a future line-up.

'I'm going to bed,' I said at last. He didn't answer, but his eyes followed me all the way up the winding stairs, and he was still watching me, long after I disappeared from view.

Daily Horoscope – Pisces

Opportunity Knocks. (It also shoots, stabs, strangles, and hangs.)

Just as I was drifting off to sleep, there was a knock on my door. Two quick hollow raps straightening my spine. I slipped on a robe and opened the door a crack. Jack was standing in my doorway. 'This is going to sound crazy,' he said.

'Try me.'

'That shovel.' He looked at me and I smiled at him as if I had no idea what he was talking about. 'Did you' – he made gestures with his hands, his best sign language of a flying shovel. 'Did you see that?'

'I think Michael flipped it,' I said, doing my own demonstrating with my hands. 'You know – just caught the end and it flipped.'

Jack looked past me, into the room, his eyes clouded with worry.

'Is something wrong?' I asked, following his gaze along the shadows of my wall.

Jack stepped into the room and closed the door before turning back to me and whispering. 'Rachel,' he said. 'She was a little worried.'

'About what?' Jack looked above my head.

'She thought this house was haunted,' he said at last.

'Haunted.'

'She's been under a lot of stress, Clair. The wedding, my mother—'

'Say no more,' I said at the thought of his mother. 'Did she tell you why she thought the house was haunted?' I sat on the bed, hoping to make him feel more comfortable in opening up to me. Jack started to pace the room as the story spilled out of him.

'Rachel moved into this room right after I proposed. My mother had gathered the wedding brigade and wanted her nearby. Not that she let her have the final say about anything.' Jack said as he continued pacing. 'But Rachel was standing her own against my mother. I was really proud of her. My mother was insisting on gardenias for the tables and Rachel said gardenias made her think of little old ladies. Isn't that cute?'

'Adorable,' I lied.

'Then she – started hearing noises. Late at night.'

'What kind of noises?'

'Small things – in the beginning anyway. Floorboards creaking, doors opening and slamming shut on their own, things like that.'

'Did you hear them, too?' I asked. Jack shrugged.

'It's an old house,' he said. 'But Rachel was really freaking out. So I stayed with her one night and yes, I heard things – but it's an old house,' he said again. 'I told her that over and over again.'

'Did that calm her down?' I asked. Jack laughed bitterly.

'Quite the opposite. She said I wasn't being supportive. She practically accused me of thinking she was – crazy.' Jack sat down on the bed next to me. I moved as far away from him as I could get. It would be easy for a girl to lose her head in this situation. Here I was wearing his engagement ring, sitting on the bed with a vulnerable, beautiful man. Mike hated me now. Maybe I should give Jack another kiss. Chance. I meant chance.

'I can't believe I'm telling you this,' Jack said. 'You of all people.'

'What do you mean me of all people?'

'You're a finance person. Logical. Organized. Am I right?'

'I'm extremely open-minded for a finance person,' I said weakly.

'I see that about you,' Jack said, staring at my lips. I licked them nervously and his eyes moved up to my hair. 'You know,' he said, moving a little closer to me. 'I'm glad you're here.' We stared at each other awkwardly as attraction hovered in the air.

'You were saying – about Rachel?' I prodded. Jack's hand was resting near my thigh. It wouldn't take much, just a little gust of wind to send it my way.

'She was really starting to act like a crazy person, Clair. I told her over and over again she was just imagining things.'

'I'm sure she loved that,' I said. Jack ran his hands through his hair.

'I know, I know,' he said. 'I didn't handle it well. But I have to admit. Part of me was wondering if I could really be with someone who believed in that kind of crap.'

'Crap?' I said, standing up, losing the fantasy of his beautiful, strong hand on my thigh.

'What's wrong?'

'You don't know if you could be with anyone who believes in that *crap*?' I said. If Jack was phased by my attitude, he didn't show it.

'I certainly don't. Do you?' he asked. I hesitated. I had never seen a ghost, but professionally I'd be a bit of a hypocrite if I wasn't at least open to the possibility.

'What about – ESP?' I asked hopefully. 'Do you believe in ESP?' Jack's face took on a serious hue. Light blue.

'No,' he said. 'And before you ask, let me assure you, I don't believe in flying saucers or leprechauns either.'

'I see,' I said. 'Then how do you explain the noises Rachel was hearing?' Jack sprang off the bed, pacing once again.

'Stress,' he said, throwing up his arms. 'Wedding stress

and an old house. And – perhaps – Grandmother might be a little bit to blame,' he said, glancing to the door as guilt swept into his sentence.

'What do you mean?'

'I think she might have – filled Rachel with some of her crazy ideas.'

'Go on,' I urged.

'Grandmother has been victimized by . . . by . . . these so-called psychics ever since she took to her room two years ago.' I felt my throat dry up.

'Huh?' I squeaked.

'She's been calling psychic hotlines if you can believe it. Running up astronomical bills as these vultures prey on her lonelines—'

I sat on the bed, knees shaking and wobbling like a baby colt. 'I tell you if I ever got anywhere near one – I'd strangle them with my bare hands,' Jack said, squeezing his hands in the air, strangling an invisible psychic. I put my hand around my own neck, reassuring it. 'Rachel told her about the noises she was hearing and the two of them started feeding off of each other's hysteria.'

'Rachel and your grandmother spent a lot of time together?' I said. 'And she still thinks I'm her?' Tears almost came to Jack's eyes.

'Mother's been trying to tell me for years that Grandmother wasn't in her right mind. She doesn't want her to have financial control anymore. I finally agree with her.'

'Jack. When Rachel spoke to you about this haunting – did you tell her you thought it was all crap?' Jack looked away sheepishly.

'Is that so wrong?' he blurted out. 'Do you think it's why she left?'

'I think it's important. Whether or not you believe in "that crap" isn't. Rachel was clearly frightened and instead of supporting her you dismissed her. Add that to the stress of the wedding and – your mother – and I'm starting to see why she ran away.' Jack looked pained again and slightly pissed off.

'So you're saying this is all my fault?'

'This isn't about fault,' I said. 'It's about perception. Whether or not you believe in her perceptions isn't necessarily the point – but how and if you validate them is.'

'That sounded like a very fancy way of saying yes, it is my fault.'

'Rachel left you on a what – Friday?'

'You just don't know when to quit do you?'

'Did anything happen right before that? Was there another incident of . . . hearing noises or anything?' I was trying not to get too excited. I had always wanted to see a ghost. As a professional in the field, it would be an incredible opportunity for professional development – communicating with energy that has crossed over. How could people not love this stuff? They could even use the rumor to promote the vodka. Everyone loves to get drunk and hear a good ghost story. They could open up the Estates as a haunted bed and breakfast! While Jack debated answering my question, I took a deep breath, trying to still my mind in case any spirits wanted to speak with me.

What if they wanted to enter my body? Okay, I might be open to new experiences, but having a dead person squeeze into me and speak in tongues wasn't my idea of a good time. Why do they have to do it that way? Do they get a sick pleasure out of being in a body again? No way was any middle-aged dead man getting inside me. Like, gag me with Brian's spoon. I crossed my arms and tried to emit a hostile 'no trespassing' energy.

'Wednesday night there was a bit of an incident,' Jack said finally. 'But it doesn't excuse her taking off like this without a word!'

'What kind of an incident?' I probed.

Jack went to the window, keeping his back to me while he spoke. He admitted that for the past year, everyone in the mansion had heard noises coming from this wing of the house late at night. Apparently, most of the noise was coming from Elizabeth's room and everyone was convinced she was the one responsible for the strange crashes and bangs heard in the middle of the night. They would come running to her room to find everything overturned – books, vases, glass.

'Grandmother was acting out in her sleep. That's what we all thought.'

'What you thought?'

'The Wednesday before Rachel left, she moved into another wing of the house.'

'And she still heard noises.'

'We both did.'

'And you still didn't believe?'

'I wasn't sleeping in the room with her. We made this decision – this is going to sound ridiculous, too—'

'You weren't going to sleep together until after the wedding.'

'How did you know?'

'It's a chick thing.'

'Anyway, so I heard all this crashing and banging – thinking it was coming from grandmother's room again, but when I peeked in, everything was absolutely quiet. So I ran to Rachel's room.'

'And it was a mess.'

'You are a mind reader. It looked like she had been robbed. Just like Grandmother's room, everything was upside down, splayed on the floor – Rachel was huddled on the bed sobbing. Completely devastated.'

I closed my eyes. Here was a woman in real supernatural distress and I just sloughed her off as a spoiled woman who wanted out of her marriage. How could I have not seen through her? I had really, really blown it. I could have at least questioned her a little further about why she wanted out of the marriage.

'Jack,' I said. 'She must have been terrified.'

'We both were. I mean imagine finding out your fiancée is – mentally unstable—'

'Whoa. What?'

'I mean – all this time – we've been blaming my

grandmother for the noises and all along it was Rachel.'

'Oh, Jack. You didn't tell her you thought she was responsible.'

'I simply suggested that we take her to see somebody. A sleep disorder expert – someone like that.'

'I take it she wasn't thrilled with your suggestion.'

'She totally flipped out on me. Totally flipped out. You've met my mother – I'm like Teflon when it comes to moody women – but Rachel, she turned on me like she was possessed. I didn't know how to handle it.'

'So how did you?'

'I just left it to Susan and my mother to help calm her down.'

'And next thing you knew, she was gone.'

'I know you think I really fucked up – and maybe I did – but I have to admit, since she's left—'

'The noises have stopped.'

'The noises have stopped,' Jack confirmed, looking at me. 'I mean once in a while you'll hear a little something from Grandmother's room, but that's because she can't hold onto things very well with her arthritis. So you'll still hear a few clunks and bangs from her room. But nothing like the tornado that swept through Rachel's.'

'And she was having nightmares, too.'

'She told you about the nightmares?' Jack shook his head. 'I apologize,' he said.

'No need to apologize.'

'Yes, there is. It's embarrassing. You're a financial advisor, not a bartender. There was no reason for her to be telling you any of that.'

Oh. Right.

'It just shows you how insane she was. She was taking it all as a sign that we weren't meant to be married. Which really pissed me off. She won't go see a doctor, but she's ready to throw us down the drain? She'd rather think we're haunted than admit she could have some kind of – sleep disorder?'

'Perception, Jack. Just remember, it's all about

perception. Rachel believed she was being haunted and in her perception, her finacé thought she was crazy. If those were the facts as you saw them, how would you feel?' Jack looked away so that I wouldn't see the guilt in his eyes.

'I really fucking blew it,' Jack said. *So did I*.

'We have to get Rachel to come back here,' I said. 'We have to get to the bottom of this.'

'We?'

'I think it will help to have a neutral third party,' I explained. 'Besides I'm the one she originally came to for help anyway.'

'Financial help. That's quite a leap for you to get involved with us personally.'

'Maybe so, but who else do you have?'

'Why would you do that for me?'

'I'm not going to do it for you,' I admitted. 'I'm going to do it for Rachel.'

Daily Horoscope – Pisces

When it comes to a cat fight, always root for the underdog.

'Well if it isn't Clair Ivars calling me from the Heron Estates.' I sat in my immaculate guest room and glared at Brian through the phone.

'Impressive hit,' I said.

'Caller ID,' Brian corrected.

'Ah. Listen, Brian, I need your help.'

'I knew it. You slept with him.'

'I didn't sleep with him.'

'Yet.'

'Brian.'

'Saving it for the marriage?' I started to cry. And, like most men, Brian can't deal with crying women.

'Clair? Are you crying? Oh, Jesus. What? What?'

'I messed everything up,' I wailed.

'Clair. Did you use a condom?'

'I didn't sleep with him, Brian. I'm talking about Rachel.'

'You slept with Rachel?'

'Brian.'

'Sorry. What are you talking about?'

'You have to find Rachel and bring her here.' I didn't have to be psychic to see Brian on the other end, fingering his spoon.

'I can't do that, Clair. I don't even know her,' Brian argued. I was ready for this and mentally stamped the word GUILT on his aura.

'Tough shit,' I said. 'You got me into this, now you're going to help me get out.'

'Just come home. Just get in your little Saturn and drive home.'

'My little Saturn is totaled.'

'What?'

'I was in a car accident.'

'Oh, God. Clair. We're city people. This is why we don't drive. Are you hurt?'

'I'm okay. Physically anyway. But – the Saturn isn't. I crashed it in the woods and they can't find it.' Just saying the words out loud set me off on a giggle. It was ludicrous. How on earth could anyone not have seen an upside down Saturn in the woods?

'What's so funny?' Brian demanded.

'If a Saturn crashes in the woods. And no one is there to hear it—' I couldn't even finish the sentence. I laid down on the ivory quilt and howled. Brian laughed, too, although his was the polite garden-variety laughter while mine was buckets and buckets of wildflower seeds.

'Sorry,' I said when I had finally calmed down. 'I've been a little stressed. There's more too – about the accident – some really strange things, but I'd rather tell you in person. How soon do you think you can get Rachel here?' Brian sighed and bared his teeth in the spoon, looking for stray bits of food. I stamped the word GUILT into his spoon.

'How am I supposed to find Rachel?' he said at last.

'Jack mentioned something about her parents. I can find out where they live and you can start there. In the meantime, I'm going to leave her a message that I think will do the trick. If we're lucky, once she hears it, she'll find you.' There was another long silence as Brian wrestled with helping me or blowing me off. I played my ace.

'Okay, Brian, I'll be honest with you. I wasn't going to tell you this – but you've left me no option.'

'What are you talking about?'

'You have to swear you won't tell anyone.'

'I swear.'

'When Rachel gets here – I think we're going to need to have a little séance.' Brian's silence said it all. His body was probably going into shock. Brian was a freak for séances. He'd always wanted to lead one – ever since Dame Diaphannie had bragged about an amazing, table-rocking séance she had held in a client's basement. I had no intention of holding a séance mind you – but I knew it was the leverage needed to get Brian to float.

'Okay,' he said excitedly. 'Text me directions. I'll find Rachel.'

'Great. It will be about an hour; I have to charge my cell phone.'

'No hurry, considering I can't get there until Tuesday.'

'Tuesday? Brian today is Friday. It's only a six-hour drive.'

'But I can't leave until Tuesday. Come on, Clair, I'm set up at a conference this week. You can't just expect me to drop everything, ride in on a white horse, and rescue you.'

'Brian. I don't care if you scoot in on a Vespa.' I lowered my voice for emphasis. 'You know how restless spirits are, Brian. I'm afraid if we don't hold this séance right away, it will be too late.' But Brian was still suspicious of my motives.

'Oh. My. God. You're falling in love, aren't you?'

'No,' I said, flicking the image of Mike out of my mind. 'I'm just trying to help a young couple in love.' He didn't buy that one either.

'Jesus, Clair,' he yelled. 'Have you called your sponsor?'

'He's in Tibet,' I explained. 'Meditating with mountain goats.'

'Tibet?' Brian laughed. 'No, he's not. I just saw him at Starbucks yesterday.' *Meditating, grass-chewing, star-gazing, goat-chasing, lying bastard.*

'Oh, that's right,' I lied. 'He was to be back this week. No worries. Just get here as soon as you can, Brian. Saturday morning would be best. That way I won't have to go to the engagement party.'

'Engagement party? Whose?'

'Jack and Rachel.'

'They're going ahead with the engagement party?'

'Yeah. I'm kind of filling in for her.'

'Come again?'

'Brian, it's complicated. Just find Rachel and get her over here.'

Susan, who unbeknownst to me had been standing in the doorway with a stack of towels, startled me with a yell. 'Rachel? You're talking to Rachel?' she yelled.

'No,' I said. 'I'm not.'

'You're not what?' Brian said.

'Brian,' I said, 'I have to go—'

'Give me that phone,' Susan said, dropping the towels and lunging for it.

'Hang up now, Brian,' I said. 'Just get here.' I didn't hear his reply, if he even had one; I was distracted by Susan's body slamming into mine from behind as she grabbed for the phone. And despite her thinness, she was still able to use speed and the element of surprise to completely knock me down. I landed on the floor near the bed while she screeched into the phone.

'Hello? Hello? Hello?'

'Can you hear me now?' I couldn't help but say from the floor. Susan slammed the phone down with a thunk. Much more satisfying anger-venting-wise than slamming a cell phone I had to admit. It's really impossible to angrily hang up your Blackberry. We always lose a little dignity with every technological gain. Susan hovered over me and glared. I made a note to myself never to look at a man like that; it was a look that could freeze the heartiest testicles.

'What was that about Rachel?' Susan demanded. I hauled myself up and moved away from her.

'I'm trying to fix things, all right?' I said.

'So you admit you're the one who messed things up?'

'Yes,' I said through clenched teeth. 'But I had some help, wouldn't you say?'

'I don't know what you mean.'

'Oh, you don't? Why didn't you tell me Rachel was frightened of a ghost?'

'What?' Susan stammered, looking like one herself.

'The noises, the crashes, the things that go bump in the night?' I said advancing on her. Susan backed up.

'I don't know what you're talking about.'

'Stop it, Susan. Rachel thought she was being haunted. And maybe if I had known it when she came to see me – we wouldn't be in this mess.'

'Well if you're so psychic why didn't you know it then?'

I hadn't planned on tripping her. I swear. Okay, maybe I did, but during subsequent retellings of this tale, I was simply stretching my foot out to stop myself from kicking her in the shin. All of my anger and stress from the past few days were accumulating in my body, turning me into someone I didn't recognize, someone who wanted to fight, someone who wanted to kick some ass.

My timing was impeccable. Just as my foot reached out, her ankle accidentally stepped into it. And if you've ever stuck your finger in a baby's hand, you know what happens, right? It instinctively curls its tiny fist around your finger and squeezes. It's an instinct we're born with. So here's how it went. Foot goes out, innocently stretching along the shag carpet to stop myself from kicking the Ice Pick in the shins, Ice Pick's ankle steps into my foot, which instinctively curls around Susan's ankle and pulls. Susan, frostiness notwithstanding, is unable to defy gravity and sinks to the floor.

Apparently, this ignites some ass-kicking fantasies of her own, because the next thing you know, she's clawing the floor like a banshee, and grabbing onto my ankle.

As the youngest child, I was always on the receiving end of abuse. And not just the run of the mill hand-me-down-clothing abuse, although there was plenty of that too.

Once, I accidentally let it slip to my brother Tommy that Kim Hayes and Melody Lions were discussing his small penis in the cafeteria. Apparently Tommy's shorts had slipped down in swim class as he hauled himself out of the side of the pool. I stared in horror as Kim held up a baby carrot for the other girls as a model. They all giggled as Kim rolled it on her tongue and crushed it to bits with her my-dad-is-an-orthodontist teeth.

'You should have used the ladder to get out of the pool, Tommy,' I made the mistake of saying. He sat on my face and farted for two solid hours.

I landed next to Susan with a thud. For a few seconds neither of us moved. The carpet smelled like dusty apples. 'I'm sorry. Okay?' I said moments later, picking myself up off the floor, trying to be the bigger person. Susan whipped around and fastened her eyes on me. Blazing and dark, it was like looking into a black hole.

Uh-oh, I thought.

She grabbed my wrist and yanked me back down. My forehead hit the carpet first and then the rest of my body somersaulted over. We lay head-to-head on our backs, one animal brain to another, breathing heavily. That really should have been the end of it.

I got on my knees, holding onto the dresser knobs for support. My head hurt and I felt dizzy. Susan grabbed my arm again, but this time I yanked it away and stopped short of slapping her across the face. We kneeled in front of each other, panting. Suddenly, she reached out and grabbed my hair. 'Ow,' I yelled. 'That hurts.' I reached out and grabbed her hair, and there we were, deadlocked by our grips on our respective locks. 'What is your problem?' I yelled, trying not to move my head even a smidge.

'Why did you come here?' Susan growled without moving her head. 'Didn't you do enough damage when you scared Rachel off from marrying my brother?'

'That's not what happened.'

'I was there. Remember? You went on and on about . . . ballerinas . . . and – and the way your husbands smelled.'

'You went out of the tent, Susan. That's when Rachel demanded I—' I stopped, realizing the truth wasn't much better than whatever else Susan wanted to think of me. 'It doesn't matter now. But believe me – Rachel already had her mind made up. And I didn't know about the haunting. I thought she was just a stuck-up – spoiled – bride who wanted out of her marriage. I was trying to help your brother!' I screamed. 'I thought he deserved better.'

'Someone like you?' Susan sneered, tugging my hair a little. I didn't answer but I tugged hers back a little harder. 'Jack's not your type,' she said, pulling once again.

'Ouch,' I said, out and out pulling hers. 'You don't know my type.'

'The minute he finds out you're some kind of psychic crackpot—'

That did it. I gave into the pain and really yanked on Susan's hair as she reciprocated and yanked on mine. We dragged each other down farther to the floor. We were both screaming in pain until finally, finally we let go, each taking several strands of the other's hair with us.

I was on my knees again, preparing to get up, when Susan rammed her elbow into my solar plexus. I doubled over in pain, trying to catch my breath. I was going to be the bigger person.

Someday.

I reached up and slapped her as hard as I could. She cried out, placed her hand against her stinging cheek, and stated the obvious. 'You slapped me.'

'You punched me in the gut.' I clutched my side.

'I'm telling Jack!'

'No. I'm telling Jack. Everything.'

'Oh no you don't. I'm getting Mike to take you home.'

'I'm not going anywhere with *him*,' I blurted out. Susan was poised to slap me again when she froze.

'Why not?' she asked slowly, bringing her hand down. 'You don't like Mike?'

'I don't need to explain myself to you,' I answered, shifting underneath her gaze and moving my cheek as far away from her hand as I could get without looking like a chicken. 'I'm not comfortable with him – enough said.'

'Most women like Mike,' she said, still staring at me. I shrugged. She stepped closer.

'Do you . . . get something off of him?'

'What do you mean?'

'I mean – like a vibe. A feeling – whatever it is that you *get*. Do you get something on Mike?'

'I thought you didn't believe in that sort of thing,' I said. It was her turn to look uncomfortable. 'How did you refer to it?' I continued. 'Oh right – nonsense – I believe it was.' Susan slumped down on the bed, taking the wind out of my superiority.

'Mike came out of nowhere,' she said. 'Just showed up last year and suddenly he's a fixture around here.'

'And that bothers you?' I said.

'It just doesn't make sense. Mother doesn't warm up to strangers – but it's as if she trusts Mike completely.'

'Well from what I understand he's been rather . . . helpful,' I said, purposely padding my words.

'If it wasn't for him, Heron Estates would have been sold off last year,' Susan admitted. As soon as it was out of her mouth, she stopped speaking and her face turned into a tomato. I didn't need to read energy waves to see she had just blurted out something she wasn't supposed to.

'What do you mean?' I asked casually.

'Nothing,' Susan answered. 'It's nothing. I just can't help thinking.'

'What?' I encouraged.

'The noises,' Susan admitted. 'They all started the day after Mike Wrench arrived.'

Daily Horoscope – Pisces

Good deeds will not go unpunished.

I tried not to show my reaction. *They all started the day after he arrived.* What part was Mike playing in this family drama? And why?

'Susan,' I said. 'I've asked my friend Brian to find Rachel and bring her back.' Susan looked at me. 'Let me help,' I pleaded. 'Let me see if I can get to the bottom of this.' She appeared to think about this for a moment and then nodded.

'If you fuck this up,' she said, sidling up to me and pointing her icicle finger in my face, 'I'm taking you down.'

After she left, I basked in an after-fight glow. Not that I'm condoning the behavior, but it did feel like I had just completed a great, albeit painful workout. I hadn't physically tried to hurt anyone since I slapped my first husband. And before you rush to judgment, it's not as bad as it sounds. It was his fault. Really.

Okay, if you must know, he *dared* me to do it. We were outside of the courthouse, admiring our mood rings.

'I'm horny,' he said, looking at the greenish tint pulsing from his ring, 'so I'm going to kiss you.' He body-slammed me against the wall and kissed me. He was all tongue, purple Bubble Yum, and drool. I was already regretting our rebellious, starter marriage, worried I had jinxed myself for marrying someone I didn't love.

'Well I'm not horny,' I said, holding my hand out to him so he could see the swirls of red clouding up in my ring. 'I'm angry.'

'Then you should slap me,' he said, popping a bubble behind his corny grin and diving for my lips again with his sticky mouth. And so I did.

You don't have to be psychic to know: It wasn't the best way to start a honeymoon.

Still, you could hardly call that my fault.

Back in the present, now that the ass-kicking was over, I had other things to think about. Like how I was going to help Rachel. Hopefully Brian would be able to find her. But in the meantime, would it hurt to check out Mike while I was at it? Susan said the noises started the day after he arrived. Was Mike the ghost? If so, why? Was he in love with Rachel? Maybe she was the 'girlfriend' he had bragged about in the truck. How dare he kiss me like that when he was in love with Rachel? Sleep was out of the question now. I needed comfort food.

I crept down the winding staircase, conscious of every creak. I just wanted to go into the kitchen and stuff my face without an audience or an inquisition. At least Brian was on his way. I was relieved to reach the bottom of the stairs and feel silence. You can smell silence, too; it's like the air on a crisp fall morning when Indian summer has finally, unwillingly released its grasp on summer like a rope slipping through a child's hand. Silence sounds like sawdust exploding from a jagged blade, existing in the frozen seconds when it hovers in the air, particles dancing and suspending gravity. Little did I know, that silence was about to be shattered.

Extra sensory perception isn't anything spectacular. It isn't mystical, it isn't evil, it isn't uncommon. We all have it. When the phone rings you know it's Uncle John. Your best friend calls you as you reach for the phone to call her. You have a dream that comes true. You have a 'funny feeling' about your next-door neighbor and the next night the police dig up twenty-four heads buried underneath his porch. It happens to all of us.

But sometimes you're just plain not in the mood. Take that evening, for example. I just wanted to make myself a sandwich and lick my wounds, but I could feel the emotionally charged energy in the kitchen before I even pushed open the swinging oak door. I hadn't realized until that very moment that I was clutching my purse.

The one that held my Tarot cards. I had been half-way down the stairs when something compelled me to go back to the room and get them. I didn't even question it; I obeyed the urge and here it was. I had gone back for my cards because I was going to need them. *I hope I get a sandwich first*. I pushed open the door to the kitchen.

As I suspected, I wasn't alone. Several Heron Estates staff members were sitting around the table. The first one to notice me, an older, plump woman with massive amounts of black and gray hair sitting atop her head like a croissant, scrambled up from her place at the table and practically threw her body in front of the sobbing young girl to her left.

I stayed where I was, taking in the scene. In addition to the sobbing girl, whose age I had yet to pin down since her long black hair obscured her face as she soaked the dining-room table with her tears, there were three other women. They must have been two aunts and a mother; they all had the same dark hair, Mediterranean skin, and plump bodies. The girl was still thin, but unless she took drastic steps to fight it, you could easily see what genetics had in store for her when she hit middle age.

'Don't mind me,' I said, heading for the fridge. 'I'm just here for a sandwich.'

I could feel them watching me as I opened the refrigerator. I ignored the heat from my cards as I spotted a nice platter of turkey. I pulled the platter out and set it on the expansive counter. This kitchen was the likes of one I had always envisioned having in a castle in France. It was open, circular, and stocked. The floors were gray, smooth stone; the walls, thick wood beams interspersed with Italian, hand-painted tiles; the counters marble and butcher block. A large black stove near a kitchen table took center stage and this is where the women hovered as I continued to raid the stainless steel fridge. I just needed bread and mayonnaise.

She needs a reading, Clair. Come on, you have your cards.

I couldn't find mayonnaise so I settled for spicy mustard. The girl suddenly wailed from behind me and the women's chatter picked up in volume and speed as I spotted green leaf lettuce.

What is the matter with you? She needs closure.

I closed the refrigerator and stepped forward. 'Is everything all right?' I said politely, since my stomach was already doing the growling for me. The girl wailed louder and the aunts wrapped their arms around her. The mother glanced at me and then at a large clock on the wall above the entrance. It was obvious I was intruding on their only personal time in the house.

'We will leave, yes?' she said, tapping her sisters on their shoulders as they hugged the young girl.

'Don't leave,' I said as my cards vibrated through my purse. 'I think I can help.' I reluctantly walked away from the platter of turkey and took a seat across from the crying girl. 'What's your name?' I said to the mass of hair hanging across from me. The girl's head stopped shaking.

'Hannah,' she finally mumbled.

'Nice to meet you, Hannah. I'm Clair. I need you to sit up straight and look at me,' I said, taking out my cards. One of the women gasped as I set them on the table.

'It's the Tarot,' the mother said. The girl's head popped up. The aunts looked at each other and then glanced at the girl who looked to her mother. The mother stared back and then finally nodded her consent. They all leaned in at once. Seeing as how I had a platter of turkey waiting for me, I decided to do a five-card spread, a much simpler version of the Celtic. This spread uses only twenty-two cards, all from the Major Arcana.

I quickly removed the Minor Arcana cards from the deck and set them aside. I have to admit a second selfish reason for using this spread with the young girl. In this type of reading, I do all the shuffling and the Querent doesn't even have to touch the cards. Despite three hankies her protectors had been dangling in front of her, she had refused all of them and had been wiping her nose with her fingers. No way was she touching my cards.

'Pick a number between one and twenty-two,' I said.

'Thirteen,' she sniffled. I counted through the cards until I reached number thirteen, then placed it on the table to the left. I continued this process until I had five cards of Hannah's choosing laid down from left to right.

'Does she have to ask a question?' the mother asked, lunging forward in her seat. Hannah stopped crying. Her beautiful, brown eyes stared at me like an inquisitive rabbit's.

'No,' I said. 'But she has to listen to the answer.' I made sure she was looking at me when I said this. We all stared at her until the girl finally nodded her consent. I turned over the first card, The High Priest. 'This is your search for truth,' I said. 'If you're religious, The High Priest can be seen as a conduit to God or to your own spiritual inquiries. Hannah, you need the moral courage to go your own road. Even if,' I snuck a glance at her aunts and mother, 'even if it goes against what others want for you.'

'Is this about the boy?' one aunt whispered across the table to the other.

'Shhh,' I said. I could tell from the slight widening of her eyes and the flush on her cheeks that Hannah understood. I gave her a little smile of encouragement and hesitated before turning over the second card.

'This card will tell us what's preventing you from embracing your own path,' I said, turning over The Magician. 'The Magician,' I explained, 'is like a juggler. He needs to be in control of his universe, he needs to

keep a strong center in order to balance.' I pointed out
the objects laid before The Magician. A cup, a sword, a
wand, a pentacle. The four suits of the Minor Arcana.
'You're not balanced right now because,' I stopped, trying
not to look at anyone but Hannah, 'you're being controlled
by others,' I said finally. 'And – even if they mean well –
you cannot continue to allow them to make decisions for
you.'

'Who are these others?' the mother demanded, looking
around the kitchen.

'Shhh,' Hannah said, to all of our surprise. Had I been
the one to shhh her, I would have been thrown out of the
kitchen on my ear. I sensed this was the first time the
daughter had taken up for herself in a long time. The
mother literally bit her bottom lip and crossed her arms,
but indeed shut up.

'Go on,' Hannah urged, looking at the third card.

'This card will tell us why you're in this situation,' I
explained, turning over Justice. The Justice card is the
epitome of fairness and strict justice. The card depicts a
female character, either standing or sitting between two
pillars. She holds a sword in one hand, perfectly balanced
scales in the other. Her eyes are wide open and all-
knowing.

'You've known the truth in your heart for a long time,' I
said softly. Hannah nodded as tears again threatened to
spill over and her lip quivered.

'Does she love the boy?' the aunt whispered again. This
time everyone at the table shh'd her, while Hannah's eyes
remained focused on mine.

'You must listen to this truth within you. You cannot
fight it any longer. This is what is causing you so much
pain. And even though others may not want to hear the
truth, it cannot be denied.'

We were almost done and even though I knew it wasn't
going to be easy for Hannah to stand up to the maternal
posse surrounding her, I could feel the burden lifting, her
shame starting to ease. She lifted her head a little higher

and wiped her eyes. 'Go on,' she said nodding. I quickly turned over the fourth card.

'This is your solution,' I said, revealing The Star, depicted by a beautiful woman pouring water back into a stream with two pitchers underneath a sky littered with stars. 'Ever since man arrived on earth, he has used the stars to find his way,' I said. 'You are not alone in this journey. You are not alone in who you are.'

Again I glanced at her conservative, traditional aunts and fretting mother. 'The Magician attempts to gain power and strength – but the stars readily give them,' I explained. 'They already have the magic. But in order to utilize their power, you have to give back. And you can't give of yourself, Hannah, until you truly claim who you are.'

Hannah nodded. I turned over the last card. It was, appropriately, The Sun. 'Your journey to claiming who you are seems overwhelming right now, Hannah, but this is a very positive card. If you will trust in what the rest have told you, then your ultimate path will be one of light and happiness.'

I felt the energy drain out of me as I swept the cards back into the deck. Hannah lunged from her seat and ambushed me with a hug. I hugged her back, feeling good for the first time all day. The two aunts and the mother stood as Hannah bounced around the room. 'Is it the boy? You love the boy?' the aunt asked. Hannah simply smiled and waltzed out of the room. The aunts shook their heads and left as well. The mother stood staring at me as I happily discarded decorum and ate a turkey leg with my fingers.

'How did you know?' she asked as I licked my fingers. 'Are you one, too?' I stopped eating, and studied the mother. I had underestimated the one intuition that usurped mine. A mother's intuition. She had known all along.

'No,' I said. 'I'm not.'

'She told you then? This,' she said gesturing back to the table where we had done the reading, 'was a game?'

'No. I just read the cards.'

'Hmm.' She pushed her hands down her ample belly like they were hot irons. 'So these cards – why do they have to be so . . . talking 'round the bush?' She blushed when she realized what she just said. 'I don't mean like this—'

'I understand.'

'Why don't these cards just come out and say "I sad because I cannot tell my mother I no like boys. I am lesbian." Why not cards just say this?'

'Because it's not the cards' job to say this,' I explained. 'It's Hannah's.' The mother looked at me while she considered this.

'I see. Same with me. I say nothing. I wait for Hannah to tell us. But her aunts are no gonna like this. Her father is going to turn over in his grave.'

'And you?' I asked. 'How will you respond?'

'You make her smile,' the mother answered at last. 'That is what matters.' She left me then, all alone with my platter of turkey in my dream kitchen.

Or so I thought.

Daily Horoscope – Pisces

If the Fourth House is passing through Jupiter at 5 trillion miles an hour and the Sixth House is passing through Jupiter from the opposite direction at 2 and 6/10th trillion miles per hour with a North Easterly wind that makes it seem like it's really traveling an additional 3 trillion miles an hour – exactly when will they collide and fuck up your day?

'Fascinating,' said a male voice from the corner of the room. I froze with my index finger still in my mouth. A deep laugh followed. 'I'm not talking about your ability to suck down an entire turkey without utensils – although that's fascinating, too – I was referring to your little séance with the kitchen help.' I didn't answer at first; instead I concentrated my anger on putting away what remained of the turkey and slamming the refrigerator door. Next I marched over to the sink and washed my hands. He remained a shadow in the corner.

'First of all,' I said without turning around. 'It wasn't a séance. It was a Tarot reading. Second, it's none of your business. And third—'

'How many are there going to be, Clair? I mean just so I'm prepared. Am I in for the long haul or can you give me the Cliffs Notes?' I didn't answer, I was too busy boiling my blood. 'Would you like a drink?' he asked when I didn't answer. I hesitated. I very much wanted a drink, but I didn't want to spend one minute longer than necessary with him.

'No.'

'Suit yourself. Do you want to hear about your car?' Despite my resolve to ignore him, this got to me. I walked to the corner, following the voice. When the shadows receded I could see him sprawled in a chair, holding a glass of golden liquid, Scotch or Bourbon, I didn't know the difference. 'I'm not much of a vodka or wine guy,' he said, reading my mind. 'I know it's downright sacrilegious in this place. Sure you won't join me?'

'They found my car?'

'You just won't let yourself warm up to me, will you?' he asked, studying me intently. *I'm warm. You're hot. I'm scalding. I'm wrong about men every time.*

'I'm tired,' I said. 'I've had a very long day.' He continued to study me while he drained his glass.

'Starting with a car accident,' he said, rattling ice cubes around.

'Exactly.' *Why am I so drawn to you? Why are lies, and secrets, and padlocks constantly floating around your aura's orbit?*

'You veered off into the woods,' he said, putting down the glass and coming closer to me. I didn't move back, I didn't move forward.

'I did.' He moved even closer. I still didn't budge. I knew this game. I was good at this game. And I liked him this close, but he didn't have to know that.

'Why?'

'Excuse me?'

'Nice weather if I remember correctly. Not too much traffic this time of year. True, the roads are curvy – you must have been speeding. Is that it?'

'Mike. I've asked you directly if they've found my car. I would appreciate a direct answer.'

'I think you're beautiful,' he said in a deep whisper. The

compliment spread through me like a shot of Southern Comfort, warming my insides. 'But you don't care about that, do you?' he continued. 'You only have eyes for Jack.' His hand came up to run through his hair and the timing was such that I stepped back. It had been exactly what I wanted to do. Reach up and run my fingers through his thick, dark, hair. Trace his jawline with my fingertips. I was also starting to bet that all those years of playing piano has made him very good with his hands.

He was staring at me. 'I'm not going to touch you, if that's what you're afraid of,' he said, misinterpreting me once again. I made no moves to correct his assumption, I didn't owe him any explanations.

'Can I ask you a question?' I said instead.

'Can I stop you?'

'How long have you been here?'

'Thirty-two years.' Despite myself, I laughed. 'Here at the estates.' Mike's smile faded slightly and he looked away. Some psychics depend on body language like this to bolster the reading. He wanted to avoid the question. It made me want to ask that many more.

'I've been here,' he said, looking away as if trying to figure out the date, 'oh, I don't know. Less than a year.' *He knows exactly how long he's been here, down to the hour.*

'That's a long time to live with another family.'

'Better than living with your own.' I laughed again, but this time he didn't join me.

'Why are you living here?' I probed.

'Why are you asking?' God he has beautiful eyes. We would have made wonderful traveling gypsy lovers. Each night in a new town, building a new bonfire, gazing at each other across the flames while he played the guitar. He's a pianist in this life but he could have been—

'I said, why are you asking me all these questions?' Mike repeated.

'I'm just curious.'

'I can see that.'

'Since you've been here,' I said, treading carefully.

'Have you . . . heard any . . . strange noises?' Mike turned his attention back to me, really looking into my eyes, and this time I was the one who looked away.

'What is your heritage?' he asked suddenly.

'Hungarian gypsy,' I said.

'Hungarian gypsy,' he repeated like he was in a trance.

'Your turn,' I prodded.

'Mostly the British Isles—'

'I was talking about the noises.' Mike's eyes lingered on my face once again before he looked away, and folded his arms over his chest. *God, I just want to bite those biceps.*

'Strange noises you say? Like floorboards creaking, doors slamming suddenly, relentless moaning?' I nodded and curled my lips around my teeth just in case they took on a mind of their own and sank into his flesh in vampiric lust.

'Nope,' he said, grinning at me. 'Can't say I have.'

'How did you save the estate?' I asked, remembering something Susan had said along these lines. *We would have been forced to sell if it hadn't been for him.*

'I don't know what you're talking about,' Mike answered.

'Someone said—'

'Someone said, someone said.' He came toward me again. He was inches away and his voice dropped to a whisper. 'I'm sorry. I'm drunk. And you're beautiful. It's always been a dangerous combination. No doubt you hate me even more now for making such a fool of myself. Regardless, I'm glad it's out in the open—'

'Do you have ownership in the estate now?' I interrupted him. 'Are they still in financial trouble?' It wasn't that I didn't like to be told I was beautiful. But if I listened to this romantic talk anymore, I was going to lose it. I was going to throw myself at his feet. I was going to rip off my clothes. I was going to let myself get sucked into the cosmos, and I'd come too far – I wasn't supposed to lose my mind this time. If I ever fell in love again, it was supposed to be healthy, sane – not this feeling of wanting to throw every caution out the window and dive in.

Apparently, my tactic did the trick. Mike stopped babbling about my beauty. His expression was no longer soft, or bumbling. He handed me a card. 'This is where the Saturn was towed,' he said. 'The police want to question you.'

'The police? Oh God. Because I drove into a national forest?' Mike started to laugh and then stopped when he saw the look on my face.

'They want to make sure you weren't drinking. Although lucky for you, it's too late for them to breathalyze you—'

'I wasn't drinking. It was eight o'clock in the morning!'

'Well you did manage to drive your car off the road and into the woods.'

'I wasn't drinking. Except coffee. A lousy twenty-five-dollar cup of coffee.' Mike raised an eyebrow but didn't say anything.

'You also walked away from the scene.'

'What else was I to do? Stick around with marsh-mallows in case the car caught on fire?'

'Call the police.'

'My cell phone was dead.'

'I understand. You were in shock. Got a little bump on the head. That's what I told the police.'

'What you told the police?'

'Yes, Clair. That's what I told the police.'

'Why are you talking to the police about me?'

'Are those your real lips?'

'Excuse me?'

'Your lips,' he said, bringing his index finger up and touching them. 'You haven't . . . had them done, have you?'

'Of course not,' I said moving my head away despite the electricity zipping down my body.

'So sorry,' he said. 'I couldn't help myself.'

'Mike. I need you to concentrate. Why were you talking to the police about me?'

'I was calling around about the car. Lucky for you, too.'

'Why is it lucky for me?'

'Because. I told them when you crawled on top of me and kissed me as if our lives depended on it, you were completely sober.'

'You did not say that.'

'I didn't?' he whispered, looking at my lips again. 'You sure about that?' The smell of his cologne, mixed with the sweetness of what I now could identify as Scotch, momentarily flooded my brain. It was Mike's turn to ruin the romantic mood.

'You'll be happy to know I left out the bit about the missing fiancée and stolen engagement ring,' he said.

'I didn't steal that ring,' I said. 'And Rachel isn't missing. She dumped Jack. It's as simple as that.'

'Nothing is ever that simple, Clair,' Mike said, reaching out to touch my hair. I told myself I didn't stop him because I wanted him to keep talking. His eyes dropped to my neck as he played with my hair. 'You of all people should know that.'

'What do you mean me of all people?' Mike ignored my question. I was disappointed when he stopped touching my hair and then I was angry with myself for being disappointed.

'The police need your statement for the report,' he said, his voice regaining composure. 'It wouldn't hurt for you to be checked out, too.'

'Checked out?'

'At a hospital.'

'I don't need to go to a hospital.'

'If they could confirm your concussion—'

'I thought you said the police believed you—'

'Calm down, Clair. It couldn't hurt, that's all.'

'I'm fine,' I insisted.

'Suit yourself. Are you ready? I told them I'd bring you straight in.'

'Now?'

'Yes, now.'

'Can't this wait until morning?' I really wanted to go to bed. And I didn't want to hang around Mike any more tonight. The verdict was in. I was incredibly, annoyingly, sexually attracted to him. It was better than wanting to suit up and marry him, but annoying nonetheless.

'No. It can't wait until morning. You're lucky they're not swarming the lawn. Let's just get it over with. The sooner you talk to the police, the sooner you can send the report into the rental car agency.'

'Oh God,' I said, suddenly remembering the rental car agency. Mike's tone softened.

'Come on,' he said, taking my arm and heading for the door.

'Wait,' I snapped, pulling away from him. He didn't stop, didn't even look back at me. 'You can't drive me anywhere, let alone the police station,' I yelled after him, 'you're drunk.'

'I'm not driving,' he answered as he disappeared out the door. 'Jack is.'

Daily Horoscope – Pisces

*Underestimating Tweedle Dee and Tweedle Dum
would be a dumb thing to do.*

Some lies you tell to protect yourself. Some lies you tell
because you're ashamed of the truth. And some lies
you tell because you're trying to save innocent people
from dying in a fiery car crash. I for one had had enough
of car accidents, and Jack Heron was speeding like a bat
out of hell. 'Slow down,' I yelled for the third time from
the back seat. Trees were whizzing by so fast they looked
like furry, green snowcones.

'She won't even answer her cell phone. I've called her
a dozen times. Why? Why is she doing this to me?'
Apparently, a few hours of stewing over being jilted had
put Jack in a foul humor and he was bound and determined
to take it out on an innocent gas pedal.

'She's a bit—' Mike started to say and then glanced
back at me. 'She's not good for you,' he said instead.

'Call her a bitch, I don't care,' I said. 'Just make him
slow down.'

'No explanation. Not one word,' Jack said. 'She wants to
dump me – fine! Dump me. Just tell me. Tell me to my face.
Tell me on the phone. E-mail me. Text me. Fax me—'

'We get it,' I said, slamming into the door as Jack took
a curve too fast.

'Just a few words of explanation—'

Now the trees looked like blurry stick people. Darkness sped by like we were in a rocket. I wrote *HELP* in the window dust. 'I thought about what you said, Clair. And you're right. I could have been more sensitive. But the punishment doesn't fit the crime here. Why won't she even talk to me? She knows the engagement party is tomorrow night. Take it out on me – fine – but my mother doesn't deserve this. She didn't even—'

The car was now officially registered in the Indy 500. 'There was a letter!' I shouted as the speedometer reached 90. The car slowed slightly as Jack took this in.

'What?' he yelled.

'Slow down so I can talk,' I yelled back as if this made perfect sense. Mike turned around and gave me a funny look, but I didn't care. 'Jack slow down and I'll tell you the truth,' I said. The car slowed down to an almost human speed. My heart was pounding in my chest like tribal drums and my palms were drenched with sweat. I felt like throwing up but I wasn't sure if I even had a stomach any longer, it felt as if it had been hollowed out like a pumpkin.

'Tell me,' Jack urged.

'Rachel gave me the ring,' I said slowly. 'And – a letter.'

'A Dear John letter?' Mike joked, 'or Dear Jack?' I glared at him.

'What does it say?' Jack asked, ignoring Mike.

'I don't know,' I said stalling for time, 'I didn't read it.'

'Where is it?'

'It's back in my room. If you promise not to drive like a complete maniac the rest of the way, I'll give it to you.' I would have felt horrendous guilt for lying like this if it weren't for the fact that the alternative was strangling him from behind while somehow wrestling the wheel out of his hands.

'A letter,' Jack repeated. 'She wrote me a letter.' I leaned back in the seat and tried to take cleansing breaths.

A letter I repeated to myself, grateful I wasn't going to

die in this car. He had a coconut air freshener. I hated coconut. I'd much rather die to the scent of citrus, or a nice, faint pine. The relief was so immediate, I almost fell asleep.

'You're sure you didn't read it?' Jack demanded, making eye contact with me through the rearview mirror.

'I didn't read it,' I repeated as I closed my eyes.

'Why on earth didn't you tell me about this letter earlier?'

'I forgot.'

'You forgot?'

'I was in a car accident,' I shouted, realizing I probably didn't have many more uses of this excuse left in my arsenal.

'Is it a thick letter or a thin letter?' Jack asked.

'Thin,' I mumbled.

'Legal size envelope or stationery?'

'Um, legal, I think.' Good God. *What have I started?*

'What did she say when she handed it to you?' Jack asked excitedly. 'I want it, word for word.'

'Jack,' Mike said.

'It could be important,' Jack said. I kept my eyes closed.

'She's asleep,' Mike answered.

'Clair? Clair?' Jack said.

'Jack, let her sleep,' Mike said.

'I just want to know if—'

'Jesus, Jack,' Mike practically yelled. 'You can read it when you get home.'

Although I was surprised Mike was coming to my rescue, this seemed to do the trick. Jack shut up. For a second at least.

'What if she's not dumping me?' he continued after a slight breather. 'Maybe she just took off for the weekend. She could have gone on one of those Pilates retreats.' Jack slapped the dashboard. Lucky for me he stayed within the speed limit or else I would have had to stop pretend-sleeping and initiate the strangling plan.

'She could be up in the mountains somewhere,' Jack

said happily. 'No cell-phone reception in the mountains,' he yelled.

'Shhh,' Mike said. Then, 'What about the ring?'

'Huh?'

'If she's just gone off on a retreat – why leave the ring with Clair? Why tell Clair she doesn't want to marry you?'

'She – didn't want the ring to be stolen.'

'From the Zenlike Pilates retreat in the mountains?'

'Some of those positions require you to press hard on your knuckles. She doesn't want to damage the ring.'

'Ah.'

'And as for her,' Jack said, referring to me, 'we don't know a thing about her. She could be lying through her teeth.'

'Then why go to all this trouble to bring you the ring? Why not just take off with it?'

'I don't know. But it will all become clear when I read the letter. I just know it.'

'Hey, man. I hope she is off in the mountains. I really do. I just think you need to consider the possibilities, that's all.' I could feel Mike's eyes on me. The heat of them licked through my eyelids again. If he didn't stop it, sooner or later he was going to sear them right off. I didn't dare open my eyes. He stared at me for a long while. I continued to pretend-sleep until I felt the car come to a stop.

The inside of the two-man station looked like a set straight out of the *Andy Griffith Show*. Two desks, overflowing with papers and toys, were situated across from two jail cells. I glanced at the messier of the two desks and wondered if they stuck me in one of the cells if they'd let me have the tennis ball, the deck of cards, or the box of Nutter Butters.

The two officers stood awkwardly side-by-side, looking more like a set of salt and pepper shakers than civil protectors. The dark-skinned one (Mr Pepper) was bald and bulky. Mr Salt was a decade younger than his counterpart and tall and lanky.

'Have a seat,' Officer Pepper said. The three of us

looked around. There were no extra chairs. The two officers sat. Officer Salt, or McGee as his nametag stated, removed a hot-pink sticky pad and a purple marker from his drawer and held them up in pristine note-taking position. Officer Pepper, or Thayer as his nametag stated, glared at McGee. 'Use the form,' he barked.

'I like to get it down here first,' McGee said. 'Then transfer it to the form.' He ripped a sheet out of the pad and stuck it on his computer screen. 'See? I just type away while reading it from the screen,' he bragged. Thayer shook his head but let it go. Mike, Jack, and I remained standing.

And then Pepper/Thayer fired questions at me while Salt/McGee marked them down, ripped them off his pad, and stuck them to the computer screen. After twenty or so who, what, where, and why questions, Salt ran out of sticky notes.

'I think we have the basics,' Pepper said, twirling around in his chair.

'Yep,' McGee said, pointing to his hot-pink splattered computer screen. 'Got 'em right here.'

'But we're still not clear on one thing,' Pepper said, salting me with a fake, slow smile.

'We're still a little unclear' – Officer Salt repeated, chewing his lip. He leaned over to Thayer and whispered, 'What's the thing?'

I didn't know about Mike or Jack, but I was using every trick in the book not to laugh. From the slight shaking of Mike's shoulders, I could tell he was going through the same thing. I bit my lip and waited. I knew what they wanted. I knew what all of them were thinking – their thoughts were swirling around my brain, conflating like a ball of yarn until I didn't know where one began and the other ended.

Someone was thinking about the bet he'd made on a football game, another was dying for lasagna, and a third was thinking about the curve of my neck. But all of them – including me – were wondering how in the hell I swerved off the road on a peaceful, sunny, quiet morning and flipped my rented Saturn upside down and inside out.

'Something flew into my windshield,' I said before they could formulate the question. 'It totally startled me. I panicked and the next thing I knew I was airborne.' McGee looked at Thayer who grabbed the box of Nutter Butters and stuck one in his mouth like it was a cigarette. He leaned back in his chair and took the Nutter Butter out of his mouth.

'Airborne?' he said. 'You're speaking metaphorically?'

'Look, I'm just saying I felt like I was flying,' I said. 'It all happened so fast. I didn't know what it was at first. I just saw this monstrous blue and black creature—'

'You saw what?' Officer McGee interjected. He popped below the desk and opened a drawer. 'Damn it,' he yelled. 'Where are the rest of my sticky notes?'

'Did ya see Big Foot?' Officer Pepper joked.

'Or some asshole from Utah in a monkey suit?' Officer Salt added as he started tossing the tennis ball in the air. I could feel Mike's breath in my ear.

'Is this for real?' he whispered.

'Anything you'd like to share with the class?' Thayer barked.

'Sorry officers,' Mike said, turning a laugh into a cough.

'No it wasn't Big Foot,' I said. 'I'm just trying to say that at the time it looked like a monster.' The men didn't respond or offer any cookies, so I continued. 'It was a blue heron. I saw him when I got out of the car. His wingspan was this big,' I splayed my arms out as far as I could, smacking Jack with my left hand and Mike with my right.

'A blue heron?' Thayer said.

'Correct.'

'Flew into your windshield.'

'Yes.'

'Did he apologize?' Salt asked. Jack and Mike both choked back a laugh. It hurt my feelings but instead of admitting this, I simply whipped my hands out again, hitting them harder this time. 'This big,' I repeated.

A yo-yo materialized in McGee's left hand. We all stopped for a second and watched the spinning disk fall to the ground. He flicked the string but the yo-yo didn't retract, it just bobbed along the dusty floor. He cleared his throat and dropped it. Thayer reached for another Nutter Butter.

'I see,' McGee said.

'Miss Ivars,' Thayer said, putting down the Nutter Butter and leaning forward. 'Have you been under any unusual stress lately?'

'You think I'm crazy?'

'Just answer the question.'

Why yes, Officer, I have. I'm thirty-two and I've been married three times. I'm a love addict. I hear other people's voices and sometimes they drown out my own. Three times is supposed to be the charm. My third marriage was supposed to stick! Three strikes and you're out. I'm out. I shouldn't even be looking at Mike. I shouldn't even be thinking about Mike. I'm done. I'm on the bench for the rest of the game. I'll have to become a whore or a nun.

'Unusual stress, Miss?' Officer Salt repeated.

'Maybe a little,' I admitted, tears coming to my eyes. Mike eased forward but I stopped him with another look.

'Did you say a blue heron?' Jack said, finally tuning into our station like a recovering television, 'flew into your windshield?' I nodded.

'That's so wild,' he said. 'Blue heron. My last name is Heron.' Mike and I exchanged looks and then turned mutual pity-smiles on Jack. We had to get him out of this station.

'Yes,' McGee said. 'It is awfully strange, isn't it? An unbelievable coincidence one might say.'

'Unbelievable,' Pepper repeated. 'Or it's a bunch of baloney.'

'Don't you have some sort of vodka-naming contest going on, Jack?' Thayer said.

'You heard?' Jack said, perking up a little.

'It's good promotion, huh?' Thayer said, looking at me. 'Ten thousand dollars. That's a nice prize. Isn't it, Miss?'

'It'll pay off,' Jack said proudly.

'Well,' Mike interjected. 'It might *not* pay off Jack. We've discussed this—'

'I'm telling you,' Jack said in a strained voice, 'it will pay off.' Jack and Mike were taking on the aura of sibling rivalry. Jack turned away from Mike and smiled at Officer Thayer. 'You thinking of entering, Sir?'

'I'm not much of an artist,' Thayer said with a slow smile. 'What about you, young lady? You much of an artist?'

'No.'

'Is that what you're doing young lady? Trying to grab attention for yourself?' Jack turned toward me and stared, as if noticing me for the first time.

'I never thought of that,' he said. 'This whole story about Rachel—'

'Wait a minute,' I said. 'Are you saying I crashed my car – because of some contest? I flew into the air! I flipped upside down! I could have been *killed*. You should be ashamed of yourselves—' I stopped midsentence. I was hearing a low hum in my ears. I saw the image of a well rising with water. Something was going on here that I wasn't picking up on.

'She has a point,' Mike said.

'It was a rental car,' I continued to shout. 'I didn't even get the extra insurance.'

'Let's take a walk,' Pepper said, pulling himself out of the seat.

'Where?' I demanded. I had visions of him throwing me into the slammer.

'We've got your car out back,' he said, heading down the hall. 'Don't you want to see it?' Oh God. The damage. The breaking of federal laws! If they nailed you for five thousand for picking a single wildflower, what were they going to do to me for slamming my Saturn into Mother Nature?

'Can I have a Nutter Butter?' I squeaked.

'You're well insured, right?' Mike whispered to me as we followed the shakers out.

'Of course she is,' Jack said. 'She's in finance.' *Now he's listening?*

'Of course I am,' I repeated like a woman walking the plank. 'What kind of idiot wouldn't insure their rental car?'

'Now. What is the real reason for your visit?' Officer Salt asked.

We were standing on a patch of grass behind the police station. Next to us, sitting upright, red paint gleaming under bright bulbs from the back of the station, was a perfectly intact, red Saturn. Not a dent, a scratch, or speck of dirt to be found. *You weren't in a car accident* slammed into me from behind, giving me whiplash. Once again I found myself at a complete loss, and underinsured. *And apparently*, I thought as I circled the pristine car, *I'm crazy to boot*.

Obviously, this wasn't my rental car. I walked around my Saturn's doppleganger like Dorothy circling Oz. 'This isn't my rental car,' I told them.

'You sure about that?' Pepper asked, patting his generous stomach. It was only now that I noticed he was waving a sheet of paper in the air like it was a bloody shoe and I was wearing the match.

'That your signature?' he said. I didn't even look at it.

'Yes.'

'This car looks pretty good for one that was flying through the air!' Officer Salt said.

'What brings you out to these parts again, Miss?' Pepper asked.

'I came to see Jack,' I admitted.

'About the contest?' he pushed.

'No,' I said loudly. 'Another matter entirely.' I was still circling the car when I was distracted by Officer Pepper/Thayer's left jacket pocket. Dancing, orange light was leaping out of it as if it were on fire. It started to twirl faster and faster, spinning like a minicolored hurricane in front of us. But I was the only one who could see it.

'Clair came to return something to Jack,' Mike offered.

'Did she now?' Thayer said, putting his hand through the hurricanes. I watched it disappear inside his left jacket pocket. I felt dizzy. 'And you're not here for any other reason?' he asked one more time.

'No other reason,' I insisted. The hand emerged from his pocket. I couldn't see what it was because of the swirling, minicolored hurricane.

'There was a bag in the car,' Thayer explained. 'Of course we had to look through it – try to obtain your identity.' We all watched as he revealed his hand, unfolding Jack's smiling face. The smiling face I had taped to my glove compartment. 'This is an article about the contest,' he said, stating the obvious. 'We found it in your bag.'

He turned the article around so we all could see it. 'It says Heron Vodka, right here,' he said, pointing to the words. 'Use your creativity to win ten thousand dollars.' He held the picture in front of us like a courtroom exhibit. But that wasn't the worst part. I had forgotten all about finding a red marker in the drawer of the motel room and in a moment of fantasizing, drawing a little red heart around Jack. Well, around a part of Jack.

You Don't Have to Be Psychic to Know: It wasn't his face.

Daily Horoscope – Pisces

Weebles wobble but they don't fall down.

There's nothing in the world like falling in love. It's a chemical high that can't be beat. Maybe my brain chemistry was more sensitive than the average gal, because when those endorphins started flying around my body, and my jaw ached from smiling all day, and I couldn't stop thinking about the person, I was a goner.

Until the relationship imploded, exploded, or was yanked out from under me. (Admittedly, a few I'd set fire to myself.) And then the falling-in-love-cycle started all over again. But this time, after the-one-I-thought-would-stick, I'd stayed away from men, I'd taken things a day at a time, thinking I'd finally, finally learned my lesson.

Apparently, I hadn't.

Why else would I draw a little red heart around Jack Heron's crotch? This was the question zipping around my brain like a revolving door on high speed while four grown men stared at me. It was like I was thirteen again and come into my room to find Tommy and Abby reading my diary.

This was worse.

My first instinct was to lie. We were back in the station standing around the desk. *I didn't do that* wanted to march out of my mouth and parade around the room, but my tongue was paralyzed. The officers were smirking and Jack had turned four shades of red and he had his arms folded tightly across his chest like the captain of a firing squad, but it was Mike's reaction that was truly making my blood feel like it was swimming in ice cubes.

He hadn't met my eyes since the officer had revealed the magazine page. I don't know why it was bothering me so much, why I cared about what Mike thought, but from the knots in my stomach, it was becoming apparent that I did care. Somehow, this ridiculous, childish whim I had when I was all alone in a musty motel room with a red marker and a bottle of wine was, in his mind, an egregious act of betrayal.

I was torn between defending myself and apologizing to him. I was warming up to Mike, starting to see him as an ally in this whole sordid mess. I had yet to think of a single thing to say in my defense. But I had better come up with something.

'A client brought that to me,' I said.

'A client?' McGee said. 'What is it that you do?'

'I'm – in futures,' I said.

'A fellow investor,' Jack offered. At least he was still talking to me.

'Fellow investor?' I asked. Jack nodded to Mike.

'Mike dabbles,' he said. Mike didn't offer any additional information.

'Why did this client bring you this?' Pepper resumed.

'She's an artist. She's going to enter the contest.'

'Why bring it to you?'

'She found out I was coming out to the Estates, so she brought me this. Thought I could put a word in for her.' Silence punctuated the end of my lame explanation.

'You never mentioned it,' Jack said.

'I never intended to,' I said honestly. 'I just came to give you the ring. I thought it would be tacky to—'

'What ring?' Officer McGee said.

'Just a piece of family jewelry the estate hired Clair to appraise,' Mike interjected quickly.

'You're an appraiser, too?' Officer Salt asked, diving into his desk drawer again.

'I dabble,' I mumbled.

'You seem to do a lot of dabbling,' Thayer said. 'You're a regular Jack-of-All-Trades,' he added, laughing loudly at his own joke.

'How are the plans for the wedding coming?' he asked Jack as I pondered how deep I was going to have to wade in my pool of lies. 'Eleanor saw Rachel and your mother in town last week going over all the arrangements. She said Madeline was a whirlwind.'

'Oh yes. Mother is very involved,' Jack said ruefully.

'How's Rachel handling that?' McGee probed. Jack exchanged a look with Mike. I tried to get in on it, but he was still shutting me out. Does he not believe that my *client*, not *I*, had drawn the little heart? For God's sake, if I was starting to believe in my own lies, why couldn't he?

'Rachel's out of town right now,' Jack said. 'She's on a Pilates retreat.'

This time Mike gave me a look. I held the look until he broke it. 'Really? Isn't your engagement party tomorrow? Eleanor hasn't stopped talking about it all week,' Thayer said, shaking his head affectionately.

'Eleanor?' Mike asked the officer politely.

'His second wife,' I answered without thinking. Thayer stopped cold and stared at me.

'Guess you've told her all about it?' he asked Jack when a moment had gone by. Jack shook his head.

'Never mentioned it,' Jack said, looking at me.

'I think *you* mentioned it earlier,' I told McGee.

'I did not,' he said. I felt excess energy dancing around me and I imagined calm, blue waters.

'Lucky guess,' I said.

'But why did you assume she was my *second* wife?' Thayer persisted. Calm, blue waters. I glanced around his desk, hoping there was a picture of her so I could explain how I had just assumed since she was so much younger than he was.

She was too. Fifteen years younger. She had a nice, musical laugh and curly blond hair. She did things to him in bed that made him feel like he was in his twenties again. She didn't like his pot belly or the little hairs around his—

I put my hands over my ears. I didn't want to know these things. 'Clair?' Mike said. 'Are you okay?'

'Tinnitus,' I lied. 'My ears are ringing.'

'That could be from your "accident,"' Thayer piped in, making air quotes on the word *accident*.

'I *was* in an accident,' I said.

'You saw the car,' Officer McGee said.

'I can't explain it. But I'm telling you the truth. I was upside down. I had to crawl out of the car.' The officers looked at each other.

'How's your head?' Thayer asked.

'My head?'

'Your noggin,' Salt clarified.

'Mrs Ivars,' Thayer took over.

'Ms—' I corrected.

'Ms,' McGee repeated loudly.

'Ever been married?' Thayer asked in a booming voice. An alarm bell went off in my head. It was so loud I almost covered my ears with my hands.

'What does my marital history have to do with the matter at hand?' I said. Thayer advanced on me.

'Ms Ivars, we're thinking you suffered from a little concussion. We did after all find your car in the woods, so at least that part was true—'

'It's all true—'

'So giving you the benefit of the doubt, that you *believe* what you're telling us – means only one of three things. You're crazy,' Pepper said, holding up one finger.

'You hit your noggin pretty damn hard,' Salt said holding up one finger. Thayer glared at him until he made it a 'two.'

'Or you're trying to bag yourself a bachelor,' Pepper said finishing up with three. Jack looked at me.

'Hit my noggin pretty damn hard,' I squeaked, holding up two fingers and feeling my head.

'Well, I guess that's it. Here are your keys,' Thayer said.

'My keys?'

'To your rental car.' He dangled them in front of me.

'I'll drive,' Mike said, taking the keys. I didn't have to ask if he was fine to drive, I knew that he was. Much better than lying, crazy, or bachelor-bagging old me anyway.

'I think you'd better get some rest,' Thayer called to me as we exited. *And I think your second wife has herpes.*

'That was just weird,' Jack said, stabbing his scattered, smothered, and covered hash browns with a bent fork. We were at a roadside Waffle House where Mike had insisted we stop. In fact, he literally screamed when he saw the yellow and black banner. So did I, since I had actually waitressed at a Waffle House the summer between my junior and senior years in high school.

Mike was actually humming as he drowned his waffle in syrup. The waitress was scowling. Jack wasn't happy either. He just wanted to get home. Since Mike and I were in the Saturn and Jack was following in his car, he could have kept going, but he opted to stay. I had the feeling he wasn't going to let me out of his sight until I handed over the letter. Which was going to be a challenge given it didn't exist and all.

'What was weird?' Mike said. 'That Clair's car was perfectly intact or that a client of Clair's drew a heart around your crotch with a red marker?'

'I was talking about Rachel and the letter. But – that other stuff is weird, too.'

'Totally. Don't *you* think it's weird, Clair?' I glared at Mike.

'There are a lot of freaks out there,' I agreed.

'Do you think this woman – your client – is dangerous?' Mike persisted.

'Dangerous?' Jack and I asked at the same time. Mine was said with alarm, Jack's with a hint of sexual anticipation.

'It just seems like a really, really juvenile thing to do. Stalkerish almost,' Mike said between sugary bites.

'Stalkerish,' Jack and I echoed. Again, mine with annoyance, Jack's laced with rapt anticipation. I looked at Mike across the table, got stuck in his eyes, and stared until I realized he was actually waiting for an answer.

'Terri's not a stalker,' I said, wondering if my voice was shooting up like a false answer on a lie detector test, 'she's just an artist.'

'Is it handwritten or typewritten?' Jack asked suddenly.

'What?' I asked.

'The letter,' Jack said.

'I told you I didn't read it.'

'Is my name on the envelope?'

'Um – no?'

'You're not sure?' Good God. Why didn't I just say she passed on a message? This was awful. Now I was going to have to find a way to type the letter. 'I can't even believe I asked that,' Jack was saying.

'No worries,' I replied, wishing he would stop obsessing over the letter, trying to write it in my head.

'Rachel hates to type! Of course it's handwritten.' Of course. I could feel Mike's pleasure as he watched me squirm.

'Waffle on three, extra smothered!' I yelled to the cook. Sometimes, there's nothing you can do but drown your sorrows in syrup.

Daily Horoscope – Pisces

Whatever you do, don't play the name game.

Mike was quiet for the first half of the drive after we left the Waffle House, but his thoughts were excruciatingly loud. He had a million questions he wanted to ask me, but he was afraid to pose them. Mostly because he thought I was a complete liar, charlatan, and stalker. I turned up the radio to drown him out. 'Jack's pretty vulnerable right now,' Mike said in the middle of 'You're No Good.' 'For his sake, I hope there really is a letter.'

You know there's no letter. You know I drew the heart around his crotch. You know I'm not in finances. And you're watching me like a hawk, waiting for me to hang myself. Not to mention the sick pleasure you're getting out of watching me sweat. And there's something else about you. Something I can't quite figure out—

Something to do with Rachel? Something to do with the strange noises in the house? *I just can't put my finger on it.*

A blast of air conditioning hit me in the face. I yelped in surprise and startled Mike. 'Jesus,' he said, swerving the car a tad. 'What is the matter?'

'I'm sorry, I'm sorry. It just came blasting on.'

'What?'

'The air conditioning. Turn it off.' Mike glanced at me. I watched his hands tighten around the wheel.

'I can never tell when you're playing games or not. Guess that must come in handy in the *finance* world, huh? Do you keep a straight face while your clients' stocks plummet?'

'Would you please help me turn this off?' *I feel like a peppermint patty on an icy tundra.*

'Clair!'

'Michael Alexander Brentworth!' I screamed back. I clamped my hand over my mouth and prayed it would go by him. No such luck. Mike pulled the car over to the side of the road, slamming on the brakes and skidding part way before jamming the car into park and turning to completely face me. I was still shivering from the schizophrenic air conditioning. It was practically blowing my hair back. We sat in silence for a minute as he wrestled with his anger.

'Who are you?' he asked. 'How did you know?'

'Why are you lying about your name?' I asked instead of answering him. I should have been appeasing him and making excuses, but I was too cold and too tired.

'Just answer my question,' he demanded. But I didn't. I suffered though the stalemate by shivering, while Mike looked out the window and tried to ignore me. I could have gotten a better read on his thoughts if my own weren't so frosted over.

'Fine,' I said when it became apparent he didn't care if I got frostbite. 'Turn off this air conditioning and I'll tell you anything you want to know,' I pleaded.

'Clair.'

'Michael, I'm begging you, okay? Please. Please just turn it off.'

'I can't—'

'You mean you won't—'

'It isn't on!'

'Of course it is. It's—' I stopped suddenly as I held my frozen fingers out in front of me. I slowly put my hand over the vent. Nothing. Mike was right. The air conditioning wasn't on. I closed my eyes and took a deep breath. What was happening to me? I needed to talk to Brian. I was having a complete breakdown.

'Clair?' Mike said, gentler this time.

'I need to get home,' I said quietly.

'I think Officer McGee may have been right,' Mike said. 'I think you've suffered a concussion.'

I put my hand on my head and rubbed. Was it possible? Is that what this was all about?

'But according to everyone else, I didn't even have an accident,' I cried. 'How did I get a concussion if I didn't have an accident?' I was really starting to worry about my sanity.

'Maybe you did lose control of the car,' Mike said. 'And you hit your head really hard – and . . . and imagined the rest.'

'I hit my head really hard on what?'

'I don't know, Clair, I'm just trying to make any sense of it I can.'

'Do you think I'm crazy?'

'Well, you're a little crazy. But in a good way,' he said, taking my hand.

'The car,' I said. 'I'm telling you, Mike, the car was upside down.'

'I'm sure there's a logical explanation,' Mike said, still holding my hand.

'That's easy for you to say.' Mike shifted in closer, took his other hand and placed it under my chin. He lifted my head until I was looking him in the eyes. He had really nice eyes.

'I want to get you to the hospital. You've got a head injury and now you're freezing for no reason.'

'I'm not going to the hospital,' I said, yanking my hand away from him. I was seconds away from throwing myself at him, dragging him into the back seat and making out with him like a teenager. Mike, not knowing all this, took it as a slight.

'Suit yourself,' he said, turning away from me.

'I will,' I said.

'Since you're well enough to stay out of the hospital, you're well enough to answer my questions,' he said.

'I'm tired—'

'How did you know my real name?'

'You must have told me,' I lied.

'I didn't.'

'It just – popped into my head, all right?' I said. 'Sometimes things just pop into my head.'

'Is this some sort of a game?' Mike asked, his anger back full force.

'I already told you—'

'It just popped into your head.'

'Yes,' I said, gritting my teeth.

'This is none of your business, Clair. You know that don't you?'

'Look. I won't say anything to anyone,' I said. *Especially since I have no idea what we're talking about.* 'I promise, okay? Just take me home.' Mike contemplated me for a moment before finally pulling back onto the road.

'You're going home all right,' he said a few minutes later. 'First thing in the morning, you're going home.'

'What took you guys so long?' Jack said as I entered my room. Mike was following at a close clip, still demanding I explain how I knew his name. 'I've been back for' – Jack stopped to look at his watch – 'thirteen and a half minutes.'

'Jack, Mike,' I said, turning to them, trying to psychically intimidate them. 'I'm really, really tired. I just need to go to sleep.' My energy was so low I couldn't even emit a slightly threatening aura.

'Of course, of course. I'll just get the letter from you and go,' Jack said, rubbing his hands together. Knowing it was useless to try and dissuade him, I dumped my overnight bag on the bed and struck a thoughtful pose. This was going to be tricky. I had told Jack the letter was in my room, but the overnight bag was the only possession I had, except for my purse. I made a show of looking through the bedside table anyway.

'Hmm,' I said, standing back with my hand on my hips when the search revealed nothing. 'Maybe it's in here after all,' I said, turning back to the bag and pawing through my clothing. 'It should be right in here,' I said. Jack was standing so close I could feel his breath on my neck.

I continued my fake search of the bag, quickly stashing underwear and a packet of extra large condoms to the side. (You draw to you the things you imagine.) It reminded me that I had an adventure to get to – one that didn't involve married men and AWOL fiancées. Mike was right. I needed to get out of here. I had promised Elizabeth I would stay for dinner, but that was before I knew I was going crazy. 'I don't understand,' I said. 'It was right here.' Jack sat on the bed and ran his hands through his hair.

'Maybe it's in the car,' he said. 'Or your purse. Do you have a purse?'

'I'm sorry, Jack,' I said. 'It's gone.' Jack stood up.

'Do you think? The staff?' He gestured weakly toward the door. I had already gotten one nanny fired, I wasn't going to go down this path again.

'No. I'm sure they didn't. I think I – threw it away.'

'Threw it away? I don't understand. You said you had it.'

'I'm sorry, Jack,' I said again. 'But it's not here.' He opened his mouth to protest again and then turned to the door like a dog who had been kicked. His heartache wrapped around my throat and squeezed. I put my hands around my neck and squeaked. Jack was at my door ready to leave. I'd made one mistake after another with this duo. There was no guarantee Brian was going to be able to convince Rachel to come, but I still had to try and help her. Ghosts or no ghosts, Jack had obviously made her feel unloved and crazy – something I could strongly identify with recently.

'Dear Jack.' He stopped in his tracks. He kept his back to me but from the stiffening of his spine I could tell he was listening. 'This is the hardest letter I've ever had to write.' He turned to me. Our eyes locked.

'You read it?' he asked. I nodded.

'I memorized it,' I said. 'I'm sorry,' I whispered when he didn't reply. 'I just—'

'Go on,' he urged.

'I know you're going to hate me for doing this, and that's the hardest bit. Because I don't think I can live with you hating me.' Jack swallowed and closed his eyes. He was trying not to cry in front of me. I was mortified, but I couldn't stop now. 'I've been searching my entire life for someone like you. Which is why this isn't going to make any sense to you – but – I can't marry you Jack.'

I glanced at Jack, he was sitting rigid on the bed, fighting his emotions. 'I can't marry you, Jack,' I continued, doing my best to tap into what Rachel must have been feeling, 'because I heard things in this house. I saw things in this house. I was frightened and confused – and you didn't believe me. You thought I was crazy – or making it up. Well, maybe my world is a little more complicated than yours, Jack. Because in my world there is room for mystery and unexplained phenomena – experiences beyond the day to day. I needed your support. I'm not crazy. I love you, Jack – but if you can't see that, then I'm obviously not the girl for you.'

We stood in silence for a moment. Thoughts were crossing over Jack's face like the scrolls on the bottom of CNN. He was moved by my letter! Now he would apologize to Rachel and my karmic debt would be paid. I couldn't wait to see her face.

'I – can't believe what I just heard,' Jack said.

'I know,' I said, smiling proudly.

'This changes everything.'

'Of course it does.'

'She's dumping me over a ghost,' Jack exploded, shaking his hands indignantly.

'Wait. What?'

'She's flushing five years down the toilet because of the

supernatural. I can't believe her. It's bad enough everyone in this house had to put up with her crazy antics – what would the public think if they got a hold of this?'

'Jack—'

'I have a reputation to protect. A business. God knows how many people Rachel has told about our so-called ghost—'

'Calm down, Jack,' I said. 'She probably hasn't told anyone.'

'I don't need this. The supernatural! Can you believe her? I need to marry someone a little more practical. Like you,' Jack said. Mike fastened his eyes on me.

'You – what?' I suddenly couldn't enunciate anything other than 'What?' Jack headed for the door.

'You and I will get through the engagement party and then I'll send a notice to the newspapers quietly announcing our decision to split,' Jack said. 'I just pray Rachel hasn't leaked this ghost nonsense to anyone else. I'm going to contact her and make that very clear.'

'No,' I yelled. 'Jack, I'm sure she didn't—'

Jack held up his hand. 'I'm sorry, Clair,' he said. 'I'm sorry you've been dragged into this mess. She's going to write a letter? Well I'm going to write a letter,' he said, spotting the sheet of stamps I had bought from the motel clerk sticking out of my bag. He walked over and pulled them out. 'It's a sign,' he laughed. 'May I?'

'Of course,' I said. 'But, Jack—' Jack took the stamps, held up his hand, and walked out the door, leaving me alone with Mike and a mountain of guilt. I sank down on the bed and looked at Mike for support. What are you waiting for? Throw me down on the bed, kiss me, get me out of this crazy estate with forlorn grooms and flying herons. Let's see if my giant condoms fit you!

'Do you think you've done him a favor?' Mike asked in a tone that conveyed he wouldn't be jumping my bones any time soon.

'What are you talking about?' I said. Mike walked over, sat down next to me, and put both of his hands in my hair.

It would have been tremendously promising, had it not been for the gut feeling that he had no intentions of going any further with me.

'Who are you?' he whispered.

'Clair,' I squeaked.

'Pretending to be Rachel—'

'Only for Jack's grandmother—'

'Pretending to write letters for Rachel—'

'How did you know?'

'Because Rachel didn't want to admit there was a ghost any more than Jack!'

'But it was upsetting her. Jack even accused her of making the noises,' I said. Mike was staring at my lips again, and his hands were still entwined in my hair. 'I had to make up the bit about the letter,' I managed to say.

'Why?' he asked, loosening his grip on my hair slightly, feeling it with his fingertips.

'He was driving that car like a maniac. He could have killed us both.' *Please kiss me. Just kiss me. I don't want to think about this anymore.*

'Which brings us to another one of your lies,' Mike said. I felt tears come to my eyes and I grabbed his wrists with my hands.

'I didn't lie about the car accident,' I said, biting back the tears. 'I thought you believed me.'

'I just don't know what to believe,' Mike said, trailing his hand along my cheek before dropping both his hands back in his own lap. I wiped my eyes, irrationally angry he couldn't see me, see how good my intentions were.

'That's not exactly my problem now is it?' I said.

'How do you know my name? And what's your plan?'

'My plan?' I said genuinely confused. 'I've actually got a friend looking for Rachel—'

'I thought you weren't friends with Rachel—'

'I'm not—'

'Then—'

'I can still help look for her. If I can get her to come here, I think I can help them straighten this out.'

'Why? Why are you getting so involved?'

'I could ask you the same question Mike *Wrench*.' Apparently, that wasn't the right thing to say. Mike frosted over like a pint glass in a freezer and moved even farther away from me on the bed that I hoped would have been rocking by now. 'Clair, I want to get close to you. I really do. But you're playing games with me. And that's the one thing I just can't stand.'

'Look who's talking,' I said, once again speaking before censoring. Mike slowly got up and walked to the door. I stood up, too, but stayed rooted to the floor, too shaky to move.

'Tell me why you changed your name,' I said.

'You see,' Mike said instead of answering. 'There you go again. If you know so much – why don't you just figure it out for yourself.'

'Mike. I didn't mean to—'

'Save it,' Mike said, and he was gone.

Daily Horoscope – Pisces

The best laid plans won't get you laid.

I was dreaming about bells. Church bells ringing in celebration of young, recently wed lovers. It was a sad, sweet sound, and when I opened my eyes and sat up in bed, I could still hear them. Only now instead of sweet and celebratory, the tones were low and fast, ringing out a warning. My heart started tripping as *gong, gong, gong* rang through the room.

If you think because I'm an empath that I'm completely immune to things that go bump in the night, think again. I loved discussing things like ghosts in the middle of the day with friends and coffee, in a removed, intellectual, any-thing-is-possible, smug, safe frame of mind. I did not, how-ever, want to hear scary bells in a strange mansion in the middle of the night. And I certainly did not want to hear—

What *was* that sound that joined it? The slapping of wood against wood. It was pounding off beat with the bells, competing in the race to scare the shit out of me.

I sat up against the headboard, pulled the covers up over my mouth, and waited for my eyes to adjust to the dark. A low, moaning sound emerged. It was the wind. It was just the wind.

Tricky how the wind was coming through the closed window. Very, very tricky.

Gong. Gong. Slap, slap. Moan. Moan. Clair. Clair. It knows my name? *Go away*, I tried to project through the room. *Go away!* I slid my eyes over to the bedside table and eyed the lamp. I just needed to scoot over in the bed and turn on the light. Ghosts hate light, don't they? Everybody knows that everything is much scarier in the dark, except sex with a stranger, which is scarier in the light, a strange, exception to the otherwise steadfast rule. Yes, most everything was better with a little light.

Go, Clair. Go to the light. Move, damn it. Move your ass over to the light. It's freezing in here. Why is it suddenly freezing in here? Clair. Slap. Slap. Gong, gong, gong, slap, slap, slap, Clair! I closed my eyes and had just revved myself up to lunge for the light when I felt fingers. Three-dimensional, bony, cold fingers touched my face. I screamed. I screamed with every ounce of breath I'd ever had in my body. The fingers went away. The gong, gong, gong went away. The slap, slap, slap went away. My name wasn't uttered again. The chill in the room was replaced by a heavy, wet warmth. It all went away, except for those who came.

Mike and Jack, Susan, Madeline, and Elizabeth were huddled in the doorway.

'I heard—' I started to say. Madeline pushed her way into the room and stood over my bed.

'Does she have any idea what time it is?' she yelled.

'You can talk directly to me, Madeline. I'm sitting right here you know,' I said.

'Mother,' Jack warned.

'She was screaming bloody murder, Jack. Has she explained yet why she was screaming bloody murder?' Elizabeth's head appeared around Madeline.

'Darling,' she said. 'Did you have a bad dream?'

'Someone—' I said, touching my neck. 'I heard—' I was stopped by the look on Jack's face. 'Rachel isn't crazy, Jack,' I said. 'I heard it, too. Noises, terrible noises in the room.' Jack looked around the room as I spoke.

'Someone is playing a hoax,' he said angrily. He whirled

around, walked over to the closet, and flung it open. We all stared at the single dress hanging in it. Jack started pawing around the inside of the closet.

'Someone has planted some type of recording,' he said. 'That has to be it.'

'Nonsense,' Madeline said. 'This girl just has an overactive imagination.'

'Rachel heard it too, Mother. Or don't you remember?' Jack yelled. 'Why do you think she's left me?'

'What exactly did you hear?' Susan asked. Everyone looked at me.

'Well,' I stammered. 'At first it just sounded like bells.'

'An angel got their wings,' Madeline said sarcastically. I hopped off the bed.

'And then it turned into a gong,' I said, advancing on Madeline, 'and then slapping noises like wood knocking together, and then I heard moaning and then I heard my name.' I was up in her face now; after facing down a ghost, I was no longer afraid of Madeline Heron. 'And then I felt cold, bony fingers touch my face!' I yelled. Madeline took a step back.

'You poor dear,' Elizabeth said, reaching out with her hand. I took it in mine. It was cold and bony. No. It couldn't have been her, could it? If so, why? Was this nothing more than a crazy old woman acting out at night?

I dropped my hand. 'I'm sorry,' I said. 'I didn't mean to wake—' I stopped. They were all dressed in night clothes, except for Madeline and Mike. The two of them were still dressed. They had been in the middle of a discussion.

'Ironic,' Susan said. 'That you'd be scared by a little ghost.'

'Why is that ironic?' Jack asked. Susan looked at me for an answer.

'Because,' I said. 'I'm a practical person. We're usually not so . . . sensitive . . . to strange noises in the night.'

'If she's through with her tantrum, I would like to go to

bed,' Madeline said. Jack was still pawing about the room, but had yet to come up with any logical explanation for the noises.

'We'll figure this out in the morning,' he said. 'Maybe you were right, Clair. I should have been more supportive when Rachel told me about the noises. I mean if it can scare a practical person like you – I can just imagine what it did to a sensitive girl like Rachel. I'd better rip up that letter and write a new one.'

'You do that, Jack,' I said. 'Tell her we're going to get to the bottom of this.' Jack nodded and kissed my cheek. One by one they left my room. Everyone that is, except Mike. We stood staring at each other.

'Are you going to be okay?' he said at last. I bit my lip and nodded, afraid that my fatigue and his kindness would reduce me to tears.

'Okay,' Mike said. 'I'll leave you alone now.'

'No,' I said with an intensity that startled us both. 'Please stay.' I walked over to him, stood on tiptoe, put my hands around the back of his neck, and kissed him. I started with a slow, gentle kiss, not wanting to scare him with years of pent-up passion. So only when I felt him kiss me back, only when he wrapped his arms around my waist and pulled me into him, only then did I press my body fully against him and start running my fingers through his hair. Only when I heard him groan did I move my hands down his chest, around his waist, over his stomach. Meanwhile, his hands were running up and down my back, and from there, exploring.

I started backing up to the bed, and he didn't miss a beat. We fell into it at the same time, and as he rolled on top of me, it flittered through my mind that mere minutes ago I had sat here with the covers pulled up over my face in pure terror, and now I was lost in pure bliss. The irony wasn't lost on me that had it not been for the terrifying noises, Mike wouldn't be on top of me right now. He rolled off of me for a second and landed so we were face-to-face, side-by-side, breathing hard and gazing into each other's eyes. He reached up and moved a strand of hair away from my mouth.

'Are you sure?' he whispered.

'Yes,' I said.

'Because I can just hold you, you know. Keep the boogie man away.' I answered him with another passionate kiss and this time my hand went straight for his pants, the bulge he couldn't hide. His hands reached out, and he teased both my nipples with his fingers. We continued to kiss through these new thrilling sensations; a whole poltergeist brigade could have come crashing through the ceiling and I wouldn't have stopped. I wanted him more than I had wanted anyone in a long time. It was hard to believe that a little less than a week ago I was drawing a heart around Jack's crotch and now I was feeling up Mike's.

He had my pajama top all the way unbuttoned and he pulled away from my kiss to lean back and look at my breasts. I always love this part, relishing the look in his eyes as he takes them in. I've always been proud of my breasts. I hoped he wasn't going to spend the same intensity and duration studying my thighs, but I've learned to feign confidence at this as well; nothing is more of a turnoff than a woman who complains about her body. Let's face it, if he's half naked and hard and you're naked and wet, he's only thinking positive things about you – so shove the negative body images off the bed!

And you can always turn off the lights. Which is exactly what I reached over to do when he grabbed my hands, pinned them down on the bed, and leaned into me. A charge of electricity zapped through me; I like my men a little on the caveman side. 'I want to see you,' he said, taking his tongue to each of my nipples. Next, his mouth trailed down my stomach, and then lower, until he was pulling off my pajama bottoms with his teeth. I was instantly grateful I hadn't worn the baggie pink underwear with green hearts. Thankfully, after getting my overnight bag back, I had switched to lacy, black panties with a satin bow. Go me! I must have known this was coming.

'God, you're beautiful,' Mike said as his mouth kissed the aforementioned black, satin bow. I arched my back and spread my legs slightly, offering him all-pass access. He gave a half growl, half laugh as his hands ran along the outside of my panties, teasing me beyond belief.

'No fair,' I said. 'You still have your clothes on.' Mike sat up and started unbuttoning his shirt.

'Allow me,' I said reaching for the buttons. His hands played along my waist as I unbuttoned him.

'So, so beautiful,' he said. 'The minute I saw you,' he added, shaking his head. I took his shirt off and let my hands run up and down his arms. I kissed him again, pushing my bare chest against his, feeling his muscles on my soft skin.

'I want you,' I said, reaching to undo his jeans.

'I want you, too,' he said, his voice catching in his throat as he wrapped his hand around my neck, kissing me into oblivion while I grappled with the button-fly on his jeans. I waited for him to come to my rescue; it had to be apparent by now that I wasn't releasing anything. And now instead of being turned on, I was cursing the inventor of the button-fly. I put both hands into it and really yanked.

'Jesus,' I said pulling for all I was worth. And then, a snap. A slight scrape. A popping sound. Metal against metal, and then a piece of glittery brilliance flew through the air like a bottle of champagne releasing its cork. I gasped as I stared down at the setting of the engagement ring; four naked prongs stared at me, a spider belly up. I wailed.

'You really do want me, don't you?' Mike said, mistaking my gasp for ecstasy.

'Oh God,' I said. 'Oh God, oh God, oh God.' I looked at the ring again, just in case in a state of presex delirium I had only imagined the diamond flying across the room. But no such luck. I was mocked by the four, angry, platinum prongs. 'Fuck,' I said. 'Fuck, fuck, fuck.' Mike growled and started to pull me back down. The look on my face stopped him. He froze with his hand reaching for me, as if he were a television actor stuck on pause.

After a few stilted seconds, Mike brought his hand down to his thick, mussed-up, ready-for-a-romp hair and ran his fingers through it. I sighed, lingering for moment on his strong chest, just lightly covered with hair – no embarrassment come summer time when we commandeered the beach and my new man whipped off his shirt. Charles had so much hair on his chest we could have made pelts for the homeless.

'That wasn't a good "fuck, fuck, fuck," was it?' Mike asked. I held up the ring, holding it steady in front of him until he realized the significance of what had just happened. 'Fuck,' he said. 'Oh fuck.' 988,968 words in the English language and, sometimes, this is the only one that will do.

Daily Horoscope – Pisces

Today you'll find a diamond in the rough or was that a rough in the diamond? We always get that one mixed up.

We sprang off opposite ends of the bed to look for the diamond. I let Mike, who was dressed, begin the search, while I regretfully threw on clothes and cast a weary look at my overnight bag. The condoms must have come with a curse. She who buys these Trojans will never ride another stallion, or some such thing. Waves of panic washed over me as I scanned the thick carpet for anything that glittered.

Breathe, Clair, just breathe. It's not here. Go to the space directly to the right of the bed and search square by square. I got on my hands and knees and started pawing the ground. After a few minutes I looked up to find Mike standing still, staring at my ass. When he caught my look, he quickly went back to examining his own square of carpet. 'They're going to kill me,' I said. 'This time, they're just going to kill me.'

'We'll find it,' Mike said encouragingly. 'It's not that big of a room. If it takes us all night, we'll find it.'

'I just can't get a break,' I said, widening my circle away from the bed. I decided to stand back against the wall and scan the room like the Bionic Woman. If only I did have x-ray vision. If only I was—

Psychic.

Angry tears came to my eyes. Luckily Mike's head was prone and gazing into the inch of space underneath the dresser. I closed my eyes and breathed in. It was time I started to tap into my abilities at will. Breathe in, breathe out. I saw the diamond in my mind's eye. Rotating, sparkling, flying. Breathe in, breathe out. Become the diamond. Become one with the diamond.

You're stuck in Levis 501 jeans. The button has you by the throat. You're ripped off your prongs. You're flying through the air. *Like the Saturn. Concentrate.* You're free! You're as free as a bird. Nobody knew what it was like to be stuck to those godawful prongs. Strangers eyeing you all the time, putting their snotty noses and stinky breath near you. Asking how many carats you are, as if size was the only thing that—

'Clair? What are you doing?' I opened one eye, startled to see Mike standing in front of me.

'I'm centering,' I snapped, irritated by the intrusion.

'I see,' Mike said. 'Is it going to take long? Because I'm not having any luck here.' I pushed past him, angry he had just destroyed my calm, psychic core. On one hand, my abilities had been even more pronounced since arriving at the Estates, on another, I had regressed. I was back to being a nine-year-old furiously scribbling down lottery numbers like I was Einstein formulating the Theory of Relativity, then changing my mind and erasing them like I was Al Capone with nothing but a pink, rubbery eraser between me and the tax man.

'If you had just helped me take off your jeans,' I yelled at Mike. 'You saw I was struggling.'

'So this is my fault?' Mike asked, following me. 'You're going to blame this on me?' I got down on the floor again and gazed underneath the bed. 'I already looked under there,' Mike said irritably. I jerked my head up to yell at him and banged it on the bed rail. I screamed in pain, as my hands went protectively to the top of my throbbing head. 'You okay?' Mike said softly.

When I'm tired or stressed, I cry. Tears, for me, are not usually about sadness, unless I'm on my period, in which case I could cry buckets over infomercials about denture cream.

But physical pain doesn't make me cry. Physical pain, such as the sharp ache that was pulsing through my noggin, made me furious. Livid. Uncontrollably angry. I stood up, clutching my head and looked around for something I could throw. 'Are you—'

'Don't touch me,' I yelled at Mike. 'Just. Leave. Me. Alone.' He backed off with his hands in the air as if I had burst into flames. A tiny, sane part of me felt sorry for him, but the angry part of me could care less. I threw myself in front of the dresser and faced my snarling mouth in the mirror. I slammed my hand down on the hairbrush quivering next to me. Luckily, Mike didn't notice it. Then the entire dresser stared to shake like a mini-earthquake. Calm down, Clair. Calm, blue waters. Calm, blue waters. I forced myself to look in the mirror.

Oh. God. That's what I looked like? No wonder men were always telling me to smile. Angry women are frightening. I took a deep breath and the dresser stopped shaking. 'I'm sorry,' I said to Mike through the mirror. 'That just really hurt.'

'I know,' he said. 'It's okay.'

'I just can't catch a break,' I said as the anger subsided and tears threatened to move in. 'I just can't catch a break.' I pounded both fists on the dresser. Something sparkly flew up and hit the mirror, like a semi on the highway sending pebbles flying into your windshield. Mike and I cried out at the same time. After bouncing off the mirror, the diamond landed right between my breasts, cradled perfectly in my cleavage. I could do nothing more than stare. Mike slowly advanced on me, and he too, simply stared.

'No fucking way,' he said at last. I started to giggle. He started to laugh. My laughter jiggled my breasts and the diamond bounced for a minute and then slowly slid down my chest and over my stomach like a slip and slide. It caught in my pajama bottoms as if it were perched on a diving board, teetering on the swimming pool that was my vagina. Mike and I howled. 'I have expensive taste in pussy,' Mike said inappropriately. I was smart enough to grab the diamond before collapsing onto him in primal, wild laughter.

It took several minutes for us to compose ourselves, step apart, and wipe the tears from our eyes. My head was still slightly throbbing and my stomach muscles had the delicious ache of the strain of laughter. As we caught our breath, I held the diamond up between us. 'I saw the whole thing,' Mike said. 'It was incredible. As soon as you pounded the dresser, it bounced up, hit the mirror – skated around the mirror without even scratching it—'

Mike and I snapped our heads to the mirror at the same time. He was right. Not a scratch. We looked at the diamond. We looked at the mirror. We looked at each other. I held the diamond up and took a step to the mirror. 'Clair,' Mike said. I closed my eye for a sec, and then before I could change my mind, I raked the diamond across the surface of the mirror. I had been keeping my eyes squeezed shut, but I heard Mike say, 'Well I'll be.'

I opened my eyes and examined the mirror. Except for a very, very faint scratch, the glass was intact. We both looked at the diamond again and spoke over each other. I said, 'He gave her a fake,' and he said, 'She gave you a fake.' We stared at each other, slowly registering each other's comments like we were an international newscast on a slight time delay.

'Rachel could have kept the real one,' I repeated to myself, mulling it over. 'Jack could have given her a fake,' Mike tested out.

'Wow,' I said.

'Wow,' Mike said.

988,968 words in the English language and, sometimes, this is the only one that will do.

Daily Horoscope – Pisces

Fake it until you make it.

We sat on my bed like two schoolgirls (an analogy I didn't share with Mike) and hashed out the scenarios. Scenario one, Rachel had given me a fake diamond to return to Jack, and she had absconded with the real one. Scenario two, Jack had pawned the real ring to finance Heron Vodka. Considering how he treated his grandmother, and it was her ring, I was hard pressed to believe he could do that.

Mike informed me that men do strange things when under pressure, and that Jack had been building up steam for the past few months over the launch of Heron Vodka. Our newly formed intimacy had loosened Mike's tongue a bit and he revealed that he and Jack had been in several rows over the financing for the project; Jack insisting they go forward, Mike adamant they couldn't afford it.

'Jack didn't want to hear that from an outsider,' Mike admitted bitterly. 'And then in complete defiance of my advice, he goes and launches the contest with the ten-thousand-dollar incentive. And between you and me, Clair, he doesn't have the money for that.'

'But this estate has to be worth millions,' I said.

'Absolutely,' Mike agreed. 'And I shouldn't be telling you this – but all of their wealth is in assets. As far as cash flow goes – this family is strapped. All the money they have goes to the maintenance and upkeep of the estate and the wine cellar. If Jack were to take ten thousand dollars away – not to mention all the advertising costs – something else has to go unpaid. We've been arguing about it for months.'

'So you think he pawned the ring?'

'It's within the realm of possibility.'

'But if Rachel has taken off with the ring, Jack and Elizabeth deserve to know.'

'And the family deserves to know if Jack did it,' Mike countered. I sighed, still clutching the phony diamond in my hand, when something else occurred to me. 'There's another possibility entirely,' I said.

'What's that?'

'Jack just recently gave me the ring back,' I said. 'Elizabeth insisted I should wear it.'

'So instead of giving you back the real one, he gave you a replacement ring?'

'Exactly. Not because he plans on pawning it – just because he doesn't want his fake fiancée wearing the family jewels.'

'Fake fiancée, fake ring,' Mike said. I looked at the ring bitterly.

'He could have told me, you know,' I sulked. 'Just so I didn't panic if anything happened.' The more I thought about it, the angrier I became. 'I'm doing him a favor,' I said, getting off the bed and pacing. 'You think it's been easy for me stuck with his crazy family? Putting up with Madeline and Susan and not being able to get a decent night's sleep because of . . . of whatever the hell is going on in this house? And he thinks I'm doing all of this to steal his precious diamond?'

'Clair,' Mike said gently.

'I returned the ring,' I cried. 'Doesn't anybody get that? If I wanted to steal the ring, why would I come all his way to return it?' Mike came up to me and pulled me into a hug.

'We don't know which scenario it is,' he said. 'Don't

forget, Rachel could have the real ring. Don't jump to any conclusions.'

'So what do we do now?' I said, hugging Mike back, thrilled I finally had someone on my side, someone to help me navigate the insanity.

'We get some superglue and we sleep on it,' Mike said. I stared at him. 'For the ring you nut,' Mike clarified. I was half relieved, half disappointed.

After Mike returned with superglue (looking like a proud cat delivering a mouse on the doorstep of its master), Mike and I spent what was left of the night in each other's arms. Neither of us made another attempt at sex. We were way too beat, way too preoccupied with our latest mystery; the possibilities of the ring had turned us into Nancy Drew and Ned Hardy.

I was preoccupied for another reason. Why hadn't I known the ring was a fake, why hadn't I felt it? I couldn't stand the possibility that Jack switched the ring because he didn't trust me. My mind filled what little was left of the night with a nightmare.

I was at the engagement dinner, sitting at a huge table festooned with gleaming gold platters piled with meats and other delectable morsels illuminated by candlelight. I was basking in the glow of the attention of being the bride-to-be, drinking champagne and staring into Jack's eyes across the table. He had been mesmerized by me all evening; we only pried our eyes away from each other long enough to chat with Grandmother Heron, who wasn't old at all anymore, she didn't look a day over thirty. My grandmother, also young and beautiful, sat next to her.

Suddenly, just as we had raised our glasses in a toast, Madeline Heron literally flew into the room with the wings of a blue heron, carrying a huge silver tray covered with a large gleaming lid. She hovered in front of me with beady, glowing eyes and in slow motion lifted the lid and let go of the platter so that it landed with a thud directly in front of me. I was struck first by the smell, the intoxicating scent of juicy, succulent, roasted turkey. It wasn't.

It was my head on a platter; my eyes were gouged out, two diamonds sparkling up at me from where they should have been. 'Cubic zirconium,' I whispered, looking into my engaged eyes. 'Fucking cubic zirconium.'

Mike snuck out of my room before the sun even filtered in through the linen curtains. We agreed to meet in the kitchen over coffee and discuss the situation with the ring.

I took my time getting ready, stretching on the sunlit bed like a cat, curling up, hugging the pillow, enjoying the feel of a permanent smile on my face. It never ceases to amaze me how unpredictable life is. Just a few days ago I was twirling around Jack's wine cellar making a fool of myself over him, and now here I was slightly crazy about Mike. Okay, more than slightly, but I was going to be cautious. But despite the diamond popping off his pants, last night was incredible. And now I could focus on helping Jack without any worry of a crush getting in the way.

My thoughts turned to Rachel as I tried to get a read on her. Either she had used me to break up with Jack so she could take off with the real ring while everyone was abuzz at her disappearance, or she had been a victim of a possible poltergeist, and Jack's insensitivity. And if that were the case, and she still loved Jack, I owed it to her to help her out.

By the time I dressed and made my way to the kitchen table, Mike was waiting for me with two steaming cups of coffee. Jack, Madeline, and Susan apparently always ate in the formal dining room so Mike and I had agreed to meet at the kitchen table, the hub of the preparations for this evening's dinner party. And even though it was only eight A.M., things were in full swing. The smell of roast and potatoes and something heavy and sweet filled the air. I sipped on my coffee and Mike and I smiled at each other like mental patients on their first outing.

'You look beautiful,' he said.

'You do, too,' I answered. I wanted to touch him. I wanted to take his hand, lead him up the winding staircase to my room, and throw him on my bed. He was wearing soft gray dress pants; they'd be much easier to remove. Besides, now that I knew I was wearing a superglued fake, I didn't have to worry how I treated the ring. Mike saw me looking at it and took my hand.

'So we have some detective work to do,' he said. 'I figured I'd start with Jack.' The thought made me uneasy. Jack was already slightly jealous of Mike, and I didn't want to be responsible for fanning the flame.

'I don't think that's a good idea. Not tonight.'

'Why not?'

'It's his engagement party, remember? I just think he's going through enough already.' Mike put his coffee cup down. It clanked on the thick pine table and sloshed over the edge. 'Jack, Jack, Jack,' he said. 'He certainly does have a way with the ladies.'

'This isn't about me and Jack—'

'Oh, it's you and Jack, now, is it? I didn't realize there *was* a you and Jack. Except of course you standing in for the bride and all.'

'Mike—'

'Forget it. I understand. He's charming.'

'I'm not interested in Jack,' I said. 'I mean at first maybe – but he's really in love with Rachel and—'

'Oh. So I'm second choice, huh? Funny. Seems to be my lot in life.'

'That's not what I said—'

'Well it's certainly not what you said last night—'

'Michael.' I took his hand and made him look me in the eye. 'I'm not pursuing anything with Jack.'

'She says, carefully crafting her words.'

'What?'

'You're not pursuing anything with Jack. Funny how you didn't say you weren't interested in Jack.' I looked away from him, watching the women at the kitchen counter in various stages of chopping, stirring, and chatting. To our left three men were unpacking boxes of tablecloths and candles, and a florist was busy wrestling with oversized vases and fresh flower arrangements. I didn't like Mike's sudden display of jealousy.

'I just think we need to get through this evening,' I said. 'Tomorrow we can get everybody in one room and confront them at the same time.'

'You've got to be kidding me.'

'No, I'm serious. It's the only way to do it. Let them argue among themselves about the ring and Rachel. I should have done it a long time ago. I'm going to tell them everything,' I said, looking directly at Mike.

'Everything?' he asked, leaning in. 'You're going to tell them about me?' His voice cracked as he stirred his coffee into a cyclone. The image of a chessboard rose in my mind. I had to answer very carefully; there were right and wrong answers to this question. Wrong move, checkmate.

'I'm only speaking to them about myself,' I said carefully. 'If you have things you want to say to them – that's your matter entirely.'

He looked away, but the relief in his face and body were obvious. What was he hiding? Was he the one after their money? Was it at all possible that he had taken the ring for himself? Was he setting me up? I was pondering all of this when he reached across the table and took both my hands in his.

'I'm sorry, Clair,' he said. 'I've been a total jerk. I'll admit – when I'm crazy about someone, I get a little jealous,' he said with a self-deprecating laugh. 'And even though I have no idea how you found out, you've kept my secret this far – you've never given me any reason not to trust you. Can you forgive me?' He leaned across the table and kissed me before I could answer. I was back to wanting to drag him upstairs. His kiss was familiar and strange, his hands on me right and wrong, the connection electric and frayed, as I chastised myself for feeling like this while momentarily losing myself in his lips.

'Ahem.' Mike broke off first and acknowledged Anderson, who had appeared behind my chair.

'How do you do that?' I cried. But he wasn't looking at

me; he was studying Mike who, I couldn't help but notice, was looking anywhere but at Anderson. Finally Anderson fastened his penny-eyes on me.

'Your guests are here,' he said with a slight bow. Mike's lips hardened at the gesture, but there was no time to decipher his reaction. Brian was here!

I was so happy at the thought of seeing a friendly face, I didn't register that Anderson had said 'guests' until I was racing across the lawn, making a beeline for the unfamiliar car parked in the driveway. The sight of Brian's lanky form bent over the trunk filled me with joy. For a second. Because if my eyes weren't deceiving me, emerging from the back seat was my sister, Abby, followed by none other than my stalker. I squinted and sure enough I could make out Terri's piercings gleaming in the sun. I was back to wanting to kill Brian.

What kind of friend gives your stalker a ride right to you? I was going to have to return to the project of finding new and exciting ways to torture him. But not now, now I was so relieved to have company in the loony bin that I wasn't going to let my irritation show.

'Brian!' I said, going in for a hug. He wasn't really the touchy-feely sort, so I got the preemptive pat on the back. Next I turned to my sister, who was gaping at the mansion. 'Abby, what a surprise,' I said, trying not to sound horrified at her presence. 'How did this happen?' I asked, throwing a psychic dart into Brian's chest. Brian coughed slightly.

'Abby and Terri showed up at my booth looking for you,' Brian said with an apologetic smile. 'When they heard about your plight, they insisted on coming along.'

'My plight?' I stammered. Terri bodyslammed me with a hug.

'Are you okay?' She pulled back and raked her charcoal-lined eyes over me. 'You look fine,' she said accusingly. 'Did you at least have an out-of-body experience?'

'Brian?' I said.

'Clair. You were in a car accident. They were worried.'

'Oh,' I said. 'That's really sweet.' Maybe I had been too

harsh on those two. Maybe I should be nicer to them.

'No offense, darling,' Terri continued, 'but didn't you see it coming?'

'Clair never gets the big things,' Abby offered. 'She's not that good.' Or maybe I should kill them. If I remembered right, there was plenty of room in the trunk of the Saturn.

'Mom is freaking out,' Abby added. 'You'd better call home.'

'Speaking of which – is that your rental car?' Brian asked accusingly, pointing at the intact Saturn.

'Yes,' I said, burning with shame and confusion once again. 'It's a long story. Where's Rachel?' I asked. I had been so excited, I had forgotten all about her.

'I tried, Clair,' Brian said. 'I really did. Her mother said she didn't want to speak to anyone. I left her a message though – told her we were going to investigate the gho—'

I clapped my hand over his mouth and glared at him. 'You weren't supposed to tell anyone that,' I whispered harshly. Luckily Abby and Terri were chatting away, oblivious to our conversation.

'Why don't we all go in,' I said, turning to Abby and Terri. 'I'm sure Anderson will be happy to fix us tea.'

'Anderson?' Brian asked.

'The butler.'

'Of course.' He gave me a funny look. Yes, when this weekend was over, he was definitely going in the trunk.

After leaving Abby and Terri under Anderson's watchful eye, I took Brian out to the fish pond where we sprawled on the bricks with mimosas, and I told him everything. He stared at the chubby, golden koi as he listened to my story. I didn't leave anything out. I told him about the car flipping and flying, the blue heron, hitching a ride with the gardeners, getting a new outfit from Anderson that just happened to fit me perfectly, falling asleep at the pond and falling in love with Jack at first sight (there was no use denying this, Brian would have accused me of it anyway), trying on the diamond ring and not being able to get it off, telling an imaginary Jack that I loved him while the real Jack listened on, being mistaken for Rachel by Jack's grandmother – everything. I even told him about my strange dreams, and most disturbing of all, the fact that I could no longer tell the difference between words in my head and the things I said out loud.

Brian listened to all of it without commenting; the story poured out of me in vivid details. I talked about Mike and Rachel and how I couldn't figure out how they fit into this strange picture, I mentioned Heron Estates being in financial trouble – Brian was such a good listener, I just kept talking. The only thing I left out was the bit about me and Mike. I certainly didn't tell him about almost sleeping with him, and I also left out the discovery of the ring being a fake, and Mike's mysterious name change. As much as I wanted Brian's take on the whole thing, I wasn't going to break my promise to Mike. And the fewer people who knew about the ring for now, the better.

'You can see why I was desperate to have you here,' I said when there was only a little bit of breath left in my body. I sat back and waited for a good dose of sympathy. I waited for my good friend Brian to tell me I wasn't going insane. Instead he rolled over and yelled, 'I thought it would be me.'

'You thought what would be you?' He rolled back toward me and glared at me. 'Did you drag me all the way out here to brag? Is that it?'

'What?'

'The vivid dreams, the clairaudience, the symbolism – this is rich, this is powerful stuff. Your psychic abilities are skyrocketing! You know I've always wanted to develop my psychic powers – way more than you ever have – this sucks! My life totally sucks.'

I bit my tongue. On the one hand I wanted the pity I deserved, on the other I knew this was a sensitive topic for Brian and I had to tread lightly. It was true that while he always wanted to be the next Edgar Cayce, or John Edward, I didn't have the slightest desire to see dead people or sketch mass murderers for overweight police officers with an attitude.

'Brian – right now I'd like to focus on more immediate things. Like the fact that I just imagined being in a *car accident*. What psychic have you ever heard of who truly thought they flipped their car upside down?'

'None,' Brian said reverently.

'Brian, I'm telling you my car flipped. *I crawled out of it*. But you saw it – there isn't a scratch on it!'

'Powerful stuff,' Brian repeated. Now I was really angry. Done walking on eggshells.

'Brian,' I yelled, 'have you considered the possibility that I'm going completely insane?'

'Yes,' he said, 'I've considered it. Many, many times.'

'Brian!'

'Clair, calm down. You should be happy you weren't really in a car accident.'

'But I was. You're not listening to me. I'm telling you that car flipped upside down.' I couldn't stay sitting any longer. I got up and started to walk away. I didn't look back, although I knew Brian would follow me. Even though we weren't dating, had never dated, never would date – Brian was still a guy. He'd follow out of guilt.

'I'm sorry, I'm sorry, I'm sorry,' he said a few minutes later, catching up to me on the path in the woods. 'You're right. A lot of strange things have happened to you in a short period of time. You're freaked out. I completely understand.'

'You do?'

'I don't mean I understand what's going on – because it's all just . . . weird – but I understand how you feel. And we're going to figure this out together.'

'Thank God.' But no sooner had I expressed relief then my body was filled with a feeling of cold, liquid dread. It was like being embalmed alive. 'Something is terribly wrong,' I said, stopping in the path. 'Something to do with Rachel.' Brian shook his fists admiringly.

'I told you – your psychic radar is off the charts!'

'What aren't you telling me, Brian?'

'Why don't you close your eyes and try to concentrate—'

I grabbed him by his collar and yanked him to me. My fight with Susan had given me a taste for blood. 'Just tell me,' I growled.

'Fine. But I have to tell you – I'm very attracted to you right now.'

'Brian,' I screeched.

'Whew,' he said. 'Attraction gone.' I concentrated all my energy on intimidating him.

'Okay, okay,' he said. 'I actually did speak with Rachel,' he admitted with a nervous laugh.

'And?' I asked, suddenly relieved and inexplicably nauseous at the same time.

'And you're not going to like what she had to say.'

Daily Horoscope – Pisces

The Rectillions Are Coming!

If you must know, Ed, the-one-I-thought-would-stick, left me. I knew it was coming. We started off the second year of our marriage fighting about my career. He didn't want me telling anyone, especially acquaintances of his, what I did for a living. When we first met he found me exotic, exciting, intoxicating. That wore off pretty quickly, and he wanted me to 'grow up.' I think he imagined me working as a psychoanalyst, wearing high heels and sexy business skirts to work, crossing my legs, chewing on a pencil, and solving other people's problems by listening to their words and childhood tragedies instead of reading their thoughts and auras.

Our marriage ended on a Saturday. Ed's best friend, Johnny, was in town, so I felt safe sneaking off to a psychic fair being held at an old warehouse in downtown Chicago. Instead of working the fair, I had decided to participate in workshops, sharpen my skills. I wonder if Ed and I would have stayed together if I had attended the seminar on auras or the class on remote-viewing instead. Would we be celebrating our tenth anniversary if he had come into the workshop to find me meditating or trying to levitate a penny? Would that have been okay with him? Not too crazy? Would he have taken me home, raced me to bed, and guided my head down to attend to him as he often did?

I'll never know. For the workshop I had decided to attend was a lecture on the ancient Egyptian pyramids. I loved Egypt and anything to do with the magical powers of the pyramids, so I eagerly crossed telekinesis off my list and headed for the pyramid lecture. I had no idea what I was in for, nor did I realize I had left a flyer for the psychic fair on our dining-room table.

The classroom was jam-packed. At the head of the class was a tall, bronze, Californian hunk standing at a table filled with crystals and miniature pyramid structures made out of gold. Blue eyes smiled at me from a tanned, handsome face, and I flushed as I took my seat. His eyes lingered on my legs as I crossed them. Suddenly, he whipped a quartz crystal from the pile and handed it to me. It was shaped like a penis.

'Healing powers,' he said. 'You're going to need it.' Embarrassed, I tucked the crystal in my pocket as he started passing out the pyramids. I examined my pyramid, turning over the 3-D structure, waiting to be mesmerized by stories of the power of the pyramids, mysterious curses, and astrological observatories in the tips of the structures, where it was rumored they could calculate the coordinates of various constellations with eerie accuracy.

I heard the crowd murmuring and looked up from the pyramid in my hands. But instead of holding them and waiting to be entertained like I was, they were all wearing the miniature pyramids on their heads. The Californian instructor looked at me and waited. One by one the participants of the workshop turned their heads – gently like they were carrying books on their heads – and waited for me to follow suit. I succumbed to peer pressure, and placed the pyramid on my head.

'What doesn't the government want you to know?' the Californian hunk shouted. I tilted my head and my pyramid toppled into my lap.

'Rectillions,' the audience shouted as I quickly picked

it up and put it on again. I wondered what in the hell a Rectillion was.

'Rectillions!' the Californian boomed again. 'The government has known about the Rectillions for over fifty years.' He started pacing back and forth, back and forth, and miraculously, the pyramid moved with him. He stopped suddenly.

'How many of you,' he said, his face glistening with sun and sweat. 'How many of you have seen their crafts?' Not daring to move my head, I slid my eyes around the room. Several hands had shot up. 'How many of you,' he said, picking up speed and intensity, 'have seen their glowing red eyes?' I slid down in my seat. Several other hands shot up. 'How many of you,' he said, stopping right in front of my seat and staring into my eyes, 'have been abducted?' He continued to stare at me. He bent down; we were eye-to-eye, pyramid-to-pyramid. 'What about you, Sister,' he said. 'Have you ever been abducted? Stolen, questioned, probed?'

And in that instant, I decided to play along. Partly for my own amusement, partly because *his* eyes were glowing red and I was slightly terrified of him, and partly because he was – after all – representing his mother ship, Los Angeles, California. He had to put on a spectacle worthy of Shirley MacLaine, and his crystal-healing, beaded, sun-fried, Birkenstock, alf-alfa sprouted, astral-projectionist friends, didn't he? And who was I to let down the RSA, or Rectillion Society of America, as I learned them to be? If I had learned anything from my supernatural experiences, it was live and let live. Judge not, least you should be judged.

And besides, it wasn't like he was shoving Nike tennis shoes on my feet and forcing poisoned Kool-Aid down my throat. Whether it was sarcasm, fear, or simply peer-pressured mass hysteria, I heard him asking me again, through rhythmic shouts, if I had been, 'Stolen! Questioned! Probed!' And suddenly, like being swept up in a massive wave that rips off your bikini top and throws you to the beach in front of the starting line of the football team,

I found myself shouting, 'Abducted yes!, Questioned yes!, Beaten, fingered, and probed, yes, yes, yes!'

The crowd cheered and clapped, offering me hankies and passing me business cards with the names of lawyers, and newspapers, and florists. I was the star. I looked up, flushed, proud that the pyramid still rested squarely on my head.

Ed was standing in the doorway with his best friend, Johnny.

They, too, looked as if they had been abducted, questioned, and probed. Especially probed. Later, Ed would kindly mumble, 'Irreconcilable differences,' whenever anyone asked him why we had parted ways.

Rectillions. Fucking Rectillions.

I hadn't felt that horrified in a long time. Until now. Now, standing in front of Brian, waiting for him to elaborate about whatever it was Rachel had to say, I felt the same feelings of shame and dread dancing in my veins. I could just go home. I didn't need to stay involved in these people's lives. Whatever Rachel had to say to Brian, I knew – I just knew it wasn't going to be good.

'What did she say, Brian?' I dared to ask when he didn't venture the information on his own.

'Just don't shoot the messenger,' Brian said, throwing up his hands like I had him at gunpoint.

'Sorry, but I'm leaving that option open,' I answered. Brian squinted at me and shook his head.

'Well first she said you predicted her marriage to Jack would be a disaster – the worst mistake she could ever make.'

'And?'

'You mean it's true?'

'We've been through this Brian – she forced me to—'

'Whoa, whoa. We have not been through this. You said Rachel freaked out on you for no reason—'

'She told me what to say in the reading, Brian. It was all a setup so Susan would overhear and Rachel could feel justified in running off.'

'And you *agreed* to it?'

'She threatened to kill herself at the wedding.'

'Really?'

'Yes, really – I told you all of this. And she said that right before she pulled the trigger, she'd say my name.'

'Say your name?'

' "*Clair Ivars has my blood on her hands*," was her exact quote.'

'Huh. How was she going to enunciate all that with a gun in her mouth?' I glared at him, refraining from telling him I had thought the exact same thing down to the word *enunciate*, but this wasn't time to inflate his psychic ego.

'What aren't you telling me? What else did she say, Brian?'

'She said she wanted to get married, fully intended to do it – but you – *putacurseonher*.'

'Brian, you're mumbling. What did you just say?'

'She said you *putacurseonher*.'

'She said I *put a CURSE on her*?'

'Shhhh, do you want the entire estate to hear you?'

'She said I PUT A CURSE ON HER?'

'Yes, yes, that's what she said. She said you put a curse on her and the wedding.'

Every job has its misconceptions; every job gets its share of slander, jokes, or labels. Take, for example, Insurance carrier, policeman, fireman, whore: bottom-feeder, donut-eater, pole-slider, pole-slider.

For us psychics, we're either quacks, fakes, or witches. That's right folks, step right up, call us a witch, burn us at the stake. No offense to Wicca, but I'm not a card-carrying member. I don't have spells, potions, herbs, voodoo dolls, or rabbit tails. I may curse the occasional date from hell, but that's simply being a woman – not a practicing witch – and I've never paid for a neon blinking sign or a 1-800-FUTURE phone number or been a card-carrying member of the psychic network.

'I can't believe she said that,' I said, clenching my fists. 'She's going to ruin my reputation.'

'You don't have a reputation.'

'That's not—'

'Nobody even knows you exist.'

'Gee thanks, Brian.'

'No problem.'

Apparently, my sarcasm had flown right past him like a Wiccan on a Hoover. I was about to grill Brian for more information, when I became aware of a shadow hovering over us. Brian realized he was there first and to my amusement, screamed and jumped like he was being prodded by a golf club in a lightning storm. 'How long were you standing there?' he asked Anderson in awe. Anderson blinked slowly, like a mastodon turtle squinting in the sun, and when he was finished looking through Brian, he turned to me.

'Madam, Elizabeth Heron requests your presence in her room,' he said.

'*Remains of the Day!*' Brian shouted. 'Has anyone ever told you you look like Anthony Hopkins?'

Anderson gave him the turtle glare again and didn't bother with a response. 'Shall we go?' he said to me.

'Certainly,' I said to Anderson. To Brian I said, 'He's more of a Mr French. Buffy and Jody?' I added when Brian didn't respond. '*Family Affair?*'

Brian covered his ears. 'Stop it, just stop.'

'What is wrong with you?'

'You're dating us,' he said. 'At least Anthony Hopkins was a cool, modern reference. God, are we really this old and still single?'

'Hey, at least I've been married three times.'

'I'll alert Elizabeth Taylor. Maybe she can squeeze in a few more to protect her record.'

All the way up to Elizabeth's room, I obsessed on Brian's revelation. I would not tolerate Rachel Morgan parading around Chicago in designer dresses telling the world I put a curse on her. Despite Brian's insistence I was a nobody, I *did* have a reputation to protect.

Thinking your psychic was going around putting curses

on people would be like finding out your accountant was embezzling money, or your personal chef was poisoning the soufflé. Here I was trying to help her, okay not purely altruistic, but still, I had returned the ring like she asked – and in return she was going to desecrate my career? I couldn't believe I had almost tried to get them back together. I was back to believing Jack really was better off without her. Yes. I had done him a huge favor and, furthermore, she had probably kept the real ring all along. That's what all this was about; she had kept the real diamond and I was the psychic scapegoat. Well, we'd just see about that.

I was dying to tell Mike about this latest development; I decided I would talk to him as soon as I was finished visiting Elizabeth. And as soon as I could, I'd call Dame Diaphannie, the Queen of Psychic Gossip. If she had wind of this 'curse' rumor, I was going to have to do major damage control.

I reached Elizabeth's door, put my hand on the knob, and felt heat burn into my palm. I pulled it away and turned my hand over. A red blister formed and burned, and then slowly disappeared. I reached out for the knob again. This time it felt normal. I turned it and opened the door.

Daily Horoscope – Pisces

Someone will let you down today.

I wasn't prepared for the scene that accosted me when I entered Elizabeth's room. Abby and Terri were sitting on her bed, drowning in dresses. I almost didn't recognize them. For one thing, they were smiling. I hadn't seen Terri smile ever, and I had to say, it suited her. Her normally sharp, contemplative face was soft and glowing and I had never noticed the flecks of yellow in her hazel eyes. For a stalker, she was suddenly very likeable. And Abby looked positively beautiful. She was a blue-eyed blonde, like Rachel, who could light up a room if she so desired. I normally didn't see this kind of smile on her unless there was a single man in the vicinity. And unless she was hot for Anderson, the thought of something or someone else was making her very, very happy.

Foolishly, I convinced myself it was the pile of dresses that lay between them like a mound of freshly raked leaves, primed for the jump. Elizabeth was propped up near the headboard, watching Abby and Terri like they were her long-lost daughters getting ready for the prom. 'Hello,' I said.

'Clair!' Abby cried. 'Look at us.'

'I'm looking,' I said. 'What are you doing?'

'Did you ever think you'd see me doing this?' Terri laughed. 'I mean even you couldn't have predicted I could be such a girly-girl, could you?' she accused me. I glanced at the frilly pink and green dress she was holding just below her chest tattoo of a Rottweiler crushing a heart in its massive, drooling jaws.

'You got me there,' I said.

'Here, here,' Elizabeth said, patting the space on the bed beside her. 'I have just the dress for you, too.'

'I feel like Cinderella going to the ball,' Abby said dreamily. 'Maybe your prediction will finally come true tonight, Clair. Maybe I'll meet my future husband.'

'And I'll win the contest,' Terri chimed in.

'Terri,' I warned.

'You must be happy you have your prince already,' Elizabeth cried, clutching my hand. Abby's smile slammed shut.

'What prince?' she demanded, turning to Elizabeth. I tried to catch Abby's eye and warn her to shut up, but unlike me, subtleties weren't her forte. 'She's been married *three* times,' Abby prattled on. 'And she's six years younger than me.'

'Well I just know this one will last,' Elizabeth said dreamily.

'Well, she'd better elope then,' Abby said. 'Because three hideous bridesmaid dresses are my limit.'

Daily Horoscope – Libra

You were born first! Your parents love you the best!

I have to stop here and explain that my sister was exaggerating. First of all, my first wedding was at a Justice of the Peace and she wore purple leg warmers. At my second wedding she wore black – complete with a veil covering her face like she was a widow. She said she was *mourning my choice* and refused to lift her dark veil the entire evening. To his credit, Charles took it in his stride; the one benefit of having a pot fiend as a husband was his slow, calm reactions to everything and anyone that was ever thrown at him. When it comes to my family, a little pot can go a long way. And finally, for my third wedding she wore her prom dress and slept with Ed's best man. Which has nothing to do with the dress, I just felt like tattle-telling on the little slut.

I approached the bed like one would advance upon a wild tiger. I loved my sister and wanted to spend time with her, but she had the glint in her eye she gets when she's on a mission. My sister's entire goal in life was to bag a husband, and somehow I was being held directly respon-sible for her deficiency in this area. You'd think the fact that I couldn't even get my own love life sorted out would have dissuaded her from using me as a matchmaker. It hadn't. And every year that went by with her sans husband made her edgier, more demanding, and, frankly – slightly crazy.

'Wait right here, darling,' Elizabeth said, heading out of the room. 'I'll get your dress.'

'I forbid you to get married again, Clair,' Abby said, shaking a blue taffeta dress at me like it was a magic wand. 'I'm the next one getting married. And I have a very strong feeling that man is close by,' she added, challenging me with a look. 'Or do you think you're the only one allowed to get premonitions?'

I suddenly wished I really did have the power to put a curse on someone. Instead I concentrated on not reacting to Abby's comment. At the moment she was waiting for me to give any indication that she was right, that I didn't believe in her intuition the way I believed in mine. But she had never worked on hers, just like I never practiced the piano. Growing up, you could count on at least once a year Abby throwing a fit over my abilities.

'Don't worry, Abby – I have no intention of getting married again,' I said right before Elizabeth came back into the room.

'Here you are, my dear. Does it look familiar?' I stared at the dress Elizabeth was holding up like it was the torch and she was the Statue of Liberty. In fact, I had seen it twice. Once in a dream, and more recently on her. The Victorian wedding dress. 'Try it on,' she said with a gleam in her eye.

'Is this like one of those surprise celebrity weddings?' Terri exclaimed. 'You know. You think you've been like – just invited to this rich BBQ where everyone wears Prada flip-flops and suddenly it's all – surprise! We're getting married. Betcha wish you had brought more than that bean spread, don't ya darlin'!'

We all stopped and looked at Terri. I spoke first. 'First of all,' I said, 'you weren't even invited. Second of all, I'm not a celebrity—'

'And third – you are not getting married,' Abby finished. 'Right? Right? Tell me – tell me this second that you are not getting married.'

'I'm not getting married,' I shouted. Then I noticed Elizabeth's crest-fallen, beautiful face.

'It's beautiful Elizabeth,' I said, gesturing to the dress. 'But tonight is just the engagement party, remember?'

'Engagement party?' Abby cried. And then, she spotted the rock on my hand.

And then, the blood-piercing screams began.

'Abby,' I yelled when I felt brave enough to remove my hands from my eardrums. 'Abby stop screaming.' I pulled her to the other side of the room. 'I didn't have time to tell you,' I whispered. 'But Elizabeth thinks I'm Rachel.'

'Who's Rachel?' Abby yelled, seconds from hyperventilating.

'Shhh. Rachel is Jack's fiancée,' I said. 'It's a long story – suffice it to say that I'm pretending to be her – just for tonight.' Terri had sidled over and was listening to our conversation. Elizabeth was still clutching the dress, waiting for me to put it on.

'You had better be telling the truth,' Abby yelled.

'Of course she's telling the truth,' Terri said. 'Clair is the most honest person I've ever met.'

'Well looks like the apple fell from the tree,' Abby huffed. 'Because impersonating a – a . . . Rachel – is not a very honest thing to do.'

'It's for a good cause,' I said, herding Abby and Terri to the door. 'Now would you give me a few minutes alone with Elizabeth so I can straighten out this dress fiasco?' As soon as they were gone I turned to Elizabeth and smiled. 'I can't wear that tonight, Elizabeth. I'm sorry. It's a beautiful dress but—'

'But it's old-fashioned. I know, it was just a thought.'

'Again – it's beautiful and if the wedding were tonight I'd be happy to wear it—'

'You would?'

'Absolutely. But remember, Elizabeth, tonight is just the engagement party.'

'I forgot. I get mixed up sometimes.'

'That's okay,' I said, kissing her on the cheek and heading for the door.

'I know why I got mixed up,' Elizabeth suddenly exclaimed. 'The wedding planner is coming today.' I stopped just as my hand was on the knob.

'The wedding planner?'

'Did you forget? Three o'clock in the greenhouse.'

'In the greenhouse?'

'Madeline conducts all business transactions in the heat.'

'I see.'

'Don't let her take over, darling. It's your wedding. You have to finalize all of the decisions.'

'Well I'm sure—'

'Cake, flower, dress, bridesmaids' dresses – it all has to be finalized today.'

A six-layer chocolate fudge cake with raspberry filling and fluffy cheese cream icing adorned with fake pink roses on top while real pink roses are stacked in between each layer like necklaces on a princess, soft shimmery pale pink satin bridesmaids' dresses, piles and piles of Cala Lilies—

'Do you think you could tell her you'll be wearing this dress?'

Vera Wang, Vera Wang, Vera Wang—

'Absolutely,' I said, lost in wedding land. 'Absolutely.'

I floated out of the room, trailing my hand along the banister, and as I gracefully descended the winding staircase, I imagined myself in that Vera Wang gown smiling at my guests who waited below, gorgeous women in beautiful gowns, handsome men in tuxedos, all lifting their golden champagne flutes while violins serenaded our happiness. I stopped on the stairs in the middle of the fantasy, wondering who I was marrying. Like many brides, I hadn't given much thought to that part of the equation. It's way easier to pick out china, cakes, and flowers than find a man with whom you can get along for six months let alone 'til death do you part.

I suddenly wanted to find Mike and finish what we started the other night. I wanted to unleash myself on him shamelessly. Weddings always made me crave sex. Until they were over of course, in which case I usually dried up like a stream in a Californian drought. Strange but true. Might as well strike while the iron's hot. *He's in the study*. I didn't argue with the voice, I simply headed for the study. Four steps from the closed door and something strange happened. My feet could barely move, as if the hall were filled with quicksand.

Underneath the stairs is a hiding nook. You can hear better in there. Sure enough, there was a tiny door in the stairs, a small storage place, the perfect hideout. I squatted down and opened the door, not even sure I'd fit.

Luckily, no one had seen the necessity to store anything under there and I fit quite nicely. It shared a common wall with the study and through the cracks I could make out two people standing close, speaking in low tones. I plastered myself against the wall and eavesdropped.

'I want her to leave.' Madeline. Talking about me no doubt.

'We've already been through this.' Mike. He's standing up for me!

'She's stirring up trouble. Disturbing a senile old woman.'

'Madeline, calm down.'

'How can I calm down? She's going to ruin everything.'

'I told you, I'm keeping an eye on her.' Keeping an eye on me? He'd kept quite a few other things on me as well.

'After all this time she comes out of her room. Now, of all times!'

'Madeline, don't be so harsh.'

'I am harsh. You'll have to accept that about me.' There was an intimacy to their conversation that went way beyond business. I felt my stomach curl. 'At least the ring is out of her grubby little hands.' Wet cement poured down my throat and hardened in my lungs.

'Madeline—'

'Michael,' Madeline interrupted. 'I'm sorry. I hate you seeing me like this. I can be, soft, too. You know?'

'I know,' Mike said gently.

'And – I love you. I love you.'

The cement broke into little pieces and spread to all my vital organs. 'I know,' Mike said. 'I love you, too.' I watched them embrace through the tiny cracks of the wall, the tiny cracks inside me.

I love you, too.

I stayed on all fours, trying to breathe. Mystery of the ring solved. I thought of how surprised Mike pretended to be when we found out the ring was a fake. How quick he had been to make me suspicious of Jack. Once again, I had been a fool. Once again, I had fallen for the wrong man.

I love you. I love you, too. I have to say, I didn't see that coming. I will not cry, I will not cry, I will not cry. I almost made love to this guy. The way he touched me, the way he looks at me – he . . . he couldn't possibly be in love with Madeline – he was worming his way into this family, using her to get to—

Do not cry! He's not really in love with Madeline. It's

preposterous. Then he's after money. He's a gigalo. Does that make you feel better, Clair? He loves you, but you aren't worth millions.

But he said they didn't have any money. It's all tied up in assets, isn't that what he said. Still, he could be after the assets. Or – maybe they do have money—

Either way, he was a parasite.

Or they were really in love.

Either option was revolting. I stayed curled in there long after I heard them leave. Then, I slowly opened the door and crawled out. And ran straight into large, black shoes.

Daily Horoscope – Pisces

Stop being so self-involved. Consider someone else's misery for a change!

It was because I was still on all fours that I saw his shoes first. Shiny and black, the right tapping away impatiently as the left pointed accusingly at my nose. My eyes traveled up the black pants, trim white shirt tucked into his waist, black fitted jacket.

'Anderson,' I said. 'This isn't what it looks like.'

'Splendid,' Anderson replied. 'Because it looks like you're crawling out of the hiding space underneath the stairs.'

'Oh,' I said. 'Well then it is what it looks like.'

'Listening in on conversations you shouldn't be privy to.' I picked myself up off the floor.

'I just like discovering new places,' I said, brushing the dirt off my body as Anderson squinted at me. 'Like the pioneers,' I added defensively.

'Perhaps I should mention this to Madeline.'

'Now why would you do that?'

'Good employees always keep the Lady of the House abreast of strange goings-on.'

'In that case,' I said, 'what do you make of all the strange noises around here at night? Is that what really drove Rachel away, or was it something – or someone – else?'

'Rachel was overexcited,' Anderson said, seemingly not batting an eye at all my accusations. 'And this is an old house—'

'Old houses make noise. Blah, blah, blah. I know old-house noises and what I heard last night was definitely not your run-of-the mill old-house noises.'

'Then what was it?' Anderson's tone, while seemingly polite, was laced with scorn.

'I haven't figured that out yet.' While I was pondering this, Anderson took me by surprise.

'I'll strike a deal with you,' he said.

'What kind of deal?'

'I won't say anything about your little hiding space—'

'It's not really my—'

'If you'll read my Tarot cards.' I stared at him, not quite believing what I had just heard. 'What?'

'You heard me.'

'How did you know?'

'The kitchen ladies like to talk.' Of course they do.

'What kinds of things are they saying?' I asked casually.

'Well you certainly lifted Hannah's spirits,' Anderson began. I thought of the young girl who didn't know how to tell her mother she was a lesbian.

'I did?' I asked greedily. Most of the times my clients took off after a reading; it was rare that I got to see the conclusion to their stories.

'Oh, yes. She's an entirely different girl. She smiles now.'

'That's so great.'

'Although rumor also has it you're responsible for the nanny being fired.'

'Oh.'

'And some even think you've something to do with Rachel's disappearance.'

'Don't these people get any work done?'

'I'm not condoning the gossip, Clair,' Anderson said piously.

'Of course not. Well, thank you for telling me.' I tried to

move around him, but when I took a step forward, he remained rooted to his spot.

'I insist you give me a reading.'

'Sure,' I said, trying to sneak around him. 'I'll read your cards sometime.' He stepped in front of me, blocking my exit strategy.

'I would like to have that reading right now.' Gee, I'd love to read your cards right now but I just found out my latest boyfriend is a liar and a cheat, pretending to be in love with an ugly old witch bent on destroying me. Rain check?

'I see,' I said when it was apparent he wasn't asking a question, he was giving an order for once in his life. 'Now it is then.'

We retreated to a quiet corner of the study and I quickly laid out the spread. I didn't know much about Anderson so it was easy to let myself go, let the cards speak through me. The Emperor told him to step up and take charge of his family. He had been hiding in the shadows, taking too much of a background role. I told him they needed him. I told him it was time he finally claimed his role as the family leader. I didn't mean this in an antifeminist, the man-wears-the-pants type of way, quite the opposite; I got the distinct impression that Anderson's voice within his family had been oppressed, squeezed shut, invalidated.

Until now I hadn't even thought of Anderson as being in love or having a family. I assumed his life was only here, at the estate, a man without an existence apart from his work. But it wasn't my job to interject myself into the reading, nor was it my place to come out and ask Anderson about his family, so I simply continued the reading. I half expected him to interrupt, to tell me that he had no one, but Anderson was all eyes, all ears, hanging on every word. I continued.

The Five of Cups shed a bit more light on things. I realized Anderson was estranged from his family. 'You long to be reunited,' I said. 'They long to be reunited. This is your job,' I insisted. Anderson gave a slight nod, and looked away. The Page of Pentacles brought us home. 'You have to stick to your guns, Anderson,' I said, laying down the card. 'The time is now. You have truth and action and justice on your side. If you want your family together – this is it. This is your last chance.' I was veering slightly from the cards now, but an insistent feeling was growing in me, pushing to get out like weeds growing through cement, wanting to reach out to Anderson and shake his reserved, immobile self to the core. 'This is the outcome,' I said, laying down the last card, The Eight of Wands. I laughed. Anderson's head jerked up. 'I'm sorry,' I said. 'It's just so concrete.'

I held up The Eight of Wands. 'Strike while the iron is hot, Anderson,' I said. 'Make your move.' I leaned in and lowered my voice. 'It's time you stop letting people walk all over you,' I said firmly. 'It's time.' A smile spread across Anderson's face as we sat with this.

Suddenly a woman was by his side. As Anderson turned to speak with the staff member, I noticed a slight change in his demeanor, how he stood slightly straighter, talked with a bit more authority. 'The wedding planner has arrived,' the woman told Anderson. 'But I can't find Madeline.' I felt my face grow hot. I knew where Madeline was, and who she was with. Anderson slowly turned to me and smiled.

'Perhaps you'd like to meet with the wedding planner, *Rachel*?' he said. 'You know. Finalize the details. The flowers. The dresses. The cake, the entrees, the music. Whatever wedding *you'd* like to have.' I was poised to say no, when I remembered. I remembered Madeline speaking to me as if I weren't in the room. Madeline manipulating the wedding, manipulating Jack, treating Elizabeth like a crazy old woman. Madeline telling Mike she loved him. I especially remembered Madeline telling Mike she loved him. A slow smile spread across my own face. Anderson had paid for his reading in full.

'I believe I would,' I said, standing up. 'I believe I would.'

I was so high after the meeting with the stunned

wedding planner, who kept stammering, 'Are you sure? Are you sure?' as she made my changes to the dress, the flowers, the music, the cake. Beads of sweat were breaking out all over her forehead. I felt sorry for her, but plunged ahead, flashing my fake ring every time she questioned my authority. I knew the moment she left she was headed for her car, to the bottle of bourbon in her glove compartment. It didn't really matter, since there wasn't going to be a wedding anyway, but it had been loads of fun, a bit of revenge, just imagining Madeline's and Rachel's faces if they were ever to find out about the replacements, the daisies instead of roses, an acoustic guitar instead of an orchestra, Elizabeth's Victorian wedding dress instead of the Vera Wang. I even changed the ice swan to an erotic statue of a couple kissing. In the end I let the fountain of champagne stay – I had a heart after all.

I was literally humming and skipping when I left the meeting, so wrapped up in my bliss that I didn't see him coming. His hands reached out for me from the shadows and pulled me into an alcove near the kitchen. He kissed me before I could formulate a thought, sent thrills down my spine before I could resist. When I did pull away, I was out of breath I couldn't stop the tears.

'Hey,' he said. 'What's wrong?'

'You,' I whispered. 'You're all wrong.' He dropped his hands from my waist, stepped back so that light from the kitchen illuminated his eyes.

'What are you talking about?' he said.

'I don't want anything to do with you,' I said.

'You don't mean that.'

I held up the ring. 'This isn't the only fake,' I said. 'You're one, too.' I walked away, my earlier happiness swept up in a tornado of hurt as Mike stared after me. Why am I'm always so blind when it comes to love? What I wouldn't give to know. Just once to look at someone and just know. And be right.

I called Rachel. As usual she didn't answer. But this time I left a message.

'Rachel, it's Clair. I've just heard from Brian that you're going around telling people I put a curse on you. And here I was about to try and help you get back together with Jack. I know all about the ghost and Jack's reaction – and I actually felt sorry for you. I was going to help you. But I've had it. Jack's a good man. And you've done your share of playing games. As far as I'm concerned you were a coward then and you're a coward now. And if you don't show up by midnight tonight – I might just take him for myself.'

I clicked the phone shut. It was time to get dressed. I had an engagement party to attend.

32

Daily Horoscope – Pisces

It's my party. I'll lie if I want to.

The appetizers came first, silver platters floating on the outstretched hands of tuxedoed waiters making their way through throngs of elegant, lively guests. Platters of crab-stuffed mushrooms, caviar, and cheese puffs sailed by, followed closely by loads and loads of champagne in crystal flutes.

Personally, I would have gone with the little plastic glasses given the number of guests, two hundred at least, and that's a modest estimate. Although after enough glasses of champagne I felt as if I were standing too close to an impressionist painting; the guests were blurring into a sea of colorful dots.

Abby, Terri, and I were standing around the gazebo in our beautiful dresses, drinking and nibbling off each and every tray that could be reached for, passed, or chased down. I was trying, in vain, to get my mind off of Mike, by way of engaging Abby in news from home.

'What about Tommy?' I asked her. 'Has anyone heard from him?' Last year, Tommy had taken off for Los Angeles, announcing his intention to finally go back to college. He was supposed to be studying economics at C-SUN, California State University, but I had my doubts. I couldn't get rid of the image of him surrounded by surfboards. So far I had kept this little tidbit to myself.

'Mmm. I think he's doing well. Mom says he loves school and is passing all his classes. Hard to imagine, isn't it?'

Surf's up, dude. 'Abby,' I said as she stared off into space.

'Hmm?'

'Who are you looking at?' Abby reluctantly dragged her eyes away from over my right shoulder and focused on me.

'Clair, I'm listening to you,' she said like a psychiatrist on a call-in radio show.

'Clair,' Terri interrupted. 'Should I show Jack my prototype before or after dinner?' A large, rolled-up canvas materialized in Terri's hand.

'Where did that come from?' I said. Terri smiled and turned around, revealing a small backpacklike apparatus slung across the back of her shoulders like a sling. She demonstrated its usefulness by sticking the rolled-up canvas through the straps. It hung from her shoulder blades to her tailbone, making her look like a self-propelled rocket.

'I made it myself,' she boasted.

'Terri. I told you again last night. You can't bother Jack about this here. You have to enter the contest like everyone else. So stick a stamp on that and—' I stopped cold. It felt as if I had just slammed into a brick wall. My head tingled and I brought my fingertips up to my forehead, gently touching the surface, probing it for a large bump or anything that might explain the sudden jolt.

'Clair?' Abby asked. 'Are you all right?'

'What was I saying?'

'She's getting drunk,' Terri exclaimed. 'I can't wait to see you drunk.'

'This is only my second glass, Terri,' I said. Abby was once again gazing over my shoulder.

'Ladies,' Brian said, popping up at my right shoulder, holding a tall, cylindrical glass of Heron Vodka. He noticed me looking at it, swirled the glass, and took a sip. 'Excellent stuff,' he purred. He leaned into my ear and whispered, 'When are we doing the séance, Clair?'

'Tell me,' Terri said, stepping right up to Brian and avoiding the two- to three-person distance we Americans are so fond of, and shoving her drawing in his face. 'What does it make you think of?' Brian stared at Terri's artistic rendering.

'It's a worm. Wearing a beret,' Brian said finally, still swirling his glass.

'Does it make you want to get drunk, darling?' Terri grilled.

'Terri,' I warned. Terri smiled, twirled her canvas by wiggling her hips, and then sauntered off into the crowd.

'What was that about?' Brian asked.

'She's illegally networking,' I said. 'And she's totally going to blow this for me.'

'She promised not to tell anyone we're psychics, Clair,' Brian said. 'Just relax. You want a sip?'

'I don't get why it's such a big secret,' Abby said. 'You've never been embarrassed about it before.'

'I'm not—'

'Not even the time the Mormons came for dinner. Remember?'

'Yes Abby—'

'Do tell,' Brian said.

'This really isn't the time or the place—'

'Clair was fifteen and she thought her psychic powers were at their peak,' she said, exaggerating the word by waving her hands in the air like she was performing a magic trick. Brian glanced at me. Abby had better watch it; she was on the verge of insulting not one, but two consummate professionals. But in the end, Brian's desire for dirt on me wore out over Abby's obvious derision over our chosen profession.

'What'd she say?' Brian's eyes were lit up like a kid's on Christmas morning.

'She told Brad Norman his fourth wife used to be a stripper—'

'Okay, Abby—'

'When she was just this mousy thing that worked at Arbys!' Abby squealed with laughter and hit me on the shoulder. 'You should have seen the look on everyone's faces.'

'Striper, okay. I meant candy striper. She volunteered in a hospital,' I explained to Brian.

'And then, our brother Tommy asked him what happened to his first three wives,' Abby continued while giggling, 'and Clair said, "Nothing happened to them, he lives with all four of them!"'

'No,' Brian squealed.

'And then – remember what you asked Dad?' Abby said as her laughter peaked and she threatened to hyperventilate.

'What? What?' Brian demanded.

'She asked him if he was going to have other wives, too.'

'She did not!'

'Right in front of our mother. You should have seen the looks on their faces.'

I gave up; once the pin is pulled on the grenade it's impossible to stuff it back in. 'And then Clair suggested Dad marry Mrs Kemp – her second-grade teacher.'

'She was a very nice woman,' I said in my defense.

'She was seventy,' Abby screeched. She and Brian fell into each other laughing.

'Looks like you're all having a good time,' Mike said, joining the group. I had never been so happy to see anyone. Neither, for that matter, had Abby. Mystery of the over-the-shoulder glances and shy smiles solved. I gave him a look, but if he noticed it, he didn't let on. 'Mike Wrench,' he said, extending his hand to my sister. He did glance at me now, as if suddenly remembering it wasn't his real last name. He held my glance until my sister's hand clamped over his.

'Abby,' she sang as she held his hand. Brian elbowed me, spilling the last of my champagne on my cleavage and down my dress. Mike glanced at the glistening spot and let go of Abby's hand.

'Nice to meet you,' he said while handing me a handkerchief. I wiped the champagne from my chest, feeling impressed despite myself; I didn't know men even carried handkerchiefs anymore. Now I didn't know what to do with it. Was I supposed to give it back? Launder it and return it with a thank-you card? Tuck it between my breasts? Mike laughed, picking up on my distress. 'You can keep it,' he said, still smiling.

'That's my sister for you,' Abby said. 'Messy.' I glanced at Abby and she raised her eyebrows at me.

'Your sister?' Mike said.

'She came along with my friend Brian,' I explained.

'Ah. Nice of you to rescue her from the likes of us,' Mike said. 'Clair's had quite the time here.' When he looked at me again, we held eye contact. Abby's arm snaked underneath his and she pulled him toward her.

'Would you mind showing me around?' she asked, batting her eyelashes so hard I was sure they were going to fall off. He was still looking at me when she dragged him away.

'Oh my God,' Brian said, turning his x-ray vision on me. 'I thought you liked Jack?'

'What are you talking about?'

'Come on, Clair. Who do you think you're talking to? Even without well-developed intuition – I just saw how the two of you were looking at each other.'

'It's not what you think,' I said. 'He's—' a cold hand wrapped around my wrist.

'We need to talk,' Madeline said, squeezing me a little too hard. 'Excuse us,' she said to Brian. I tried to send him mental SOS signals as she dragged me away, but he was already looking for his next glass of vodka.

From the look on Madeline's face, I was worried she had heard from Rachel. I imagined the news of me sprinkling curses on people like it was fairy dust coursing through the information highway and landing in everyone's e-mail box like a vacation giveaway. Madeline was towering over me like a giant stick insect. I decided to preemptively defend myself.

'I know what you've heard,' I said. 'And it isn't true.'

'Exactly what isn't true?' Madeline responded.

'I didn't put a curse on her,' I blurted out. 'No matter what she says, this whole thing was her idea.'

'Her idea?'

'Down to every last detail.'

'And by her you mean?'

'Rachel,' I said getting slightly irritated. 'The entire thing was Rachel's idea.' I waited for Madeline to explode, or call me a liar, but to my surprise, she seemed to shrink slightly under the weight of the news.

'Why? Why would she do this to me?'

'It's Jack you should be feeling sorry for, don't you think?' I said.

'Oh I think she must want all of us to suffer. And you – you don't even know us. Why would you do this?'

'I didn't do anything—'

'How can you say that? You come all the way out here—'

'To return the ring.' I showed her the cubic zirconium. 'Which you now have back in your possession,' I added. Madeline's worry lines arched into a frown.

'Is that what all this about?' she demanded. 'You thought you were going to keep the real thing – or . . . or . . . reap some kind of reward?'

'No,' I said, horrified she was bringing this all back to money. 'I'm telling you the truth. I never meant for any of this to happen. I just came out here to return the ring – which you now have—'

'And threaten us.'

'What? No, I would never—'

'I've spoken to Mike,' Madeline said.

'About what?' I said, trying to shake the image of the two of them locked in a passionate embrace. Madeline took a step closer and pointed her long, bony index finger at me.

'The two of you aren't going to get a dime. Do you understand me? Not a single dime. I will not be blackmailed.'

'Madeline, nobody is blackmailing you—'

'How dare you call me Madeline.'

'I'm sorry – would you prefer, Mrs Robinson?' I clamped my hand over my mouth. I really hadn't meant to blurt that out.

'Excuse me?'

'No,' I said pulling away from her. 'Excuse *me*.' I tried to get away, but she grabbed my arm again.

'You think I'm a horrible mother, don't you?' Of all the possible things I had imagined coming out of her mouth, this wasn't one of them. I stared at her, trying to get a read, but all I could think of was Mike. I hated him. I hated her.

'I just want my children to be happy. After all these years. Is that too much to ask?' Madeline yelled. A buzzing noise filled my head, obscuring the rest of her words. I could see her mouth moving but I couldn't make out a thing. And then a hand touched the small of my back. I was grateful for the interruption, but it added ten years to my already fragile existence.

'I'm sorry,' Jack said as Madeline's mouth abruptly stopped moving. 'I didn't mean to scare you,' he said gently, his hand still on my back.

'It's all right,' I said.

'Grandmother would like to see you,' Jack continued.

'Tell her I'll be right there,' Madeline replied.

'Mother,' Jack said, his hand still on my back, 'I'm sorry but it's Clair she wants to see.' Jack steered me away from Madeline. But Madeline was faster; she grabbed Jack's face with both her hands and kissed him.

'I love you,' she said. Jack laughed uncomfortably and I looked away. No matter how old you were, nobody wanted anyone else to see their mother mauling them in public. I'd have to think of a polite way to tell him about the smear of bright red lipstick on his chin. I was grateful he was getting me away from her. So grateful, I didn't have the slightest premonition of what was about to come.

Daily Horoscope – Pisces

You've been summoned.

Being psychic doesn't stop you from being stupid. It doesn't stop you from constantly wanting what you don't have – always worrying about tomorrow instead of living in the now. Perfect example: Here I was alone with Jack as the sun slowly made its descent and the stars were sprinkling themselves across the night sky like someone lightly salting a baked potato, but I couldn't have cared less. I was too busy stewing about Mike.

Did *he* tell Madeline I was blackmailing her? What would I be blackmailing them about? The only dirt I had on them was their little tryst, and that's the one thing they didn't know I knew! It had to be about his mysterious name change, something I had very little interest in – until now.

And then there was the fact that my sister was probably at this very minute pulling out all the stops to seduce Mike. I was going to have to get her to stay away from him. She would go ballistic, of course, but I couldn't worry about that now. There was no way in hell I was going to let him seduce her, too.

'Abby and Mike seem to be getting along famously,' Jack said in the middle of my brooding. As I've said, we're all psychic to one degree or the other, and without even realizing it, Jack had just picked up on my thoughts.

'I'm sure they're just being polite,' I said irritably. *Besides, he's too busy bonking your mother*. Jack gave me a funny look, but I didn't say anything more. 'It's a beautiful night,' I lied.

'It is indeed,' Jack said softly. I instantly felt guilty. This was supposed to be his engagement party. How could they be going on with this charade? That must have been what Madeline meant when she asked if I thought she was a horrible mother. Look at us. We were all being horrible.

'Jack,' I said. 'I'm sorry. This can't be easy for you.' Jack studied me for a moment and then looked away when he spoke. He put his hands in his pockets and I saw his face contort for a second, as he prepared to go through the motions of being 'strong.'

'I'm just looking at it as a business gathering,' he lied. 'Be forewarned, there are going to be a lot of geeky, drunk investor types among us tonight.'

'There goes the neighborhood,' I said. We both laughed.

'I forgot,' Jack exclaimed, 'you're one yourself. Right? Although you're more of an advisor than investor, right?'

'Exactly,' I said. 'I advise people to the best of my ability, but ultimately it's up to them to invest in their own future.'

'Well if I do say so myself, Heron Vodka is going to be a wise investment. The contest alone is drumming up a ton of publicity.'

'That's wonderful,' I said. I wonder if Mike has figured out by now that I know about him and Madeline? I mean I wasn't exactly nice to him. Is he going to try and deny it? Or is he going to out and out lie? Make up some excuse as to why they're privately confessing their love to each other while innocent people crouch in tiny hiding places underneath the stairs and eavesdrop—

'Take that friend of yours,' Jack said as we reached the house.

'What friend?' I asked, paranoid that Jack was picking up on my feelings for Mike.

'Um . . . that girl – with the canvas sling,' Jack said.

'Oh, no,' I said picturing Terri ambushing Jack, 'I told her not to bother you. I am so sorry.' Jack laughed, took my arm, and walked me up the steps.

'It's okay,' he said. 'I can honestly say – never in a million years did I expect somebody to draw a French worm for Heron Vodka.' Jack and I laughed again, and this time when I tried to stop, I couldn't.

'I – tried – to – tell her that,' I managed to choke out in between laughs. We were standing on the porch, neither of us making a move to go inside yet.

'Ah, you advised her?'

'I predicted a dismal outcome,' I said. We laughed some more. It felt good after all the stress, all the secrets and worry – and frankly all the champagne – it felt good to just let go and laugh. What a release.

'Of course I shouldn't have been surprised,' Jack said, shaking his head.

'Why is that?'

'Well isn't she the psycho who drew a heart around my crotch?'

'Right,' I said, laughing without heart this time. 'That was a psycho thing to do.'

'Seriously immature for someone her age—'

'I get it,' I said. Jack gave me another funny look. I managed a giggle, completely fabricated this time.

'I love your laugh,' Jack said. I stopped laughing when he said this and our eyes met across the shadows of the porch. Something flickered between us and then Jack looked away. 'We'd better get inside,' he said. 'Grandmother will have a fit if I keep you any longer.'

The interior of the house sucked all the blossoming intimacy out of us; Jack and I retreated to familiar, politer forms of interaction. 'Mike and your mom seem to get along,' I said, trying to get a read on Jack's take on him.

'Ah, back to Mike are we?' Jack said. He was trying to sound goodnatured, but if I wasn't mistaken, I was picking up on some jealousy.

'He's single,' Jack said. 'If that's what you're really after.' Yes, the green-eyed monster was definitely lurking right beneath the surface.

'I'm not after Mike,' I said.

'I was talking about your sister,' Jack replied. 'Definitely not talking about you.'

'Oh. Of course.' I laughed and Jack laughed and I studied the grain of wood on the floor. 'Just curious,' I said lightly, 'why were you "definitely" not talking about me?'

'You're not his type.'

'Oh. I know that,' I said quickly. I took in the oil paintings in the narrow hall. I wondered who the old man in the painting was. He had a stern face, but nice blue eyes, and soft wrinkles ran down his cheeks like streaks of rain lingering on a window after a hard storm. This was going to be a lovely evening. I needed more champagne. 'Why aren't I his type?' I asked.

'Because Mike's ideal woman is more of a gypsy,' Jack laughed. I stopped walking.

'He said that?'

'Yeah. He said something like that the other day. Strange, huh?' My heart leapt in my chest until I remembered him seducing Madeline. It was inconceivable. Was he referring to her as a gypsy? No. He was making fun of me. Mocking me.

'So I guess you're way too conservative for him,' Jack said. 'Although your sister seems a bit more – creative. Free-flowing. That's his type.'

I was close to blurting out that bitter middle-aged stick insects were his type, when the door at the end of the corridor swung open, and Elizabeth Heron called out to us. 'There you are, my dear,' she cried, arms extended like a child reaching for a parent.

'She's so taken with you,' Jack whispered in my ear.

'Rachel, Rachel, Rachel,' Elizabeth sang. 'You look beautiful.' I looked down at my dress, trying to see me through her eyes. My gown was emerald green with tiny little beads sewn around the empire waist, and a long train that kissed the floor. Once again, it was as if the gown had been made for me.

'Thank you,' I said. 'You look beautiful, too.' A blush crawled up her cheeks, accompanied by a shy smile.

'Don't lie to an old woman,' she said, waving the compliment off with her hand, although the smile betrayed her glee.

'She's right, Grandmother,' Jack said, leaning in to kiss her cheek. 'You do look beautiful.'

'And you're such a handsome grandson,' Elizabeth said, staring at him affectionately. 'Would you mind giving us some time alone, dear?'

'Of course,' I said taking a step back. Elizabeth grabbed my arm.

'I was speaking to Jack, my dear.'

'Told you,' Jack whispered in my ear. 'Somebody likes you.' It was my turn to blush, but not for the reasons Jack thought. His soft voice in my ear made me feel like I was cheating on Mike. *His ideal woman is a gypsy.* I thought about kissing him in the truck, in my bedroom, in the alcove. I'd been replaying those moments a lot lately, wanting to savor them, relive them, wanting every second of them back. I wish we had life remote controls. There were so many things I'd delete, or fast-forward through, like my marriages, but moments like those, with Mike, I'd play over and over again.

What was wrong with me? *He's seducing Madeline, he's seducing Madeline, he's seducing Madeline.*

And as we speak, Abby was chasing after him like he was the last prom date in the neighborhood.

'Shall I come back up in a while and escort you two lovely ladies to dinner?' Jack was asking.

'Isn't he the perfect gentleman?' Elizabeth said as she scooted him out. 'Thanks, but we'll find our way down, dear.' She closed the door on him, and smiled at me briefly before swiftly heading to a writing desk in the corner of the room. I suddenly felt awkward, uneasy. I looked around the room to distract myself. Other than a four-poster bed with an ivory spread, and the writing desk where Elizabeth was hunched over, the only other pieces of furniture were two dusty end-tables and a dresser. Pale green walls, bare of decoration except for a single oil painting, stood out against an ivory, shag carpet.

I advanced on the painting, a portrait of a young girl staring out a window. She looked lost. She looked lovesick and lonely. She looked, a little bit, like me.

'Don't just stand there, Clair,' Elizabeth said, with her back to me, sitting straight up, spine like a rod, chin tilted up like the valedictorian of a finishing school. 'We need to talk.' I took a step toward her and then froze, her words ringing in my ears.

Clair.

She had just called me Clair.

Daily Horoscope – Pisces

Get off your ass and do something. But first, you'd better be sitting down.

'Young lady, I asked you to come over here,' Elizabeth said. I moved toward her while my mind rewound her last statement like an answering machine replaying an unintelligible message. I had, in fact, told her my real name several times, but she had never once reacted to it or referred to me as anything other than Rachel. Was this a rare moment of lucidity?

Elizabeth finally turned to me, motioning to the bed. I obediently took my seat. 'Tell me,' she said, clasping her hands in her lap and turning so that our faces were only inches apart. 'How is it going with my grandson? Are you making any progress?'

'I – uh,' I said. *Progress?*

'I know it's a difficult situation. Such a pity to have to rush it.'

'Grandma Heron—'

'In my day, we didn't dally like the young people do now. You met someone and weeks later you'd be engaged. All this dating around and getting to know each other. Ridiculous. No wonder there are so many divorces. By the time young people get together they already know everything there is to know about the person. Insanity!

How can a relationship last when all the mystery is gone? You of all people should know that,' she said with a slow, secret smile.

Me, of all people?

'In my day, you met, you didn't hate him, he didn't hate you, your parents approved, and you married. End of story.'

'Sounds romantic,' I clipped.

'Romance evolves, Clair,' Elizabeth scolded. 'It's not the only ingredient for a successful marriage. Haven't you learned that by now?'

'What do you mean?' I asked, totally thrown by the change in her demeanor, the way her eyes were fixed on me, as if I were a mirror reflecting back an exact image.

'I don't mean to hurt your feelings, my dear,' she said gently. 'But you're making things difficult with your heady ideals.'

'My heady ideals?' I said, almost choking.

'Jack will make a wonderful husband you know.'

'I'm not who you think I am—'

'Please, Clair. Let's drop the pretense,' Elizabeth said, holding out her hands.

'You know I'm not Rachel,' I said, mostly to myself. Elizabeth leaned forward and took my hand.

'I know this is happening fast. I apologize. I thought we'd have more time. But we don't. I'm afraid we just don't.'

I still didn't know what to say, what exactly she wanted me to do, or even if she was in fact in her right mind. I decided to proceed cautiously. 'Elizabeth,' I said, squeezing and releasing her hand before moving back slightly, 'Jack is in love with Rachel. Not me. Rachel.' *And I'm in love with Mike*. Stop it! There's your addiction again. You don't even know Mike—

'So you'll just have to get him to change his mind.'

'Mike?'

'Mike? Who said anything about Mike? I was talking about Jack, my dear. Remember him?' Elizabeth said, pointing a wrinkled index finger at my fake engagement ring. 'The man whose fiancée you're pretending to be?'

'We were just pretending because you—'

Elizabeth bent down and retrieved a dog-eared folder from the bottom drawer of her writing desk. She cradled it in her lap and looked at me. Tiny sparks of blue light were zipping in and out of it like fruit flies. I was transfixed. It was as if I was holding onto an electric fence, but no matter how much electricity was zipping through my body, I couldn't let go. 'Do you believe in fate, Clair?' Elizabeth whispered. 'Love at first sight?'

I opened my mouth to say, 'Yes, of course I believe, it's a job requirement,' but my jaw was locked shut. Then I opened my mouth to say something profound and mature, like how women these days weren't all naïve little Cinderellas waiting with our bare, manicured foot stuck outside our front door, toes painted red and pointing up, like the stiff, red flag on a mailbox, signaling our desire to be picked up. More resilient, in fact, than the mailman, because no matter how much rain, sleet, or snow pummeled our naked foot, we refused to bring it inside until the prince arrived, with his slippers, preferably Jimmy Choos.

Of course I believed in love, in fate, didn't I? At the time I married each of my three husbands, I had convinced myself I was in love. And I had already done enough postmortem on my marriages, it was time to stop beating myself up about the past. And, let's face it, we're not exactly thinking rationally when we're in love. Our bodies are flooded with chemicals when we first fall in love; it's like being on Ecstasy and suddenly everything the other person says or does is blissful, perfect.

And not that I'm condoning drugs like X, but let's face it, most likely when you wake up from that little high, the most you're going to be stuck with the next day is a bottle of Advil and a gallon of water, instead of a government-backed certificate uniting you to the snoring stranger next to you for the rest of your happy, little lives.

Finding true love should follow the unwritten rules of going to the grocery store. Any fool knows you don't go grocery shopping when you're hungry, much less starving. You'll throw any old thing in your cart if your stomach is in the throes of a grumbling delirium. But the second you get home and get a little something into your system, you're going to think – why the hell did I buy Cajun pork dumplings, garlic soy sauce, and imitation crab-stuffed, wheat-infused, pesto-rainbow raviolis?

You know why you did it, you were starving and delirious. The real question is – why didn't any rational, satiated fellow shoppers stop you? Even if they feared you'd get violent, they could have at least kindly removed the bizarre items from your cart when you weren't looking.

Why didn't anyone tell me a mood ring wasn't a romantic engagement ring, and neither was a freaking infinity tattoo on your middle finger? People 'in love' should be locked in a cage together until they get a glimpse of what it will feel like to truly hate each other. We should all be forced to spend time with several of the ones-of-thousands-of-potential ONES, locked in a Waiting-to-Hate-You-So-I-Can-See-If-I-Can-Stand-to-Love-You-Cage with them, and after being held captive with fifty or so men, the one you hated the least would be the one you could grow to love the most.

But what if you did find the guy you hated the least, and after a couple of decades of lukewarm bliss, he dies in a freak accident and you *still* spend the majority of your life alone because you lost him in old age, at a time when neither the cloak of beauty nor the burden of loyalty was there to protect you? Funny how similar love was to the stock market. No matter how wisely you invested, you just couldn't predict whether your portfolio was going to grow steady and pay off, or crash and burn.

But if you didn't invest at all, you didn't even get a chance. Even I knew that. Zero investments yield zero profits, every time. Yet can you stand the heartache of losing absolutely everything? If spreading out your investments were your safest bet, what did that mean when it came to love?

You couldn't exactly keep several other men waiting in the wings in case Mr-after-Spending-Twenty-Days-Locked-in-a-Cage-with-You-I-Hated-You-the-Least doesn't work out.

Could you?

After all, I was currently attracted to two very different men – Jack and Mike – and I was at a small, private estate in the middle of nowhere. Multiply that by the number of possible ONES in the world and you can't argue the logic. There *are* hundreds of thousands of potential ONES. But it wasn't exactly conducive to romance to start lining up men and locking them in cages, like securing your stock portfolio.

Unless you traded on a mutual understanding that you were simply using each other as backup in case your preferred cage-mate's stock plummeted. No wonder we were so messed up when it came to matters of the heart. With so many variations and questions marks, it wasn't surprising that even we psychics couldn't predict the millions of love permeations in a given portfolio.

'Clair,' Elizabeth said, grabbing my face in her hands and focusing my attention back on her. 'Jack has to fall in love with you tonight.' That woke me up. I didn't know whether to laugh or throw cold water on her in case she was teetering on the brink of insanity.

'Elizabeth,' I said. 'I'm very confused.'

'It's simple, Clair. I've been waiting for you. I've been waiting for you for a very, long time.' I opened my mouth to ask another question, but she stopped me by handing me the folder. 'Have a look,' she said, settling back in the chair and waiting. I opened the folder.

It was filled with a stack of newspaper clippings. The top article was slightly faded but perfectly pressed. I didn't even have to look in the upper-right-hand corner to know the date. May 31, 1994.

It was a picture of me and my first husband, Steve.

We were dressed in jeans and matching I MARRIED STUPID
- - -> T-shirts, holding hands on the front lawn of my
parents' house. My mother had sent the article to the local
papers after the wedding, trying to compensate for missing
the 'celebration.' After weeks of communicating with me
only through Tommy, Abby, and my father, it was her
attempt to acknowledge us as a married couple.

Steve Winds, son of Margaret and James Winds,
married Clair Ivars, daughter of Anna and George Ivars, on
May 31, 1994, on a beautiful, sunny, afternoon—

This line cut into me when I read it; Mom couldn't
bring herself to admit that I had married at the courthouse
on a gray day without inviting any of them, but she still
found a way to put a positive spin on it. It made my heart
break all over again to read this, and needless to say she
was invited to the next two weddings. I stopped reading
the announcement, turned it over in the folder and picked
up the next one.

Charles Lanes and Clair Ivars are pleased to announce
their engagement. The wedding will be held at Saint Francis
Church on Sunday, September 23, followed by a reception
in the grand home of Naomi and Harold Lanes, parents of
the groom—

Grand home all right. At the reception Charles
succeeded for the first and only time in getting me to
smoke pot with him, and we ended up in the laundry room,
having sex on top of the washing machine. His parents had
just bought a top-of-the-line Maytag, and Charles planted
me on top of it and eagerly attacked me. It would have
been a lot more satisfying had I not been lying on top of a
bottle of Clorox, but between the pot and Charles'
enthusiasm, I didn't bother to mention it. Unfortunately for
Charles, between the joint, champagne, and gyrating
motions of the washer, I fell right to sleep and woke up
with a bleached ass.

I knew what the third article would be, but I had to
look anyway.

Edward Grand and Clair Ivars tied the knot last week

in an elegant ceremony attended by more than two hundred guests—

Mom thought the more witnesses she could round up for this one, the better the chances the marriage would last. I put the article back in the folder, closed it up, and tried to hand it back to Elizabeth. I couldn't look anymore.

'At least I always kept my name,' I said, trying to lighten the lead I felt in my stomach. 'Can you imagine? I'd be Clair Winds Lanes Grand Ivars.' Elizabeth smiled kindly but didn't make a move to take the folder back.

'You missed one,' she said softly.

'I was only married three times,' I said piously, suddenly afraid to look at the last item as if it had been penned by the Ghost-of-Relationships-Future. But Elizabeth was determined to wait me out, and as she predicted, my curiosity outwon my fear.

I reopened the folder, quickly turned over my three wedding announcements, and gingerly held up the last item in the folder, a piece of faded, pink stationery with beautiful, cursive handwriting.

Curly circles on top of the 'S,' the long looping 'Ls,' and oval 'Os.' I knew her handwriting as well as I knew my own. Tears came to my eyes and my hands began to shake. There was no doubt, this had been written by my grandmother, Isabella Ivars. But it was the title at the top of the page that had made me sprout roots and dig into the bed:

My granddaughter Clair and the Man She Will Marry

March 4, 1984. My ninth birthday. The day my grandmother died.

Daily Horoscope – Pisces

You should have had a V-8.

My grandmother taught me the Tarot. Every Saturday morning we would sit in her kitchen with steaming cups of black tea and while I drowned mine in milk and sugar, she would turn the cards over one by one, as a matter of teaching. Before explaining the card, or the meaning, she'd ask me to look at it first and tell her my thoughts.

'But I don't know what it really means,' I said that first morning as I held The Queen of Swords. 'She's very pretty,' I added, feeling a little foolish, even for a seven-year-old.

'That's it,' my grandmother encouraged. 'You think she's pretty. Do you like her?' I opened my mouth to say yes, but the long, sharp sword in her hand stopped me.

'I like her,' I said slowly. 'But she's a little bit scary, too,' I said finally. My grandmother smiled.

'Reverence,' she said. 'You're describing reverence.'

'Who?' I asked, genuinely puzzled. My grandmother laughed, a warm twinkling sound that never failed to warm me up and love her even more.

'Reverence is a feeling of great respect, mixed with a little bit of healthy fear.'

'That's it,' I said as the tingling feeling in my stomach grew. 'That's how I feel.'

'Very good,' said my grandmother. 'The suit of swords is a powerful suit. Power is not something to take lightly, Clair. Neither should you take The Queen of Swords lightly.' I nodded, holding the card in my hand, marveling at this feeling, rolling the new word in my mouth, curling it around my tongue. Reverence.

'That's enough of her for now. Find another card and tell me how you feel.'

And so it went, bit by bit, every Saturday. I would drink tea with my grandmother and study the cards. She always wanted to know how they made me feel. Afterward, she would offer me insight as to their real meaning, but she was careful never to negate my first instinct, my base feelings about the cards. I'm convinced it's why I'm such a strong reader today. All children possess this feeling, but they gradually learn to distrust it, or hide in the face of adults telling them what they should think or feel instead.

My grandmother believed in that little voice; how could she not? It was her guiding light.

I looked back at the page in my hand and read what she had written underneath the line about the man I should marry.

The winds of fortune will change lanes until a grand finishing brings her home to your grandson who will be lost, until he finds her.

I didn't have to read it again. The words had already leapt off of the page and struck me in the chest. Winds. Lanes. Grand. My three ex-husbands. My mind was reeling.

'You knew my grandmother?' My voice was barely a whisper. I didn't trust my words, the rolling sensation in my stomach, or the free-falling fear tumbling through my veins.

'Isabella Ivars,' Elizabeth whispered. The tears that had swelled in my eyes broke free and ran down my cheeks.

'How?' I said. 'When?'

'Perhaps I should take it from the beginning,' Elizabeth said softly. 'I was nineteen years old,' she said. 'I was working as a seamstress in Chicago.' I leaned back against the headboard as Elizabeth's story poured out. She had just gotten engaged to a young man by the name of Robert Heron. He was barely making ends meet, working in the kitchen of a nearby restaurant, and Elizabeth's parents were dead set against the marriage. When Robert announced his intention to buy land down South in order to start a winery, her father out and out forbade Elizabeth to have anything else to do with him.

Elizabeth was torn. She and Robert were desperately in love, but Elizabeth was terrified at the prospect of disobeying her father. Six days had gone by since the proposal, and although Elizabeth was still sneaking out to see him, she had yet to give him an answer. She found herself unable to concentrate at work, her usual smooth line of stitching jagged and marred with droplets of blood from repeatedly stabbing her palm with the needle. One day after work, she found herself wandering aimlessly down the street, praying the right answer would come to her.

It came in the form of a sign hanging in the window of a small apartment building. Written in black marker, on a piece of paper no bigger than a postcard, the sign read: Spiritual Reader. $1. After she'd paced in front of the sign for two solid hours, the front door swung open and Isabella Ivars welcomed her in.

'I almost turned and fled,' Elizabeth said, lost in the memory. 'I was taught not to believe in those people,' she said. 'My mother called them devil worshippers.' She glanced to see my reaction, but my face remained neutral. Of course I'd been accused of such things myself, but it was hard to be defensive when you knew in your heart you were simply using the cards to tap into the inner workings of your mind and the energy of the Universe. Assured that I had taken no offense, Elizabeth continued. 'Besides, she was so sweet-looking. She was younger than me by a smidge and much more beautiful. But it was when she took my hand and this incredible feeling of peace came over me that I allowed her to lead me inside.'

My grandmother read Elizabeth's cards and predicted that she and Robert Heron would be very happy. She told her that in time her father would soften, and her husband's business would 'bear fruit,' although in a slightly different direction than he had planned. Elizabeth, who hadn't said a word to my grandmother about wine or grapes, was convinced of my grandmother's gift.

'I left feeling like a great weight had been lifted off of me. I ran directly to the restaurant, burst in, and shouted to Robert that I'd marry him.' A girlish blush swarmed her cheeks as she lost herself in the memory. She collapsed in giggles.

'What?' I encouraged.

'When he turned around, I saw it wasn't my Robert at all,' she admitted. 'It was the cook.' I laughed along with her. 'You should have seen the look on his face. Horrified, I tell you.'

'I'm sure he wasn't,' I laughed.

'Then my Robert came into room and I got a chance to say it all over again.' She paused, savoring the memory before continuing with the rest of the story. 'The first three years of marriage were bliss. There were problems, of course – there weren't any wineries in this area at the time and the first few crops failed miserably. I have to admit, I started to think your grandmother's reading had no merit at all. My father still wasn't speaking to me, and we were suffering so badly.

'Then Robert got an idea. He built the wine cellar in the woods and started ordering fine liquors and wines from other regions of the world – places we had never been – villages in Italy, mountain communities in Spain, families in the South of France. Little by little he started collecting amazing wines, talking about them to the restaurants where he used to work, and word started to spread. The fanciest restaurants in Chicago starting contacting us to supply their most lavish affairs. And that year we even had a crop good enough to bottle some of our own. Heron Estates was off and running. And about six months later, true to your grandmother's prediction, my father came around to make amends.'

But although their livelihood had taken off, Elizabeth admitted they were struggling to conceive. They wanted children desperately, and it was this desperation that brought Elizabeth once again to my grandmother's doorstep. Isabella had married my grandfather by this time and had given birth to my mother. Luckily, she only lived a few blocks from her original apartment, and after a couple of discreet inquiries, Elizabeth was able to locate the gifted reader. At this second reading, my grandmother told her she would bear only one child – a son – and he would be conceived within the year. True to form, her son, Robert Junior, was born eleven months later.

So Elizabeth was thrilled when she discovered she was pregnant for a second time, and this time she sought out my grandmother to tease her for being wrong.

'She was very delicate with me, your grandmother,' Elizabeth said as she wrung her hands in her lap. 'She didn't come out and tell me the child would never grow in my womb; she simply congratulated me, but added she would be here when I needed her.' Elizabeth left, puzzled by the statement, but it all made sense the next week when Elizabeth miscarried.

'I was extremely angry with your grandmother,' Elizabeth admitted. 'I thought if she had warned me – that maybe I could have prevented it. I had been working in the field that morning' – she stopped in midsentence and looked away. 'No matter, I knew it wasn't her fault. She was my friend by then and I wouldn't have believed her if she had told me. But it didn't stop me from behaving like a child,' Elizabeth said. 'Isabella wrote me letter after letter over the years, but I refused to even speak to her.'

Time passed. True to Isabella's word, Robert Junior was the only son. He grew up and married and the Heron Estates prospered just as Isabella had predicted. A granddaughter was born – Susan. And then a few years later there was Jack.

'It's not that I didn't love my granddaughter, Susan. I adored her. Still do. But I'm old-fashioned, Clair. I wanted a grandson. I wanted him to take over the business from my son – who wasn't exactly a whiz at the books,' she laughed. 'For that matter, neither is Jack. But I was absolutely thrilled when he was born. He was the light of my life. And he brought your grandmother back into my life.'

Elizabeth continued her story, telling me how when Jack was three years old he was stricken with a severe case of measles. Madeline and Elizabeth were at his bedside around the clock, but despite medication, his fever had spiked and nothing was working. The doctors told them to fear the worst. Elizabeth didn't know if my grandmother was alive, or would even speak to her again, but she had to find her.

'I couldn't bear the pain of waiting. I was going to make her tell me the news, no matter how bad it was. I was going to tell her, too, that I was sorry. For all my anger. For rejecting her. For all the years of friendship I had wasted.' Elizabeth stopped to wipe tears from her eyes. 'She was still there,' she continued. 'And when I contacted her, she didn't even hesitate. She came to the estates straight away and sat with Jack.'

I knew my mouth was hanging open at this point, just knowing my grandmother had been here, in this house, and had met the same people I had been getting to know over the past few days was enough to make me dissolve. 'I'm glad she was there to support you,' I said quietly.

'Oh, she did much more than that, Clair. She saved Jack's life.'

'What do you mean?'

Elizabeth reached out and took my hand. 'She held his hand,' she said. 'And twenty-four hours after your grandmother arrived, Jack's fever broke. He sat up in bed and asked for a popsicle,' she said, clapping her hands together and allowing the tears to run down her face. 'She wasn't just a reader your grandmother, she was a healer too.'

I didn't know what I thought of this revelation, but there were too many other questions swimming around my brain to even try and process it.

'And this?' I said, holding up the piece of pink stationery. 'How did you get this?'

'It arrived in the mail,' Elizabeth said. 'It was the last time I ever heard from her.'

I could barely get the words out. 'That's because – she wrote this the day she died.' Elizabeth squeezed my hand as I wiped away the tears.

'How old were you then, dear?'

'Nine,' I said. 'I was nine.' The day was seared in my memory. I had been at school, sitting at my desk, when the room started to spin and suddenly my eyes were filled with tears. 'No,' I screamed in front of the entire class.

'What is it, Clair?' the teacher asked irritably. We were supposed to be reading silently.

'My grandmother,' I yelled through tears. 'I have to go home and see my grandmother.' My school wasn't within walking distance, or I would have run out of the classroom and never looked back.

'And why is that?' the teacher asked as I sobbed at my desk.

'Because,' I yelled. 'She's dying.'

When the teacher refused to let me leave, I threw an all-out fit, not stopping to think of the consequences – not only for the fit, which was bad enough, but also the reaction when people learned that my grandmother had died ten minutes after I arrived home, exactly two hours from the time I started crying at my desk. My reputation as a freak was signed, sealed, and delivered.

'But it was worth it,' I told Elizabeth. 'I got to hold her hand, and say good-bye.'

'She waited for you,' Elizabeth said.

'She waited for me,' I agreed.

You have my gift, Clair. Always trust it. Always trust your instincts.

'I'm afraid I've let her down,' I said quietly.

'Nonsense,' Elizabeth barked. 'Why would you say that?'

'Three failed marriages – that's not exactly something to be proud of—' I stopped as Elizabeth gingerly held up the faded pink stationery.

'Winds, Lanes, Grand,' she whispered. 'It's how it was supposed to go.' I stared at the words again. *Until she comes home to your grandson—*

I stood up. It was too much to take in sitting down. Elizabeth stood up, too, following me to the window.

'I didn't understand it right away either, of course. I knew Isabella had a granddaughter, Clair, but I certainly didn't know what it all meant. I put it in a drawer and forgot all about it. It really wasn't until Jack brought Rachel home and announced his intention to marry her that I even remembered the letter. You had just divorced for the third time. That's when I realized—'

'How did you know that?' I interrupted.

'The wedding announcements,' Elizabeth said, waving the folder. 'I saw each and every wedding announcement. Your grandmother made sure of it.'

'Made sure of it? How?'

'The first one I came across by accident. Jack and Susan had taken me into Chicago for the weekend. They were going out to a jazz club, and I was too tired to stay up that late – so Jack brought me the paper. I loved the crosswords. I opened the page right to this,' she said, pointing at the picture of Steve and me.

'You looked just like her,' she said. 'And of course there was no mistaking it – Clair Ivars,' she said. 'I still didn't connect it to the letter. Until that night – when I dreamt of your grandmother and pink stationery. I cut out the article and placed it in this folder. I subscribed to the paper the very next day. And I waited,' she said, holding up the other two articles. 'To see if there would be two more.' I was standing and pacing once again. My entire body was tingling.

'And here you are,' Elizabeth said, coming up behind me. 'And you're meant to be with Jack,' she said, putting her hand on my shoulder and turning me around. 'Don't you see? You're meant to be with Jack.'

'Rachel coming to see me,' I said pacing the room. 'How did that come about?' Elizabeth looked away, but I had already caught her expression. It was that of a child caught doing something naughty. Elizabeth shrugged.

'It took me six months to find you. I called every psychic in Chicago.' *She started calling psychics, racking up bills—*

'I finally got a hold of someone who knew you. Dame something—'

'Dame Diaphannie.'

'That's her. Strange girl. But she was willing to call me when you registered at the same psychic fair.'

'For a price, I'm sure.'

'Well worth it, darling. Even the two years I spent locked in this room—'

'What?' I cried. 'What does that have to do with it?'

'I shouldn't have said that, darling. It was my choice. I begged Jack not to marry Rachel, but he wasn't listening to me. So I told him I wouldn't come out of my room until he broke it off—'

'Oh God—'

'It's okay. Because here you are. Here you are at last.'

'How did you persuade Rachel to come and see me?'

'Well I didn't have to do much persuading, darling. She was already at her wit's end.'

'Because of the noises.'

'You heard them yourself.'

'Elizabeth . . . Jack doesn't love me. He loves Rachel.' *Not to mention, I can't stop thinking about Mike*.

'But she's all wrong for him. Look at her – she left him!'

'Because of me,' I confessed. 'I lied. I lied in her reading. I told her the marriage would be a disaster.'

'And it would have been. You're the one he's supposed to be with.'

I headed for the door. Elizabeth hurled herself in front of it with surprising force.

'Where are you going?' she demanded.

'I'm going to find Jack. I'm telling him the truth. About everything.'

'No. Clair, don't.' Elizabeth's voice caught like a sweater snared on barbed wire.

'There's something you're not telling me,' I said as a low hum filled my ears.

'You have to make it stop,' she begged. 'You have to marry Jack and make her stop.'

'Make who stop?' I implored, horrified at the terror in her voice.

'Your grandmother,' Elizabeth cried. 'She's been haunting this house since the day Jack brought Rachel home.' I stared at Elizabeth as fear played across her face like a five o'clock shadow. She grabbed my shoulders like they were life jackets. 'Don't you see?' she said. 'You have to marry Jack. It's the only way she'll stop.'

I sank onto the bed, once again convinced that Elizabeth wasn't running at full mental capacity. My grandmother the healer, possible. My grandmother the poltergeist – not in a million years. But still, the letter – it was my grandmother's handwriting.

'So you're telling me that Rachel wanted to cancel the wedding because,' I stopped, as I needed to take a deep breath in order to speak the rest of it out loud, 'because my grandmother was haunting her?'

'Well,' Elizabeth said, gazing out the window. 'There's that.'

'And?' I said as a feeling of panic crawled up both arms and invaded my skull.

'And then there's the check I gave her for a hundred thousand dollars.'

Daily Horoscope – Pisces

Like a good neighbor hard drugs are there.

'A hundred thousand dollars?' I squeaked, trying to sound calm when what I really wanted to do was run after the first glass of champagne I could find. Or Jägermeister even. I hated Jägermeister, but at this point I would drink it out of a bucket through a straw.

'Well you didn't think she was going to give Jack up just because of a few squeaky floorboards and a couple of nightmares, do you?'

'So you bribed her?'

'I told her the truth. I told her she wasn't meant to marry Jack. The money was just . . . a consolation prize. She didn't want to take it at first. But then she started having nightmares – just like I was having – and that's when I convinced her to go see you.'

'How did you explain who I was?'

'I just told her you were a very gifted psychic. I told her if a reading were to say they weren't supposed to marry—'

'But the reading didn't say that, Elizabeth. I lied. Rachel blackmailed me into lying to her – just so Susan would hear—'

'You see. In the end she chose the money over Jack.'

'But Mike said Heron Estates doesn't have cash flow.

That . . . there have been money problems. The wealth is tied up in assets.'

'Mike?' Elizabeth said, suddenly looking confused. 'What about Mike?'

'Jack told me he was hired to clean up the books,' I said, trudging lightly. She obviously had no clue what I was talking about.

'Did he now?' Elizabeth said, staring off into space as if scanning a card table for a missing puzzle piece. Of course Mike could have been lying about their finances. Of course! He's using Madeline to get his hands on their money.

No, you're wrong, Clair – he's not like that.

'It doesn't matter anyway,' Elizabeth said, throwing her hands up. 'Rachel never cashed the check.'

'That means – she changed her mind. She does love Jack.' Elizabeth looked away from me and started puttering around her writing desk while invisible pins stuck themselves into the back of my neck, leaping on and off like ballet dancers on acid. 'Elizabeth,' I said. And waited.

'Rachel's coming back,' Elizabeth said at last.

'Well, good. Maybe she and Jack can work this out. I mean taking the check wasn't cool – but she didn't cash it so—'

'Rachel's worked up a bit of a story since you last saw her,' Elizabeth interrupted. 'And it makes you out to be—'.

'I know, I know. A psychic who put a curse on her. Brian told me.'

'I'm afraid it's a little worse than that,' Elizabeth said in a wobbly voice. 'She's going to say you're blackmailing her.'

'What?'

'She's going to say you concocted the whole thing – even the haunting – just to get Jack and his estate for yourself.'

'Even if she tries to say that,' I said, 'no one is going to believe her. She's the one who accepted a check for a hundred thousand dollars,' I argued.

'And then there's that,' Elizabeth said as I watched her literally shrink before my eyes. 'Oh, Clair. I'm so sorry. I'm getting old. My mind – doesn't work as well as it should sometimes.' She started to shake and tears came to her eyes. I sat next to her on the bed and put my arms around her.

'Shh,' I said. 'It's okay. Whatever it is, it's okay.'

Elizabeth pulled away and looked me in the eyes. 'Didn't you hear me?' she whispered. 'Rachel never cashed the check.'

'I heard you,' I said as the pinpricks returned. 'It means she chose Jack.' Elizabeth shook her head and moaned. 'Elizabeth. What's wrong?' Now that I knew about her relationship with my grandmother I felt even closer to her. I wanted to protect her, I hated seeing her this upset. 'Whatever it is, I'll help you fix it. I promise.' Elizabeth started sobbing. There was nothing worse than seeing this beautiful elderly woman break down.

'Elizabeth,' I said. 'It's okay. I promise – whatever it is—'

The door swung open and Madeline Heron barged in. 'Grandmother Heron, you're crying. What's the matter? What did you do to her?' she yelled at me. 'What is going on here?'

'These are happy tears,' Elizabeth said, even though she was as white as a sheet. 'Rachel and I were just talking about my Robert.'

'I see,' Madeline said, already losing interest. 'We need *Rachel* downstairs,' she continued, choking on the name, 'people are starting to arrive.'

I walked over to Elizabeth. 'What were you saying?' I asked. 'About the check?'

'Check?' Madeline said. 'What check?'

'I was just telling Rachel to check on Jack,' Elizabeth said. She looked at me and I felt a chill run down my spine. I wasn't going to get it out of her now, not with Madeline around, but I knew whatever she had to say about Rachel and the check wasn't going to be good.

Forget the champagne or Jägermeister through a straw, I thought as I headed down to the party. I needed a good old-fashioned brick wall to ram my head into. How did I get myself into this mess?

Over a stupid crush, that's how. I didn't have to come all the way out here to return Jack's ring. FedEx would have done the job just fine. I'm in this mess because three divorces and another dozen road-kill relationships hadn't taught me a darn thing. I still fell in love like a twelve-year-old with a picture of Jack in a magazine article.

And what about my grandmother's prediction? Was Jack the man I was meant to spend the rest of my life with? Then why was I still thinking about Mike? And how could I still be thinking about Mike when he was after Madeline? The thought made me literally sick. He was either really in love with her, which was a nauseating thought, or he was after Heron Estates. Both deal-breakers. So why did I still want to see him, touch him, beg him to tell me it wasn't true?

Your grandson. My granddaughter.

If you had told me just days ago that I was meant to spend the rest of my life with Jack Heron, I would have been ecstatic. Now I didn't know what to do. I reached the bottom of the stairs feeling completely paralyzed at my limited, conflicting options. I didn't know how I was going to get through this, but I did know it was going to be while clutching a very expensive glass, or twelve, of first-rate bubbly.

I set out first to find Brian; I needed his take on this latest bombshell, but Abby got to me first. She tackled me from behind the minute I stepped out into the summer night air. The party was in full swing; the patio lights illuminated what the darkness failed to hide – throngs of well-dressed guests mingling, chatting, and lubricating themselves senseless. The air was thick with the smell of crab cakes, designer perfume, and cheap laughter. The expensive red wine on my sister's breath was so strong I could almost taste it.

Cabernet Sauvignon 1982 Reserve.

Why did the senseless psychic tidbits always insist on threading their way through my brain while the major ones – like *Don't marry that guy, he paints his toenails black when there's a full moon* – always eluded me?

Abby looked deliriously happy and I was suddenly extremely jealous and feeling sorry for myself. Here was a lavish affair like a party straight out of *The Great Gatsby*, and I wasn't even going to get to enjoy it.

You have to hurry. You're the one who is supposed to marry Jack—

'He's Canadian!' Abby was yelling in my ear. 'And an entrepreneurial.'

'Who?' I said, graciously ignoring her incorrect grammar while trying to unhook her sweaty grip from my shoulders before her overexcited fingers walked their way across my neck like two daddy long legs and squeezed.

Rachel's coming – and what did Elizabeth want to tell me about the check?

'Mike Wrench,' she said breathlessly. 'He's amazing. You are psychic Clair De Lune,' she floated. 'He's exactly who you described.' The end of her sentence was swallowed up in an indecipherable squeal, but I understood her in the way family members can read each other's minds, regardless of their psychic proclivities. My sister's language was embedded in my DNA.

Michael Alexander Brentwood.

'Abby, listen,' I said, putting my hands on her shoulders and looking her in the eye. 'Mike Wrench isn't available.' Her face was that of a child told she could never eat cookies again. Ever.

'And why is that?' she said with her hands on her hips. I had to play this carefully. Abby would turn into a raving lunatic if she got so much as a whiff of my feelings about Mike.

'I just – you don't know him that well – and . . . you deserve the best,' I stammered.

'Clair. If I'm going to get pregnant with twins, there's

no time to waste,' she said like I was personally responsible for the wasted time.

'Abby. I was – what – nine years old when I gave you that reading? It didn't mean anything. You have to stop this – you have to stop living your life based on something a nine-year-old predicted!'

'He's the one, Clair. Mike Wrench is the one.'

'That's not even his name,' I shouted. Her animated face suddenly imploded. 'What do you mean?'

Oh God. Where's the Veuve Cliquot? 'Abby, I'm going to get a glass of champagne. We'll talk about this later.' I didn't give her the chance to ask any more questions; with a little luck and a lot more red wine, she'd forget all about my comment. Probably not a chance in hell of that, but I had bigger fish to fry.

'Champagne?' a roving waiter said to me as he glided by with an outstretched tray. I took two and weaved my way through the crowd, heading for a plate of cheese.

I felt him before I saw him; I felt his eyes bore into me like they had since that first day he confronted me on the lawn. 'There you are,' he said as his eyes wandered up and down my dress, lingered on my chest, up my neck, and hovered on my lips before they finally landed on my eyes and he gave me a lazy, sexy smile. 'You look beautiful, Clair,' he said, reaching for one of my glasses of champagne.

'Sorry,' I said, pulling my hand back protectively. 'They're both for me.' He raised his eyebrow and laughed as I downed the first glass.

'See?' I said.

'Have you always been a two-fister or do you save that classy habit for swanky parties like this one?'

'When in Rome,' I said, setting the first glass down and drinking from the second. I was thrilled to see him, and furious with him, and angry at myself that I was thrilled to see him, and if he looked at me like that two seconds longer I was going to bury my face in his neck and happily suffocate. God what was that cologne he was wearing?

'Slow down, lady,' Mike said, taking my hand. I tried to ignore the electricity shooting through my palms. 'Here,' he said. 'Have some cheese.' I opened my mouth to protest, but he stuck a wedge of white cheddar in it. I hated its creamy tart taste, hated that it tasted so good, hated that from now on nothing would taste as good if his hand weren't on the other end of it. He put that hand up to my face and wiped off a tiny speck that remained stuck to my bottom lip.

'You've certainly made an impression on my sister,' I blurted out like a schoolgirl tattling. Mike dropped his hand, and looked at me.

'What about you?' he said without missing a beat. 'What impression have I made on you?'

Before I had a chance to formulate a safe, most likely sarcastic answer, Mike pulled me to him and kissed me.

It doesn't matter how great the guy is, if he's not a good kisser, or if the two of you together are not good kissers, the relationship doesn't stand a chance. Unless you think you can do without kissing. Which I never could. Which is why this would be so much easier if it weren't for the fact that he was the best kisser I'd ever – well – kissed. My first husband was a complete amateur, lots of cold tongue thrusting, my second husband always tasted like pot, and my third one had ADD and although he was a good kisser, he didn't like to spend much time smooching. Much more important things to do like scream at hockey games and review opening chess moves.

But Mike was an A++ kisser. Otherwise, I could easily cross him off my list, yank him away from Madeline, and hand him over to my sister to breed a couple of twins.

But God, our lips melted into each other and pushed so many buttons I was lit up like a call girl in a Navy yard. If it hadn't been for spilling my champagne down my cleavage again, I probably would have begged him to take me underneath the cheese table. I pulled away and looked down at my chest.

'I'm sorry,' Mike said in a low, very un-sorry voice.

'Want me to get that for you?' He asked as he leaned his mouth toward my chest. The thought of Madeline flashed through my mind. I pushed Mike away just as his lips grazed the space between my cleavage.

'How could you?' I whispered, unable to ignore it any longer. 'You've been lying to me this whole time.' Mike looked genuinely confused. 'I heard you,' I said, afraid of my own voice, afraid of my flailing words. 'I heard you.'

'Clair,' he said, reaching for my waist. I pulled away. He registered my resistance and folded his arms across his chest. 'What are you talking about?' he said. I met his eyes, and willed myself to be strong. Think steel. Think two-ply Hefty bags, think of all the breakups you've survived – I couldn't delay this any longer. His actions were unforgivable and I had to take this to the point of no return.

I love that you play piano, I love the dimple in your chin, I love that you have beers with the gardeners, I love your laugh, I love, love, love the way you look at me—

'Clair?'

'I think you're a liar,' I said, barely containing tears. 'And a user. I don't want you anywhere near me or my sister.'

'You're kidding me.'

'Do I sound like I'm kidding? Do I look like I'm kidding?'

'Where is this coming from?'

'You've been lying,' I shouted. He flinched at the tone of my voice, but relegated his own so that his reply was urgent, but quiet.

'I've been lying? What about you?'

'What about me?'

'Ms Financial Advisor—'

'Clair,' Jack boomed, stepping up behind me and slipping a hand around my waist. 'Mother sent me to find you.' Mike and I held eye contact. 'The seating for dinner has begun,' Jack continued like a game show host. 'You're a few chairs down from us, buddy. Next to Abby,' he said, grinning at Mike and giving him a punch to the shoulder.

'You okay, Jack?' Mike asked returning the punch. 'You seem a little – wired.' I looked at Jack. Mike was right. Jack's eyes were dilated and his right foot was tap dancing.

'I'm great. I'm feeling great,' he said loudly. Mike and I exchanged a look as Jack led me to the table. An unwelcome image of Mike sitting across from Abby rose to mind, followed by an even more unwelcome image of him kissing Madeline. Maybe Elizabeth was right. Maybe Jack was my destiny. Regardless, I was going to have to come clean. About everything.

'Jack,' I said. 'I have something to tell you.' Jack looked at me with his huge pupils and an even bigger grin.

'What up?' What up? I was so thrown by his vernacular, I couldn't respond.

What up? Well – my grandmother and your grandmother I think were soulmates. Only problem is, your grandmother is a senile agoraphobic and mine's been dead for twenty plus years. Furthermore, your fiancée is on her way here to accuse me of being a witch who put a curse on her and I'm in love with Mike who's bangin' yo mama. That what up, Bro!

We had reached the table and Jack was pulling out my chair. Elizabeth was already seated across from us. 'There you are,' she said like an excited child. 'Here we all are.' I looked down the length of the candle-lit table adorned with deep wine glasses, glittery china, and napkins folded into swans. The smell of bread and sweet potatoes and roasted meat filled the air. I didn't dare look at Mike, but I could feel him; it was like we were connected by a rope of heat.

'Sorry I'm late,' Anderson said, suddenly appearing at the table. Instead of his usual black suit with a white shirt, Anderson was dressed in blue. To everyone's astonishment, he pulled out the seat next to Madeline and sat down. It took Madeline a moment to speak; she was staring at Anderson, not believing her eyes. *She's in love with him, too.* Then why is she involved with Mike? A red X rose into my mind, blocking my thoughts.

'Anderson, what are you doing?' Madeline asked out of the corner of her mouth. Anderson smiled. 'I'm taking my rightful place at the table,' he said with a wink to me. I slid down in my seat and looked the other way. 'I think that's wonderful,' Jack shouted beaming at Anderson. 'It's about time.' He turned to me. 'You said you had something to tell me?' Everyone within a five-mile radius was staring at us. I shook my head no.

A platter of sizzling steak floated in front of me surrounded by fluffy twice-baked potatoes and grilled asparagus with shitake mushrooms. *Confessions*, I thought, *will go over better on a full stomach*. Maybe Rachel wouldn't even show. Besides, if this was going to be my last meal, I was going to enjoy every morsel of it. If for no other reason than to distract myself from my sister's future twin-producing, entrepreneurial, Canadian husband-to-be.

Daily Horoscope – Pisces

Buy high, sell low or is that buy low, sell high?

I don't know why they sat the eager investors at our end of the table, but I shouldn't have been surprised when Mike, who was seated a mere four seats across from my sister, suddenly leaned over and motioned to the five or six men who were discussing their latest investments, and said loudly, 'You should ask Rachel. She's a financial advisor, too. A real whiz with futures.'

Suddenly ten males in black suits and white shirts swiveled their heads toward me, leaning in my direction one at a time, like dominos falling down the long dining-room table.

'I forget, *Rachel*,' Mike continued, as Abby frowned at me from behind him, 'do you deal primarily with organizations or individual investors?'

I looked away from Mike and talked to my field greens. 'Oh,' I said, 'don't get me talking shop. I'm sure it would bore everyone at the table.' Before I even got the rest of the sentence out, the suits protested loudly, assuring me there was nothing they'd rather discuss than the stock market. I could have ended it all by announcing certain secrets swirling around the table that I found really fascinating: one of the investors ate peanut butter and pickle sandwiches at exactly 9:15 every night; another was up to his eyeballs in debt, despite his five-million-dollar home; and yet a third had set Tivo to record porn from midnight to six A.M.

But these guys didn't want me delving into the hidden files of their minds, they wanted to discuss money, money, money, a subject I had avoided for most of my life.

Granted, I accepted it was a necessary evil, a form of energy we have to deal with or it will deal with us, but I had never invested myself in it, figuratively or literally, the way these men had. I was thirty-two and I didn't have a retirement fund. I glanced at Mike again who looked like he was thoroughly enjoying spearheading this inquisition, goading me as if he knew I was touring a dark cave without a flashlight.

'Do tell us,' the suit farthest from me shouted up the table. 'What stocks do you recommend?'

'Oh,' I said as the conversation around me suddenly stilled. Abby looked at me; she was wrestling between two impossible choices: out me as a liar, or watch me squirm. I didn't have to be psychic to know which one she'd choose.

'Well, I usually charge a lot of money for specific investment advice,' I said, smiling and drinking more champagne as a way of signaling the end of the conversation.

'Give us some general advice then,' someone shouted.

Get to the dentist; you have gum disease.

'Um, well, I'd hold steady gentlemen,' I said. 'These are unpredictable times.' There, that should do it. Waiters were removing the salad plates and a bowl of broth was placed in front of me while another hand finally refilled my champagne glass.

'But say we have a little extra to invest,' the domino nearest me said. 'What do you think will be the next big thing?'

'What are you investing in these days?' Mike added.

'Um I – uh – I do a lot of hedging,' I said, turning to Brian for support. He of all people should be able to read the absolute panic on my face.

'Rachel,' Brian said, pronouncing the name like an ESL student on the first day of class, 'is an excellent hedger.' Mike covered his face with a linen napkin. I started humming 'Mrs Robinson' to see if he would pick up on it and flush with guilt, but all it elicited was a curious frown on his part. And then I was too distracted to continue the experiment. The suits weren't finished with me.

'But what specifically should we be looking out for?' an insistent voice asked.

'Middle Eastern plums,' I blurted out before anyone could stop me. *Where in the hell did that come from?*

'Middle Eastern plums?' Jack asked, joining into the portion of the conversation for the first time. From his tone of voice, he was completely baffled. Elizabeth smiled at me while Madeline and Susan squinted.

'Middle Eastern plums?' the line of dominos repeated, leaning back like the little black and white squares were falling up instead of down.

'Middle Eastern plums,' I said confidently. 'By a landslide.'

Cell phones, Blackberrys, and other hand-held computers popped up around the table as the information made its way down the line of bewildered guests. I buried myself in my broth, scalding myself in the process, and then cooled my throat with more champagne. 'Excellent,' Jack cried. 'Let's all invest in Middle Eastern plums!' I studied his face. It was flushed. His eyes and fingertips were dancing. *He's high as a kite*.

A hand shot up among the suits.

'Yes?'

'Um. Is there any particular company ... um ... harvesting the plums?' He asked with a stylus poised in one hand and his hand-held in the other. His eyeglasses had worked their way down his long nose and he was peering over them intently.

'Yes, Rachel,' Mike said. 'What company would that be?'

'Well,' I said, starting to sweat and looking around for

support. I turned to Brian again, but he had his face buried in a bread basket, clearly done bailing me out.

'You've all heard of Florida oranges, right?' I said after downing my entire glass of champagne in one swallow. I had never seen so many people squinting at me in my life.

'Minute Maid?' Jack shouted, pounding the table. This time, I wasn't the only one giving him concerned looks.

'Exactly,' I said loudly. 'Minute Maid.' Heads bowed down to cell phones and styli tapped furiously on tiny screens until someone looked up and spoke. By now they were nameless, faceless, investing voices, floating at me from the dark depths of the table.

'Are you saying Minute Maid is going to start making . . . Middle Eastern plum juice?'

'Um,' I said, realizing this could be fact-checked by one of these buggers pretty easily, 'not Minute Maid per se – but a smaller company similar in nature.'

'Who?'

'Jenga Juice,' I said, remembering the orange flyer that had been slipped under my door a month or so ago – or a lifetime as it felt now. Had I really only been here a few days?

'Jenga Juice?' someone asked.

'Jenga Juice,' I repeated. 'I think they're really going places.'

'And they're investing in Middle Eastern plum juice?'

'Rumor has it,' I said mysteriously, 'they're – uh – trying to come up with something to help our digestive systems as well as improve our relations with the Middle East.' More stares. Mike's hands were obscuring his face and his shoulders were shaking. Little swirls of red light clouded my eyes and I took a deep breath. *Don't get angry, Clair*. 'They're going to start making plum wine, too,' I said now that I was on a roll. 'Well, rumor has it,' I added again.

'Rumor?' Susan joined in with a clear warning in her tone. 'You're suggesting these men invest in a company based on a rumor?'

'I seem to remember you've made a decision or two

based on rumors, Susan,' Harold suddenly piped up.

'Excuse me?' Susan lashed back. 'What rumor would that be?' *That you were fucking the nanny?* she added silently. Harold's face blanched.

'It's nothing, dear. Just joking,' he said.

'I don't think this is appropriate dinner discussion,' Madeline said as the meat was carved and the side dishes started their parade around the table. The energy coming at me from across the table was getting too hot to ignore. I met Elizabeth's eyes. *Rachel is on her way—*

'So you're saying that Jenga Juice,' Jack said, irrationally happy, 'is getting into the plum wine business?'

'Jack,' Madeline warned.

'Jenga,' Abby said. 'Are they Asian?'

'She said it was a rumor, Jack,' Susan interjected. 'Just a rumor.' I should have kept my mouth shut, but stress, champagne, and scorned-woman syndrome were getting in my way. I could feel Mike staring at me like the Bionic Man. I didn't dare return the look.

'Organic plum wine, Jack,' I whispered, leaning across the table. 'That's all I'm saying.'

'That's all you'd better say, young lady,' Madeline said, cutting me off.

'Clair,' Brian's floated from somewhere to my right, 'would you like more potatoes?'

'Clair?' Elizabeth said loudly. 'Who are you calling Clair, my dear?' Brian turned twelve shades of red. Elizabeth winked at me. Jack's arm snaked around my shoulders and he suddenly pulled me in for a kiss.

'This is Rachel,' he said loudly. 'My lovely Rachel.'

'Looking plumper than usual,' Harold added, making red clouds appear before my eyes. Tongue hanging out, he eyed my breasts. The red clouds turned into swirling tornadoes. *Don't get angry, don't get angry, don't get angry—*

I stole a glance at the kids table where Mathew and Conrad were playing tug-of-war with a wishbone.

I wish we could go swimming.

'I didn't know you were a financial advisor, too,' Terri piped in just when we thought the conversation had been dropped.

'Too?' Jack said. 'What do you mean, "too"?' Sweat was pouring down his cheeks.

'You know, in addition to her readings,' Terri said.

'Potatoes,' I shouted. 'I would like more potatoes!'

'Me, too!' Jack shouted. 'I love potatoes!'

Madeline shoved the platter in my hands while Susan glared at me and Abby's eyes were fixed on me like I was the bull's-eye on a dartboard.

'Readings?' Jack persisted. 'What kind of readings?'

'Don't you read to kindergarten children, Rachel?' Susan said, trying to finally get into the game. Kindergarten children?

'I think she means investment readings, Susan,' I said.

'Oh,' Susan answered. 'That makes much more sense.'

'So this thing with Jenga Juice,' someone shouted. 'How big of an opportunity do you think this is?'

I should have just kept my mouth shut, but truthfully, I couldn't get Jenga Juice out of my head either. An image of their company charts had been flashing through my head the last few minutes like a traffic light stuck on WALK, and I saw a red arrow pointing up, up, up. So why shouldn't I give them a little advice? There were astrologers who made a living investing in stocks based on what sign was passing through which house on any given day. How was this any different than telling them how to stay happily married or what job to take or whether or not to risk investing their heart in a new love? What is the stock market anyway but legalized gambling?

It's not like I'd be held liable if I lost their money. And most of the people here had plenty.

'Buy, buy, buy gentlemen,' I shouted. 'Buy up Jenga Juice before it's too late,' I said, waggling my finger at Jack. 'You might want to think about growing plums, too,' I said. 'Just think about it.'

'Jack, would you take that champagne bottle out of her

hands?' Madeline insisted. 'She's spilling it all over the table.' Jack tried to swipe the glass, but his hand caught air instead.

'I'm seeing double,' he admitted. 'Is anyone else seeing double?'

'Good God,' Madeline exclaimed. 'Jack, you're white as a sheet.'

'Mike,' Jack asked excitedly. 'What do you think?'

'I think she's right. You are white as a sheet.' Jack laughed like it was the funniest thing he'd ever heard.

'I'm talking about Jenga Juice, my friend,' Jack exclaimed. 'I want to buy plenty of shares.'

'I . . . uh . . . don't think this is a good time to be taking any chances,' Mike said carefully.

'Well I do,' Jack said. 'And it's not like I need your permission to invest. Right, Mother?' It was quick, but Madeline and Mike exchanged a glance between them before she focused on Jack.

'Darling, it's bad form to discuss business at the table,' Madeline said, avoiding his question. How dare the two of them share an intimate glance in public? Did Anderson notice it? I tried to break into his thoughts, but they remained under lock and key.

'Well I think you should listen to your future wife, Jack,' I slurred.

'Take it easy, Miss Plum,' Mike whispered loudly. A whistle from a departing cruise ship went off inside my head.

'Are you saying that Mike holds the power over the Heron family investments now?' Jack yelled at Madeline.

'Jack,' Mike said. 'You're not in any shape to discuss this right now.'

'I'm not talking to you, Mike. I'm speaking with my mother.'

'This is neither the time nor the place for this conversation,' Madeline said tightly.

'Oh, it's not?' Jack asked. 'You're so right. I had forgotten. This is a celebration, right? An engagement party.' He took a fork and banged on his champagne glass.

'Time for a toast!'

'Jack, sit down,' Madeline hissed. Jack wobbled on his feet. He held the glass up, like a torch. Then he sat down and drank the rest of it without uttering a word.

'What?' he asked Madeline who was staring at him from across the table. Her accusing eyes slid to me and latched on. *What have you done to my son?*

The negative energy at the table was building up in my body, reaching lethal levels, and no amount of deep breathing or imagining the color blue was decreasing it. Anxiety poured out of me like lava spewing from a volcano.

'My spoon,' Brian shouted. 'Oh my God. Look, Clair. My spoon!' One by one, heads turned to Brian's spoon, which was hovering several inches off his neck, straining at the end of his chain like a dog on the end of its leash.

'A parlor trick,' one of the suits cried. 'Wonderful!' He started clapping, and soon others around the table joined in. Brian was beaming. Then he spotted my utensils. My knife, fork, and spoon were curling in on themselves, bending like anorexic yoga masters trying to wrap their ankles around their necks. Shame roared in my ears, and I shut my eyes, but I knew there was no stopping it.

'It's you,' Brian yelled, pointing at my gnarled utensils. 'You're doing it.' Exclamations and gasps cascaded down the table as every eye fastened on me and my violently vibrating plate. I clamped my hand down on it.

'She made my shovel fly, too,' Conrad yelled from the kids table.

'Did not,' Mathew said.

'Did, too,' Conrad sulked.

My eyes slid down the table to the investors. Every single one of them were holding their spoons up. Some of them were blowing on them, others were rubbing them in their palms, and one kept tossing it in the air and frowning every time it clunked back down on the table. *Calm down, calm down, calm down. Breathe in, breathe out. Breathe in, breathe out.*

'Clair?' Mike's voice cut across the table. 'Are you all

right?' I opened my eyes and slowly lifted my hand off my plate. Jack reached over, grabbed my mangled spoon, and banged it against his champagne glass again.

'I'd like to ask my beautiful bride-to-be a question,' he slurred with a pointed look to his mother. 'Will you marry me?' he said to me.

'She already said yes,' one of the investors shouted. Laughter erupted. Jack hauled me to my feet. 'I want her to marry me,' he said, squeezing my waist until I could barely breathe, 'right here, right now.'

Daily Horoscope – Pisces

Sticks and stones may break your bones but the ball and chain will kill you.

I didn't have to throw a fit, Madeline did that for me. She literally flew out of her chair and stopped short of physically attacking her son. 'What are you doing, Jack?' He wobbled a bit on his heels, forward and back. 'What did you do to him?' Madeline said, turning on me. 'What is he on?'

'I have no idea,' I said honestly. 'And don't worry, I'm not marrying anyone tonight.'

'What's the matter, Mother?' Jack asked. 'Don't like how it feels when you have no control over something?'

'You're actually considering marrying this . . . this—'

'Watch it,' I said.

'Just to spite me? Fine, you want to invest in – oh what the hell was it?' she asked, turning on me again.

'Jenga Juice.'

'Jenga Juice? Fine – you get your way, Jack. Now will you please sit down?' She glanced toward the investors who were still buried in their various electronic toys.

'You know what I want, Mother?' Jack said, not bothering to lower his voice. 'I want him gone.' We all followed the end of his finger. It was pointed directly at Mike. *Does he know about the two of them?*

Mike looked at me before returning Jack's glare. 'Why don't we all calm down,' he said.

'I just love a good wedding,' Elizabeth sang. 'As soon as the two of you marry, I can die in peace.' She looked at me and winked.

'Jack,' Madeline said. 'Can I talk to you in private?'

'Why, we're all family here,' Jack said, pulling me into him. 'Whatever you have to say, you can say in front of my beautiful bride-to-be.'

'Hear, hear,' Elizabeth said.

'Jack—'

'Mother – if I remember correctly, this is exactly what you wanted. This dinner,' he said, holding his arms out, 'those investors,' he said, pointing down the table, 'and my fiancée,' he said, squeezing me. 'Am I wrong?' Jack picked up his glass and banged it with a fork. Everyone at our table looked up. 'I'd like to make an announcement,' Jack said.

'How many of these are there going to be, Jack?' Mike said irritably. This time I did meet his eyes. *What are you doing?* he mouthed. Jack was still banging on his glass.

'My beautiful fiancée and I,' he shouted, 'are getting married – right after dessert!' Jack shouted. The table erupted in cheers. I stood like a statue. And then common sense kicked in.

'Jack,' I said quietly. 'I'm not marrying you tonight.'

'Why not?' he asked.

'Because we're not really engaged,' I said. 'Remember?' Jack lifted my hand and kissed the ring.

'Could've fooled me,' he said.

'It's not even real,' I blurted. There was a gasp and suddenly Elizabeth was reaching across the table for my hand.

'What do you mean it's not real?' I felt horrible; I hadn't meant for her to hear that.

'Don't worry,' I said. 'The real one is safe and sound with Madeline. Isn't it, Madeline?' Elizabeth turned on Madeline.

'Rachel is – clumsy,' Madeline stammered. 'I couldn't have her losing your ring, now could I?' She finished her sentence by shooting daggers at Mike. Jack reached into his pocket and pulled out a diamond ring.

'We can fix that,' Jack said. He took my hand and removed the cubic zirconium and replaced it with the real diamond.

'*You* took it?' I said.

'Who else?' Jack answered. I flushed, knowing that Mike was staring at me harder than ever. Mike didn't take the diamond from me. *See, Clair? You were wrong about him. He still told Madeline he loved her. He told her he loved her!*

'Who's going to marry us?' I joked. 'Anderson?' Anderson traded my laughter for a long, long stare.

'He is an ordained minister, my dear,' Elizabeth said.

'You are?' Mike and I asked at the same time.

'Universal Life Church,' Anderson admitted. 'Nine ninety-nine on the Internet.' Jack was slowly leading me away from the table, to the gazebo. As we passed the other tables he started whispering, *There's going to be a wedding*, and soon we were swept up in a mob, heading for the tent.

'Jack,' I said, gasping for breath. 'You have to tell me – what did you take?'

'I didn't take anything,' he said happily. 'I think it's you. You make me feel – incredibly high.' He stopped, swung me around. 'I think I'm in love with you, Clair,' he said. 'All night – just looking at you – I've been euphoric.'

Euphoric. Just like I felt in the car on the way out here.

'One minute I was writing that letter to Rachel—'

Oh. My. God.

'– getting ready to mail it—'

'Jack,' I interrupted. 'The stamps you borrowed from me. How many did you lick?'

Jack stuck out his tongue and blew his lips out like a horse. 'Tree,' Jack said, holding up two fingers. 'Hey,' he shouted. 'Let's get married under the willow tree.' He pulled my hand and started running with me. Two stamps. And he was this high. I had licked a total of . . . twenty. Enough to make me think I'd flipped my Saturn. No wonder Sammy grinned like an idiot when he gave me the stamps. What kind of hallucinogenic lab was he running out of the King's Ransom motel? If I used twenty and Jack used two—

Jack pulled me to the willow tree. 'Jack,' I said. 'Where are the rest of the stamps?'

'Don't know,' Jack said. 'Here we are.' He leaned against the willow tree, pulled me to him, and kissed me. *I want Mike*. I didn't know the crowd had reached us until I heard clapping.

'Where's Anderson?' Jack bellowed. Anderson stepped up with Elizabeth on his arm. 'Let's do it, my man,' Jack said, punching Anderson on the shoulder.

'Jack,' Madeline said, pushing through the crowd, 'don't do this. I'm begging you, don't marry this woman.'

'I'm not getting married,' I said for the umpteenth time. I felt a hand in mine.

'Your grandmother predicted this, Clair,' Elizabeth whispered in my ear. 'This is your destiny.'

And there it was, the question I'd pondered all my life, is there any such thing as love-at-first-sight, meant-to-be, THE-ONE, destiny, or fate?

I always thought I believed. That when I knew, I'd just know. That it would be so easy. And here – standing underneath the willow tree – is a man like Jack Heron. And yes, he's higher than Dan Quayle after the spelling bee, but he wants to marry me. I've certainly married worse. And you all know how much I love vodka. And my grandmother – my grandmother hand-picked him. She reached out from *the other side* – just so I wouldn't screw it up this time. This should be a no-brainer.

I looked at Jack. 'You really want to marry me?' I asked.

'I do,' he said. I tried to ignore the shadow puppet he was making with his left hand while he said it. 'It's a swan,' he said. 'For you.' *We'd better hurry. Before the drugs wear off.*

'Grandma Heron,' Madeline exclaimed, marching Elizabeth in front of me. 'Look at this woman – take a good look at her – she's not Rachel.'

Elizabeth looked at me and smiled. 'I know that, dear,' she told Madeline. 'She's Clair Ivars. And she's meant to marry Jack.'

'Ivars?' Madeline said. 'Why does that name sound familiar?'

Elizabeth smiled at me. 'She's Isabella Ivars' granddaughter.' For the first time in her life, Madeline Heron was struck dumb.

'Isabella?' she said. 'The woman who saved Jack's life?'

'The very one,' Elizabeth said. Jack pulled a willow tree branch down and started chewing on it.

'Oh, my, God,' Madeline said. 'You planned this Elizabeth – didn't you?'

'Clair,' Mike said, stepping up. 'I have to talk to you.'

'Not now,' Elizabeth said. 'These two lovebirds are ready to tie the knot.' *Around my neck, like a noose.*

'I want to talk to you, too,' I said to Mike. It was time I let him have it. Mike and I tried to make our way to a private spot, but the crowd wouldn't part.

'What are you doing?' Mike shouted over them. 'Have you totally lost your mind?'

'I could do worse than Jack,' I said defensively. We glanced at him; he was now using the willow branch to scratch his nose. Mike and I politely looked away when he actually stuck it up his nostril.

'Somebody worse?' Mike repeated. 'Like me?'

'Mike,' I said. Mike barged through the crowd and had his lips on me before I could even finish the sentence. He pushed me against the tree, the bark digging into my shoulder blades as his tongue explored mine. Time fell away. I forgot about the 'wedding party' behind us, I forgot about him and Madeline, I forgot about Rachel. I forgot about the check. I forgot about everything – except a pink sheet of faded stationery.

'Stop it,' I said, pulling away. 'What if . . . what if I'm just a relationship junkie?' Mike smiled at me.

'What does it matter,' he said, 'if it's a great relationship?'

'What if . . . what if you don't stick?' I whispered. Mike took a step toward me.

'Then I'll staple myself to you,' he said.

'What if – what if we aren't meant to be?'

'What do you mean?' he asked. 'We're perfect you and I.' I took the piece of stationery out of my little beaded purse.

'Do you believe in fate?' I asked him. He looked at me. Waited. 'I think I'm meant to marry Jack,' I said, handing him the paper.

'Because of this?' he said when he finished reading it. 'You want to marry a man just because of this?'

'My grandmother wrote that,' I said. 'She was an intuitive. She knew things.'

'Like you?' Mike said. I studied him. 'I heard you do that reading in the kitchen – remember?'

'Yes. Like me – only her gift was much stronger.'

'And because of this,' Mike said, waving the stationery. 'Just because of this – you're going to marry Jack?'

'This isn't just a little thing, Mike,' I said. 'It's not like a horoscope that could apply to anyone or – or some kind of vague prediction. This is my grandmother. Writing about me – this is huge.'

'I suppose it is.'

'And – it's not like you're available—'

'You don't know that.'

'Then tell me. What is going on between you and Madeline?'

'That's none of your business,' Madeline answered for him. I looked at Mike.

'Mike?' I asked. He closed his eyes for a moment, looked at Madeline, looked at me. But remained silent.

'I see,' I said. 'Well if you'll excuse me, I have a wedding to get to.'

'You don't even have to move,' Jack said, dragging Anderson behind him, the rest of the dinner guests in tow. Jack grabbed my hand. 'Go ahead Raggedy Andy Man,' he said.

'Um – we are gathered here today' – Anderson licked his lips and looked around – 'I've uh, never actually done one of these before,' he admitted to the crowd. They applauded encouragingly and he bowed. I'd forgotten his thespian past.

'Clair,' Mike said, taking advantage of the rocky start, 'did it ever dawn on you – you're not the marrying type?'

'Of course it did,' I retorted. 'Three times.'

'Then what the devil are you doing?' he asked. Anderson held up his hand and turned to Mike.

'I think you should say that when I say "Is there anyone here who knows any secret why these two should not be wed."'

'Secret?' I said.

'I think he means "reason,"' Jack said, clapping Anderson on the back.

'Why don't you let Clair do the ceremony,' Mike said. 'She's been through it three times herself.'

'Three times?' Jack asked, taking a step back. 'You've been married three times?'

'Low blow Mike,' I said. 'You think you know me?'

'Yes. I think I *do* know you, Clair,' Mike said, taking a step forward. 'And I *still* like you.' It was the most romantic thing anyone had ever said to me.

'You're sleeping with Madeline,' I blurted out.

'What did she say?' Madeline said, snapping to attention.

'She,' I shouted at her, 'is right here. Right in front of you. Stop talking about me in the third person. Stop treating me like I don't even exist!'

'Clair,' Mike said. 'Whatever you think is going on between Madeline and me—'

'I heard you two,' I said.

'Young lady—' Madeline said.

'Clair,' I interrupted. 'My name is Clair.'

'Shame on you, Clair,' Madeline shouted, shaking her finger at me.

'Me?' I shouted back. 'You're the one sleeping with a man young enough to be your son.' Everyone erupted at once. 'You told her you loved her,' I yelled at Mike. 'I heard you.'

'You son of a bitch.' Jack released the willow branch and rushed Mike like a linebacker. He slammed him against the tree trunk. 'You – and my mother?' he yelled. He pulled his fist back. I threw myself on Jack, but it was too late. Mike stepped out of the way and Jack punched the tree. Madeline tried to intercept, but Jack rushed Mike again, knocking him to the ground. They rolled around the grass.

'Your suits,' Madeline shouted. 'You're wearing nice suits.' They didn't stop. Madeline roared over them like a locomotion searing down the tracks. 'Jack,' she shouted, 'get off your brother this instant!' The rolling stopped with Jack on the bottom. Jack looked up from underneath Mike. He was wearing a grass mustache and his lips and teeth were covered in dirt.

'My what?' he said, spitting out a twig.

'Your brother,' Madeline repeated. 'Mike is my son.' Mike crawled off of Jack, and the two of them lay side-by-side panting. From this angle, you really could see the resemblance.

'I should have told you two a long time ago,' Madeline said as Susan stepped forward.

'How is this possible?' Susan asked as Mike got up off the ground and then extended his hand to Jack.

'Didn't see this one coming – did you, Ms Psychic?' Mike whispered in my ear. He pulled back and nailed me with a god-awful, smug, sexier-than-hell grin.

'How can he be – Mike's younger than me—' Jack sputtered. 'Dad was already—'

Anderson stepped up to Madeline and put his arm around her waist.

'I'm Mike's father,' he announced. 'But I want you and Susan to know that even though I've loved your mother for years – I didn't make any kind of a move until your father died.'

'I just couldn't keep you,' Madeline said, turning to Mike. 'It was so soon after the death of my husband. I didn't want to hurt my kids, my husband's reputation—'

'And I knew a great family who wanted to adopt,' Anderson added.

'Oh my God,' Susan said. 'That's why you told us you were going to fat camp?' Madeline looked at the ground. 'I haven't eaten dessert in twenty years because you said we had fat genes!'

'I'm so sorry, darling,' Madeline said. 'I've regretted that decision ever since.'

'Well you certainly should. Twenty-two years without cake and ice cream!'

'Susan,' Madeline said. 'I was talking to your brother.'

'I continued to eat cake and ice cream, Mother,' Jack said.

'Your other brother,' Madeline clarified. 'Mike – I regretted giving you up. Times were so different then. Women were judged so harshly.'

'And I didn't know how to stand up like a man,' Anderson admitted. 'I'm so sorry.'

'It's okay,' Mike said. 'I had a good life. I wouldn't have wanted it any other way.'

'Anderson Brentworth,' I said to myself, pulling the handkerchief from my cleavage. AB.

Mike leaned into me and whispered, 'You were wrong about the Alexander; my middle name is Anderson.'

You see? Close never gets you any credit.

'I can't believe this,' Susan said.

'I'll second that,' Jack said. 'Have you always known you were adopted?' he asked Mike.

'Yes, I always knew,' Mike answered. 'But I didn't set out to find my mother – until a few years ago, when the adoption laws changed.'

'I'm so sorry, I'm so sorry,' Madeline kept repeating to everyone.

'It's okay, Madeline,' Mike said. 'I mean it. I had a good life.' Elizabeth snuck up behind me.

'I guess that makes Mike my grandson, too,' she whispered. 'Not by blood, but still. Do you think your grandmother meant—' I turned to Elizabeth and gently hugged her.

'I don't think this is about me at all,' I said. 'I think this is their moment.' I turned to leave. And slammed into Rachel.

Daily Horoscope – Pisces

She's baaaaaaaaaackkkk

You would have thought a princess had arrived, the way the crowd parted and Jack sank to his knees, although granted, she definitely could pass for one. I was once again struck at what a beautiful woman she was. The only difference this time was that instead of looking like a frightened poodle, she looked confident and enraged.

And she was looking at me.

Which caused everybody but Jack (who couldn't take his eyes off her) to look at me as well. Her long, lean arm, draped in Chanel, was pointed straight at me; I half expected sparks to fly out of her French-manicured nails like a Wizard zapping me into a block of ice. Susan, meanwhile, had ushered the rest of the guests back to dessert, and part of me feared it was so they could murder and bury me underneath the willow tree without too many witnesses. Abby, Brian, and Terri had happily ditched our little fucked-up wedding ceremony for cheesecake.

'She's the reason I wasn't here,' Rachel yelled. 'It's all her fault.'

'What is she talking about?' Mike whispered in my ear.

'Long story,' I tried to whisper back, but I couldn't find my voice.

'Were you on a Pilates retreat?' Jack squeaked.

'No,' I said, stepping up. 'She wasn't.' Jack, the man who seconds ago wanted to marry me, wouldn't even look at me now. 'Jack,' I said. 'I'm a Tarot—'

And there was that outstretched hand again – but this time it was holding a check. Why did I feel so clammy? What had Elizabeth tried to tell me about this check? Why was Rachel going to admit to accepting a check worth a hundred thousand dollars? Is she insane?

Jack picked up the check and examined it. He lifted his head slowly and now he looked at me. Why was he looking at me like that? Wordlessly, he passed it to Susan, who reacted with the same horrified expression. Then—

She looked at me.

One by one they passed it around and looked at me like they were smoking a joint after a Move-On.org gathering and I was the only one who forgot to wear their Bush Sucks pin. I caught Elizabeth's eyes. To my surprise I found them filled with tears.

Madeline was the only one to immediately verbalize.

'A hundred thousand dollars?' she spit out. 'You disgusting little girl,' she yelled. Mike glanced at me and then left my side to see what they were talking about. He, too, looked at the check, looked at me.

'What is this, Clair?' he asked, handing me the check: *Pay to the Order of* Clair Ivars.

'Oh my God,' I said.

'She planned this all along,' Rachel squealed, pointing at me. 'She's been blackmailing Elizabeth!'

'That's not true,' I said. 'This check was supposed to be made out to you and you know it.'

'Clair's telling the truth,' Elizabeth cried, clutching my arm. 'I made a terrible mistake.'

'Grandmother Heron, what are you talking about?' Rachel said with the perfect mix of concern and defensiveness.

'Don't play any more games, Rachel,' Elizabeth said. 'The jig is up.'

'Grandmother,' Jack said. 'Rachel isn't playing games with you. Clair is. She's been blackmailing you. We all know it now. You don't have to be afraid.'

'She's not afraid of me, Jack,' I said, unable to bite back a reply. 'And I never blackmailed anyone.'

'What do you call this?' Jack barked, pointing at the check.

I was still holding the check. And wearing the ring. I didn't notice it until I saw Rachel looking at it. And then the floodgates opened. The princess opened her mouth and screamed. I could hear the champagne glasses breaking over at the dinner table, and even slapping my hands over my ears didn't diminish the pain. The next thing I knew, she was yanking on my finger, and this one had no qualms about taking my poor little digit with her. Luckily, Mike pulled her off and allowed me to slip the ring off myself. I held it up like a hostage.

'I'm Clair Ivars,' I said. 'I'm a Tarot card reader. Rachel came to me, wanting me to give her a bad reading, wanting me to give her an excuse not to marry Jack.'

'That's not true—'

I turned to Susan, she was my only hope. 'Susan,' I said, 'Tell them.' Susan sighed, wrestling with her words. I saw lies perched at the tip of the tongue and, miraculously, watched them die.

'Clair's just a tarot card reader,' she said. 'A really bad one.'

'Hey—'

'Rachel insisted we go see her. She heard about her from Elizabeth. I tried to talk her out if it,' she told Jack. 'Rachel was really freaking out – and Clair just made it worse!' I looked at the ground. 'She went on and on about hacking people up with hatchets – and – and how bad her ex-husbands smelled.'

Mike was staring at me. 'That's a little skewed,' I said with a shrug.

'But she's not after money, I'll tell you that. She didn't even take money for the reading.'

'It's true,' Elizabeth said. 'I was supposed to make that check out to Rachel.'

'Rachel,' Jack said. 'Is it true? You wanted out of the wedding? You thought the check was for you?' Tears poured from Rachel's eyes. Real ones this time.

'She was terrified, Jack,' I said. 'Remember all the noises?'

'Back to the ghost again, are we?' Jack said. 'Rachel – I should have supported you more on that, and I'm sorry. But – taking a check not to marry me? I can't forgive you for that.'

'Rachel had no intention of cashing the check,' I cut in. 'She didn't even look at this check – until recently – did you Rachel?'

'How did you know that?' Rachel asked. Did nobody understand what I did for a living? 'It's true Jack. I wasn't going to cash it. I was just waiting for you – to – fight for me, I guess. But then tonight when Clair called me and said she wanted you for herself—'

I turned to Mike on this and whispered, 'That's a little—'

'Skewed?' he whispered back.

'Exactly.'

I missed the rest of what Rachel had to say to Jack. No matter. It must have worked, because he was on one knee putting the ring back on her finger.

'I promise. I'll spend the rest of our life together chasing away your ghosts,' Jack said.

'The ghost was Clair's grandmother,' Elizabeth piped in. 'Isabella.'

No, it wasn't. It was Anderson. Jack was always like a son to him. So when Elizabeth begged for his help, convincing him that Jack and I were meant to be, he stepped right in. His theatrical experience gave him the know-how to rig the sound effects.

I didn't say any of this. He had enough of an uphill climb in repairing this dysfunctional family. I looked at Anderson for a long time

'It's okay,' I said. 'It's going to stop now. I'm sure of it,' I said, keeping eye contract with Anderson until I saw a slight nod. I turned back to Elizabeth. 'I can't tell you how happy I am to have met you. You're the reason I was meant to come out here. And I don't want to hear you've locked yourself in your room again, or I'm going to come and haunt you. You got that?'

'Got it, darling,' Elizabeth said. She turned to Rachel.

'I'm sorry, dear,' she said. 'You must think I'm horrible. Can you forgive me?'

'I already have,' Rachel said with her mesmerizing smile. Mike slipped his hand in mine and started leading us away from the crowd. We didn't get far. Hannah's mother stormed toward us with her two sisters in tow.

'Hannah's gone,' the mother yelled. 'This is all your fault.'

'What do you mean gone?' Mike asked, stepping up to protect me.

'This woman told her to follow her heart – so she's going after her lover – Aimee.'

'Aimee?' I said.

'The nanny,' the mother yelled. 'Her lover.' From ten feet away, I heard Susan gasp. Uh-oh. I turned twelve shades of red as Susan advanced on me. We stared at each other until I shrugged. 'Sometimes I'm a little off,' I said. Susan walked up to Harold.

'You weren't sleeping with the nanny?' she asked.

'Good God,' Harold said. 'Of course not.'

'I think I'm going to go get dessert,' I said to Mike. He laughed and slipped his hand around my waist. 'Good idea, Madam Ivars,' he said.

'Jack,' I said as we were leaving. 'Your contest.'

'Oh no,' Jack said, breaking away from Rachel. 'I was supposed to announce the winner. I've barely even looked at the applications. Everything's been so insane—'

'It's okay,' I said. 'You're going to call it Blue Heron Vodka. Do invest in Jenga Juice. And lock the rest of my stamps in a drawer. They're laced with some kind of super-strength, futuristic LSD and the police will be taking them as evidence.'

'Wait,' Susan said. 'You just admitted you were often a little – off. So how do we know what to believe?'

'You don't,' I said looking at Mike. 'But sometimes you just have to take a chance. Otherwise, life just isn't worth living, is it?' I turned to Mike and smiled.

'Should I go get my stapler?' he whispered.

'No,' I said. 'I've got something better.' And then, I put the rest of the world on pause, and kissed Mike like our lives depended on it.

Daily Horoscope – Pisces

Today is the first day of the rest of your life. Then again, so was yesterday.

I had just put my bag in the trunk and leaned in to say goodbye. I was finally going home. Without Mike. He had enough to catch up on here. But he'd be joining me soon in Chicago. And I was counting the days. We had spent last night together in the wine cellar; we had made love near the pond and dissected our incredible past week together like children telling each other the same bedtime stories over and over again. I had been grinning ear to ear all morning. Until now. I could feel my lungs filling with water.

'Clair?' Abby said. 'What's the matter?'

'Good God,' Brian said. 'You're turning blue.'

I'll give him credit for this, it wasn't until he said turning blue that I associated the feelings in my body with the wine cellar. I turned and fled.

I could feel the grass beneath my feet, the smell of dirt, of earth. I ignored the tears streaming down my face and the phantom gravestones of my dream, this time with a name other than Rachel's on the headstone. This was my fault. If I hadn't done Rachel's reading, if I hadn't sent the nanny away, if I hadn't distracted everyone so at the dinner – if, if, if, and more if – maybe, just maybe, someone would have been paying more attention.

'Clair?' someone shouted at me as I ran past. I didn't stop. I just ran.

Perhaps in a normal situation, Jack or Mike or Brian could have run faster. But I had adrenaline on my side, and perhaps other forces, for like my experience in the Saturn, I felt like I was being lifted, like I was flying through the air. Just as I ran into the woods, Mathew was running out. Dirty face streaked with tears, mouth open in horror. 'I know,' I said as I flew past him. 'Tell your mother.'

And then I was there. Through the wine cellar to the patio. The bricks cutting into my feet. Finally, I spotted him. His little hands were barely clinging to the edge of the pond with his tiny fingers, seconds from slipping away. I knelt down and grabbed him underneath the arms, pulled him out, and cradled his wet, shivering body in my arms. I couldn't tell who was crying louder.

'I just wanted to swim,' Conrad said.

'I know,' I said.

'Like a fish.'

'Like a fish,' I repeated. Susan was screaming somewhere behind me as everyone else converged on the tiny patio. She took him out of my arms.

'My baby, my baby,' she said.

'He's okay,' I said.

'I wanted to swim, Mommy.'

'My baby, my poor baby.'

And then, someone wrapped their arms around me. I leaned back as Mike kissed my neck.

'Not bad,' he whispered as Brian and Abby ran up.

'Is he okay?' Abby shouted.

'He's fine,' Mike said. 'Clair saved him.'

'Oh my God,' Abby said, 'you just saved an innocent child from drowning in bubbles. You're legit!' Abby grinned at me. 'Wait until I tell Mom.'

'See?' Brian said. 'You're the real thing.' I looked at the pond.

'Those aren't exactly bubbles,' I said.

'We'll give it to you,' Abby said.

'Kind of like a psychic sliding scale,' Brian added.

'I'll take it,' I said.

'Good adventure, eh?' Brian answered.

'Eh?' Abby said, turning to Brian. If I wasn't mistaken, a blush crept up his cheeks.

'Sorry,' he said. 'Us Canadians.' Abby's aura ignited as she beamed at me. I laughed, turned around, and threw myself shamelessly at Mike. He hugged me like we were touching for the first time. He hugged me like we'd been touching for a million years. I didn't know – *exactly* – what was going to happen from here, but I knew it was going to be good. I just knew.

You can buy any of these other
Little Black Dress titles from your
bookshop or *direct from the publisher*.

FREE P&P AND UK DELIVERY
(Overseas and Ireland £3.50 per book)

TO ORDER SIMPLY CALL THIS NUMBER

01235 400 414

or visit our website: www.madaboutbooks.com

Prices and availability subject to change without notice.